Susan Hurley has worked in medical research and the pharmaceutical industry for more than thirty years. Her research has been published in high-profile medical journals like *The Lancet* and her writing has appeared in *Kill Your Darlings, The Australian, The Big Issue* and *Mascara Literary Review*. She was shortlisted for the 2017 Peter Carey Short Story Award and *Eight Lives*, her first novel, was shortlisted for the 2018 UK Caledonia Novel Award for an unpublished manuscript. She lives in Melbourne with her husband and labradoodle.

PRAISE FOR *EIGHT LIVES*

'A powerful and pacy thriller that had me hooked until
the very end.'
Christian White

'Clever, complex, suspenseful – *Eight Lives* is the scientific thriller
I've been hoping for.'
Toni Jordan

'A cautionary tale of greed and hubris, of inherited violence and
the lengths we all go to for family. So many conversations will be
started by this breakneck medical thriller. A big debut from a huge
literary talent.'
J.P. Pomare

'Vey well written, with compelling characters and a totally
engrossing plot.'
Thuy On

'Susan Hurley's expertise in the world of clinical research informs
a strong, suspenseful plot of intriguing detours and unexpected
alliances that leads to a shocking conclusion.'
Susan Kurosawa

'A thrilling account of a drug trial gone bad.'
Madeline Milburn, Judge of the 2018 Caledonia Novel Award.

Published by Affirm Press in 2019
28 Thistlethwaite Street, South Melbourne, VIC 3205
www.affirmpress.com.au
10 9 8 7 6 5 4 3 2 1

Title: Eight Lives / Susan Hurley, author.
ISBN: 9781925712766 (paperback)

A catalogue record for this
book is available from the
National Library of Australia

Cover design by Design by Committee
Typeset in Minion Pro 12.75 / 19 by J&M Typesetting
Proudly printed in Australia by Griffin Press

MIX
Paper from
responsible sources
FSC® C009448

The paper this book is printed on is certified against the Forest Stewardship
Council® Standards. Griffin Press holds FSC chain of custody certification
SGS-COC-005088. FSC promotes environmentally responsible, socially
beneficial and economically viable management of the world's forests.

EIGHT
LIVES

SUSAN
HURLEY

For Sunny

Prologue

THE AUSTRALIAN TIMES

A mother and son reach safety. The Vietnamese refugee crisis worsens.

Milton Krum, Immigration and Social Affairs Writer

15 August 1979

HONG KONG. Dung (pronounced 'Yoong') is a six-year-old Vietnamese boy whose emaciated condition brings tears to the eyes of his doctor at the Jubilee Refugee Camp's hospital. Dung's skeleton is conspicuous, his skin sunburned and ulcer-ravaged, exposing bone at his wrists. He weighs only fourteen kilograms.

Dung and his mother, Mai, were found staggering through the streets of downtown Hong Kong six days ago, their clothes filthy and tattered. Mai was delirious, but, with the assistance of a camp inmate who recognised her, authorities have now established that she and Dung escaped from the southern Vietnamese district of Ba Tri in a small boat. Fishermen rescued the pair at sea and dropped them on shore under cover of darkness. The head of the United Nations High Commission for Refugees' Support Services, Ivan Hadley, says Mai and Dung would almost certainly have died without the fishermen's intervention. It is illegal for citizens of Hong Kong to assist refugees in this way.

Refugee camps in Hong Kong, Malaysia, Thailand, Indonesia and the Philippines now hold almost 200,000 people, and the exodus from Vietnam shows no signs of abating. Boats packed with more escapees continue to arrive in Hong Kong harbour each week, and Hadley says each brings another harrowing tale of hardship. Although most refugees flee Vietnam on large, overcrowded boats, in other respects Mai and Dung's story is typical. Mai claims that Thai pirates stole their engine and fuel, as well as their water and rice, forcing her to row much of the journey. Then she had to contend with a severe storm. July is typhoon season in the South China Sea and waves over nine metres high are common. Mai bound her son and herself to the mast to avoid being washed overboard.

Passing ships ignored their plight. Hadley says skippers have been instructed by their vessels' owners not to pick up escapees, as Southeast Asian countries are now refusing to accept refugees rescued at sea. Many of these so-called 'boat people' are believed to have lost their lives on the ocean as a consequence.

But even for those, like Mai and Dung, who survive the sea journey, the struggle is far from over. Western nations have been slow to accept boat people as permanent settlers, frustrating the countries that have given them refuge. Last month, after Malaysia threatened to expel the 75,000 refugees now living in its camps and to shoot on sight any further refugees trying to land, the UN convened an international conference in Geneva to discuss the worsening crisis. A proposal for an international island camp, where all the region's refugees would be temporarily confined, was discussed. Hadley fears that solution would create a dumping ground for the unwanted. He claims Western nations have been creaming off the skilled, educated refugees. After the Geneva conference, the Australian government announced it would consider raising our annual refugee quota of 10,500.

Mai and her young son have reached land and safety. Now their wait for resettlement begins. But since being rescued, the only word Dung has spoken is 'Ma'.

Rosa

Golden Boy, that's what we called him. Not to his face, but not in a mean way either. He was my boss at the biotech start-up that was developing the drug he invented. Golden Boy was brilliant – effortlessly so, it seemed – and already a star of the medical research world when he died at the ridiculously young age of thirty-three. He was universally acknowledged as an all-round good guy too, although of course the truth was more complicated.

His name was Dung, but I only learned that at his funeral. While he was alive I never heard a soul call him by that name, a name chosen by someone who loved him. I hadn't expected to cry at his funeral, but that realisation undid me.

Golden Boy. Dung. I still think of him every day, even now, ten years after he died. Because he's the reason I'm where I am today. And because what I did killed him.

Melbourne, 2006

Part 1

I mean, shit, we learn by climbing over the bodies
of humans ...

– Murray Gardner, MD, University of California, in
*Shots in the Dark: The Wayward Search for an
AIDS Vaccine* by Jon Cohen.

Dear Ly,

I've tried to make my mother proud. Ăn quả nhớ kẻ trồng cây, she would say. When eating the fruit, think of the person who planted the tree. I've tried to do that, and more. I've tried to live honourably, to treat people well, even when they've treated me badly. I've tried to be different from my father, to look after the women in my life, like he didn't. Especially you, little sister. I've tried to look after you. I've been trying to atone for what I did, without even knowing what it was.

Ly (Natalie)

It started when Dung went on TV with Charlie Cunningham. I saw them, on the news. It was a Saturday in May, and my salon was the only business in the lane still open when the news came on. I normally shut at six, but my last client had come late. I was sweeping the floor and Trà My was putting clippers in the steriliser when Wendy arrived, almost thirty minutes late. Wendy didn't care that we were packing up. 'I need a full pedi,' she said, 'and a manicure too, darl.' She'd only booked a toenail file and paint, but, no problem, business is business.

Trà My started applying remover to the chipped polish on Wendy's fingernails. Wendy wouldn't try shellac, even though I'd told her – many times too – that it would last longer than the Big Apple Red polish she always went with. Shellac would be worth the extra money, but Wendy is cheap. I was on feet, even though I am the boss. Trà My says smelly feet make her want to puke. So I was sitting on the stool checking Wendy's feet, which are always bad news because she squeezes them into pointy stilettos, when Wendy said, 'Let's catch the news.'

'The Trouble with Mr Bean' was playing on my new TV, a fifty-inch flat screen. I got it on a plan and didn't have to make the first payment until January. I hadn't told Dung about the TV.

He was my partner in the salon, so I suppose I should have, but he would have said it was silly to spend money on a fancy TV. He would have been mad about the payment plan too.

Mr Bean was my favourite TV show when I was little, and Dung had given me a box set for Christmas. 'The Trouble with Mr Bean' is the best episode. Even though I've seen it heaps of times, I still laugh out loud when Mr Bean chucks a cupcake full of wasps into the car that a thief is trying to steal. The thief squirms like a worm, but he can't escape the wasp.

Trà My switched the TV over to the news like Wendy wanted, but I wasn't watching or even listening when Dung came on. I was hungry. I was thinking about the *canh chua* Má would have waiting at home. On Saturday it was always *canh chua*.

Trà My saw him first. '*Ly*,' she shouted, '*Nhìn kìa!*'

I looked up, pissed. I'd told her heaps of times: 'Call me Natalie in front of clients, not Ly. And speak English.' Speak Vietnamese, then clients want a cheap price. I give good prices, good Aussie prices. A mani and a pedi? Fifty dollars. But if clients hear Trà My speaking Vietnamese, they say: 'Oh, it was only twenty in Phuket,' or 'Really? The nice girl in Bali only charged me fifteen.' They want the same price in my salon that they got wherever they last went on holiday. No way is that happening, so speak English, I tell Trà My.

'*Anh của Ly trên TV kìa,*' she said, pointing. I turned to look, and Trà My was right. There was my brother, on TV, on the news.

I picked up Wendy's right foot and put it in the footbath, then the left foot with the bulging bunion. 'Soak for five minutes, Wendy,' I said, and stood up to see Dung better.

It looked like he was at the hospital. He had a white coat on and his stethoscope around his neck. He was talking to an old lady who was lying in bed. Sick, I suppose, but she looked okay. What was going on? Dung didn't look after sick people any more. Now he worked in research. He did experiments, and he'd discovered a new medicine.

Wendy sighed. 'I *am* in a bit of a hurry,' she said.

My brother often gave me advice: 'Always call your clients by their name,' he said when I opened my salon. 'You know how Aussies love to hear their name.' He was making a joke, but still I try to follow his advice. I make jokes too. Jokes to myself. Jokes to remember the names of clients. Sourpuss Samantha. Moustache Michelle. And Wino Wendy, who smelled of wine that night. She must have had time for drinks with friends before her appointment, then decided she needed a mani *and* a pedi. Now, she was in a bit of a hurry. Well, too bad. 'Your callouses are hard. You have to soak,' I told her. The water in the footbath was warm and bubbly. Wendy could relax. Enjoy!

But Trà My said, 'No problem, Lady, we quick.'

Lady! Trà My had already been in Australia for two years then, but she was still such a fob. I only hired her because her Auntie Kim got Má a job when we arrived here. Cleaning the houses of Aussies was the job. Má said that now it was our family's obligation to help Kim. Má meant that it was *my* obligation. And it wasn't just Kim's family I had to help. Now I had to return all the favours that were done for Má. Otherwise she said she would feel shame. There were lots of things I had to do so that Má would not feel shame. And also lots of things I mustn't do.

On TV, Dung was somewhere else now – where he worked, I suppose. 'The lab.' He had taken off his white coat and was sitting on a stool in front of a bench. There was an Aussie man on the stool next to him – young like Dung, but fat. At the bottom of the screen were their names: Charlie Cunningham and David Tran.

Trà My yapped: 'Lady Wendy, that's Natalie's brother. Dung …' She stopped and corrected herself. 'David. David is a doctor.'

'Really, Natalie, your brother is a doctor?' Wendy asked.

What was her problem? Did she think I was too stupid to have a doctor brother? It's true that I am not smart enough to be a doctor like Dung was, but that doesn't mean I'm stupid. Anyway, Dung thought it was okay for me to be a manicurist. He said that ladies need to have nice nails as well as be healthy. He said there were too many doctors anyway. And when I finished my training he said: 'You should start your own business, Ly. I'll help you.' So that's what happened. Dung paid the key money for my salon. 'I'm your silent partner now,' he said. But then the agent wouldn't give me the key. He said the landlord had changed his mind and wouldn't rent his shop to me.

When I was little, an Aussie girl at school called me a 'slope'. I didn't even know what a slope was, but I knew she was being mean. I cried so much Má had to come and take me home from school. Má was angry. 'Stupid girl. Why you cry?' she said.

Dung was kind though. 'When someone's mean, turn the other cheek,' he said. But when the landlord wouldn't rent his shop to me, I told Dung that I didn't want to turn the other cheek. So my brother didn't stay the silent partner. He came to the agent's office with me and he sorted it out. We got the key and walked back together to the shop that would be my salon.

It wasn't nice then. It was dirty. I had to work hard to clean it. It had been a jewellery shop, and the jewellery it sold was cheap. I told Dung there would be nothing cheap in my salon. Nothing tacky. No plastic flowers. No golden cat waving its hand.

'But, Ly, they bring good luck, those cats,' Dung said. No, I told my brother, no cat.

Now here was Wendy looking at Dung on the TV, then back at me, then at Dung again. 'He doesn't look like you,' she said.

'Agree with your clients' was another piece of advice Dung gave when I opened my salon. 'The customer is always right. Make that your motto.'

But I didn't want to agree with Wendy, even though she was right: Dung didn't look like me. 'He's tall,' was all I said. Dung was six foot one, very tall for a Vietnamese. Dung said that was because of all the protein he ate when he was little, all the beef steak Má fed him when they lived in Vietnam and all the chicken he was given in Hong Kong when he was so thin the doctors thought he might die. Má never gave me beef steak, and only little bits of chicken, so Dung was much taller than me. I'm five foot nothing. And even though they were sitting on stools, I could see that my brother was also much taller than Charlie Cunningham. Dung's neck started where Charlie Cunningham's potato head finished.

'Handsome too,' Trà My said.

Trà My was right about that at least. Dung was handsome, and on TV that night he looked good. I'd done his buzz-cut the week before, in my salon, even though I'm not a hairdresser. Number four, just how he liked it. His clothes looked smart too, even though his girlfriend, Abigail, helped him buy his clothes now, not me. A nice white shirt, a maroon tie, navy stovepipe trousers that suited his giraffe legs. And on TV Dung was smiling, happy. But Dung was always happy.

'What you think, Lady? Handsome?' Trà My asked Wendy.

'Mmm … he's not really my type,' Wendy said.

Not her type! Did Wendy think that she was Dung's type? As if! I grabbed the remote from Trà My and turned the sound up on the TV. A woman was asking Dung and Charlie Cunningham questions, but I couldn't see her. Charlie Cunningham was saying he had started a company that would sell the medicine Dr Tran had discovered. The name of the company was SuperMab. I knew that already, even though I hadn't known Dung was going on TV.

'What say?' Trà My asked Wendy.

'Natalie's brother is going to be very rich,' Wendy told her. 'Charlie Cunningham is saying sales of the drug he discovered will be a billion dollars a year.'

'Wow!'

'Yes, wow,' Wendy said. 'What's the problem, Natalie? You don't look happy.'

I pulled the plug from the footbath. 'No. No problem.' I picked up the scalpel. 'All good.' I began to scrape the still-hard dead skin from Wino Wendy's heels.

Trà My blabbed on: 'Lady, other one, Aussie man, get rich too?'

Wendy laughed. 'Charlie Cunningham? He's already rich.'

'Your type?' Trà My asked.

I looked at Charlie Cunningham on the screen again. His face was covered in orange freckles. His thin, straight hair looked greasy.

'Darl, Charlie Cunningham's so rich he's everybody's type,' Wendy said.

So that was how it started. Dung, going on TV with Charlie Cunningham. Charlie Cunningham saying 'a billion dollars'. And the stupid thing is that it wasn't even true. The fat Aussie, Charlie Cunningham, made up the billion dollars.

'But if it was on TV, on the news, it must be true,' I said to my brother. 'It wasn't as if it was an ad.'

'No Ly, it *was* an ad,' Dung said, 'an ad for our company, an ad for us.'

So Charlie Cunningham had made up the billion dollars. He made the movie of him and my brother talking. He sent his movie to the TV and they put it on the news, as if it really *was* the news. That was how it started.

It was dark when we finished Wendy. 'You go,' I told Trà My. 'I'll clean up.'

I knew that the man I used to call Pa would be waiting at home for me. He would have heard Charlie Cunningham talk about the billion dollars on TV, or someone would have told him. He would already be sitting in Má's kitchen, his snake eyes ready to watch me slurp my *canh chua*.

I had been too busy that Saturday to eat lunch. Now I was hungry. I still had the *cá kho tộ* Má had given me. Aussies don't like its fishy smell, so usually when Má gave me *cá kho tộ* I had to chuck it in the bin and pay nine dollars fifty for a sandwich. But the night Dung went on TV with Charlie Cunningham, I put my *cá kho tộ* in the microwave, I switched off the lights in my salon, I sat in the dark and ate it.

It was raining when I got off the bus, so I walked the four blocks to our street fast and didn't slow down until I was outside number eight. I could see the number-eight Nguyens inside, sitting at their table, talking and laughing while they ate their supper.

I kept walking. When I got to number fourteen I stopped and lit the cigarette I'd taken from the pack I keep at my salon. Má would smell it on me when I went inside, but too bad.

I could see the number-fourteen Nguyens inside watching TV. I stood on their nature strip and looked across the road to my house. The man I used to call Pa had parked his black Merc outside. It was parked crooked, staring at me like a tiger. He would be inside, sitting at our table, playing with his big, ugly ring. His foot would be resting on the yellow wall, making a dirty mark. Má would have to scrub hard to get that mark off – so hard the paint would come off. She would have taken the Johnnie Walker whisky out from the back of the cupboard and poured him two fingers. She would have made him a sandwich too. Peanut butter. His favourite. Má would be sitting with him, quiet, while he sipped his whisky and ate his snack, but her hands would be underneath the table, her thin fingers picking her cuticles. She would pick till her cuticles bled. Then she would pick some more.

The rain had stopped, but my denim jacket had got wet. I was cold. I chucked my cigarette butt onto the number-fourteen Nguyens' grass. I thought about Dung, my tall, handsome, smart brother. That day, not so smart. I crossed the road and opened our gate. That was how it started. Seven months later, Dung was dead.

Rosa

It was 2006 when I started working for Golden Boy, aka Dave Tran, but I'd known him for a few years before that. He'd been a medical fellow at the research institute where I'd been a PhD candidate: The Bill and Erica Sandburg-Tate Centre for Excellence in Immunology Research. It's always called 'BEST'. It was, it still is, the go-to place for doctors training for specialities that involve immunology – like oncology or rheumatology – as well as for scientists, like me, aiming for a research career. Medicos and scientists from all over the globe dream of adding a stint at BEST to their CVs.

Unlike BEST, the biotech start-up where I worked for Dave was a small-scale enterprise: my hiring brought the headcount to a meagre four. Apart from Dave, there was Charlie Cunningham and Yvette Jackson. Charlie was the CEO. His father and a band of deep-pocket mates, who Dave once described to me as 'high-net-worth individuals', had stumped up the moolah to start the company, which was called SuperMab. SuperMab was Charlie's first stint as boss cocky. His own mini-kingdom to rule.

Yvette was the admin, on secondment from the Cunningham Family Office, the organisation apparently charged with counting and multiplying the Cunningham money. Yvette was not happy about her deployment. SuperMab wasn't where I wanted to be either. It's the one thing we had in common. It didn't bring us close.

My first assignment, my first week on the job, was to perform in a promotional video Charlie had commissioned. The day before the shoot. The planning meeting. Me, Charlie, Dave, and the video director – whose name I didn't know because we were never introduced – seated around the conference table in Charlie's office. Charlie to me: 'We need you to do some legit science shit.'

I couldn't afford to fuck this job up, but 'legit science shit'? Seriously? I looked at the video director. He seemed suddenly fascinated by the notes on his lap. I looked at Dave. His lips were pressed together, a slight downturn at the corners. An I'm-sorry-about-this expression. Then, a slight nod of his head. Do it.

Okay. I was doing it. I donned a clean white smock, the uniform of the jobbing scientist. The director yelled, 'Action.' I strode purposefully into the lab's room-sized fridge, where I selected a flask of red liquid. Although Dave's drug was actually colourless, the director thought that a red liquid would work best 'visually'.

The camera rolled while I carried the telegenic flask back to the lab bench, where I pipetted out aliquots of the red liquid into a tray of mini-wells – efficiently, no spills. 'Nice choreography,' the director said. It was nice pipetting too. Even Jude, the head of the lab where I moonlighted as an undergrad, said so when she saw the video on TV a week later. And she was a stickler for sharp lab technique.

I'm not someone you'd expect to see on TV. I've been Italian earth mama material since puberty. I'm the girl looking at the boys looking at the other girls. I'm solid verging on stout, and my skin tone's olive verging on swarthy. I don't fight it. My grooming routine's super minimalist: Nivea face moisturiser, morning and night; lip-gloss for special occasions; a hard-plastic headband to keep my thick curly hair out of my eyes. But despite all that, when, at the planning meeting, the video director asked Charlie, *sotto voce*: 'Hair and make-up for the talent?' I'd been thrilled. Rosa Giannini, the talent! Then, a pang of humiliation when Charlie said, 'No need.' Humiliation and confusion. I was the talent, right, so why no hair and make-up?

I found out when I saw the video air. I watched it at home with my aunt, Frankie, and uncle, Pep. I'd moved back in with them a couple of weeks before, when I split from my boyfriend, Nico – or, more precisely, when he dumped me. I was back living where I was raised. The bush. Strangeways. A place that barely qualifies as a town. It had been a thriving five-pub hub for the surrounding goldfields a century and a half ago, but at the last census there were seventy-seven residents. These days Strangeways doesn't even boast a milk bar. It's scrubby country that's never fully gotten over the gold rush, the mounds of mine diggings now colonised by weeds, the abandoned mine shafts covered by rusty wire mesh. There are trees, sure, but they're mainly box-ironbark: wimpy gums that drop their branches at a gust of wind and not uncommonly give up the ghost completely after a hot spell, crashing to the ground, or sometimes raining their dry leaves down on the parched dirt and then, skeletal remnants of their former selves, dropping dead standing up. Even hardcore residents like Pep couldn't describe Strangeways as bucolic and keep a straight face. I sound harsh. So is Strangeways.

But it's home, and I wasn't unhappy to be back. Sure, the hundred-plus-kilometre commute to Melbourne each day was a bummer – a half hour on my bike, an hour on the train, another ten minutes on the bike – but I wasn't unhappy to be sleeping in my little-girl bedroom again, waking to the sound of Pep's kelpie barking at our resident wallaby's black-ops-style morning raid on the veggie garden. Sure, I'd been gutted by the break-up with Nico, but I was liking the spin that Jude, who'd segued from boss to often-bossy friend, was putting on it: he didn't deserve me.

And it was May, the best time of the Strangeways year. Summer was over, another bushfire season survived. The tomatoes had ripened and been turned into sauce, the apple crop stewed, the pears preserved, the peppers and cucumbers pickled. All summer and autumn's produce was stacked under the house to see us through the winter. Seasonal eating of local produce: Arcadia! Meh. We were locavores by necessity, and making it all happen was a slog. But May was a brief respite before winter's routines and what Pep insisted on calling 'brass monkey weather'. Soon I would be sleeping in my beanie and scarf, and, come July, Pep and I would be holed up in the shed, elbow-deep in pig and beef mince, making bull boar salami. A year's supply of panini filling.

So there I was, once again the third wheel in my aunt and uncle's rituals – including watching the news every night before dinner, Frankie perched on the edge of the couch ready to dash to the kitchen if the ragu sounded like it needed a stir, Pep slumped in his armchair necking his first VB of the night. Although not the night Charlie's video aired. When Dave told me it would be on the Channel 12 news, I'd been surprised and – once the intel sunk in – horrified. I'd somehow assumed that the whole video thing was done when the director shouted 'cut'. Obviously I wasn't thinking clearly. Now I had to face the reality that my family would see me on TV. But first they had to sit through the breaking news. An earthquake in Indonesia, the worst in twenty years. Another gene for breast cancer sequenced. A preview of the night's footy match. The Doggies were playing the Swans and set to lose. 'Put the moz on them, why don't you,' Pep growled. He tapped his foot, impatient. He only watches the news for the weather report. Rain. We were nine years into the worst drought Australia had ever known, and Pep was obsessed.

Next up, the newsreader announced that an exciting new treatment for melanoma was being developed, right here in Melbourne. The video. It opened with my nice pipetting, but it looked like only over-the-shoulder shots of my forearms and hands had made the final cut. Neither Frankie nor Pep said a word. They didn't recognise those body parts as mine, and they had no reason to look closely. They didn't know I was working for the company that, the newsreader announced, was 'poised to take the drug invented by Dr David Tran from lab bench to patients' bedsides', words that came verbatim from the script concocted by the video director and Charlie. While viewers watched my hands do their best work, the voiceover dutifully forecast that Dave's drug would transform the lives of people suffering from melanoma.

The next clip showed Dave at a woman's bedside. He was looking down at her, kindly, while somehow maintaining his typical ramrod-straight stance. Maybe she was suffering from melanoma, because viewers were informed that: 'There are almost 13,000 new cases of melanoma diagnosed in Australia each year, and every five hours, one person dies from the disease.' Or maybe she didn't have melanoma. Because melanoma wasn't one of the conditions Dave's drug was slated to treat. During the prep for the video shoot, Charlie had asked Dave if it was possible his wonder drug would be used for melanoma. Melanoma scared people, Charlie said, and the stats sounded awesome. Dave said he guessed it was a possibility. Suddenly, a new disease that Golden Boy's drug might cure. Which was crazy, because his drug didn't need Charlie's hype. Despite my newbie status at SuperMab I knew all about Dave's discovery. I'd seen him present his data at BEST seminars, and his drug was looking like a winner. If it worked as well in people as it had done in the lab and animal tests, it would be a blockbuster and its inventor would be the perennial Golden Boy.

But now on TV it was Charlie who was being asked the preordained questions, while Dave sat on a stool at his side, smiling but silent. On and on Charlie waffled about all the money Dave's drug would make – presumably for the 'high-net-worth individuals' – and finally, it was a wrap. 'Eight men will participate in the first human trial of this exciting new drug, scheduled to start in December,' the newsreader announced.

I breathed the proverbial sigh of relief. There'd been no headshots of me. No body shots of my perp walk from the fridge with the red liquid. That night an explanation of why

I was working at a newly famous biotech company would not be required. Which was awesome, because that explanation would have involved a confession: I'd bombed out of the BEST PhD program.

When I'd made it into that program, I'd told my family that I would soon be Dr Giannini, a real doctor. Frankie had been proud-as, albeit a little confused. Her Rosa, a real doctor? Wasn't her GP – Dr Righetti – a real doctor? Pep, just as proud, had gone with a high-five and his standard shout-out on all matters Rosa: '*Il capo!*' One of the few Italian phrases he knew. The boss. That would be me.

Then, almost three years in, a stuff-up. Telling Frankie and Pep all about it was not something I was up for: my break-up with Nico was more than enough bad news for now. They'd both liked him, but Frankie especially. He'd won her over by not only fronting to her annual making-of-the-tomato-sauce day, but also hand-cranking almost two hundred kilos of tomatoes through the moulis. What a man! How could I not hold on to him? Of course my darling aunt didn't pose that question, nor do I suspect for a moment that she thought it. I did though.

So, this further instalment of 'The Trials and Tribulations of Rosa Giannini' could wait. Maybe forever. Because maybe now that I was standing shoulder-to-shoulder with Golden Boy in the lab, some of his stardust would waft in my direction and pave the way to the illustrious scientific future I longed for.

Maybe the drought would break too. Or maybe not. Even the perky weather girl wasn't calling it: 'Rainfall for May has been the lowest ever recorded,' she announced.

Miles

The night Davey went on TV spruiking his miracle drug was the first I heard about him hooking up with Charlie Cunningham. I didn't see the show the two of them put on, but Mother did. Davey had told her he would be on the news. No way would she have missed it.

He was her protégé, a project she took up some twenty years before his TV debut. She nabbed him – Dung, as he was known then – for herself in the uniform shop at school where she used to volunteer occasional afternoons of her time. I can picture it: the skinny scholarship kid rocking up solo for his hand-me-downs; the ladies-who-lunch eyeing him off; Mother, Lady Bountiful incarnate, pouncing, giving him the third degree. 'When did you arrive in our country, Dung? What class are you in? Year Seven? My son's in Year Seven too! Do you know any of the other boys yet? No? Well don't worry, darling, my Milesy will be your friend.'

Jesus Christ, was my first thought when I heard I'd been friended. Mother felt 'under-occupied'. Yeah, I got that. Spending the old man's hard-earned decorating the house and herself, hosting book club, nailing French, organising the gallery spring lunch: those activities filled her days, but they weren't meaningful enough. She wanted to 'give back'.

Okay. More power to you, Mother. But why couldn't she find an 'authentic' little project that didn't involve me? What about a trip to the orphanage in Kenya where all the pre-loved shit that couldn't be palmed off on the scholarship boys got sent? That could work.

'No, darling,' she said when I made that – rather constructive, I thought – suggestion. 'Phoebe went last year, remember? She asked me to be her plus-one, but I had to go to Fiji with Daddy for the firm's conference. She made a film of the darling little African boys singing the school song. It was gorgeous – and they were even singing in tune! – but it did seem rather touristic.'

So Mother went with the less touristic option: Dung. She became his personal social worker. She devoted herself to helping him 'realise his potential'. One of her first steps was to change his name. By Mother's decree, Dung became David. 'He'll integrate much better at school with an anglicised name,' she predicted, 'and David references his Vietnamese name.'

The name thing sorted, Mother began inviting Davey home. First it was for 'nutritious meals', then sleepovers. Davey was more than presentable from the get-go. He was clean. He was quick to smile, and that smile displayed straight teeth. He was polite and engaging with adults. A total winner.

His sleepovers became a weekly gig, during which Mother took pleasure in displaying him to her girlfriends. Whenever Davey was in residence, one of her intimates who 'just happened to be driving by' would pop in for a late-afternoon Savvy B and refugee viewing. There was probably a roster.

Despite that weird start, Davey and I were soon best buds. Because it was hard to sustain animosity to Davey. I would ignore him, mock him, bait him – obviously behaviour I'm not proud of now – but Davey had nailed the art of turning the other cheek. Davey's default expression was his emoji-worthy smile, which should have made him annoying, but somehow didn't. And he seemed to forgive me. In Davey's version of our shared adolescence I was his loyal friend from the get-go.

But that was Davey. He never showed any sign of the angst or anger that I now know must have plagued him. And his agreeable demeanour made it easy for others, me included, to believe he was whoever they wanted him to be.

For Mother, the waif in need of school kit became a second son, and, like all the best sons do, he kept in touch, dropping in for a coffee when it wasn't even her birthday, bringing appropriate gifts when it was: often flowers, never chocolates. Their little chats kept Mother up to speed on Davey's triumphs, the details of which she conscientiously relayed to me. The night of Davey's TV appearance, she was on the phone, I'm guessing the second he faded from the screen.

I was rostered on at the Oxford Hospital. 'I'm busy,' I told her when I picked up. I wasn't. I was on a break, in the caf, tucking into a slurry that the hospital cooks claimed contained chicken. I expected to be busy very soon though. I was the Admitting Officer, the controller of the hospital's beds, which were always in short supply. Large chunks of an AO's time are spent interrogating interns who pitch to get their patients one of those beds. Interns – I knew having been one myself the previous year – are so risk-averse they want to hospitalise any punter with a blip on their ECG (imminent heart attack!) or a high creatinine (looming kidney failure!). The AO's task is to sort the serious from the ambit claims, and they're typically flat chat doing so. As well as that core business it was a Saturday, so in a few hours there would be an influx of customers who had overindulged in their poison of choice. Many would need a bed for the night.

So I wasn't really bullshitting when I said I was busy, but I was also thirty-three years old and, for fuck's sake, my mother was calling me at work. 'Seriously, I can't talk right now,' I told her.

Right on cue my pager went off. It was Sharon Earls, the nurse in charge of the Emergency Department. Shaz is famous at the Oxford for her cool, competent moves in the resus cubicle; her slap-downs of any doc who displays up-himself, or herself, tendencies; and the tattoo that dominates her forearm: *STEVE*, her now ex-husband's name, around which her tattooist inked a snake when Steve left her for his favourite pole dancer.

MCA. Standby, Shaz's message said. A motor car accident. The ambos would have called it in. Only a specific category of bingle warrants a heads-up like that. I needed to get my arse into gear.

Mother had prattled on while I checked the message. 'It was such a thrill, seeing him on the news … His drug really does sound marvellous … It's so clever of him … Davey's going to be famous.'

Yeah? Where I was spending my days he was already famous.

Although he was a few years gone from the Oxford by the time I started out there as an intern, he'd made a big impression. The hospital grapevine hung heavy with amazing-Davey stories, and I heard often – *ad nauseam,* in fact – what a beautiful surgeon and faultless proceduralist Davey was. Which made sense. Although he'd displayed zip hand–eye coordination at school when it came to sports – Davey couldn't have caught a ball if his life depended on it – in the science lab he was deft. A toad that needed pithing? Davey was your man. One stab and, bullseye: they were brain-dead. Every time. Teenage Davey's task-specific dexterity had apparently translated into a skill that had stood working-doc Davey in good stead. Whatever piece of equipment needed to be stuck up or down whatever misbehaving body orifice was presented to him, he could do it – quickly, competently, no drama.

I was chuffed that my buddy had aced his time at the Oxford – I was, hand on heart – even though I was doing it tough. My first year there had been a shocker. An intern is everyone's girl. The consultants' flunkey. The registrars' gofer. Shit, even nurses boss interns around. And, because I took time out to play the pro tennis circuit once I graduated medicine, I was noticeably older than the other fledgling docs. After nearly eight years chasing fluffy balls around rectangles of various varieties, I quit and came back home to kickstart my hopefully soon-to-be-stellar medical career. But by then I was practically a geriatric in the eyes of my fellow interns, so never really one of the gang. And to my contemporaries, who by that time were senior registrars, or even junior consultants, I was just another often worse-than-useless underling. Long story short, I wasn't getting much love.

And by then Davey had moved on from the Oxford to medical research, a gig that he was apparently also acing. It seemed he had moved on from me too. When I chucked tennis in and came back to Oz, I'd expected to spend serious bro time with Davey. It hadn't turned out that way. Maybe it was me. My hospital roster was cruel – we're talking sixty-hour weeks, minimum – and off-duty I was rarely in the right headspace to pick up the phone and call him. My down time was spent partying or binge-watching sports. Neither was Davey's scene.

Cosy casseroles with him and his girlfriend, Abigail, weren't a possibility either. They'd been together forever, but she'd only recently graduated to live-in status. I could say I wanted to give the lovebirds their space, but the truth is more complicated. When Abigail didn't like someone, or something, she didn't hesitate to make that clear. On any measure of agreeability, she and Davey were at opposite ends of the spectrum. I don't know, maybe they had some sort of good-cop, bad-cop thing going on. What I do know is that I was someone Abigail didn't think much of. Was it my bro-ishness, or my family's 'arrangement' with Davey? Probably both. And I returned her antipathy. I couldn't see what Davey saw in her, apart from her high-cheekbone good looks, which, I'll admit, were magnetic, albeit full-on ice-maiden. She bossed him around and Davey let her. I didn't like it. Davey was the guru, not her. He should have been calling the shots.

Anyway, bottom line – and I wish it were otherwise – Davey and I rarely caught up in the two years between my return home and the so-called 'incident' and his death.

But I knew about his shit-hot discovery. As well as Mother's bulletins, I'd heard all about it at Christmas. Davey, being the second son, always attended Southcott family celebrations. At least the food had been better than the muck I was ingesting in the caf. Mother hires top caterers, even for family dinners.

I gave up on the 'curry' and pushed the plate away. I had a stash of energy jubes if a hypo hit later.

My pager pinged again. An update from Shaz. *ETA 5. F 40 y. ICU stat. xx*

'Duty calls, Mother,' I said, and hung up.

In five minutes a forty-year-old female who'd smashed her car, or whose car had been smashed into, would be arriving by ambulance. Shaz's shorthand – *ICU stat* – told me that the patient had arrested. The paramedics would be doing CPR, but it was a lost cause. Their passenger's age made her a candidate for organ donation, and the ambos had decided that her injuries didn't rule out that possibility. She needed to be taken straight to the Intensive Care Unit and put on life support. Hell of a start to Saturday night. Shaz had signed off with a kiss kiss in solidarity.

Almost two hours later I swiped myself into Emergency. The patient had been scanned. Her head injury wasn't survivable. Her brain had coned. But I'd done my job and sorted the bed. Conversations with families about their loved one's body parts go better in ICU. The organ donation coordinator had kissed his kids goodnight and arrived to make his pitch to the patient's husband and two teenage daughters, seated at her bedside, holding hands, hoping for a miracle. No, there was no hope, he would tell them, but many lives could be transformed – and some saved – if his team harvested her organs. He'd done the maths. Eight lives, if her soon-to-be-widowed hubby agreed to the patient's heart, lungs, liver, bowel, kidneys and corneas being transplanted. He would close his pitch with the suggestion that, despite the tragic loss, hubby and his daughters might find comfort in the gift his wife, their mother, would be giving to those transplant recipients. *Good luck with that*, I thought as I left him to it.

I could see the ambulance parked outside, its rear doors open. The unfortunate woman's transportation was being cleaned. When I rounded the corner, one of the ambos was slumped in a chair outside a cubicle. He looked like he needed talking down. I took the chair next to him and snuck a look at his name tag. *Josh*.

'Bad luck, mate,' I said. 'So, I didn't hear the deets …'

'Not much to tell. Wrapped her Beemer around a power pole just off the West Gate. Whacked her head on the steering wheel,' Josh said. 'Smelled like a point one five.' Ambos pride themselves on guessing the blood-alcohol level of their passengers, based on their smell. Josh's guess was three times the legal limit. 'Her pupils blew just as we hung a right onto Footscray Road,' he added.

'Bad luck,' I said again, racking my brain for more comforting words and coming up short.

'Yeah, well, she was never gonna make it,' Josh said.

Emergency was quiet. I looked around its overlit spaces for conversational inspiration. I could see Shaz standing in the nurses' station, speaking and gesticulating to what looked like an audience: a couple of nurselings in their navy scrubs and a young female intern. The TV on the wall behind Shaz was playing the Doggies–Swans match. The sound was muted, but I could see the score. Seventeen goals to one and it wasn't even halftime. The Doggies were getting thrashed. I could hear random words but couldn't get the gist of Shaz's speech. 'What's the deal?' I asked Josh, pointing in her direction.

'Apparently Dave Tran was on the news just before we rolled in,' Josh said. 'One of your mates, isn't he?'

'Indeed.'

'Top bloke, our Dave,' Josh said.

I nodded. Davey was a top bloke, there was no denying it.

'I'm guessing she's telling the newbies about one of his wins,' Josh said.

Yeah. She would be. Davey's dexterity combined with his encyclopaedic medical knowledge, not to mention his general willingness to give even hopeless situations a crack, had made him a top doctor as well as a top bloke. He'd been good at saving people, and that had delivered him an adoring fan base at the Oxford, with Shaz the cheerleader-in-chief. Her tales of Davey's wins on her patch were a core component of every nurse's and every intern's induction to Emergency.

'I'm going for a smoko,' Josh said and sauntered off outside to join his hopefully more empathetic colleagues.

I stood up and moved within earshot of Shaz.

' … he'd made the shed himself … ' she was saying.

It was her go-to episode in the top-doc-Davey series: his save of the punter who walked through the glass door of his backyard man cave after a full day holed-up woodworking, listening to the cricket on the radio and sinking tinnies from his beer fridge. I knew the story word for word.

The patient was a fifty-year-old male – a big guy, a hundred and twenty kilos and counting. He was a do-it-yourselfer, one of Emergency's core customer groups, and, as Shaz had just told her audience, he'd made the shed himself, from scavenged materials. The glass in its door was not the safety variety. The wife had found him with a big shard protruding from his chest. Her screams roused their son from a TV-watching torpor. Son snapped into action and pulled out the glass. Bad idea. Dad looked worse, not better, so wife and son shoved him in the back of the family wagon – they didn't have insurance to cover an ambulance – and drove to the hospital. When they pulled up, Mr DIY was flat as a tack.

Shaz was doing door-bitch duty that night. She got the story from the by-then-hysterical wife, the orderlies got Mr DIY into a cubicle, and Shaz rounded up her favourite resident: Davey, then just three years out of med school. The patient arrested in front of them. Davey didn't even try CPR. He reasoned that the glass shard had penetrated Mr DIY's heart, so he sliced into his chest with a scalpel from the suture set. Just like that.

Davey told one of the other residents, who'd rocked up for a gawk, to pitch in. The resident eased the patient's ribs apart with a retractor while Davey kept cutting to open up the pericardium. His guess was right. Blood poured out, exposing the patient's heart, complete with a one-centimetre hole. Shaz's hero pulled the hole closed with one hand and massaged the heart with the other. It started beating. The patient woke up. So there they were, Davey with both hands in an open chest, cranking up a heart, and the heart's owner staring right back at him.

I knew Shaz had got to this point of the story by the responses from her audience that drifted my way: 'Are you serious?' 'You're kidding!' I'd had thoughts along the same lines the first time I'd stood to attention while Shaz got on her soapbox. 'Enough already,' had been my reaction.

But nah, there was more. A team of sorts assembled. An anaesthetist intubated and sedated the patient. Blood was transfused – twenty litres of it, according to Shaz – and Davey stood there, hand plugging the hole, waiting for the duty cardiac surgeon to arrive and take charge. At last the call came. The surgeon was otherwise occupied. He couldn't get away. The word on the wards is that he thought the scenario a lost cause. Mr DIY was a goner. The surgeon did not want to be in charge when the patient bled out.

So Davey got his orders: sew up yourself. Dr Davey had done just one surgical rotation by this stage of his career, which qualified him to put in the final stitch in theatre, or perhaps tie off the knot. That didn't stop our Davey. He sewed up.

Shaz had stopped talking. She was looking at me and wiggling her fingers in a wave. I wiggled back. She must have got to the happy conclusion. Mr DIY lived. His saviour became a legend. The End.

My phone buzzed. I dug it out of my pocket. I'd missed an earlier message that Mother must have sent after I hung up on her. *Davey on TV with Charlie Cunningham.* And then the news that sealed his fate, and mine: *Charlie is his business partner.*

Foxy

Hindsight is such a cheap sight. When things pan out less than perfectly I try to resist the temptation to cogitate over what I might have done differently. Onward and upward, I say. Yet as I potter about packing up my office, as I prepare to embrace retirement, despite its prematurity, I have to admit to pondering the 'if onlys' of the incident. What a shocking business that chain of events was. A tragedy of the first order. Calling what happened an 'incident' is like calling Gallipoli a skirmish. But I needed to take some heat out of the situation – I was the spin-doctor on the case – so that's how I positioned it. Thanks to *moi*, it's always referred to as 'the incident'.

Public relations is the official name of what's been my game for the past forty years. Lobbying, crisis management, reputation protection: yes, my firm, Harry Renard and Associates, does all that. But fundamentally, I'm a *consigliere* at large. A fixer. Foxy's here to help, I tell my clients. And I do. I step up to the plate. I deal with whatever mess they find themselves in. I clean up and wash away any inconvenient facts. I bury the bodies, *sans* drama, and with absolute discretion, naturally.

Well, at least I *did*. Now I suppose I'll have to get used to speaking in the past tense. It's certainly not what I envisaged for myself at this point in time. Christ, I've still got a full head of hair, I can almost fit into the dinner suit I got married in, I can play eighteen holes without breaking a sweat, and, until this blasted incident at least, people were still talking about my sixtieth, an excellent night at the Long Room, organised superbly by my good wife Edwina, during which she and I convincingly demonstrated to the assembled throng that we still know how to rock and roll.

But I've faced the facts. I don't have a choice – not with young Charlie Cunningham in jail and CC, his father, one of my most cherished clients, dead. A heart attack in his sleep is the official line. A broken heart is the reality. I could have weathered the young Vietnamese fellow's death, but the fiasco that followed? No. Melbourne is a small town when the chips are down. Everyone whose name has ever been mentioned in the same sentence as young Cunningham's now has *l'odeur de Charlie* about them. So I've steeled myself to take down my shingle.

I'll be sorry to let my office go, of course, but I've promised Edwina I'll never be home for lunch. Not that it's come to that yet. I'm still popping in to the city every day, working through my files, culling anything that would be embarrassing, or incriminating, if it fell into the wrong hands. I've never been one for file notes, memos, records of any sort, but there *are* snippets of information lying around that I need to destroy. Because I can't have anything leaking out. Not now. Yes, most of my clients have run for the hills, and, yes, our fairweather friends have crossed Edwina and me off their Christmas lists, but I think our core social circle will survive this Charlie business. Anything explicit though, anything linking me directly to the boy's shenanigans – well, we could end up being rather lonely on festive occasions, and that would so disappoint my good wife. She's taken this like a trooper. I don't want her to suffer any more.

So I had Deidre, my secretary, sort all the incident ephemera into a box for my perusal before I sent her off on a cruise. A gift from me. Noumea. I've always treated my staff well: it instils loyalty. And there, right on top of the box, acting as a rather ironic paperweight, is a DVD. On it is a video news release that my nemesis not only commissioned, but also performed in. Charlie. Urgh.

Until the incident I'd had little to do with him directly. I'd seen him at Cunningham parties, of course. They always had a Christmas bash at their Toorak compound, and Easter Monday was 'games day' down at the Portsea bolthole, something CC's wife, Mary-Lou, seemed to take great pleasure in organising: egg-and-spoon races for the kiddies, humiliating three-legged events for the unfortunate adults who failed to escape her clutches.

I'd watched Charlie over the years, dashing his father's hopes and dreams. There was his threatened expulsion from school, aged fourteen, allegedly for making lewd suggestions to a female teacher while he was liquored up, an occasion when I was called upon to help. The school's Cunningham Music Wing, with its exorbitantly priced state-of-the-art acoustics, was the fix to that problem. Then there was his gap year overseas, during which he was mostly incommunicado. I'm sure there were other missteps too painful for his father to share. CC put on a brave face, feigning indulgence, but he didn't fool old Foxy. Charlie was the quintessential third-generation fuck-up.

Case in point: the ghastly video he took it upon himself to produce. The DVD is an advance copy that my contact at Channel 12 sent over, which was jolly thoughtful of her. I was horrified before I'd even watched the thing. A video news release? Oh, my PR colleagues tell me they're quite the thing these days, and I suppose they do have a place in some communication strategies. Apparently the mums and dads believe they're watching real news. But I find them crass.

The one that young Charlie had gussied up featured him displaying like the peacock he'd grown up to be, pimping the little venture he'd been given to run. So energetically too, and yet so pointlessly because, for Christ's sake, what value was there in the hoi polloi hearing about Charlie's dreams – or, as it turned out, delusions? I could have asked the Channel 12 lass not to run it and I'm sure she would have obliged. But why bother, I thought. One way or another Charlie was going to crash and burn. Why not let him be the director of his own demise.

I knew the other two lads involved in the incident as well: the unfortunate Tran and the Southcott's boy, Miles. Miles was the one I knew best though, and by far. There's even a photo of him on my desk, taken when he won the Junior Open, holding the trophy cup above his head, pleased as punch with himself. He must have been only twelve or thirteen. What a handsome lad he was. And still is. The athletic physique – toned without being cut and intimidating – the baby face, the deep mid-chin dimple, the thick tousled hair – dirty blond, I'm told, a colour Edwina describes as 'to die for'. He has quite the surfer look about him, although I've never heard so much as a whisper that surfing is one of his passions, and I do make it my business to know such things. No, tennis has always been his game. That Junior Open win was a, if not *the*, highlight of his career. He's even signed the photo: *To Foxy. With my best wishes.* A moment of pretentiousness that I'll overlook.

Because he's a nice lad, Miles. I'm genuinely fond of him. As a matter of fact he would be my pick for the son I never had. Not that I would ever say as much to Edwina. She tried for a boy, bless her, but after the second miscarriage I drew a line in the sand. 'I'm happy,' I reassured her, 'our Katie's perfect.' And she was. Katie was a toddler at the time, an adorable one, the spitting image of Shirley Temple, complete with rosebud lips and corkscrew curls. 'We'll let it be,' I said, 'our little threesome will make a beautiful family.' And it has. We've been able to give Katie everything she's needed, everything she's wanted. She's done us proud too: head girl at Burgess Hall, straight As in her law degree. What's more we had absolutely no angst during the teenage years, which can sometimes be so awkward with girls.

Yet every chap hankers for a son, and it's Miles who taps those unrequited paternal urges in me. What it is about him that presses those buttons I can't pinpoint readily. He's very charming, certainly. He captivates the ladies – Edwina included. Perhaps I see something of myself in him.

I've known his parents, Kip and Sally, for yonks. I've been jolly helpful to them over the years too. Because it's not just paying clients who've benefited from my expert assistance. Foxy's here to help, I tell all my friends and acquaintances. And I've always walked that talk.

Yes, they're good people, the Southcotts: good value and pleasant enough company, solid members of my friend portfolio. That said, Sally *can* go on about her oddball causes, of which there are many. Strewth, the last time I saw her she was raising funds for the Friends of the Disabled Acrobats! Kip's philosophical about her do-gooding. Happy wife, happy life, he says, and I have to agree with him there. Keeping Edwina happy is one of my top priorities. The alternative is simply too ghastly to contemplate.

It must be twenty years since I first helped the Southcotts out. It would have been just after Miles won that trophy. The business of tennis was outside his father's comfort zone. Kip isn't a particularly high flyer – oh, I'm sure he's made more good investments than bad, but he's not far enough in the black to give up his day job. I would say he's in the lowest stratum of our city's high-net-worth individuals. So when it looked like Miles had a talent that could be monetised, I was there to help. I arranged a couple of sponsorships. The contract with Bouncey was a particularly sweet deal as I recall, for me as well as the Southcotts.

Then, when Miles was poised to move to the international circuit, I bowed out. I was sure there would be a crowd of seemingly impressive young fellows lurking in the wings, jostling to take my place, and I decided that Miles wasn't a battle worth winning. I told Kip his boy needed different representation. 'Miles needs a team, more people to look after him, people with contacts and experience I don't have,' I said. Kip, no doubt dazzled by my competitors, was appreciative. I'd let him and Miles off the hook without any awkward conversations. But to be frank, I couldn't see Miles making a go of tennis once he left the safety of our shores. Strewth, if I'd thought he had a future I would have put some effort into making myself indispensable to the boy. No, I knew Miles was simply not hungry enough to succeed out in the big wide world. 'I like hitting the fun shots,' I recall him telling me. He still thought of tennis as a game! I suspect Kip also knew, perhaps not even that deep down, that his boy wasn't destined to make it on centre court. Why else would he have insisted Miles do medicine? 'It's our Plan B,' Kip told me. 'He can fall back on it if necessary.' Medicine. Plan B. Right.

It was through the Southcotts that David Tran first came into my orbit. I'm not a sentimental chap – except of course when it comes to Edwina and Katie – but thinking about that young fellow does make me a trifle melancholy. What a tragedy. Dead at thirty-three. At least CC got in his three-score years and ten.

But I didn't know Tran well. I would see him out and about with the Southcotts from time to time when he and Miles were at school, and he was at the Cunninghams' last 'Christmas in Winter' soiree with his girlfriend. They were a striking pair, I must say. Both over six-foot tall and skeletally slim. Tran with his rather exotic backstory, a 'boat person' made good. The lass, Abigail, almost ethereal, although possibly anaemic, with quite astonishing waist-length, straight honey-blonde hair. SuperMab had just been set up, so I sent Edwina over to chat with the two of them. Abigail was a social worker, my wife reported back, and not one who clocked off for the weekend. The plight of refugees and the urgent need for an apology to Indigenous folk, as well as the perils of deforestation and the doomed Great Barrier Reef, were all mentioned during their brief tête-à-tête. Oh, and golf courses. Abigail considered the quantities of water devoted to keeping them green scandalous. 'She sounds like Sally unplugged,' I said to Edwina at the time, an observation that rather amused us both.

But even though I doubt that I spoke more than a dozen words, total, to Tran, I heard a great deal about him over the years, from Sally in particular. I have to say, he always sounded just a tad too good to be true. As it turned out, I was right about that. I actually had quite a major influence on his life. At Kip's behest, I greased the wheels for him to get into medicine. Tran and Miles were finishing school and getting their university applications in order. Then, that very year, and seemingly out of the blue, an interview was added to the entry requirements for medicine. As well as jumping the exam hurdles, anyone aspiring to be a doctor now had to be interviewed by a couple of chaps from the medical faculty. The official line was that the university wanted to ensure that their students, our future surgeons, would be empathetic individuals as well as hotshot cutters. Everyone in the know recognised that explanation for the poppycock it was. The real problem was that the Asians were topping class after class. Our kids were drowning in their wake. And the new arrivals all wanted to be lawyers or doctors. Good luck to them, one might be tempted to say. But the prospect that, just by way of example, the Dean of Medicine's mother might soon have only two options when she was feeling poorly – the clever young Cambodian doctor or the even smarter Vietnamese – well, that was simply a bridge too far.

The Southcotts were anxious that Tran might miss out on the place he so coveted, and I could see it would have been awkward for them if Miles got a guernsey but the extremely smart refugee they'd nurtured so assiduously missed out. Heavens, they even had the lad living with them.

'I'm here to help,' I told Kip when he outlined the dilemma to me during our weekly luncheon at the club. And that's precisely what I did. A quiet word in the ear of someone who was in my debt, and it was fixed. Tran was in.

It's rather sad, thinking about that assignment. If I hadn't stepped up – well, things might have turned out quite differently. But how could I, or anyone else for that matter, have predicted how it would all play out down the track? Tran discovering a purported wonder drug. The Cunninghams dabbling in biotech – something they knew bugger all about. CC putting Charlie in charge of that endeavour, a boy who had Buckley's of running so much as a chook raffle. And then the drug trial: the plan for eight men to become human guinea pigs. Christ! It was a perfect storm, and, I maintain, an unforeseeable one. Although, with that bright light of hindsight, I will admit that Charlie's video was a harbinger of events to come. Even though I'd had an advance viewing I still watched it on TV, at home with Edwina, a glass of vino in hand. And seeing Charlie make such a first-rate fool of himself, I expected to soon land a new, high-value client. 'Edwina,' I said, 'that boy will be my retirement ticket.' Yes, how very ironic.

Abigail

I never called him 'Davey', like Miles and Sally Southcott did. It's the patois of their class, not mine. Nor did I call him 'Dave', like his colleagues at the hospital and BEST. He was far too cerebral for that. I never called him 'Dung' either. He said he remembered nothing about his escape from Vietnam, nothing about his life there. Being dropped off by two fishermen on a sandy Hong Kong beach at night was his first memory. I doubt that was true. Just like he covered up the scars he bore from his time on the boat, I suspect he suppressed his memories of those and earlier times. But my attempts to jog those memories always prompted a little sideways movement of his right hand, signifying that the discussion was over. I gave up; reluctantly though, because I'm sure he would have benefited from talking about those harrowing years. But I decided that if he wanted to forget what were no doubt horrific experiences, he was entitled to. And Dung was a name from that forgotten time.

We met in college, early in term one of my second year and his first, when I was assigned to waitress his table. I worked my way around the antique oak trestle, leaning in from the right side, like I'd been trained to do, careful not to give any of the testosterone-fuelled diners an opportunity for a covert touch-up, something I'd trained myself to do, whisking away the greasy plates, but not before I'd aligned the knives and forks together at twelve o'clock position, fork prongs pointing upward. I liked to remind the boys of the table etiquette most of them spurned.

He stood before I got to him, holding a small stack of plates, his own and those of his table neighbours, and followed me back to the kitchen. 'I'm David,' he said when the swing doors closed behind us, blocking the stares and whistles. He waited until I'd put my plate-laden tray down, then held out his hand.

I already knew who he was. He was impossible not to notice. Preternaturally unperturbed, he stood out from the college scrum. His handsome Asian looks were like a mating call for the girls, some keen to horrify their parents, others, like me, merely smitten. Now here he was, up close, his beautiful, soft brown eyes staring into mine, telegraphing something. I'll rescue you, if you want, from yourself? Or, please rescue me? Or, simply, I fancy you?

I brushed him off. 'Thanks for helping me clear,' I said, 'but don't do it again. You'll make me a target.' I only had to tell him once.

He was a paying resident. The Southcotts had funded his place. I was one of the waitresses. Six nights a week, I, and five other cash-strapped female students, served dinner to around two hundred young men. Lunch was a make-your-own-sandwich affair, but we were also required to set up the buffet breakfast and bus the tables after the boys had hoovered up their eggs and bacon.

In return we were granted room and board. We ate before the meal service with the cooks and the dish pig and got to live on campus in a place my parents would never have been able to afford, even if their youthful antipathy to such institutions had dissipated as they'd aged – which it hadn't. It was all rather *Upstairs, Downstairs*, the century-old college buildings Gothic in style. There was even a turret, where we waitresses lived. 'The Virgins' Wing', the boys dubbed it. Inaccurately, of course. We also got tutoring, like the boys, but only if at least one paying resident was taking the same subject. For me, that was a big 'but'. My degree is in social work, a girl's occupation.

Waitressing was hard work, the heckling incessant. The residents were mostly private-school boys from the proximate Eastern suburbs who were only in college for the social life. Miles Southcott was one such, Charlie Cunningham, who resurfaced as David's feckless business partner some fifteen years later, another.

I got myself into a headspace that made waitressing tolerable. I gave the boys no encouragement, although I'll admit I wasn't above giving them something to look at. I dressed Annie Hall-style. Op shop stuff, by necessity, accessorised to catch the eye. Two splashes of the same hue: one near my neck, the other near my ankles. If my outfit included a cerulean silk scarf, I would applique violets onto my socks.

Unlike me, the other waitresses fraternised intensively, and so it was that my waitressing stint, and theirs, ended prematurely on the night of the Winter Ball. Even more than the usual river of booze flowed, it was said later, as if that was an excuse. Jacqueline, my turret neighbour, knocked on my door at three am, her mascara and tears a muddy mix, the black-lace ball gown I'd admired seven hours previously ripped from its hem to her bust. Hughie. She'd said no, but that hadn't stopped him. She thought she might have been drugged, that perhaps he'd spiked her drink, because she didn't feel 'just drunk'.

I laid her down on my bed and fetched Matron, whose response was of the 'there, there, dear' ilk. 'Are you sure that's what it was?' she asked, when Jacqueline said the word rape. 'Weren't you dating Hughie? Or was it Howie? Or Harry? Or Hamish?' Or, by implication, all of them, concurrently. In other words: shut up, slut.

I took Jacqueline to hospital, came to understand what 'rape kit' means, sat with her while the policewomen asked their questions. They would investigate, they assured us, but they suspected Hughie might argue that the act – because, yes, even without sending the samples off, the doctors could confirm there had been a sexual act, and a violent one – had been consensual. Think about getting a lawyer, Jacqueline, one policewoman suggested, while the other nodded encouragement.

I've always been determined not to be that person whose contribution to the issues of the day is to sit around mouthing platitudes: 'How terrible!' 'Something must be done!' I see myself as someone who follows through. An activist. But Jacqueline was unsure about pursuing Hughie. It was starting to sound too hard, maybe too embarrassing, probably futile anyway. I persuaded her to at least talk with Legal Aid, and the Legal Aid lawyer persuaded her to file a formal complaint with the university.

I suspect the college Grand Poohbahs had hoped they could shut their eyes and pretend it never happened, but, faced with the complaint, they suspended Hughie and came to the negotiating table. Hughie's parents came along too. Jacqueline was into design. She dreamed of going to the Parsons School in New York. Courtesy of her rapist's parents, that dream came true. She didn't even tell me herself. Matron did. Jacqueline was whisked away quicker than the dirty dinner plates.

There was also a hasty review of the whole waitressing deal. It was declared anachronistic, incompatible with the college's plan to go co-ed the following year. Professional waiters were hired from the catering company that provided the food for old boys' functions. The incumbent waitresses were offered room and board, gratis, until the end of the academic year. We all accepted.

But before I was compulsorily retired, there was the dinner service on the day of Hughie's reinstatement to get through. The boys I was assigned to serve were too cunning to try anything that might have been visible from the Masters' table. When I leaned in to tidy the first diner's cutlery, he grabbed his meat-bloodied knife and held it at his groin, blade facing out and up. The next boy followed suit. And so on, until they all had metal phalluses. As smoothly executed as a synchronised swimming move, and just as ridiculous.

That night it was David knocking on my door in the Virgins' Wing. He'd heard about the knife stunt. This time I didn't rebuff him.

We talked for hours. I was more upset by Jacqueline's capitulation than the boys' puerile performance. My first attempt at righting a serious wrong in the adult world had failed. Jacqueline should have stayed and fought.

David disagreed. She was the victim, not me, he said, and she'd made her own decision. It was inexcusable, what she said had happened, but if she wanted to spare herself the angst of telling her side of the story over and over, of being subjected to scepticism, disparagement and taunting of the sort I'd experienced that night, that was fair enough. And she seemed to have got something she wanted. It was a victory of sorts, he said.

Perhaps. The activist in me still felt thwarted.

'Think of it this way,' David insisted. 'You stood up for someone, and something, important, and you made a difference. Be proud of that. Now, use that experience in your next battle.'

And what would that battle be? What cause would I take on next, David asked. Such a good question, but so difficult to answer, because I was troubled by so many things. All the uneaten food I scraped into the bin every night, while so many people outside the college gates went hungry. And water – how much of such a scarce resource is wasted. The craziness of importing mineral water from Italy. All the fossil fuels used to do that. Deforestation. Trees are living beings. They communicate with one another, even warning their neighbours when caterpillars are attacking. But every decade we cut down forests the size of New South Wales. We cut them down to grow crops, which are then used to feed animals, sentient beings that we humans kill to eat. Monoculture, genetically modified food, population growth, and, of course, refugees and climate change: I worried about all those issues.

In the years that followed the night of the knives I came to know that David was a wonderful, patient listener. He listened intently that night.

'You can't fix all the problems of the world,' he said, finally. 'You can't save everyone. It's too great a burden. But I love that you want to.' And he wrapped his arms around me.

That night I felt that he was my soul mate. In the end, I was wrong. And in my low moments I sometimes even wonder how genuine his empathic persona actually was. But he was still the love of my life, and that status is unlikely to ever be updated to 'first love', even if I wanted it to be. Given my role in his death, I'm a no-go zone for men now. I'm the black widow spider.

Rosa

Imagine a drug that could target whichever cell in your body's gone rogue and is making you sick. Imagine that drug stops the tiny troublemaker portion of the rogue cell from behaving badly, and, *voila*, you don't feel so sick, or maybe you're cured. And, added bonus, this imaginary drug doesn't affect any of the surrounding portions of the cell that aren't misbehaving. So, no side effects. A magic bullet. Sound awesome? Actually, that drug's real. It's a monoclonal antibody, aka, a mAb.

Dave's drug was a mAb, and until I bombed out of my PhD, I was working on a mAb too. In fact, at the time, most immunologists were working on mAbs, and those who weren't wanted to be. Because monoclonals are basically this century's penicillin. 'The miraculous mAbs', is what Prof – aka Professor Ian Patterson, the Director of BEST – calls them, and that's not puffery.

Scientists had been mucking around with mAbs in labs for years, but by 2006 their moment had arrived. They were revolutionising the treatment of not just one, but a bunch of diseases. Like cancer. After treatment with a mAb, tumours were melting away. Women with metastatic breast cancer were living way longer than their doctor 'gave' them, courtesy of a mAb. The extra time was good time too, not time spent suspecting that the treatment was worse than the disease. Arthritis sufferers, their muscle and joint stiffness gone thanks to a mAb, could now dress themselves, reach up and take a coffee mug from the cupboard, live a normal life. I'm not gilding the lily. For patients, mAbs are a dream come true.

And mAbs were making their inventors serious moolah. Pretty much every mAb that reached the market was becoming a blockbuster, which means annual sales topped a billion dollars. Enter the Cunninghams and their high-net-worth-individual mates, stage right.

And enter Dave Tran and Rosa Giannini, stage left. The promise of mAbs is what drew the young and ambitious to BEST, where Prof Patterson held court. Prof was in on monoclonals from close to year dot. We used to call him 'the mAb Meister' – 'we' being the PhD students, medical fellows and post docs. Prof did a lot of the groundbreaking basic mAb science, so, when mAbs became flavour of the century, BEST became mecca for would-be immunologists. There was a queue to become one of the mAb Meister's apprentices.

Dave was one of the chosen few. So was I. Prof didn't reach out to me personally – as if. He didn't do proactive recruitment. Distinctions or higher in all subjects of your degree; a 'top of' prize – top of something, anything, humanities electives excluded, naturally; a published paper before graduation: those were just the prerequisites. Then candidates had to grovel.

What got me started on the pilgrimage to anointment as an immunologist was a guest lecture the mAb Meister gave to a bunch of green-behind-the-ears undergrad science students.

Heckling from the back: 'Hey Prof, any of this on the exam?'
The airspace in the lecture theatre congested with paper planes.
Prof, centre stage and untroubled by the melee.

And there I was. Rosa Giannini. The science tragic. Nerd
enough not just to sit up front, but to pay attention, to take *notes*.
The bright-eyed girl from the bush, thrilled to have made it to
the big city, to university – and not a Mickey Mouse one either.

But I was there under false pretences. My alma mater had
wanted to diversify its student body. It wanted to get more
students from 'regional areas', and it wanted more girls to enrol
in science. So it gave country bumpkins and aspiring science
sisters a free kick, lowering the entry score required for those
underdogs to walk its hallowed halls. With me it got double the
bang for its buck.

'The New Age Dawns: a Potted History of the Miraculous
mAbs' was the title of Prof's lecture. That potted history
started back in the mid-1970s, when two seriously smart
scientists at Cambridge University had a light-bulb moment.
They figured out how to make mAbs. In so doing, they
transformed immunology.

Here's why. Back to the cells. Think of the rogue cell, or
cells, as terrorists that are running amok. The immunologist
is the CIA analyst, someone who can work out which portion
of which cell is the terrorist mastermind. Let's call that portion
of the cell a 'molecule', because that's what it is. That molecule
is the target. If you can take out the target, its fellow terrorists,
lacking a leader, become good guys. So, the immunologist
designs a miniature, drone-controlled, state-of-the-art missile:
a monoclonal antibody. It hits the target and only the target,

disabling the terrorist molecule without destroying innocent bystanders in the process. So, few nasty side effects. Monoclonals are kickass CIA assassins (think *Homeland*'s Peter Quinn) and sweet-as peacekeepers, rolled into one.

It sounds easy. It isn't. Identifying the terrorist mastermind, aka the rogue molecule, is super hard. So it wasn't until the 1980s that a mAb was first used to treat patients. Those patients were people who'd had a kidney transplant. The mAb they were given stopped their immune system rejecting the new organ. They survived. I thought that was awesome.

The scientific paper that brought this news to the world was published in 1981, the year I was born. I'm Sicilian, and the lead author on that paper was Italian. With Cosimi for a *cognome* he had to be, right? Benedict Cosimi. In the year I was born, one of my compatriots had done groundbreaking research on the first of an amazing new class of drugs.

The stars were aligned. And there was more. In 1984 the two Cambridge scientists who figured out how to make mAbs – César Milstein and Georges Köhler were their names – won the Nobel Prize for their efforts. Immunology? I was in.

A couple of years later I met the prerequisites to become a mAb Meister's apprentice. I did the grovelling too. As an undergrad, I got a part-time job at BEST: lab assistant in the facility where the mAbs are made for the BEST scientists. Jude's lab. I was already working weekends as a barista, but, *nessun problema*, I would work two jobs. I knew that I'd be no more than a bottle washer, mouse-cage cleaner and general dogsbody. But I was okay with that. I'd be in the same building as Prof, the place where he and his followers had brilliant ideas and did cutting-edge science. Prof would see all my hard work and decide I should be one of his PhD students, right?

Wrong. During my lab assistant years, I didn't even sight Prof, or any of the serious scientists. The antibody facility isn't co-located with BEST proper. It's in an industrial park in the western suburbs. BEST scientists don't go there. Their goodies are picked up and transported to the real BEST by courier, or personally delivered by Jude, who makes the trip into the city every day to network with her customers. Still, maybe my slog in Jude's lab helped get me over the line. In 2003 I was accepted into the PhD program with Prof as my supervisor. Yay me and my brilliant career.

Miles

Unsurprisingly, Mother wasn't the only person Davey impressed when his SuperMab promo aired. 'Did you see Dave on TV?' Shaz asked that night when I ambled over to see what life-or-death matter she was going to entrust me with next.

'Nah, I was sorting the ICU bed,' I said. 'Did he sing and dance?'

'Absolutely. He'll be the next Australian Idol.' Shaz laughed at her own joke. 'But in the meantime he's started a company. I guess you know that though?'

'Heard something about it.'

'I recognised his business partner. Charlie Cunningham.'

'Yeah? Did he ... what? OD and get brought in here?'

'Nasty!' Shaz reached out and pinched my cheek, not quite affectionately. 'Charlie's the one who married the model – Mercedes Janney. It was in all the mags.'

It was no surprise that Shaz recognised Charlie and no surprise that she was impressed. The Cunninghams were well known around town, for a shitload of reasons. Mother, for example, was fascinated by the social accomplishments of Charlie's mother, Mary-Lou, who had recently been awarded the Order of Australia for all her good work on the Friends of the Australian Native Gardens board. Mother had taken to wondering, aloud, how Mary-Lou got to be on that board, because Mary-Lou knew nothing about plants, native or otherwise. Mother probably hoped that if she mused about this mystery often enough the old man would crack and tell her what she already knew: Charlie's father, whom the old man referred to as CC, must have given the Friends a very large donation. Once this fact was out in the open, perhaps the old man would feel obliged to buy Mother a seat on that board too. But he didn't bite. The Cunninghams were rolling in dough and several rungs higher than us on the Melbourne social ladder. The old man knew better than to try competing with CC.

To the old man, the Cunningham name epitomised business smarts. His Cunningham riff pivoted on the fact that CC had managed to call the peak of the commercial real estate market. CC sold his chain of hardware stores at what turned out to be just the right time. Property prices were going gangbusters, and CC divested the freeholds as well as the businesses. A few months later, the bubble burst. 'The deal of a lifetime', I'd heard the old man call that transaction.

'So, how did CC know the property market was about to crash?' I asked him once.

'CC's very canny,' is all he could come up with.

My Cunningham story was an old one too. Charlie was at school with me and Davey, and he was an A-grade arsehole. The stand-out demonstration of this burgeoning trait was when he ratted on the boarders, who, almost to a boy, hailed from Western District sheep stations. There they'd grown up slumming it with the shearers and playing more than the occasional game of two-up, a pastime many were loath to abandon once they were sent to school in the big smoke. There was a regular Saturday-night game in the boarding house. Why anyone would want to spend hours standing around in a circle watching some dude chuck a couple of pennies in the air – not to mention betting money on the outcome – I have no idea. It was also against the school rules, as well as illegal, but the Master had decided to look the other way. Unfortunately, after the boys from the bush let Charlie Cunningham in on their game, that was no longer an option. Charlie lost a packet. So he dobbed in the game's convener and his fellow players. Expulsions followed – although not Charlie's.

Okay, that was probably twenty years ago. Maybe Charlie had now seen the error of his adolescent ways. More likely he hadn't. So as far as I was concerned, the words 'Charlie Cunningham' and 'business partner' did not belong in the same sentence, and certainly not a sentence that included my buddy's name. No way could I fake enthusiasm for this latest Davey news.

'Come on, Miles. Be pleased for your friend,' Shaz said. 'It sounds like he'll make some serious money at last. God knows he deserves it.'

She looked at the clock. 'Anyway, I'm off.' Her shift was over. 'Give Dave a hug from me when you see him. Tell him not to be a stranger. And tell him he's still my favourite boy.' She went to the sink, pumped the hand sanitiser, wiped away some of the germs she'd accumulated in the past eight hours. 'But don't worry, Miles, you're my second-favourite.'

'Good to know,' I said, like I meant it – and, actually, I did.

I'm ashamed to say that I hadn't seen Davey for five months before his TV debut. In a spectacular admin move, the Oxford had rostered two years of my annual leave back-to-back, giving me eight consecutive weeks' vacation, February and March of 2006, which I spent in South America. So Christmas was the last time Davey and I had caught up, if you can call dinner with Mother, the old man and Abigail 'catching up'. Christmas Eve dinner. Mother likes to celebrate European style.

There'd been no talk about Charlie on that occasion, although there'd been plenty of talk about Davey's discovery. It kicked off when we were sitting outside on the terrace beside the pool, having pre-dinner champers. 'Tell us about your research, Davey,' Mother said, apropos of nothing. It had been a stinker of a day with no cool change in sight. The pool's chlorine had evaporated to a haze that hovered just above the surface. The temperature was still in the mid-thirties. I was looking forward to dinner, which Mother's running sheet specified would be served inside, where the aircon was running full bore.

'This drug you've discovered,' Mother continued, 'I've told Kip and Milesy how marvellous it sounds, but I probably haven't done it justice. I've always been more an arty person than a science person, haven't I, Kip?'

The old man smiled indulgently.

'Not that I think science isn't important. Quite the contrary. Where would we be without scientists like you,' she looked at Davey, then me and added, 'two.'

Mother was trying too hard. Abigail had rocked up in a long, cream-coloured lacy dress, which, although it kind of resembled a tablecloth, gave her a virginal vibe. When she'd made her entrance holding Davey's hand, I'd felt a pang of sympathy for Mother, who, despite her weight watching, has been a victim of post-menopausal kilogram creep. Now she favours caftans, and Christmas Eve she'd gone with a floral, sequinned number in blue-green tones. Her vibe was more Christmas-tree bauble to Abigail's tree-topper angel. Mother had been outclassed by a younger player, but she was determined to stay in the game.

'Darling, you told me that when people who have cancer are given a drug like the one you've invented, when they're given one of these mAbs rather than chemo, they don't lose their hair,' Mother said.

'That's right, Mrs S,' darling said.

'That's so clever. Kip, remember when Roz had breast cancer and her hair fell out? It was awful. She had such beautiful thick, wavy hair too. The wig she got wasn't anywhere near as nice, and she said it was terribly itchy. So not having your hair fall out would be brilliant, wouldn't it, Kip?'

Who could argue with that? Not the old man.

'So, Davey, your drug, your mAb. You told me it was called EIGHT. I thought that was so clever. Tell Kip and Milesy how you came up with its name,' Mother said, pointedly excluding Abigail from her enumeration of those who needed a briefing.

'Well, its scientific name is SMB1412. The SMB stands for super mAb, because it's a special type of mAb,' Davey said. 'But SMB1412 is kind of a geeky name, so, because the numbers one, four, one and two sum to eight, and because eight's an auspicious number, a lucky number, I call it EIGHT.'

'Tell me again why eight's a lucky number?' Mother said.

'Because in Chinese the word for eight sounds like the word for wealth,' Davey told her.

Who knew? Perhaps Abigail, who chose that moment to insist on being included. 'Let's find a more fun topic of conversation,' Davey's beloved said.

I choked on my mouthful of champagne. I was actually on the same page as Abigail, although not for the same reason. I suspected that this interrogation about 'EIGHT's' clever name and likely lack of side effects, as far as wavy hair went anyway, was merely a teaser for the far more complex expose Mother was about to insist on. I wasn't up for it. Apart from the fact that it was freaking Christmas Eve, immunology has always been way too complicated for me. And I've never been able to see the point. A patient rocks up with an allergic reaction? Treat 'em symptomatically, I say. A rash? Bring on the steroids. Something more serious, like a peanut allergy? The EpiPen will be your friend. I figured that was all the immunology I needed to know, and if it wasn't, Christmas Eve was not the time for an education program.

But I also knew better than to think that my thoughts were relevant. This was Mother's gig. As usual she had curated the evening exhaustively. She'd had the family silver polished. The table had been decorated with the holly she has her florist import every year. Soon we would be eating a menu she'd spent hours workshopping with the caterer and drinking wine, sourced from the old man's cellar, matched to the food by the caterer's sommelier. If Mother wanted to talk about Davey's research, we would. I knew it. The old man knew it. Davey knew it. We sat silent, three would-be wise men, trying not to laugh, waiting for the two women to duke it out.

'What could be more fun than hearing about Davey's important work?' Mother said, flashing her trademark know-your-place-bitch smile at Abigail.

But, like Mother, Abigail is someone you don't mess with. Christmas Eve she wasn't dialling it back. 'Maybe we could talk about how to help all the people in the world who won't get to enjoy a lovely Christmas meal like I'm sure you've got organised for us, Sally,' she said. 'That might be fun.'

The evening was certainly shaping up to be more fun than *I'd* anticipated, but the old man rallied before it got even better. He had to go in to bat for Mother. Any slip in loyalty, perceived or actual, and he would be looking down the barrel of the Christmas–New Year break from hell. 'I'd like to hear about your work, David,' he said. 'But I, for one, need some more champagne before we turn our attention to solving global poverty.' He skolled his glass and poured himself another.

'Of course, Mr S,' Davey said. I saw him take Abigail's hand under the table. Poor bugger. Davey liked to keep everyone happy.

'Tell me, David,' the old man said, 'what is it about your drug that makes it "super"?'

I can personally vouch for Davey's ability to explain techy concepts to airheads, but that night he seemed off his game, perhaps distracted, anticipating the earful he was going to get from Abigail later on. He gave a long-winded answer.

Still, I got the gist. It turned out that when the lucky EIGHT reacted with some special molecule on some special blood cell, the immune system magically produced some even more special blood cells, which, it further turned out, were the immune system's good cops. If the immune system was misbehaving, these special good-cop cells brought it into line. So, it looked like EIGHT would be used to treat a bunch of diseases – possibly all diseases that involve the immune system, and even I know there's a shitload of those. It looked like Davey had basically invented the master switch for the immune system. 'I was lucky,' my modest buddy said at the conclusion of his impromptu immunology-for-dummies lecture.

Yeah? Or maybe it was his natural brilliance and killer work ethic.

The old man wasn't faking his interest in Davey's latest accomplishment. Although not as overtly effusive as Mother, he too was proud of Davey. Twenty-something years ago it was a different story. In the weeks and months after Davey entered Mother's line of sight in the uniform shop, the old man hadn't seemed to mind his occasional presence at the breakfast table. But once the sleepovers looked like becoming a thing, he baulked. 'We need to back up, Sally,' he said. The old man told Mother he didn't trust the government's vetting of refugees. So 'Mr S', the peacemaker now so eager to hear about his work, had Davey investigated by a private detective. It sounds Marlowesque. And paranoid. I mean, what deep, dark secrets did the old man suspect Davey and his clan were hiding? But that's what went down. The private eye did his sleuthing and turned in a report.

By then I had more than a passing interest in the outcome of the investigation. My tennis commitments were already intense. Mornings, I ran or worked out in the gym, and every night I trained. I was drilled senseless by a succession of coaches hired by Mother, each supposedly better than his predecessor. I kept doing okay, and the old man was proud, no question, but he insisted my grades mustn't suffer.

I had a problem: I could barely stay awake in class. Davey was the solution. He had started tutoring me. Maths, Chem, Physics, even English: he knew the material chapter and verse, and he was a natural teacher. When he stayed over at ours he gave me more help than I even knew I needed. I didn't want those visits curtailed.

So, when the old man read the detective's report to Mother one evening during their mummy-and-daddy time, the two of them holed up in the parents' retreat, I eavesdropped from the very terrace on which the report's commissioner was now throwing down a bottle of French.

The report gave a rundown on Davey's family – his 'family of origin' Mother took to calling the Trans, once, in her opinion, he was part of *our* family. The detective had discovered that Davey was not true-blue Vietnamese. He *was* from Vietnam, but he and his mother, whom Davey always called 'Ma', were Hoa, which basically meant Chinese. This was news to Mother. Still, she didn't miss a beat: 'Kip, you know how hardworking the Chinese are,' she said.

According to the report, Ma had worked as a live-in maid for a wealthy family. When she became a mother, they let her bring little Davey to live with them. His father was long gone by the time he was born, but otherwise the report made it all sound pretty cruisey until the Yanks shipped out of Saigon and Ma's employers fell on hard times – or hard times fell on them. If the report went into the deets, the old man wasn't sharing them with Mother.

'It says there's a half-sister called Ly,' the old man said.

'Yes,' Mother said. She and I already knew about Ly. Davey was devoted to her and had decided she would benefit from an integration program similar to his own. He'd renamed her Natalie. 'She sounds so sweet,' Mother said, 'I must drop over to Davey's one afternoon and meet her, and their Ma.'

'Don't get carried away, Sally,' the old man said, 'One refugee is all we can handle.'

I wouldn't have minded a sister, but although Mother and I did drop over one afternoon soon after this conversation, and did eyeball Natalie – who *was* sweet, and cute, with saucer-sized brown eyes set deep in a little round, worried face, and shiny black seemingly basin-cut hair – Mother didn't get carried away.

There was no in-house man in the picture. Natalie's father, a Kevin Tran, had come to Australia with them, but the old man's private eye hadn't been able to sniff him out. Like Davey's father before him, Kevin Tran had gone to ground, his surname the only legacy he left for Davey, Natalie and Ma.

'See, Kip, there's no father figure. Davey's got no male role model,' Mother said. 'He needs to spend time with us. Time with *you*, Kip.'

The old man gave his yeah-right grunt and moved on to the story of Davey's long journey to the land of Oz. The report referred to a newspaper clipping from *The Australian Times*.

I heard the old man shuffle the papers to find the copy the detective had provided. He read it aloud. It could have been a movie. The escape from Vietnam in a little boat. The setback – Thai pirates steal their food, water and the boat's motor. Hungry and thirsty, they start rowing. Then, a fierce storm. Facing it down, Ma binds Davey and herself to the mast.

Most of the deets in the report were news to me, and many, I learned later from Davey, weren't true. It turned out that my old man's suspicions were well founded. The Trans had secrets, which the private detective hadn't uncovered. He hadn't tracked down Kevin Tran and hadn't got Davey's backstory right. He'd done a crap job.

The storm at sea wasn't fiction though, and I already knew about it. Davey's wrists and ankles still bore the scars from Ma's mast-tying move, and his torso and thighs were liberally sprinkled with deep pockmarks, a consequence of the infection that had ravaged his starving body once he made it to Hong Kong.

But Davey hadn't taken Mother into his confidence. He wore long-sleeved shirts and long pants to conceal his scars. He never donned bathers, maintaining he couldn't swim, and, no thank you, Mrs S, he didn't want to learn. Davey chose to present undamaged to his new compatriots – apart from me and, I assume, Abigail, who I'm pretty sure was his one and only.

But, until the report's reading, all Mother had known was that Davey was a 'boat person'. On hearing what that actually meant, she spat the dummy. 'Kip, enough,' she said.

More shuffling of papers. 'The report talks about the refugee camp they were in …' the old man protested weakly.

'No. Enough,' Mother said. 'A six-year-old going through that ...' The nightmare sea sector of Davey's escape from his homeland sealed his fate. If the old man had hoped the detective's background check would be a get-out-of-jail-free card, he was about to be disappointed. There was no deal-breaking dirt, no grounds to veto Mother's project. Davey was on the second-son track.

And there he was on TV, twenty years after the background check and five months after that memorable Christmas Eve, impressing Mother, Shaz and who knew who else. While there I was: the first son, the failed tennis champ and failing doctor, looking out through the one-way glass at a hospital waiting room full of grim-faced punters, their eyes fixed on the door, willing it to open and reveal a nurse who would call their name.

I knew who I should call: my best friend, who'd named his wonder drug EIGHT because eight was a lucky number. Yeah, well, he'd sure be needing luck now that he'd thrown in his lot with Charlie freaking Cunningham.

I had to call him. When I was on the tour he'd texted or called me before every one of my matches. As daggy teens we'd got into a conversational groove heavy on military slang, and Davey always signed off our pre-game chat with the order: *Stay frosty, my friend.*

Now I needed to tell him to do the same. *Stay sharp, watch your six.* But what I also wanted to say was: *Jesus Christ buddy, Charlie Cunningham! What the fuck are you thinking?* Then again, what would I know? I was eating Davey's dust. I should probably stay in my own court.

My phone rang. It was him.

'Hey, the TV star,' I said.

'Funny. You still at the hospital?'

'Yeah. I'm on the disco shift. Here till O dark hundred.'

'Great. I mean, that sucks. But listen, I need a favour. Natalie's cut her head open. I need a suture set, and some local.'

'She okay?'

'Yeah. She slipped getting out of the shower. She probably only needs a half-dozen stitches. It's bleeding like stink though, so make it xylocaine with adrenaline.'

'Why don't you bring her in? I'll let you pull rank and jump the queue. I'll do the sewing.' I wasn't serious, and Davey knew it. No way would he let an amateur stitch up his precious sister.

'Yeah, very funny, my friend. I'm at Ma's. I'll be Oscar Mike in five. Okay if I do a drive-by, and you run it out to me?'

'Roger that,' I said, remembering the good old days, not focusing, like I should have, on the fact that for a cut that was no big deal, Davey sounded spooked.

Ly (Natalie)

When I was little, the other Vietnamese kids at school had so many aunties they had to give them numbers. One girl even had an Auntie Nine. I was jealous. I had no aunties, no uncles, no cousins. 'Can I have an auntie?' I asked Má.

That question made her mad. 'Stupid girl,' she said. But Dung said that Má's friend Han could be my auntie. I could call her Auntie Only One if I wanted her to have a number.

When Auntie came to drink tea with Má, she'd say: 'You lucky. *Con chị thông minh.*' You have smart son. And Má would nod, happy. It's true. Dung was smart. Má was lucky.

But after Auntie said, 'You have smart son,' she and Má would put their cups down. *Clink.* Back on the saucers. And they would look at me. Even if I was washing the dishes with my back to Má and Auntie, I'd know that they were looking at me when I heard the teacups clink. Má would be shaking her head. No. Ly is not smart like Dung. For a long time I thought that was why she liked Dung more than me.

Dung *was* smart, like Auntie said, so he should have known that there would be trouble if Mrs Southcott drove him home from school. He should have known that the man I used to call Pa would come back. But Dung was kind. He wouldn't have wanted to disappoint Mrs Southcott when she said, 'Let's drive you home.' But I wish he'd said, 'No. No thank you, Mrs Southcott, I'll take the train.'

I was sitting at the table in our kitchen eating a Nutella sandwich when they arrived. I heard a car stop and ran to the door. Dung was walking towards our gate. Mrs Southcott and her son, Miles, were following him, single file, like I followed my teacher into the classroom every morning.

Dung saw me at the door and waved. I waved back, but Mrs Southcott saw me and waved too. I felt stupid. Mrs Southcott looked pretty though. She had a long plait, like the Snow Queen in the story my teacher used to read to the class, and a white dress that almost came to her ankles. She'd pushed her sunglasses up onto her head, like movie stars do, and she was carrying a big, black leather bag over her arm. It looked heavy.

I ran back to the kitchen. Auntie was the only visitor we ever had, and Má always cleaned and tidied before she came. I was little, but I still knew Má would feel shame to have Aussies see our house when she hadn't cleaned and tidied. Má was busy, getting our supper ready. Dung brought Mrs Southcott and Miles into the kitchen and stood beside them. He was already tall, but Miles was even taller, and Mrs Southcott taller still. They were like three giants. I stood next to Má and took her hand. She didn't push me away like she usually did.

'I make tea,' Má said. Mrs Southcott looked around the kitchen. There were only three chairs. 'Thank you, Mrs Tran, but we can't stay,' she said. 'We just wanted to pop in and say hello.'

After they left, Má sat at the table and put her head in her hands.

The next day, the man I used to call Pa came back. He had come to Australia from Hong Kong with Dung, Má and me, and he stayed with us in our room at the hostel, but he left soon after we moved to the house that the hostel people found for us.

Má had known him in Saigon. She'd been the maid for a rich family and he'd been their driver. He got out of Vietnam before Má, and when she and Dung were brought to the hospital in Hong Kong, of course he recognised them. He came to visit her. He said he would help her, and look after her and Dung. He was lying. After they got married he turned mean. He probably only married Má so that a Western country would accept him. Countries liked to take families rather than single men.

Once we were in Australia he became *really* mean. A bad man. He joined a gang.

They called themselves 'Born to Kill'. Dung said that was what some American soldiers in the war wrote on their helmets. The members of the Born to Kill gang gave themselves crazy names. Pistol, Revolver, Fire: the names of what they would use to kill someone who wouldn't pay them for the drugs they were selling. When he joined the gang, the man I used to call Pa picked the name Hands. He told me and Dung that we had to call him Hands now too. I wanted to call him dickhead, but Dung said not to. He said I should call him Hands, but I could think *dickhead* when I said it.

When Hands moved out of our house after he joined his stupid gang, Má said: '*Đi cho khuất mắt.*' Good riddance. But she only said that after he had gone, when only Dung and I could hear. When she said *Đi cho khuất mắt*, Dung put his arm around her. Má cried, but it was happy crying.

The day after Mrs Southcott drove Dung home, Hands walked right into our house as if it was still his house. We were eating supper. He swiped Dung across his head from behind. 'I hear you a big shot now,' he said. 'New school. Rich friends.'

At my school that day, Binh, the boy who lived next door, told me that he'd seen a big white car parked outside his family's house. The car was a Range Rover. He was impressed. It was Mrs Southcott's car. I suppose Binh must have told his father, and his father must have told Hands.

'Go to our room, sis,' Dung said to me. 'He'll be gone soon.'

'Sis.' Hands lifted one side of his lip. I could see his front tooth that used to be broken. Now it was covered in gold.

Dung took my hand under the table. He squeezed it, then let go. 'It's okay, Ly. Go,' my brother said.

Hands leaned over in front of Dung and me. His face was so close I could see the blackheads on his nose. 'He's not your brother, Ly. Dung here,' Hands jabbed Dung's chest. 'Not,' *jab*, 'your,' *jab*, 'brother.'

Dung, not my brother? I looked at Má. She was looking down at her hands in her lap. I looked at Dung. He was angry, glaring at Hands.

'*Mai, nói cho nó biết*,' Hands said. Tell her, Mai. '*Nói cho nó biết thằng thòng minh này không phải là nanh của nó.*' Tell her smart boy here is not her brother.

Má kept looking down. Why didn't she say: 'Don't be stupid, of course Dung is Ly's brother. You stupid. Get out.'

I could feel tears coming. I stood up. Hands was looking at Má. Tell her, he said again to Má. I tucked my head in and charged like a bull at his belly.

It wasn't what he was expecting. He fell back against the kitchen bench. '*Đụ má mày,*' he snarled. Fuck your mother. He got up and stepped towards me. '*Con ranh này,*' he shouted. This brat, this spirit of a stillborn baby. His hand was a fist ready to punch me.

But Dung was quick. My brother jumped up and pushed me out of the way. 'Don't touch her,' he yelled. Then Hands' fist with its ugly ring landed on Dung's face, right above his eye.

Má had many secrets, and one of them was that Dung was not her son. Dung and Má said that if Hands told the Aussie government this secret they would send us all back to Hong Kong, or Vietnam. Dung and Má didn't want that to happen. So they made a plan, and because my English was already better than Má's I had to help with the plan.

Má took me down to the phone outside the shops and made me call Mrs Southcott. 'Would you please visit us again, Mrs Southcott?' I said when she answered. 'But this time without your son.'

'Okay, sweetheart, I guess I can do that,' she said, 'but what's this about?'

She sounded so nice. 'My Má needs to talk to you, that's all,' I said.

Mrs Southcott came a few days later. I had to stay home from school because she came in the morning. This time, she had her hair in a ponytail and she was wearing skinny jeans. She still looked pretty.

Má made tea, and the three of us sat at the kitchen table. Má and Dung had told me what to do. Má would talk first. When she was finished talking, she would look at me and blink. Then I must say, 'Mrs Southcott, my Má is working three jobs already, and still we do not have enough money for the Australian life.'

I am not stupid. I knew Má was going to ask Mrs Southcott for money. But I didn't know what Má was going to give Mrs Southcott in return. Dung and Má hadn't told me.

So when Má said to Mrs Southcott, 'What about Dung go live with you? He help your son with the homework and you pay me,' it was not what I was expecting. I knew Dung helped Miles with his homework. Miles was Dung's friend now. Miles had looked after Dung when some boys at his new school put jam on his seat in class. My brother didn't see the jam and he sat on the seat. But he didn't just get sticky. The jam had pieces of glass in it that went through Dung's pants into his bottom. Miles got some tweezers and picked all the pieces of glass out. Then he painted the cuts with yellow antiseptic. Miles had been kind to Dung, so of course Dung would help Miles with his homework if he needed help. But Dung couldn't go to live with the Southcotts. That was crazy. I wanted to shout at Má. I wanted to shout *No*.

Mrs Southcott bit her lip. She was unhappy too. I suppose it wasn't what she was expecting either. She'd taken Dung to have an operation on his face where Hands' ring had split it open. The first operation hadn't worked, and now he needed another one. I suppose she expected Má to just say: 'Thank you, Mrs Southcott.'

Má looked at me and blinked both eyes, like we'd practised. I looked down at the tea in my cup. No. I did not want Dung to go and live with the Southcotts. I didn't care if that meant we had to go back to Hong Kong. Hong Kong would be okay if the man who called himself Hands now wasn't there. I would be with Dung and Má. I didn't care that Dung wasn't my blood brother.

But it didn't matter what I wanted. Má and Dung didn't want to be sent back to where they came from. So Má had to have money to give to Hands, and Dung had to live with the Southcott family and help Miles with his homework. Every month, Mr and Mrs Southcott paid Má. And the first Monday of every month, dickhead Hands came to our house to collect the money. He said he was paying Má and me a visit, but it was Má who was paying him.

So now our family had another secret. Of course, everyone, all our neighbours, knew that Dung had gone to live with the Southcotts. 'Sad for you, Mai,' Auntie would say when she came to drink tea with Má, 'but good for Dung. He will have many opportunities now.' But no one, not even Auntie, knew that Má was taking money from the Southcotts in return for Dung. Má said no one could know, because if they did she would feel shame.

The night Dung went on TV with Charlie Cunningham was a Saturday, but Hands didn't wait until Monday to pay us a visit. He was already sitting at our table when I walked in. 'Get Dung here,' he said. 'Get your *brother* here.' He sneered at me, showing his stupid gold tooth.

That was when Má started to go crazy. Má knew what Hands was going to tell Dung. Má had many secrets, and Hands knew the secret that she'd kept from Dung ever since they arrived in

Hong Kong. Hands had waited a long time. Now he would use the secret to get some of the billion dollars.

Dung was living with Abigail then, so I called him and told him he must come. But Dung said, 'No. I've had enough of this bullshit, Ly.' There was no way the government would deport him and Má now. And Dung didn't even have the money that Charlie Cunningham had talked about on TV. 'It was just an ad, an ad for our company,' my brother said. So he wouldn't come.

He had said 'enough' before. When he first met Abigail, he said she would help him with the government. Together they would get Hands out of our lives. But Má went crazy. She wouldn't let him tell Abigail that she wasn't his real mother. In the end, Dung did what Má wanted, like he always did, so that she wouldn't feel shame. Now he was saying 'enough' again. I hoped he meant it this time.

'*Dung nói gì?*' What did Dung say? Hands asked when I hung up the phone.

'He said you're a *mặt lồn*,' I told him. Pussy face.

Dung did come that night. He was leaning over me when I woke up on the floor. He was holding my wrist in his hand, checking my pulse, I suppose. I could feel something sticky running into my eye.

Abigail

Apart from one break-up, David and I were together all through uni and his time at the Oxford. Ten years. A whole decade during which we didn't live together, something that more than disappointed me.

When my fee-free college stint ended, I moved into a terrace house in Fitzroy with the other three former waitresses. We all started waitressing again to cover the rent, me at the Vegie Tavern, my housemates at higher-end restaurants. Their tips were good, mine non-existent, but serving people meat to make money wasn't something I could do anymore. Animal welfare had become my project. Like David said, I couldn't right all the world's wrongs, so that's the cause I chose.

I grew up vegetarian. I'd only ever eaten free-range eggs. But why should I feel self-satisfied about that? Why should chickens be restrained at all, even on an ethical farm, just so I can have a boiled egg for breakfast? And why should cattle be domesticated so that I can eat camembert? So I went vegan. I stopped wearing animal products too. Leather shoes were out, as was anything woollen: blankets, coats, sweaters. There were downsides. Plastic sandals make for sweaty feet in summer. And I was often cold in winter. Cotton isn't as warm as wool, and down jackets were out because ducks and geese are plucked alive to source the down feathers. But I was living by my principles.

David stayed on in college. His 'arrangement' with the Southcotts required him to be there, on standby, ready to coach Miles whenever he deigned to grace the country and the college with his presence. The arrangement enraged me, but it was a non-negotiable part of David's life.

He also refused to go vegan. The hunger he felt during his escape from Vietnam had a permanent impact on his appetite, even though he chose not to remember the horrors he experienced as a so-called 'boat person'.

David was unwilling to deny himself any type of food or any extra helping he desired, yet, magically, he remained pencil thin. Food was his indulgence, steak his favourite meal. The one memory he had – or chose to share – of his life in Vietnam, was of eating what he called 'beef steak'. In a sort of prequel to David's arrangement with the Southcotts, he and Mai had lived with a well-to-do family: the Phams. Mai was their maid. The family imported foie gras, cheese and wine from France, and beef, which Madame Pham adored, from England. 'They shared it with you?' I asked, surprised, when David told me about this luxury.

'Why wouldn't they?' David asked. Then, understanding my question, 'Madame Pham was always generous, as well as beautiful.' And, I could see, adored by her maid's son.

But, despite his enthusiasm for beef, and the woman who first provided it, David seemed happy to eat whatever I cooked. The night we broke up, I'd made a vegetarian version of *mapo doufo*. It's a tofu dish, Sichuan in origin and spicy. I substituted mushrooms for the minced pork in the traditional Chinese recipe. It was just the two of us that night, which was rare. My housemates usually made sure they were around when David was. He would chat charmingly with them, seemingly oblivious to their flirting, and always brought wine, although he didn't drink and couldn't afford that generosity. He gave Mai a large portion of the allowance the Southcotts gave him.

It was a mild late-summer night, and we were eating outside in the little backyard space where I'd managed to grow some herbs in pots to create a courtyard ambience. David scraped his plate clean, then blew our night, and us, up. 'Those mushrooms tasted almost as good as pork,' he said.

I was incensed. His compliment on my painstakingly prepared meal rested on a comparison to meat. He was being honest, and, with the insight into our relationship I have now, my reaction to his praise must have floored him.

David was everyone's rock. In the absence of his father and stepfather he'd become the provider for his family, as well as Natalie's life coach, Miles's tutor and Sally Southcott's flagship project. But in our relationship, I'd become the rock. He'd comforted me on the night of the knives, but now I looked after him, almost *tended* to him, to an extent that's embarrassing to recall. Though he rarely complained, even when people treated him badly, whenever I sensed his frustration or disappointment, I was there for him, ready to listen. Almost like a good wife. And I protected him, leaping in to save his feelings when I thought it necessary. Once, circa 2001, when John Howard alleged that asylum seekers had purposefully thrown their children overboard in a ruthless bid to get rescued and brought to Australia, a now former friend had the gall to ask David, 'As a boat person, does that sound plausible?'

I saw his horrified look before he could mask it. 'No, it does not sound plausible at all,' I said, quickly and sharply. I made sure we never saw that 'friend' again. Now here I was, slipping further into the woman-as-nurturer role: I was feeding him. And this was my reward? The mushrooms tasted almost as good as meat?

I picked a fight. Going vegan was a trivial contribution to animal welfare – I knew that – and I'd turned my attention to animal experimentation. Animals suffering, more than 100 million losing their lives every year: all so that someone's theory could be tested, or their face cream deemed safe, or a new medicine – often something people might not even really need – cleared for human use. Imagine the outcry if all those lives being lost were human.

David and I had talked about it many times before that night. Testing medicines on animals before humans was essential, he said. The drug that kept my dad's cholesterol down and prevented him from having a heart attack had been carefully tested to ensure it was safe. The insulin that kept one of my housemates alive came about through experiments on dogs and rabbits. A million monkeys died during the development of the polio vaccine, but that vaccine has since saved many millions of human lives. The end justifies the means, David argued. I'd be able to live as an ethical vegan for twenty, maybe thirty years longer than I would have without all the medical advances animal experimentation has brought.

I wasn't convinced. Scientists consider it unethical to experiment on humans unless they've tested their theory, or drug, on animals first. They believe that it's acceptable to use animals first because they're lesser beings. But then, the whole point of animal experiments is to extrapolate the results to humans. It's possible to do that extrapolation because apes and humans, mice and men, are alike in many ways. So, why do we humans have special privileges? David didn't have an answer, but he'd heard me and he hadn't rolled his eyes. Tacitly, we agreed to disagree.

I broke that truce the night of the *mapo doufo*. I knew it wasn't only research scientists who were doing animal experiments: med students did them too. That night I asked him about the experiments he'd done that week. Probably not realising that I was seething, David told me about the 'hotplate test', during which medical students get to see for themselves how morphine alleviates pain. They warm up a hotplate. They get their stopwatches ready. Then they drop a mouse onto the plate and measure how long it takes the mouse to jump off. Because it's painful, standing on that hotplate. Then they give the mouse a dose of morphine. It doesn't jump? They got the dose right. How long does the morphine last? Back on the hotplate, mousey. When it starts jumping, the morphine has worn off.

What a pointless experiment! Why couldn't all these aspiring doctors just read about the pain-killing properties of morphine without subjecting mice to such cruelty?

They could, David said, but the experiment was part of the syllabus. He wanted to be a doctor. He couldn't risk rocking the boat.

And I couldn't be with someone who had that attitude. We broke up. I broke us up.

I lasted three months. I told him not to call and, always the courteous one, he didn't. I missed him, and I was unnerved when one of my housemates – the prettiest one – asked whether, if David and I were really over, she could have him. But I held out. How could I be involved with, sleep with, someone who tortured mice and was okay with it?

My dad got us back together. He and David got on well, which wasn't saying much because David got along well with everyone. But my dad was a conscientious objector to the Vietnam War. When I'd first taken David to meet my parents, I'd feared his unremitting amiability might falter. My dad, after all, hadn't been willing to fight for David's countrymen and women's freedom.

But it wasn't a problem. It was a stupid war, David said. If he'd been in my dad's shoes, he wouldn't have gone either – which I wasn't sure was really the point.

Three months after David's faux pas and my meltdown, Dad suggested lunch at the Hare Krishna restaurant, one of our haunts. I'd never doubted that my dad lived scrupulously by his principles. Over the dhal, I found out I was wrong. He reminded me that he'd had his weak heart valve replaced the year before. I remembered. I'd been worried in the lead-up to the surgery and relieved when he came through okay. What I didn't know was that the valve that now kept his heart pumping was porcine in origin. A pig had lost its life to save my dad's.

'I guess you had no choice?' I asked. It wasn't really a question, but again, I was wrong. He could have opted for a metal valve. But then he would have had to take anticoagulants all his life to stop his blood clotting as it passed through the metal. And with anticoagulants, as well as the inconvenience of small cuts bleeding profusely, came the risk of stroke. My dad chose to accept the pig valve rather than face that inconvenience and take on that risk.

Don't be so judgemental, Abby. Dad didn't need to say it. His morality tale got me and David back together.

Although it wasn't something we really talked about, I expected we'd live together once David graduated medicine and his arrangement with the Southcotts ended. Instead, he moved back home with his mother and sister. He hadn't lived with them since he was fourteen, and he regretted being separated from Natalie when she was little. Now, he wanted to buy them a house. Living with them saved him paying rent.

I'm ashamed of how annoyed I was about these plans. Mai had rowed across the South China Sea to deliver him to safety. Here in Australia she'd sacrificed the comfort his company would have brought her, the family time they could have enjoyed, so that he could get a good education. The worst childhood deprivations I'd endured were the limited mango season and my parents' admirable refusal to buy me a Barbie doll.

David logged long hours at the hospital, first as an intern, then a resident, registrar, and finally Chief Resident. I rarely saw him more than once a week, sometimes less often. Most of my girlfriends, including all my housemates, got married during David's years at the Oxford. He wasn't my plus-one at a single wedding.

After his four years at the Oxford, David was on track to be a consultant. Instead, he chose research. He had an idea for a drug that he thought might cure diseases of the immune system. If his idea worked, the drug would save many more lives than he ever could as a doctor.

It sounds so noble. In fact, his motivation was mercenary. A junior hospital doctor isn't well paid, and as a consultant it would take time for his practice and income to build up. But if his drug were successful, he would make an insane amount of money, quickly. That was the theory. He would be able to buy the house sooner. He didn't want Mai and Natalie to have to get a loan like everyone else did. I never understood that, but I wasn't *his* social worker, and even if I had been I wouldn't have been able to dissuade him. I willed myself to continue finding his concern for Mai and Natalie's welfare as endearing as I did when I first met him.

I'd been working at the Refugee Centre since I graduated. My clients were mainly Sudanese people who'd fled their country's civil war. I helped the new arrivals negotiate with the government agencies that supported them here. I worked out what they needed and qualified for, filled out the forms and made the follow-up calls when those forms got lost or went un-actioned. Getting the refugees housed, fed, clothed and on track to a new life was satisfying work, and I was trained not to expect them to always be grateful, which they weren't.

But it wasn't enough. I needed a change. Although the wedding invitations had slowed to a trickle, baby showers were starting to appear on my calendar. Now David was heading down an exciting new path in the research world.

I felt like I was waiting for something. But what? It wasn't for David to propose. I don't believe in marriage. I didn't need the state, or church, to sanction our relationship. And it wasn't children. Population growth is placing an overwhelming burden on our planet. I'd decided that procreation wasn't a responsible choice. But perhaps I *was* waiting for some kind of validation, of us. I am sure of one thing: I felt humiliated.

I decided to do what I would have counselled against if I'd been my own social worker: run away. I packed up the contents of the studio apartment I'd rented when my share house disbanded and I moved to Rwanda.

I was away for three years, all the time David was at BEST. If I hadn't gone away, I suspect David would be alive today. I know he'd be alive if I hadn't come back.

Rosa

Flash forward three years from my admission to BEST. I'm a city girl now, living in Collingwood with Nico, who's a fellow PhD student at BEST. A lab romance, our eyes locking over the Bunsen burners? Nope, we bonded over pizza and Coronas one Friday beer o'clock. We had the same ambitions – become an immunologist, discover something worth discovering – and we both needed to live near BEST. Experiments don't run on time like trains are supposed to, so 'research scientist' isn't a nine-to-five job. Commuting late at night to Strangeways (me) or Ringwood (Nico) was a bummer. Rents being what they were, co-habitation seemed the way to go. I know, super romantic.

So, it's 2006 and we're not quite living the inner-city dream. We're in a studio apartment. We wake to the sound of our neighbour flushing his loo, or worse. And although, as Jude, the *Pride and Prejudice* tragic, kept reminding me, Nico does resemble Colin Firth – if you squint – he isn't shaping up to be the gentlemanly Mr Darcy. How surprising, given the prosaic start to our relationship.

There's a problem with my research too. My results, my data, aren't making sense. I know it, but I can't bring myself to admit it. Why? What about that 'we're totally objective, we call it as we see it' image that scientists put out? In reality, not so much. Scientists are optimists. We believe in our work. We believe our work will work out. When it doesn't, sand looks like a top place to bury your head.

Here's the thing, no scientist wants to publish a paper in the *Journal of Negative Results*. For a start, no one will read it. Breaking news: 'Refuted my hypothesis. Proved myself wrong.' Cue the yawns. No one will reference it in their own papers either. And that's a problem, because a scientist's career is all about publishing papers in high-profile journals. Promotions, tenure, grants – they're all about your number: the number of papers you've published.

Like every other researcher pipetting away at the BEST lab benches, I dreamed of publishing my results in *Nature*, a journal as important to scientists as *Vogue* is to fashionistas. A scientist who makes a paradigm-shifting discovery and scores the *Nature* publication is a winner. If all you can crack is the *Journal of Negative Results*, you're a loser. Simple as that.

So, scientists mine their data for positives. If your experiments don't prove your original hypothesis, there must be something to see, something interesting, some new theory that your results do support. Scientists are positive thinkers, pathological optimists.

And that was me. Until it wasn't. My six-monthly 'catch-up' with Prof at the Patterson *casa*. Prof always reviews his apprentices' progress at his place, late at night, usually on a Friday. Why does he choose a venue and time so totally inconvenient for his students? Because he can.

The mAb Meister lives in Doncaster. The outer-Melbourne 'burbs, and not famous for its public transport. Nico usually drove me there, even though Prof wasn't his supervisor, and waited until I was done to drive me home – audiences with the mAb Meister are brief. But this night, Nico 'had something on'.

'Oh,' was all I said. Not, 'What have you got on?' or 'But you always drive me.' Just 'Oh.' We still fought.

'So where are you at with your driving lessons?' Nico asked.

Nowhere, was where I was at. I wasn't taking driving lessons.

'Come on, Rosa. You need to get over this driving thing,' he said.

This driving thing? My parents were killed in a car accident. A three-car pileup. Heading to work, my papa was in the driver's seat, probably humming 'Sweet Caroline', a song he claimed Neil Diamond wrote for my mama, Carolina. Or maybe Papa wasn't humming. Maybe he was belting out a line or two – *Good times never seemed so good* – while my mama in the passenger seat snapped open her treasured gold compact and powdered her nose. Whatever. A car behind them pulls out to overtake, its driver probably momentarily blinded by the Sicilian morning sun. The driver swerves sideways into my parents' Fiat, when he finally sees the oncoming car. Too late. A head-on collision. My parents' car spins, then, momentum gained, crashes back into the other two already mangled cars. The explosion. Quadruple fatalities. Closed-casket funerals. Me, aged six, an orphan.

Nico had previously pointed out that my aversion to driving stemmed from this tragedy. I mean, seriously, no shit, Sherlock. And now that I'd been the recipient of his insightful psychoanalysis, I was supposed to – what? – oh right, get over it.

I'm an independent, resourceful woman. There's a bus to Doncaster. I rode it. I walked the block and a bit to Prof's. I knew the drill. The door was left unlocked for students. I let myself in. Three chairs were lined up in the hallway, none occupied. I took the middle one, just for fun. My review was scheduled for nine-thirty pm. Nine-thirty came and went. Canned laughter from the adjacent room where, I guessed, Prof's wife and the children he was reputed to have spawned were watching TV. Then, the music that heralded the news bulletin. Ten o'clock. The apprentice before me was taking way more than their allotted fifteen minutes. The last bus home left at ten-thirty. A taxi would cost forty bucks. I checked my purse. Twenty-seven dollars, fifteen cents. I didn't own a credit card.

Ten-thirty passed. Ten-forty. Real laughter now, from the inner sanctum. At last the door opened and Golden Boy walked out of Prof's study. Although he'd already left BEST to set up SuperMab, he was apparently still subject to the Friday-night summons.

'Terrific, Dave,' Prof said, slapping him on the back. Golden Boy smiled in my direction and held the door open for me. No greeting from Prof, not that I expected one. He'd turned on his heel and was back behind his massive desk before I was even in the room. I took the seat opposite, where he could look down on me. I'd submitted my progress report – or, more precisely, my lack-of-progress report – a week before, as Prof insisted his students do. He never gave any sign of having read these reports in advance, and now he started flipping through mine. I reacquainted myself with his home office. Mid-calf-high piles of papers stacked on the floor, ringing the room's perimeter. Floor-to-ceiling bookshelves filled with binders. Old projects? Files on former students? I couldn't read the labels. I focused on the one binder-free shelf. It was devoted to framed pics of Prof receiving accolades at conferences all over the world. A lei around his neck in Hawaii. A sombrero on his head in Mexico. A spear in his hand in Africa. It didn't look like he was having fun yet.

Then he spoke: 'You haven't had a positive result with your mouse model since ... August.'

I hadn't. I was working on a mAb to treat Alzheimer's disease. At first it had seemed to work, reducing the nasty amyloid plaques in the brains of Alzheimer's-affected mice. Then it seemed not to be working. These things happen. I was worried, sure, and investigating why, but ...

'And you got a new batch of your mAb around that time?' Prof asked.

Did I? Yes. I did.

Prof doesn't often make eye contact, but he made it that night. 'Your hybridoma's stopped producing your mAb,' he announced.

Shit. Worse than shit. Total disaster. Because an immunologist's hybridoma is basically their right arm. It's a particular sort of cell that Milstein and Köhler, the two Cambridge scientists who won the Nobel prize, worked out how to make. Like its name implies, it's a hybrid of two different types of cells that the researcher fuses together. One cell in the combo produces your mAb, the other's a cancer cell that gives the hybridoma the ability to multiply and grow, forever – basically like cancer does if it goes untreated. A hybridoma pumps out your experimental material, your mAb, in perpetuity. Unless it doesn't. My hybridoma didn't.

What went wrong? I have no idea, which, I know, sounds weird. But the whole process of making mAbs is a bit random. They're biological products, made from living cells, and sometimes living cells just go rogue.

Think of it this way: think of a hybridoma like the starter for making bread, the sourdough variety. I'm not a cook, but Frankie – ever hopeful of turning that situation around – has told me all about it. The starter – 'the mother dough', Frankie calls it – is a mixture of flour, water and microbes. A hybridoma produces a mAb, which treats disease; the starter produces carbon dioxide gas, which makes bread rise. You fire up the oven, pop in the loaf, the starter does its best work, and out comes a beautiful loaf. You break out the butter. Other times, your loaf is a flat rock. The starter, stored in the fridge between baking days, has lost its mojo.

And with a hybridoma it's pretty much the same deal. At BEST, the hybridomas are stored in a freezer in Jude's lab. When you need some more mAb, you call up her up, she defrosts your tube of hybridoma, adds some culture medium – which is basically cell food – heats the mix up and *voila*, the hybridoma starts pumping out your mAb.

But my hybridoma had turned dud starter. Carked it. The fresh batch of mAb I'd had delivered in August was, as Prof so astutely intuited, no better than murky water.

Shit happens, and I wasn't the first scientist to experience what Jude was soon referring to as 'a setback'. Normal cells have a fixed amount of DNA, but a hybridoma is a combo of two cells. It's got twice the normal amount of DNA. Cells don't like having extra DNA, and they sometimes chuck out the excess.

Sometimes that excess contains the DNA for your mAb, so the hybridoma stops producing it. But when shit like that happens, top scientists know it. Not me. I spent five months running experiments on some random gunk.

It was an epic fail, and Prof, the bearer of the sad tidings, looked like he'd swallowed something quite unpleasant – possibly the experimental material that this would-be immunologist before him had been working on for almost half a year.

So, what now? As stuff-ups go, 'my hybridoma carked it' was mega, and even Prof seemed stumped. 'Let's speak next week,' he said. 'I'll see if I can find some way forward.' He sounded almost compassionate, and Prof doesn't do compassion. But he wasn't going to roll with it. He stood up. My catch-up was over. He walked to the door, opened it. No pat on the back for me.

My thoughts returned to transportation. That should be an easier dilemma to solve than the fallout from a dud hybridoma. Twenty-seven dollars would probably cover a cab to Camberwell station. From there I could catch the train to Collingwood. That would work.

And there was Dave, slouched on the seat I'd vacated fifteen life-changing minutes ago, his legs stretched out, his feet almost touching the opposite wall. 'I thought you might need a lift,' he said.

Golden Boy rescued me, and not just from a wallet-emptying trip home.

Foxy

Until I opened the file marked 'Professor Patterson', in the box of tricks I'm working my way through, I'd almost forgotten the genesis of SuperMab. At the top of the Professor's file was a printout of a *New York Financial Journal* piece from back in 2004. Joe Unger, CC's right-hand man at the Cunningham Family Office, had faxed it over to me, the blanks in the document stamp completed in his handwriting and OCD style:

    From: JU
    To: Foxy
    Action: JU will call to discuss.

'JU will call to discuss'! Joe often refers to himself in the third person. Rather chichi of him, I've always thought.

LIFEMAB announces $1.5 billion deal with the Federal Government, the headline reads.

The Californian biotech company LIFEMAB has signed a contract with the Federal Government to provide 30 million doses of the monoclonal antibody Pandaid®. Dr Thomas Norbert, LIFEMAB's Chief Executive Officer, said the government will stockpile Pandaid® as a precaution against a possible influenza pandemic.

More details of the deal followed, but Joe was obviously focused on the penultimate sentence, which he'd underlined: *Norbert developed Pandaid® after returning from postdoctoral studies in Australia with Professor Ian Patterson.*

Joe called me later that day, excited – or at least excited for Joe. He's a lawyer by training but his humourlessness is so Olympian he could easily be mistaken for an accountant, and he dresses just as unimaginatively, in a style one could describe as 'funeral-ready'. A mid-grey suit – in a rare confiding moment Joe told me he has three, identical – a white shirt and a diagonally striped tie that, curiously, resembles that of a school he didn't attend.

'What a transaction,' Joe enthused down the phone line. 'Foxy, I have to hand it to this bloke Norbert. I mean, it's been nearly a hundred years since the last flu pandemic and he's persuaded the US government to spend one and a half bill on this Pandaid in case it happens again!'

The *Financial Journal* piece hadn't caught either of us completely off guard. We knew that the monoclonal antibody 'Norbert developed' was set to be a success. We'd been expecting a good-news announcement of some sort. But the specifics of the deal, and the number – $1.5 billion – cripes!

'And you know what's so brilliant?' Joe continued. He didn't expect me to know and he didn't wait for an answer. 'The stuff has to be chucked out every three years because of its expiry date. It's money for jam.'

Yes. That was what set the ball rolling: the *ka-ching* of the cash register reverberating in Joe's ears. He became determined that the Cunninghams would be the ones cashing in when the Professor pulled another blockbuster out of the hat.

Because it was true. Norbert had developed Pandaid after a stint 'Down Under', as I'm sure he refers to our wide brown land. What the *Financial Journal* piece didn't say, but what everyone in the know knew, was that Pandaid was an infinitesimally tweaked version of one of the Professor's very own discoveries. Norbert had claimed the tweaked version as his own. No, it wasn't cricket. But, to be fair, the Professor had only himself to blame. He didn't file a patent for his original discovery, and so Norbert was legally entitled to tweak to his heart's content. Who could blame him for doing so?

But how embarrassing it was for the Professor to have his nose rubbed in the *merde*, and so publicly. Oh, he put on a brave face. In fact, the next paper in the Professor's file is a clipping from a local rag, the *Australian Financial Daily*. It's a story based around an interview with the Professor, and the journalist asks how he feels about not sharing in Pandaid's windfall profits. 'I'm pleased that so many lives will be saved if, God forbid, there's ever another influenza pandemic,' the Professor is quoted as saying.

I was helping him by this stage, at CC's request. Those two were old school chums. I had coached the Professor well, and he was right on message. The *Fin Daily* article concludes with the 'speech-to-camera' I had him memorise: 'Our mission at BEST is to develop many more medicines in this exciting drug class and, in so doing, to reduce human suffering wherever we can. We can't let ourselves be distracted by commercial considerations. We're scientists. We must, and will, remain absolutely focused on the science.' The words sound convincing on the page. They have an almost Churchillian ring, dare I say.

When we'd rehearsed before his interview, that was far from the case. I suggested the Professor practise in front of the mirror. Perhaps he did.

But Patterson was far from the only Australian babe in the commercial woods. Our country has always had its share of wunderkind researchers – in fact, more than its share. We punch well above our weight in terms of game-changing inventions. The black box flight recorder, Wi-Fi, and that rather neat little contraption to get honey on tap from beehives, to name just a few.

And there had been other missteps by other business dunderheads. We were letting opportunities slip away. Other chaps of Norbert's ilk had cashed in on our discoveries. Australian scientists simply had to lift their game. I mean, strewth – this Norbert fellow making a motser from the Professor's work: it was a national humiliation!

When the Pandaid business became public knowledge, biotech was booming overseas and our government decided Australia needed to become a global player. The term 'knowledge economy' was being bandied about, although I doubt any of the bandy-ers knew what it meant. The government threw money at anything that would make the science crowd *au fait* with the grubby, scary commercial world. It reached out to the business community as well. There were even 'listening tours' to conferences in the States, to get us chaps up to speed on biotechnology. As a matter of fact, Edwina and I went on one. The itinerary included Los Angeles, and Edwina, who adores gardens, was keen to see the Getty Villa. So, I said yes, fine, we would accept the government's kind invitation, and in fact it was rather fun, but, goodness me, *what* a junket.

The government did more than fund mini-breaks for the likes of *moi*. They introduced extraordinarily generous tax breaks for R&D. That was what caught Joe Unger's attention. Joe's speciality is tax law. He plays it like a game of chess. The tax office makes a move, clamping down on the Rich List's latest investment strategy, and Joe starts working on counter moves. His skill was what endeared him to CC, whose aversion to paying tax was well-known. The much-copied Bottom of the Lake scheme was Joe's handiwork: strip a company of its assets and before-tax profits, then dump it in the 'bottom of the lake', where it couldn't pay its creditors – including the tax office. The Cunninghams made quite a tidy sum before the scheme was outlawed.

The R&D tax breaks prompted Joe to suggest venture capital as the next destination for Cunningham money. At first CC was uncomfortable at the prospect. He liked cash-cow businesses. Venture capital? It's all about start-ups, companies – one can hardly call them businesses – that burn cash. They quite literally churn through the dollars until they either take off like a rocket or self-combust.

Joe got his team busy researching probabilities. They found that, on average, one start-up in five succeeds – twenty per cent – which at first blush sounds like a jolly unattractive investment proposition. But, in fact, the payoff for the venture capitalists almost always exceeds the losses on the companies that fail, and by a significant margin too. Still, CC wasn't comfortable putting serious dollars on the table when eighty per cent of the lucky recipients would crash and burn. It was simply against his nature. CC's first business rule: Don't lose money. His second rule: Don't lose money. His third: If you're going to lose money, lose other people's.

And that third rule is how Joe got CC to dip his toe in the venture capital pond. Joe's pitch emphasised how the government would be a big contributor to the new Cunningham initiative. I'm sure his cashflow projections involved a rejig of the Cunningham Family Office accounts so that every possible expense, right down to the last paperclip, was suddenly reclassified as R&D.

My contribution? Well, CC felt the need to have some additional private money in the mix. Foxy was there to help. I finessed Joe's team's numbers into an irresistible sell for investors. I played the role I love: the schmoozer.

I brought nine players on board – high-net-worth individuals, mostly old money. Chaps who were looking for that elusive investment alpha and had at least a couple of mill to put on the table. They were the fortunate few. They'd been offered the chance to get into bed with CC, the wily old codger who everyone knew had the Midas touch. They would get at least a thirty or forty per cent return, probably a lot more. They knew some of the investments would come to naught. They knew because I told them. But they were persuaded that it wouldn't matter in the long run. I convinced them it was par for the course.

Rosa

'My career's over,' I said to Dave. We were tooling down the Eastern Freeway towards the city. *I thought you might need a lift*, he'd said in the hallway at Prof's. Struck dumb by the mAb Meister's insightful analysis of my data, I'd nodded and followed him out to his car.

It was April and maybe an unseasonably warm night, because I was sweating. Or maybe it was stress sweat. Smelly sweat anyway, because Dave lowered the windows. 'Let's get some flow-through ventilation happening until the aircon kicks in,' he said. I took deep, calming breaths of suburban air while he negotiated the back streets that led to the freeway on-ramp. Unlike Nico, Dave was a sedate driver who slowed down when traffic lights turned amber, rather than trying to run them and slamming on the brakes if that strategy failed. By the time we reached the freeway, I was capable of speech.

I wasn't being a drama queen. My career was over. As stuff-ups go, 'my hybridoma carked it' was like landing on a snake a few squares from the finish in a game of snakes and ladders. This snake had taken me back to square one. My mAb would need to be made again from scratch. That would take months. Then I would need to repeat my experiments. By then my funding, aka my stipend, would have run out. My stipend. How Dickensian it sounds, and was. Fewer dollars than I would have made working a couple of barista shifts a week. But, I wanted to be *Dr* Giannini. I sucked it up. So now what? Prof had said he'd try to 'find some way forward'. Realistically, he'd needed to get me out of his house.

And then there was Nico. We were on track to finish our theses at the same time, and we'd planned to do post docs in America together. Nico favoured Seattle. I favoured Boston. A discussion was pending. Or a coin toss. Now what?

'How did it start?' Dave asked.

My need for a ride home had trumped my need to process Prof's revelation alone and weepily. I'd lapsed into a private doom-and-gloom-themed reverie. 'How did what start?'

'Your career. What got you interested in science?' Dave asked patiently.

I wasn't up for sharing my scientist origin story, which I hadn't told anybody before, because nobody had ever asked. No, not even Nico. Yes, how telling. But when Dave said: 'I thought you might need a lift', I didn't go down the 'are you sure?' or 'is it on your way?' path. I just nodded. For all I knew he was circumnavigating Melbourne to get us both home. I owed him an answer.

'With my uncle's bees,' I told him.

Most men who've crossed my path would have responded autobiographically. 'I'm allergic to bees,' they would have said, or 'I love honey,' or maybe 'Yeah, my mate's dad's a beekeeper too.' Sub-text, and not very sub: enough about you, let's talk about me. Not Dave. 'Tell me more,' he said.

Okay, why not. 'I loved the way they flew into their hive, did some secret stuff and *voila*, honey!' I said. 'The hive was like a magic box. So, I asked Pep, my uncle: "How do they do that? How do bees make honey?" I hung out with him when I was little, helping him with chores around the place, sometimes little-girl stuff, like collecting the eggs the chooks laid, other times big-girl stuff, like plucking the chook's feathers when he killed one for dinner. I asked him that sort of "Why is it so?" question all the time: "Why does the chook still run around when it doesn't have a head?", "Why do the leeches bite me when I walk into the dam but not when I jump in from the pontoon?" I probably drove him crazy.'

'And what did he say?' Dave asked.

'Always the same thing: "You tell me, *capo*." That's what he calls me. *Il capo*. The boss.'

Dave laughed. 'So he trained you to be a scientist. You posed a question. You had to answer it.'

'Exactly.'

'So how old were you when your training started?'

'I was seven.'

'A child prodigy,' said Golden Boy.

No. An orphan exile. I was seven when Frankie and I washed up in Strangeways and I started hanging out with Pep. When my parents died, she became my guardian. My grandparents on both sides had already passed away. Frankie decided we should get out of Sicily. Her solution? Become a mail-order bride. Marry a fella she hadn't met who lived on the other side of the world. Frankie's no beauty – I look like her, not my mama – but, still, once she put herself on the marriage market, two or three long-distance suitors put up their hands. Pep had to persuade her that he was the one. In his pitch letter he said his family were from Bergamo. That appealed to his future bride. Northern Italians? The aristocracy as far as Frankie was concerned. Pep also hyped the Strangeways environs. Frankie would live in the two-storey stone villa built by his grandfather. (True, if you count the storeroom as a storey.) There was an Italian community at Strangeways who loved the mother country's traditions. (True, if you count two other families as a community.) And, his trump card, he had two beehives with Ligurian Queens, descended from the bees his family brought out from Italy last century. (True, but the weirdest pick-up line of all time.)

Father Bianco from St Augustine's in Strangeways and his counterpart in Cefalù, where Frankie and I are from, brokered the deal. The two wedding photos hang side-by-side next to the TV at Strangeways: Frankie, on the steps of the Cefalù Cathedral, unrecognisable beneath her black-lace veil, still mourning for her sister. Pep, some sixteen thousand kilometres away in Strangeways, wearing the only suit he's ever owned, with a bunch of mates all crowded around a keg that they clearly couldn't wait to get stuck into. Father Bianco, distinguished from the other mates by his dog collar, cassock and gold cross, gives the gathering nominal gravitas.

It was Father who wrote the marry-me-Frankie letter for Pep, because Pep doesn't know more than a dozen Italian words. Pep was pulling the wool over Frankie's eyes. His family *were* from Bergamo, but they came to Australia more than a hundred and fifty years ago, in the gold rush. They didn't find gold, and by the time Frankie and I arrived, any Italian blue blood had been well and truly bred out of him. He's so bogan he could pass for a skip.

But Frankie hadn't told Pep the whole truth either. She brought me with her, the little black-clad flower girl clutching her hand in the wedding pic. If that worried Pep, he's never shown it. He was either happy to have me shadow him, asking dumb questions, or he gave a good impression of it.

While I was hanging out with Pep, my aunt was spending her days in a darkened room, having a nervous breakdown. The effort of getting the two of us here had been massive, and Strangeways was a huge culture shock. For a start there was no *paseggiata* in which to participate, or even to watch seated on a stool outside her front door. Sure, there were the two other families of Italian descent living nearby, and they welcomed us. The Tognettis live closest, but closest is nearly a kilometre away. Walking up the dirt road past their place in the evening dressed in your second-best would have been seriously weird. And Frankie was used to the sea. Cefalù has a beach, fifty metres from where we lived. Frankie had looked Strangeways up on the map before she married Pep, and it seemed pretty close to the ocean. Scale is a foreign concept to my aunt. The closest beach is two hundred kilometres away.

I'd told Dave all this by the time we pulled up in Collingwood. He was a nice guy, I thought then – and still think, even after everything that happened. He was unlike most of the medicos who parachuted into BEST for a fellowship year or two before heading off for consultant land. 'Celebrity scientists', those of us in the serious-scientist, PhD-candidate camp used to call them: too up themselves to bother with the nitty-gritty of lab life. Reordering the reagents you just used? Why bother. Need a piece of equipment and need it now? Nick it from another lab. Not Dave though. He was a considerate colleague as well as a Golden Boy.

Dave hadn't laughed or curled his lip in distaste at Frankie's exit-Sicily strategy, like the high school friend I'd confided in had done. 'How could your Aunt do that?' she asked. 'That's like being a prostitute.' No, Dave had been solicitous. 'How is she now? How did it work out for her and your uncle?' he'd asked. I'd reassured him that Frankie was fine. She'd recreated as much of her Sicilian life in Strangeways as was humanly possible. And I'd told him that she and Pep stuck it out – that, despite the unusual start to their relationship, they're good together.

We'd laughed over my youthful stab, heavy on Sicilian superstition, at explaining the chooks' post-mortem dance: they're running away from the evil eye in their severed head, was my explanation. But I hadn't told Dave why I tried so desperately to get right the answers to the questions I posed to Pep. A little dag, in my gumboots and floppy sunhat, trailing around this new man in my aunt's and my life, I feared that if I got anything wrong we'd be sent back to where we came from.

It was after midnight. The windows in my apartment were dark and Nico's car was absent from the parking lot. Whatever he had on had segued into a big night.

We sat parked outside while I told Dave why I hadn't known that my hybridoma had carked it. And we were still parked, still talking, when Nico burned up the street, swung his car into the parking lot – stuffing the turn – and knocked over a rubbish bin on the footpath. By then, I had a job at SuperMab.

Foxy

CC agreed to establish a venture capital fund. The idea was that it would ferret out Australian inventions, license them from the inventor, add value in some clever way and then launch them on world markets, primarily the US and Europe. Yes indeed, it was an ambitious plan.

CC brought the Professor in as the science man on the board. The Professor's first contribution was to propose calling the fund 'Capella'. Capella is a star, the northernmost in Melbourne's sky, apparently. It sits low on our horizon and twinkles wildly because of the haze, but it's one of the brightest stars in the Northern Hemisphere. Our Professor is fond of a good metaphor.

He also proposed Capella's first project: the drug that Tran had invented. Capella would set up a company and finance the drug's development, take it from the lab bench to the patient's bed, the Professor said. How poetic that sounded at the time. And it seemed that the idea might also have legs, because after the debacle with Norbert, the Professor, quite understandably, made sure that none of his acolytes would get so much as a sliver of the commercial action arising from any clever ideas that surfaced on the BEST campus. Tran's ownership of the so-called 'super mAb' was purely ceremonial: the patent belonged to BEST.

I had qualms. Oh, I know, I know, the bright light of hindsight. But it seemed to me that drug development was a giant leap from flogging nuts and bolts and flipping property, which was how CC had made his money. I was sure that there was quite a bit more involved in getting a drug to market than the look-at-me headlines about Pandaid implied.

Interestingly, Joe was on the same page, and his anxiety ratcheted up a few notches when he learned that the first step would be to run a human trial of this drug, which Tran apparently called 'EIGHT', for good luck – hardly an encouraging sign. The drug had been tested on animals, but never before on people, so the men who volunteered for this trial would, for all intents and purposes, be human guinea pigs. Joe didn't like the sound of it. Yes, his own business development team had crunched the numbers, and, yes, Joe had personally made, and won, the argument with CC that a twenty per cent success rate for tech start-ups was an excellent norm. But now, faced with the possibility that an experiment on human guinea pigs, in his hometown, that he'd implicitly championed, had an eighty per cent chance of failing, he baulked.

Joe decided that he needed to know what was actually involved in drug 'development', apart from this first human trial. What were the traps for young players? He got his biz dev boys to do some more analysis. They duly produced what Joe rather pretentiously referred to as a 'white paper'. There it sits, accusingly, in the SuperMab box, now somewhat yellowed and dog-eared.

When it was still fresh off the printer, Joe decided he would drop by my office and take me through it, which was how I learned that there need to be three clinical trials before a drug can be prescribed by doctors and sold in pharmacies. The trials are called, terribly unimaginatively: the phase one, the phase two and the phase three. The phase one, which needs to show that the drug's not toxic, almost always involves healthy volunteers – the human guinea pigs – rather than patients. The phase two and phase three trials are much larger in scope and involve patients suffering the disease the drug is intended to treat. During phase two, the boffins try to get an idea of whether the drug will be effective, and what dose should be used. The phase three is the big kahuna. It demonstrates whether or not the drug is better than current treatments, or safer, or hopefully both.

I remember being somewhat peeved when Joe explained all this. It didn't seem terribly complicated, even for a basic fellow like me. I could have read his bloody white paper at home, with a stiff drink in hand, and still got the gist.

'Now comes the good and bad news,' Joe said. A natural grim reaper, he started with the bad. He'd got his staff to research the question, 'How often does a drug that's tested in a phase one trial make it to the pharmacy shelves?' It was apparently a difficult question to answer. Joe's biz dev boys said that it was hard to know how many of these damn trials are done, because when a trial fails the scientists involved typically say no more about it. Understandably, but inconveniently for us, they bury the results. The lads did manage to come up with a figure though. About fifteen per cent of drugs like this EIGHT that are tested in a phase one trial eventually come to market. The remainder fall by the wayside during one of the three trials. The twenty per cent success rate that Joe had previously trumpeted was for projects like the development of solar batteries, 3D-printing, miniature robots.

'Honestly, Joe,' I said, 'I wouldn't worry about that. There's really no difference between fifteen per cent and the twenty per cent success rate you pitched. No one cares.'

He looked at me like I was a fool. 'Of course they don't, Foxy. That's not the bad news. The bad news is how expensive these bloody trials are. The whole development process is likely to cost around $400 million!'

'Cripes!' I said.

'Exactly. There's no way we can do it. We're not Big Pharma. We can't spend four hundred mill on something that's only got a fifteen per cent chance of success, even if we had that much to splash around.'

'Quite. So then, what's the good news?' I asked him.

'Well the first trial, the phase one, has a much higher chance of success. Sixty to seventy per cent. And if it is successful, the value of the patent increases quite substantially.' Joe permitted himself a thin smile.

I could see where he was heading. 'So the smart move would be to flip SuperMab after the human guinea pig trial,' I said.

'Exactly,' Joe said. But he didn't look as pleased with himself as I would have expected.

'Joe, it sounds like a jolly good plan,' I said. 'The Professor won't like it, of course. He's got a lot of ego invested in the idea that he'll personally see this drug used to cure the sick. But c'est la vie. He'll come around.'

Up until this point Joe had been clutching the white paper, reading portions of it to me as if it were a child's bedtime story. 'There's a problem,' he said, at last passing the document over, pointing to the real bad news. It was his staff's summary of the not-insignificant number of instances when drug trials had ended in tears. I scanned it in horror. A very unfortunate young man dead after being given a supposedly you-beaut gene therapy. The researcher, who had stood to gain financially, sued by the family. One dead and four others brain damaged after the trial of a drug that sounded suspiciously like EIGHT – a purported miracle treatment for a whole raft of diseases. Strewth! There were more examples, but I didn't need to read further.

Joe, of course, had read on, and, despite the possibility that a successful phase one could turn a quick profit for Capella, he was now having second thoughts. But he was staring down the barrel of a very awkward conversation with CC, whom he'd personally persuaded to get involved in biotech. 'Why don't you have a powwow with the Professor first?' I suggested. 'He might be able to provide some comfort.'

So, Joe duly set up a meeting. He asked me to sit in, thinking my presence would dampen the niggling tension between himself and the Professor. Because there was certainly tension. At one of the Cunningham parties – Christmas 2003, I believe – Joe made the mistake of expressing scorn for the Professor's decision to name his research institution 'BEST'. Joe, perhaps after one too many of Mary-Lou's sangrias, wondered aloud, and within earshot of the Professor, why he couldn't have just called his place of work 'EST'. According to Joe, Bill Sandberg-Tate, who was one of his chums, was happy to hand over his generous founding donation for the research centre, but 'couldn't give a flying fuck about having his name on the door'. Bill was happy for his wife, Erica, to get the kudos. I'm not so sure about that, although I do agree that the name BEST was an inappropriately immodest, and fate-tempting, choice.

Unfortunately, Joe's logic about my tempering influence on the Professor was flawed. I'd seen the Professor at his nadir after the Norbert-Pandaid story broke. No doubt embarrassed, he'd been slightly distant with me ever since and, *mea culpa*, I hadn't put the elbow grease into excising that residual awkwardness. So I was very much the third wheel at Joe's sit-down, which did not go well.

'Where's CC?' the Professor asked when he arrived, noticeably breathless. Quite understandably he'd expected that, after being summoned to the Cunningham Family Office, the boss, his old friend, would be there to greet him. The temperature in the room dropped a few more degrees when Joe offered coffee and his secretary brought in three cups of instant. The Professor chain-drinks double espressos to get by on four hours of sleep per night, which, he boasts, are all he needs.

Oh, the Professor gave us his stump speech. Monoclonal antibodies were the best thing since sliced bread. Every mAb that's come to market has racked up at least a billion dollars in annual sales. And, hold the phone, mAbs were being used to treat yet another condition: macular degeneration, which, the Professor explained to Joe and me, means blindness. After treatment with a miraculous mAb, those afflicted could now see again.

'He'll be walking on fucking water next,' Joe remarked glumly when the Professor excused himself and tootled off back to BEST.

Still, Joe took several deep breaths and decided he would try to dissuade CC from the project, which the Professor was now calling SuperMab. I bowed out at this point. My core business has always been extricating clients from holes they've dug for themselves. When I observe the digging, my modus operandi is to stand back and await the inevitable SOS.

Joe had no luck. We'd given the Professor a heads-up that his project was under threat and he'd made a pre-emptive strike. He'd arranged to spend a weekend down at CC's farm, after which CC was fully committed.

CC argued to Joe that the Professor had credibility in the drug discovery world. Joe couldn't deny that. Pandaid apparently worked – why else would the Yanks be spending so many greenbacks on it? The Professor had invented one wonder drug with Norbert looking over his shoulder, ergo this next discovery that he'd invented with Tran would be similarly successful. The Cunninghams' lack of experience running drug trials wouldn't be a problem because the trial would be outsourced to professionals. And the risk involved in a first human trial for the fellows who volunteer? CC had an answer for that too: drug trials are regulated to buggery, he told Joe. If the government said the trial could go ahead, well then, it must be safe.

'CC's determined to put his balls on the table,' a despondent Joe told me. So Joe and I had no choice but to line up with him. SuperMab was set up and we crossed our fingers that this first project of Capella's would be a winner. Then CC proceeded to make a misstep entirely of his own volition. Oh, let's call a spade a bloody shovel: CC stuffed it. He indulged his first-born. Much to Joe Unger's chagrin, CC made Charlie CEO not only of SuperMab but Capella too. CC gave young Charlie enough rope to hang himself.

Rosa

The SuperMab offices were about a kilometre from BEST, in a new building that was stylish and super luxe. A copper facade – laser-cut in a complex pattern that supposedly resembled DNA – a ginormous marble reception desk in the moodily-lit foyer, the works, all funded by the government as part of its let's-invest-in-science push. The building was touted as a 'biotech hub', a home for start-ups like SuperMab and all the ancillary services they needed to become a commercial success. But it had no labs for actual experiments, which was a bummer if you were a biotech company and your core business was – duh – science. So Dave rented lab space back at BEST, and that was mainly where I worked.

But it was at the glam SuperMab offices that I learned what that work would be. I already knew I would be working on the first clinical trial of Dave's mAb. I would way rather have been finishing up my PhD and arguing with Nico about where to do our tandem post docs. But after my PhD stuff-up, Nico and I had 'the discussion'. It would be at least another couple of years before I submitted my thesis. I understood that Nico needed to keep his career plan moving, didn't I? I wouldn't want to hold him back, would I? And long-distance relationships don't work, do they?

It would be best if we took a break, Nico thought. That was the fairest thing, for both of us. He would still do his post doc in the US. He'd just go stag. And I would return to Strangeways.

Still marking time at SuperMab, helping to run a first-in-human trial was a pretty good second prize. Except for Pandaid, which nobody at BEST ever mentioned – within earshot of Prof anyway – no BEST discovery had got that far along the drug-development path before.

And EIGHT wasn't just any drug. It was special because it was a mAb, and it was special in that special class of drugs. It was a *super* mAb. It earned that rep from one of the experiments Dave did with rats. Before drugs are trialled on humans, they're tested in what's known as 'animal models', which means the scientist simulates, in animals, the disease she's hoping her drug will treat in humans. In other words, she makes the animals sick. (Of course, it's mostly 'he' who's doing the simulating and hoping, not 'she'. Fempower has gained no more traction in science than elsewhere, but humour me my example.)

So, one of Dave's experiments had involved making rats sick with rheumatoid arthritis. Their joints became inflamed, their hind paws swelled, they lost weight. Then he gave them EIGHT. They regained weight and their arthritis improved. What also happened was that their immune systems produced some special blood cells known as 'regulatory T cells', or 'TREGS'. When the immune system's running amok, like it does in autoimmune diseases like rheumatoid, TREGS bring it back into line. In other words, magically, EIGHT managed to get the immune system to fix itself – which, for immunologists, made EIGHT the Holy Grail.

So, I've flunked out of my PhD but I'm helping Dave prep for the first human trial of the Holy Grail. I'd hoped that I'd be pivotal to that trial's success. I wasn't sure what vital role I'd play, but I expected to at least be there on the day, maybe labelling the blood samples that Dave took from the volunteers, maybe testing those samples, maybe being the first person to see the amazing TREGS – they'd be a bunch of purple dots on the read-out from a flow cytometer – that Dave expected that EIGHT would produce in humans, like it had done in the rats.

I was dreaming. Charlie had hired an organisation called ClinHelp to run the trial. And they weren't just helping: they were totally in charge. The Monday after the video featuring my nice pipetting went live, I met Gigi Johansen, the manager ClinHelp had assigned to SuperMab, and she told me, Dave and Charlie how it would all work.

I was late for the meeting. Commuting to the city from Strangeways, more mornings than not the train sector of the journey is punctuated by an almighty thump. A kangaroo, out for a peri-dawn hop and blinded by the train's lights, meets its maker. The train slows briefly in sympathy. Then the driver floors it to make up the lost time. That morning, a girl I'd never seen on the train before – a city girl newly relocated to the bush, I guessed – freaked out at the thump. What was going on? A train veteran mimed a kangaroo hopping, by way of explanation. She wasn't getting it. 'Skippy,' he yelled. Now totally freaked out, she pressed the emergency button and the train screeched to a halt.

So I slunk into the meeting twenty minutes late. I wasn't planning to offer up my excuse, with its 'the dog ate my homework' vibe, and I didn't need to. No one seemed to have missed me. Only Dave acknowledged my arrival, and barely, looking up briefly from the pile of papers in front of him. A slight nod of his head, an even slighter stretch of his lips into something that only slightly resembled his usual smile, and back to the papers. There was a similar stack in front of the vacant seat opposite him, next to Gigi. My seat.

Gigi, a Scandinavian blonde born in Denmark, suited up in a navy pencil skirt and tailored jacket, was telling Charlie that she had worked all over the world. Charlie, sitting opposite her, was ogling her black lacy bra, which, in his defence, was clearly visible beneath her sheer, white, probably-silk blouse.

Charlie, sensing my presence, swivelled his head in my direction. 'I need a double-shot latte,' he said. 'From the joint across the road,' he added, returning his attention to Gigi's underwear.

Mmm. 'Any sugar?' I could have asked, or, 'Dave, Gigi, can I get you guys something too?' But I'd done his legit-science-shit bidding without so much as a protest peep. I couldn't let this BS escalate. 'Fetching coffee is above my pay grade,' I told him, and, weirdly, he didn't push back. Charlie Cunningham stood up, went to the drinks cupboard and poured himself a morning whisky.

I felt a flush colonise my face and creep down my neck. I needed this job. Dave looked up from his papers and winked at me. Good, I hadn't screwed up.

Gigi ignored the episode. Once Charlie drained his refreshment, she stood up and powered through her slides. She explained that ClinHelp would file applications for all the approvals needed to run the trial. ClinHelp would write the protocol and recruit the trial participants. They would hire the doctor and nurse who would administer EIGHT to those participants. The protocol would tell ClinHelp's doctor and nurse how to prepare and inject EIGHT, when to draw blood for testing, when to measure the participants' vital signs and when to send them home. ClinHelp would contract labs to analyse the blood, statisticians to crunch the data. They had writers on staff who would cut and paste the statisticians' analysis into templates and prepare some explanatory text. *Voila,* the study report and a paper for publication would appear on Dave's and Charlie's desks.

Gigi had set up the trial workflow in special ClinHelp project management software. Tasks. A timeline. Milestones. It was all laid out in the papers she'd given Dave and me. Gigi was counting on 'the team' – aka Dave and Rosa – to complete our assigned tasks so that 'we' could hit the milestones.

My job was to repeat experiments for which Gigi believed the government drug regulator, Safe Medicines, would require duplicate results before they green-lit the trial. I was to consolidate all the data on EIGHT and prepare a summary for the doctor and nurse who would run the trial. The summary was called the 'Investigators' Brochure', and Gigi would supply the template for it.

Tasks assigned, Gigi proposed a tour of the newly commissioned ClinHelp trial facility, conveniently co-located with SuperMab in the biotech hub. Our entourage took the central, cantilevered staircase up four flights to the top floor where ClinHelp was housed. Gigi and Charlie led the way, bride and groom style. Dave and I followed like loser cousins pressed into best-man and bridesmaid service.

'Are you okay with all this?' I whispered to Dave.

'With what?'

'ClinHelp. The whole outsourcing thing. I thought we would be doing the work.'

'No, it's fine. Don't worry. That's the way trials are done,' he said, not sounding even vaguely interested.

Okay. I was obviously an idiot.

Our walkthrough began in the dosing room, a window-less cube with slippery linoleum and a central, glassed-in observation station. Ten gurneys were spaced around the perimeter, each with a stand on which to hang intravenous fluids and a sphygmomanometer to measure blood pressure. It looked like a plush hospital ward. Gigi pointed to the gurneys. 'That's where the trial subjects will lie while they receive their infusion of EIGHT. Your lucky number, I believe,' Gigi said to Dave, who looked away.

Gigi explained that the subjects would be 'healthies', so-called because to participate in the trial they had to be healthy. The healthies would be men in their early twenties. Eight of them would be randomly selected to receive EIGHT. Another two subjects – the controls – would receive a saline infusion. 'A placebo,' Gigi explained to Charlie.

'So you, what, roll a dice to figure out who gets the good stuff?' Charlie asked.

'Kind of,' Gigi said. 'The computer generates the random numbers that tell the investigator, our doctor, who gets what.'

The gurneys were stripped back to their blue, plastic-clad

mattresses. The sphygmomanometers read zero. The observation station, with its ergonomically correct kneeling chairs, was deserted, the three computer consoles not even flashing a screen saver. It was eerie.

Gigi seemed to sense that Charlie's interest was waning. She herded us through to the trial-participants' lounge. A billiard table, sectional sofas arranged in clusters, wall-mounted flat screens and game consoles at the ready on the low coffee tables. A stainless-steel bench stretched along one wall, bookended by a glass-doored fridge stocked with juices and soft drinks, and a cafe-standard espresso machine. Even Charlie gawked. This was where the healthies would hang out after the immediate post-infusion monitoring period.

Gigi must have known she had to justify the luxurious digs. 'There's no upside for healthies to enrol in a drug trial, because they're not afflicted by the disease the drug is designed to treat, so we roll out the red carpet.' She opened a door off the lounge and – ta-dah – pointed to ClinHelp's 'unique selling point'. A mini laundromat: two washers and two dryers. They weren't coin-operated.

'A few retrenched factory workers guinea pig on phase ones like the SuperMab trial, but it's mostly students. It's become quite a popular thing for them to do,' Gigi said. 'They'll love the laundromat.'

Just as Gigi was loving her tour-guide role. She explained that ClinHelp had competitors, other international companies with offices in Melbourne that ran trials for biotechs. At least one new trial 'opened' – that is, started enrolling – every week, and competition between companies for subjects, who weren't allowed to be in more than one trial at a time, was becoming fierce.

'Some students just do the occasional trial to fund their mid-year trip to Bali. The newly unemployed might do a study or two to tide them over until they land a new job. But others make a habit of it. They treat it as a part-time job.'

'So … what … these dudes are going to be paid, like, money?' Charlie asked, suddenly interested.

'Of course. Yes,' Gigi said. 'We call it an honorarium. For this trial it's two thousand dollars per participant.'

'Two thousand bucks? For hanging … here …?' Charlie flapped his arm in the direction of the espresso machine, a top-line La Marzocco. 'After being lucky enough to receive my man Tran's wonder drug,' he jerked his thumb at Dave, 'they get two grand as well?'

After just three brief face-to-faces with Charlie I had no doubt: we were not simpatico. But I was with him on this. Two thousand dollars! Maybe I could volunteer. Although I was now a private-sector employee, I wasn't making the big biotech bucks. The plan was for me to work for a year at SuperMab, who would then give BEST a grant for me to resume my PhD. Stipend funding all the way. That was the deal Dave and Prof had come up with. I was okay with it, but two thousand dollars for a few days hanging out here? Seriously tempting. But I knew I was dreaming. At BEST we weren't even permitted to take our own blood for our experiments. It had to be against the SuperMab rules for a staff member to volunteer for the trial. And if it wasn't, there was the inconvenient fact of my gender. Women usually aren't permitted to participate in first human trials in case they're pregnant.

While I pondered the unfairness of all this, Gigi had leaped to the defence of the honorarium. 'ClinHelp head office sets the proposed reimbursement, the honorarium,' she said, 'not me. They have a scale to work it out. It considers the inconvenience to the participants. How long they have to stay at the study centre. What sort of samples have to be taken. Blood, urine or if they have to provide faeces or have a spinal tap ...' she looked at Charlie, probably saw she was losing him, 'and what sort of drug's being trialled.' She turned to Dave. For moral support? 'And, Dave, I know I'm not telling you anything you don't already know, but your drug, EIGHT, is regarded as "first-in-class", because no other drug has been found, yet, to stimulate TREGS in humans. So, according to the ClinHelp scale, participants should be reimbursed for the greater risk of something going wrong. I mean, it's obviously very unlikely ... it's something we hope, and believe, won't ever happen.'

Gigi took a deep breath, then seemed to exhale her defensiveness. 'But I have to say, Charlie, I think two thousand is a good level for us to be at with the honorarium. In the US, not long ago, there was a strike in the middle of a clinical trial. The subjects banded together and decided the reimbursement was too low. It was all resolved pretty quickly, but it *was* awkward, and we don't want anything like that to happen here. Ultimately though, the honorarium will be decided by the ethics committee.'

Now Charlie looked totally confused. Gigi tried to explain. 'All clinical trials have to be approved by an ethics committee as well as the government regulator. Ethics committees are made up of clinicians, academics, members of the general public. All the committee members have to be completely independent, they can't have any interest in the outcome of the trial, and one of their roles is to make sure that the honorarium we're suggesting is neither too high, giving the volunteers an inappropriate incentive to participate, nor too low, taking advantage of them.'

'So … what … these ethics dudes get to tell us what to do?' Charlie said.

'Yes,' Gigi admitted.

'So, eight guys off the street get two grand each. Sixteen grand?' he said, looking at Gigi kind of expectantly, wanting – what? – a koala stamp for his maths? 'And there's nothing we can do about it?'

'No, it's twenty thousand,' Gigi said. 'The two men who get the placebo get the honorarium as well.'

Charlie shook his head in disapproval. 'Fucking unbelievable,' he said.

'I'm sorry,' Gigi said, her clipped tone giving the impression she was sorrier about having to work for a moron like Charlie.

'So, are we still on budget, with this "honorarium"?' he asked.

He'd got her. An awkward silence. 'We are slightly over what you and Dave had allowed,' she admitted.

'Well, that's not good enough,' Charlie said. At last he had something to lord over her. 'I'm not having that. You'll have to scale back somewhere. I'm not having us run over budget.'

I looked at Dave. Was he 'not having' us run over budget too? He wasn't saying. I thought maybe he'd taken a vow of silence that day, because not a word from Golden Boy had been heard for the duration of the walkthrough. But in fact it was an omen for our future as a 'team'. He turned out not to be the person I thought I was signing up to work with.

But, whatever. Our tour was over. 'Lunch?' Charlie said, looking at Gigi. 'You can run me through some budget options while we eat.'

'Will Dave and Rosa be joining us?' she asked, sounding like she would genuinely welcome our presence.

But it wasn't her party. 'They have to get back to work,' Charlie said.

I took another look at the participants' lounge, tried to picture it on the day of the trial: the healthies firing up the espresso machine, folding their laundry, surfing the cable TV channels, getting on with their lives, only eight of them having really earned their honorarium, as far as Charlie Cunningham was concerned. Would they have already banked it, I wondered? Somehow, I doubted they would get paid in advance.

Miles

I got Davey's second I-need-a-favour call in early October. I hadn't seen him since his SOS for a suture kit the night of his TV appearance.

'Are you still dealing hospital beds?' he asked. I was. I disliked the Admitting Officer job less than the others I'd had to hack. There was no laying-on of hands, which suited *me* fine, but not my colleagues who were hell-bent on spending their lives ministering to the sick. So I'd made an aspiring urologist happy by trading him my assigned surgical rotation.

'I expect you're a good AO,' Davey said.

Davey was on the money. On my watch, not a single patient who was sent home from Emergency died in the subsequent 48 hours. That was the key 'performance indicator' for incumbents. I'd managed the politics okay too. Doctors like getting their way more than most other people, so when a bed-seeking intern is knocked back they often refer up. Their registrar or consultant gets on the phone if they think their underling's pitch has been unreasonably rejected, or sometimes if they just feel like bitching. Somehow, I'd managed to work out who had power and who didn't. I'd kept the right people happy.

The Admitting Officer gig also comes with a significant perk: out-of-hours custodianship of the keys to the hospital pharmacy. Those keys make the AO popular with co-workers seeking free, no-questions-asked meds – usually knockout pills for when they're doing night duty tough. Seroquel's the go-to. But Davey's ask wasn't a downer. Ma had been put on a new heart med that was difficult to source outside hospital circles. Could I help? Of course I could. Happy to.

More than happy to, because as well as giving me the chance to play Happy Helpful, Davey's call gave me a shot at raising the subject of his choice of business partner. The night Natalie needed stitching hadn't been the time, even if I'd had something more useful to say than *Stay frosty. Watch your six.* Now I had a hot-off-the press Charlie update to share.

A bunch of my old school buddies get together the last Friday of the month. It's always the same plan: drinks at the Corner, steaks at Vlad's, then more drinks at the bar du jour. In summer, the proceedings kick off with a pick-up game of frisbee in Como Park. Davey was never part of this particular gang, and I'm not a steadfast attendee, but I show my face at one or other of the venues when I've got nothing else on. It's usually a good night.

I'd rocked up to the September gathering, as had Rupert Stone, back in town from Hong Kong for his sister's wedding. Stone's not a bad bloke. He's made a shitload working for Clifton Bates Investment Banking. And good luck to him. He's a smart operator. But he's just a bit too fond of bragging about it, and not humbly.

Stone joined the party at the Corner just as we were about to move on. He sidled over to me at the bar. 'I hear your refugee's gone into business with Cunningham,' he said in lieu of a 'Hey, Southcott'. When I didn't bite, he added, 'That's going to be tricky.'

'Maybe Charlie's changed,' I said. Not that I thought he had, but Stone needed to. *Your refugee*, is how the lads at school referred to Davey. Stone needed to grow up.

'Yeah, Cunningham's a big boy now, but word on the street is he's still not a smart one,' Stone said.

It turned out that Stone had called in on the local Clifton Bates operation while he was in town. One of his investment banker mates, knowing that Stone went to school with Charlie, had given him the lowdown. An engineer had been doing the rounds of Melbourne and Sydney's venture capital outfits, trying to flog some new technology he'd invented. The technology was a suite of computer algorithms for manipulating videos. All of which meant fuck-all to me.

Stone explained: the algorithms were for 'Photoshopping' videos. The engineer claimed that, given a ten-minute clip of any punter talking any shit, he could wave his magic algorithms and produce a new clip of the same punter talking whatever shit you wanted.

The algorithms sounded awesome to me. I could have used them to trick up a video I knew still existed in at least one location – Mother's trophy stash – of me being interviewed for a TV sports show after I won the Junior Open. 'The Oz Open will be my next win,' I say. I mean, Jesus Christ, what the fuck was I thinking?

But algorithm-touting engineers are apparently the used-car salesmen of the venture capital world, so Stone's mate's bullshit radar was on. Still, he met the guy, watched his fake video of George W Bush declaring war on North Korea and had a good laugh. However, the engineer demoed the technology on a massive computer that he rolled into the Clifton Bates offices in a case sized to schlepp kitchen sinks around, reinforcing Stone's mate's suspicion that the whole proposition was dodgy. That, and the fact that the $21-million ask was way too cheap for such a technology, which, if it worked, movie studios would be fighting over. They'd save on reshoots, big-time.

Despite his reservations, Stone's mate played the good corporate citizen and referred the opportunity up the Clifton Bates hierarchy. His instructions eventually filtered back down: take a look. The higher-ups told him to get cracking on some due diligence. But there was a problem: the engineer had gone no contact. Wouldn't return Stone's mate's calls. After a week of heavy dialling he got the 'this number has been disconnected' message. Then Stone's mate heard a whisper on the top-end-of-town grapevine that Charlie Cunningham had bought the algorithms. Yet there'd been no smug shout-out about the deal from the Cunningham clan. Stone's mate's theory was that his own reservations had been well-founded. The algorithms were a scam, the equivalent of a written-off car rebirthed and flogged by a slick salesman as brand-spanking new. Stone's mate reckoned the Cunninghams now knew they'd been dudded and were busy workshopping how to spin what should have been a *mea culpa* as a win.

'Or maybe they're rejigging the algorithms so that they run on a phone?' I suggested.

Stone snorted. 'Or maybe not,' he said.

Yeah, it all sounded inconclusive. Still, I told Stone to keep me in the loop if he heard anything more, and I decided to include Davey in that loop.

So, when he called in his pharmacy order, I suggested we do burgers after work. He was a red-hot meat-lover and had to be struggling with the extreme vego diet I suspect Abigail enforced. 'I can give you Ma's meds while you get an iron hit,' I told him.

Davey laughed. 'Tempting, but Ma isn't doing great. I drop by most nights after work to help Natalie out with her.'

Davey's devotion to Natalie and Ma hadn't waned in the couple of decades I'd known him. Which was interesting, because – big reveal – neither were biological family. Somehow the old's man's crack private detective had failed to uncover that minor detail. Ma was his *amah*, which is what the Chinese call their children's nanny, and Natalie was her daughter. Davey's real parents were the Phams: his mother a beautiful, elegant woman; his father a successful businessman, although possibly a dodgy one. They'd both been casualties of the Vietnam War, leaving Davey with only Ma to look after him, which she did assiduously. At least the private detective had got that right.

Davey had sworn me to secrecy when he told me his backstory and no one else in his Australian circle knew – not even Abigail, my buddy had assured me when I'd asked. All of which might have made me wonder how it was working out for the two of them. Because to state the bleeding obvious, it was a big thing to be concealing from your significant other. But, never one for deep-and-meaningfuls, the only thought that I can recall crossing my mind at the time, and then only fleetingly, was: now Davey's looking after Ma like she looked after him. Which was regulation Davey, but meant we weren't doing burgers.

'Let's make it coffee,' Davey said. 'My office. Do you mind?'

Of course I didn't. It was less than a five-minute walk from the Oxford, across the road from a cafe where I sometimes picked up feta and roast veg muffins for the nurses. The day I played pharmacy delivery boy for Ma's meds, I grabbed a takeaway latte and an Americano to lubricate our chat.

Arriving bearing caffeine, I was greeted by a heavily made-up receptionist not long out of high school. 'Oh, you're the tennis player!' she said. 'Maybe I should, like, get an autograph.' I made a show of looking behind me. In a glass-walled conference room off the reception area, two women were seated at the corner of a large table: a brunette in her twenties and a blonde, probably early thirties. It looked like Davey had a bit of a harem happening.

'You're confusing me with someone else,' I told the teenage receptionist. She shrugged, didn't press the point, and buzzed Davey on the intercom. He emerged from an office two arm-lengths from her desk. I passed him the Americano and we drifted across the reception area to look in on the blonde and the brunette.

The door was shut, but we could hear the blonde shouting out numbers to the brunette, who was moving her finger down a column, calling out 'yes' after each one. 'The clinical trial manager, Gigi,' Davey said, pointing to the blonde, 'and my research assistant, Rosa Giannini.' The brunette. From the receptionist's desk Rosa Giannini had looked a bit like Frida

Kahlo minus the flowery headpiece, but up close she just looked pissed off.

'Should I get another couple of coffees?' I asked Davey, pointing my cup in the direction of the two women.

'No, they're busy. Let's talk in my office,' Davey said, and turned on his heel.

Back we went past the receptionist, now yacking on the phone, and talk we did. I laid out my Charlie story, but Davey wasn't interested. He seemed restless, struggling to concentrate on what I had to say, at one point getting up and walking to the window, standing there with his back to me, arms crossed, staring out at his admittedly awesome view of the park.

It wasn't the Davey I knew. Was he worried about Ma? The meds I was delivering confirmed what Davey had said: she wasn't doing great. Or *was* it woman troubles? For the last few years Abigail had been in Africa, his girlfriend in name only. Now that she was back in town and they were live again, I wouldn't have been surprised if he was struggling with the whole set-up.

'Earth to Davey,' I said to his back.

He turned to face me. 'This is Davey, Earth,' he said, smiling.

'Interrogative: Everything okay?' I asked.

'Everything's frosty,' he said. 'And I hear you, Lima Charlie. But you've got no evidence.'

He was right. All I had was Dude A (Stone's mate) shooting the breeze with Dude B (Stone) who shot the breeze with Dude C (me) who was now attempting to shoot the breeze with Dude D (Davey). I had nothing.

'And it sounds to me like Stone's friend's suffering green-eye, big-time,' Davey added.

Milesy, you're paranoid about Charlie, Davey didn't say, but obviously thought. Maybe I was. But just because you're paranoid doesn't mean they're not out to get you, I thought but also didn't say. Maybe I could have asked around, got something Davey would have accepted as evidence. Maybe I should also have quizzed him about what was going on for him. I tell myself that it wouldn't have made any difference though, that Davey's course was set by then.

Rosa

SuperMab's lab at BEST was just a couple of benches that weren't even locked off from the other labs on the same floor. Our space was only distinguished from Laycock Lab on one side and Tingle Lab on the other by the 'SMB Lab' that I was required by BEST law to write on yellow tape and stick on anything moveable: the hotplate, the shaker, my chair, whatever. The rule had gone meta: we even labelled the yellow-tape dispensers. It didn't stop people nicking stuff. The tape peeled off, real easy.

There was also the plaque on the door: *SuperMab. A Capella Company*. And next to the plaque, someone had taped a page, printed out from an astrology website:

Capella the Star

Capella is only forty light-years from Earth and is thought to have a planetary system similar to ours, with a strong possibility of intelligent life.

Capella gives honour, wealth, renown, a public position of trust and eminent friends, and grants a nature that is careful, timorous, inquisitive and very fond of knowledge. Those connected to Capella will become popular, receive honours and have success in material enterprises.

Below the last line, someone had scrawled *Go Rosa!* in red pen. I loved that scrawl, those words. *Go Rosa!* They were evidence that someone was still rooting for me, evidence I sorely needed. Because after my PhD stuff-up, the received wisdom at BEST had been that Rosa Giannini was a slack-arse. She spent how long experimenting on water? Five months? No, longer than that – more like eight. The magnitude of my alleged idiocy grew daily, exponentially.

My co-workers had a point. My hybridoma carking it *was* one of those random shit-happens things, but it need not have derailed my PhD. I made a major contribution to that outcome.

'So what happened with the assays?' Golden Boy asked the night he drove me home from Prof's.

What a good question. What had happened with the assays, the quality-control tests that every immunologist worth knowing runs? When you get a new batch of your mAb, standard operating procedure is to rerun the QC assays before you start experimenting with the fresh stuff, so you know that your mAb is still there and working as it's supposed to. Jude had promised me her team would run them before they sent me new batches. She'd offered, *insisted*. She wanted to give my rise through the BEST ranks a helping hand.

'She sounds like a good friend,' Dave said.

Yes. So, after I told her what had gone down at Prof's, Jude investigated. The answer: there'd been a communication breakdown. The team member she'd assigned to run my assays went on maternity leave. The mat leave fill-in didn't get the memo and didn't run my assays. My hybridoma carks it and no one does the work that would have sounded the alarm bell. A perfect storm.

Jude and her team learned from the episode though. Checks and balances were put in place to make sure it never happened again. Which was awesome.

I didn't point the finger at Jude. Blaming her would only have made it worse. The manager of the antibody facility doing favours for a lowly PhD student? A lowly PhD student maybe seeking those favours? Those optics looked seriously bad. I took the fall.

And when the 'Rosa's PhD aborted' newsflash did the rounds of BEST, I felt the cold wind of rejection. Science is for winners. I was a loser. Some co-workers gave me the side-eye. Others looked away when they saw me coming. The floor, some object on the horizon, the random splatter on their lab coat, whatever commonplace entered their line of sight – suddenly fascinating. Others laughed. I know, incredible, that anyone would laugh – and out loud – but it happened, and more than once.

Some of my co-workers were sympathetic. There were a few die-hard softies who gave me a hug, or tried – the urge to hug is the one Italian trait I missed out on in the DNA lottery. And there was my anonymous fan who scrawled *Go Rosa!* on the Capella printout.

SuperMab was a fresh start. No way was I going to stuff up again. No way was I going to let Dave down. He'd rescued me from a return to barista world or lab assistant duties at Jude's. I was grateful. Okay, once I started working with him, he did seem different. Not the considerate Dave who'd driven me home. Not the polite, unselfish man about whom his former co-workers at BEST never had a bad word to say. When I worked for him, he was aloof and, when I tried to engage, verging on snippy. I thought maybe he was struggling with the reality of working for a cretin like Charlie. I mean, who wouldn't struggle with that? Especially with people knowing it too, which, after Charlie's video ran on TV, they did. Charlie came across as the boss, not Dave, because Charlie *was* the boss. But so what if Dave had hit the nice-guy wall? I had to focus.

My role was way lower-profile than I'd expected, but I was taking it super seriously. I would focus on the data, pay attention to every detail like a good scientist should. Eight men's lives depended on me getting everything one-hundred-per-cent right.

And, just in case I needed reminding, one of my former fellow PhD students told me the same thing. Kenny. A few weeks into my SuperMab stint he dropped by the lab for a chat. Yay, I was out of the sin bin! Actually, no. Kenny's visit wasn't a social one. His luckless cousin, a commerce undergrad with a penchant for the pokies, was pressuring Kenny for a loan. Kenny had fallen for that before and wasn't going to be suckered a second time. He was thinking about suggesting his cousin enrol in a drug trial. And cuz stood a good chance of making the cut. Kenny had done his research. The homeless often volunteer for trials, he said. News to me, but okay. Kenny said students are preferred though, and cuz, despite being a dipshit, was still a student. Kenny had discovered that two grand might be on offer for EIGHT's trial. Easy money, and EIGHT had to be a shoo-in, being Golden Boy's invention and all. But then, Rosa was working on the trial now, and look how well her PhD had turned out.

Kenny paced around the lab, fingering the equipment. He picked up my lab notebook, started to flip through it.

I snatched it off him. 'Piss off,' I said.

'Relax, Rosie,' Kenny said, holding his hands up in surrender. 'Look, my cousin's seriously bad news. He's even stolen from his folks to pay his gambling debts. Nicked the vintage port they put down the year he was born and flogged it. But he's family, and I don't want anything bad to happen to him. Especially if he enrols in this trial on my say-so. If something bad *did* happen to him, it'd kinda be on me. So, just tell me the trial's going to be safe. That's all I want to know.'

'Don't be dumb,' I said. 'You know as well as I do that things can go wrong.' Kenny was an idiot, but still, I saw his dilemma. 'You don't have to worry about me stuffing up, though,' I told him. 'Safe Medicines will review the protocol and look at all the data. They'll have the final say. Not me.'

Which was what Gigi said when I called her a few weeks later. She'd emailed me the protocol for the trial that she and her ClinHelp team had written. It specified that the eight healthies would get their dose of EIGHT virtually simultaneously. The ClinHelp doctor would inject the first subject, wash his hands, and ten minutes later it would be subject number two's turn. And so on. All the eight subjects would be done in just over an hour.

I'd never run a clinical trial, but, like I reminded Kenny, I knew that things could go wrong. It's a sad fact: drugs can have unforeseen toxicity. It doesn't matter how many animals, or how many different types of animals, you've experimented on before the first clinical trial. Humans are different from animals. Sometimes shit happens. But if shit did happen, according to the protocol eight men would be stuffed.

I emailed Gigi back: *Shouldn't we be waiting at least an hour, maybe two, after the first participant receives their first dose before the next participant gets theirs?*

No reply. So, I called her. 'Yes, I got your email, Rosa, thanks, but dosing an hour apart would cost substantially more. With the last subject getting their dose eight hours after the first, we'd need staff for an extra day and night and the trial facility would be tied up for that time. This way we come in on budget and Charlie's happy,' she said.

'Charlie?' Was I meant to feel reassured about dosing the healthies ten minutes apart because it made Charlie happy?

'Look. It's all we could come up with, given the budget over-run for the honorarium. Rosa, Safe Medicines will review all the data, and the protocol. The ethics committee will too. They'll let us know if they have a problem. You don't need to worry.'

But I did worry. I sat on my stool in the lab for weeks, reading all the material Dave gave me, every word on EIGHT he'd ever written. I tabulated the results and crosschecked the numbers. I cut and pasted sections from Dave's papers into the template for the Investigators' Brochure I'd been assigned to write. Then I read what I'd compiled, from start to finish. Closely. And I realised there was a problem with EIGHT, something that neither Dave nor Gigi, nor Prof for that matter, seemed to have thought of.

'Remember, Mother Nature can be a nasty bitch,' the mAb Meister had said at the conclusion of the lecture that turned me on to immunology and the miraculous mAbs. 'Mess with the immune system and be ready for what she'll throw right back at you,' Prof warned me and the few other undergrads who'd gone the distance in the lecture theatre.

I realised that on the day of the clinical trial, once the healthies had arrived with their toothbrushes and dirty laundry, after Gigi's team hooked up the IVs, once doses of Dave's super mAb dripped into their veins, there was a real chance that Mother Nature would reveal herself to be that nasty bitch. Eight men's lives, Kenny's gambler cousin's included, would be on the line. Shit. How was I going to break that news to Golden Boy?

Part 2

We had to do it to ourselves before we did it on others ... If anything goes wrong and the skid row bum dies, and the experimenter has not done the experiment on himself, he is liable for murder. It's as simple as that. A man is entitled to risk his own life. He is not entitled to risk somebody else's.

– Dr Stephen D. Elek, who injected staphylococci into his own skin in order to study wound infections, quoted in *Who Goes First? The Story of Self-Experimentation in Medicine* by Lawrence K. Altman, MD.

My one regret, Ly, is that I couldn't take you into my confidence. But I know I'm doing the right thing. My atonement will be complete. I expect there will be shock and confusion at first. Cruel words might even be spoken about me. Turn the other cheek, little sister. Be proud of me, and know that what I did will eventually be seen as honourable. And if things don't go exactly the way I expect, Miles will look after you. I know he will pay back his debt.

Miles

I always told Davey I owed him, but I never thought he'd call in the debt. 'No, Miles, my friend,' he would say, 'it is me who is indebted to you, and your family.' When he realised what a tool that made him sound, he changed the words, but not the sentiment. 'Nah, mate,' he'd say, 'it's frosty.'

I was sixteen when I won the Junior Open. The next year I made the Junior Davis Cup team and we cracked the semis. But the old man wasn't convinced I could finesse that success into a career. He insisted on a Plan B. Medicine or law, my call. I couldn't imagine being a doctor, or a lawyer. But I didn't have any better ideas, and Davey, even then, was the man with a plan. Medicine was Davey's goal, so that became my pick too.

Things have always fallen into place for me, and that's the way it went down at school. I guess I was smart enough to get into medicine, but tennis didn't leave enough time for an only-smart-enough dude to make the cut. Then some committee of bureaucrats gave me a beautiful gift. They decided to scrap the system of full-on, your-whole-future-depends-on-your-score final exams, just as my turn to take a shot at them came up.

A new 'certificate of education' was introduced in its place. A big chunk of the certificate of education score was based on assignments. Mother's second son, my best buddy, did mine. All of them. And the assignments he produced for me were different from those he turned in for himself. Davey was street smart as well as book smart. Yeah, there were still exams, which Davey coached me for, and, nah, I didn't score as well on those exams as I did on 'my' assignments, but the differences weren't large enough to trigger one of the 'please explains' from certificate of education central command that our school came to dread. Because I was far from the only student enjoying the benefits of 'coaching'. I just had the best tutor.

Davey and I both got into medicine and our arrangement continued through med school. We lived together in college, courtesy of my old man. We graduated together, courtesy of Davey's note-taking while I played the second-tier tournaments overseas, and his tutoring when I flew back home to sit the exams.

Once I was Dr Southcott, I gave tennis a serious shot. When I gave it away, I even had a ranking – number ninety-seven. Yeah, ninety-seventh in the world. But by then, even in my most upbeat moments, I couldn't see myself cracking the top fifty. And I was over the life. Playing tennis in Paris? Sounds cool, but I spent most of my time in the City of Light eating bananas in the change rooms at Roland-Garros, waiting for my match to start. Reality bit. I just wasn't good enough. I quit. It was time to take a shot at Plan B, which, thanks to Davey, had been lobbed in my court.

His third I-need-a-favour call came late at night, Friday the 24th of November, a date I've now had to state so often I may as well have had it tattooed on my forehead.

'Ma need a refill?' I asked when I picked up.

'What?' Davey said.

'The meds. The flecainide. Is she doing okay?'

'Ah. Right. No, it didn't agree with her,' Davey said. 'And she's fine now anyway. Her ECG's back to normal. It must have been a virus. But thanks for asking, my friend.'

This time Davey was calling to set up a meet. He quizzed me about my roster and decided he'd drop by Emergency the next morning. I would have preferred something more convivial, but all Mother's good work hadn't turned him into a drinker. So, no biggie, we went with his plan.

I was sitting in the procedure room, reading the paper, when he rocked up on the Saturday morning. It was about seven-thirty. I know because two male nurses had just clocked on seriously hungover. The shift was already short-staffed because a bunch of nurses had called in sick. It was the day of the state election and they could earn twice as much working as voting scrutineers as they could at the Oxford. We couldn't risk these two going home due to genuine sickness, albeit self-inflicted, so I'd set up IVs for them. They were lying on gurneys, clutching ice packs to their throbbing foreheads, waiting for the rehydration to kick in.

Davey didn't look like he was travelling that well either. He was flushed and sweaty, but his greeting, 'How's it going, my friend?', was regulation Davey.

His outfit, not so much. He was kitted out in Fila gear. 'What's with the designer threads?' I asked.

'I've been in the States,' he said. 'I bought a bunch of stuff at the outlet stores.'

Okay, Davey would never pay brand-name prices. But why was he shelling out for workout gear, even if it was going cheap?

'I've taken up jogging,' he said.

Jogging? That did not compute. I'd never seen Davey willingly work out. At school he'd say real work was his exercise – he didn't need to play games or heft weights. And I got that. When Davey first entered the Southcott circle, his schedule was punishing. Mornings he delivered papers on a clapped-out bike, then rode a couple of k to the station and caught the train to school. Saturdays he schlepped boxes of fruit and veg at the market with his fresh-off-the-boat clan. But when he no longer had to do any of that, Davey still wouldn't have a bar of exercise that didn't have 'a point'. 'I've got a finite number of heartbeats,' he used to say. 'I'm not wasting them running around in circles.'

Twenty-something years later, Davey knew he had to put out an explanation for the about-face. 'I've been feeling stressed,' he said. 'Running relaxes me.'

That was new too. Davey, stressed?

'Let's hit the caf,' he said, before I could amp up the interrogation.

When Davey had called the night before, he'd said he wanted to talk privately. At seven-thirty in the morning we'd have the doctors' table in the caf to ourselves. The night-duty staff would be heading out for post-shift Bloody Marys at the café du jour, and no one on the day shift would be hungry enough yet to face the rubber eggs and black bacon the hospital chefs called breakfast.

'You guys doing okay?' I asked the pair on the gurneys. One gave me the thumbs up, the other moaned, and Davey and I were Oscar Mike.

He was carrying a blue foam esky when he walked back into Emergency the next day, the Sunday. I'd proposed a quieter day of the week, but Davey wanted it done, stat.

He was wearing jeans and a T-shirt. Maybe he'd given up the jogging.

He strode up to the triage desk, where Shaz was standing in front of me. 'Darl, what a lovely surprise,' she said, looking expectantly at the esky, 'and you've brought us some rolls. Yum!' Apart from his reputation as a superstar doc, Davey's other claim to Oxford fame was the rice paper rolls made by his Ma, filled with prawns and served with a secret sauce that resembled peanut butter. Davey would bring them in for Shaz – who was always ready to eat – whenever they worked the same shift. Today she was shit out of luck.

Davey put down the esky and held out his arms to hug her. 'Shaz, great to see you.' Davey was the only doc – the only staff member – at the Oxford who'd ever been game enough to call Sharon 'Shaz' to her face. 'But I'm sorry, no rolls. If only I'd known you were on ...' He raised his eyebrows to me, his nonverbal querying why the hell she *was* on.

'I shouldn't be,' Shaz said, 'but two of my team called in sick. Bank couldn't help us. Lots of early Christmas parties, they said.' The team members in question had probably been too far-gone for even a litre of normal saline to turn their hangovers around. 'I didn't want to leave my second-favourite boy here in the lurch,' she said puckering her lips and air kissing in my general direction.

Shaz took a break, yacking with Davey, bringing him up to speed on the latest staff couplings and uncouplings. Finally, the question I was dreading: 'So, what brings you here, sweetheart, away from the lovely Abigail on a Sunday? And so early?'

'I'm here to see my friend,' he said, cocking his fingers at me like a gun.

Shaz likes to be in the know. Davey, in Emergency, on Sunday, to visit his friend Miles? Something was not quite kosher. She looked from Davey and his esky to me.

'Secret men's business,' I said, and gave her a wink.

During the Davey-Shaz love-in, a line of nurselings had formed, all needing something from Shaz. Duty called. She let the mystery go, and we headed for the procedure room. With Shaz on the prowl, I thought Davey might bail. 'Rain check?' I asked.

'No way. It's on, my friend,' Davey said.

He shut the door, opened his esky and took out a vial.

'So, that's the super juice?' I asked. 'Guess it'll sell for what … a thousand bucks a dose?'

'At least twice that.' Davey was preoccupied, checking off the drugs and equipment on the IV trolley. 'Is there a butterfly?' he asked.

I pointed out the cannula. 'Let me do this for you,' I said.

'No. Thanks. But no thanks. I told you, I'm doing it myself. I'm not getting you into trouble.'

'So, what … I'm only here for the bragging rights? "I, Miles Southcott, saw the Nobel Prize-winning David Tran prove that EIGHT really is a wonder drug".'

'Either that or you'll be boasting you resuscitated the dickhead who tested the poison he invented on himself,' Davey said.

I laughed. I had complete faith in Davey. I'd never known him to be wrong about – well – anything. I wasn't buying his Doomsday scenario. And that Sunday he was his typical calm, confidence-inspiring self. Signs of the anxiety that had prompted his apparently fleeting flirtation with jogging were gone-baby-gone.

While we talked he'd found a butterfly and set up the trolley with all the gear: normal saline, his vial of super juice, a tourniquet, a couple of syringes and swabs. He'd filled out his name on a drug chart and an observation chart. He'd set up a syringe driver and an IV pole. My meticulous buddy.

'So, any advice if things do go pear-shaped?' I asked.

'Good question.' Davey looked thoughtful. 'You'll probably need to phone a friend.'

We laughed. Davey was a big *Who Wants to be a Millionaire?* fan and under no illusions about my doctoring skills.

'Rosa Giannini, my research assistant. Phone her,' Davey said. 'She knows more about EIGHT than I do.'

The brunette with the Frida Kahlo vibe? Davey must have seen my confusion. 'Just treat me symptomatically,' he said. 'I'll probably get cold after a few minutes.' He walked over to the crash trolley, looked on the shelf below the meds. 'Yeah, here's a space blanket. Chuck that on me if I start shivering. You'll need some adrenaline if I have a reaction.' He rummaged through the drugs. 'Plenty here. And you'll need some normal saline if I go into shock.'

His crash trolley check sorted, Davey put his arm around me. 'I want you to look after Ma and Natalie if this turns out to be my final act,' he said and glanced back at the crash trolley. 'Oh, and Abigail too. Please look after her too, my friend.'

We both laughed. This was going to work. Pear-shaped was not a possibility. No way would Davey entrust his Ma and precious sister to a flake like me. And no one looked after Abigail but Abigail.

'Solid copy,' I said.

Davey went back to the drug chart. 'Let's get kinetic. I'm recording what I'm administering. All you need to do is take my blood pressure, pulse and temperature every ten minutes for the first hour, and every half hour after that for the rest of the day.'

'You're kidding? This is an all-day gig?' I asked.

'Affirmative. I need eight hours of post-dose obs. I've brought some reading.' He pulled a thick paperback out of the esky. *Animal Liberation: Towards an End to Man's Inhumanity to Animals.*

'Looks like a real page-turner,' I said. 'So … what … you've stopped eating dogs?'

The lads at school had taunted Davey big time about his clan's dog- and cat-eating traditions. 'What's it like to eat Spot and Pussy?' they'd ask, smirking like the adolescents they were. 'Delicious. Dog Nine Ways is my favourite meal,' Davey would tell them, smiling like the inexplicably cheerful dude he was. November the 26th he'd dialled up the funny.

'Maybe I'll give the dogs a rest,' he said. 'Abigail's planning a re-education program for me. This is my pre-read. Anyway, let's get cracking. You need to take my baseline obs now.'

I did as instructed. His BP was one-twenty on seventy-five; heart rate sixty beats per minute. 'You'll live forever,' I told him.

Davey resumed his prepping. He soaped and rinsed his hands, drew up a couple of mls of his precious mAb, injected it into a vial of saline, shook it, then drew up some of the now-diluted drug into another syringe, which he attached to the syringe driver. He sat on the gurney, put a tourniquet strap on his left arm, just above the elbow, and pulled the strap tight through the buckle.

It's not easy to give yourself an IV injection. I guess junkies nail it, and Davey had too. He wiped an alcohol swab over the top of his left hand, picked up the butterfly with his right, took the needle cover off with his left, then pinched the butterfly wings together with his right thumb and forefinger, and smoothly guided the needle into a vein on his left hand. Blood trickled down the tubing. He released the butterfly, and I undid his tourniquet. At least he let me do that. Davey unscrewed the cap on the tubing and squirted in a couple of mls of normal saline to flush through the blood. Then he attached the tubing to the syringe driver and taped the butterfly wings to his hand.

'I've set it to infuse two mls per minute for five minutes,' he said.

'Drum roll?' I asked.

Davey snorted and pressed the start button. We sat in silence while the super juice dripped into its creator. *One small step for man, one giant leap for mankind*, I thought but didn't say. Davey looked serious. The fun part was over.

Shaz paged me fifty minutes after the infusion finished. I'd done Davey's obs every ten minutes, as he'd instructed. He seemed fine. He had started shivering so I'd covered him with the space blanket, but his vitals were tracking fine. His BP had dropped slightly, but only to one fifteen on seventy, and his heart rate was up a bit. I wasn't worried.

I called Shaz. One of the consultant orthopods had arrived in Emergency unannounced. 'He's with the fractured tibia in cubicle seven,' she said. 'He wants the kid in a bed upstairs, stat.'

'Duty calls, buddy,' I said to Davey.

'Will it take long?' he asked.

'It shouldn't. But you're doing okay, aren't you?'

'Yeah. I'm fine. But I need to tell you some stuff.'

'Stuff?'

'About Rosa.'

The science chick again. 'What about her? I thought you and Abigail were tight?'

'We are. It's not that. I just want to talk. You know, "share". Like when we were at school and we used to hang out in your room and tell each other stuff.'

My memory of those times involved Davey telling me how to solve quadratic equations and conjugate French verbs. I didn't need a refresher. With the clarity that the retrospectoscope brings, I know that I should have stayed with him. Davey wasn't making sense. He may have been slurring his words.

Instead, I did Shaz's bidding. 'You can share big-time when I sort this,' I said.

The fractured tibia in cubicle seven was sixteen years old. He'd broken his leg skateboarding the day before. His mates had called an ambulance, and one of them had hitched a ride to the hospital, arriving seriously bummed that the ambos had declined to turn on the siren. The kid's fracture was closed but displaced, and he was booked for surgery Monday. It was sorted. His leg was splinted. The kid was happy. A big fan of his morphine pump.

But that wasn't enough for Mummy and Daddy, who'd surfaced after all the drama. They'd had a boozy day at the races, felt guilty about being incommunicado during the crisis and grateful that the fruit of their loins was okay. Now that was all over red rover. Stockbroker Daddy's blood alcohol level had fallen low enough for his real personality to kick in, and it was ugly. Today, the words and work of the unbelievably young, thus inexperienced and incompetent, residents and registrars weren't good enough. His boy shouldn't have had to lie on a gurney in Emergency overnight. Why wasn't junior in surgery today?

Then the penny dropped. Stockbroker Daddy twigged that the orthopaedic surgeon responsible for his boy happened to be one of his clients. So, said surgeon was summoned from his Sunday-morning Bay Road cycling gig. Now he was strutting around Shaz's domain, the cleats from his shoes clacking, his mood as black as his Lycra cycling knicks.

'Get them all out of here,' Shaz demanded.

'There's no bed for the kid,' I said.

'I don't care. Discharge one of the fractured NOFs to a nursing home. Send someone from neurosurg to the vegetable garden. Bump the young son and heir to oncology if you have to. I don't need this aggro.'

I paged the orthopaedic registrar, who was sleepy enough after an all-nighter patching up bikies to admit that he'd been hiding a bed. One of his hip replacements was good to go, and there was a place for her in rehab. Cool. But the registrar needed his boss's okay to discharge the old girl, and his boss, who just happened to be – what a happy coincidence – the very surgeon now raising hell in Emergency, hadn't answered his page on Friday. So the hip replacement was still on the ward, clogging the system. 'Your man is right here,' I told the reg. I got the Cadel Evans wannabe and his lackey talking and soon all parties were happy, or happy enough.

It had taken me nearly an hour to sort it. I'd missed a set of Davey's obs. He would not be happy.

I heard retching when I opened the procedure-room door. Jesus Christ! Davey was on the floor, on all fours, a pool of vomit seeping back towards his knees. The sphyg had fallen over and was propped on his back. He was still attached to it. Maybe he'd been trying to take his own blood pressure and had – what? His butterfly had come out and blood was trickling from his hand. The saline bottle was smashed on the floor, its contents diluting the chuck. Davey looked up at me. His face was beetroot. He looked out of it.

As I got closer the smell hit me. He'd shat himself. 'Let's get you off the floor,' I said. I put my arms around his back and pulled him to his feet, untangling the tubing. 'What happened?' I asked when I had him on the gurney.

No answer. My pulse was racing as I took Davey's with my fingers. I counted thirty-five beats in fifteen seconds. His heart rate was a hundred and forty. I inflated the sphyg cuff. 'Dave. Davey. What's going on?' I yelled. 'Talk to me, buddy!' I wasn't sure if he could hear, if he was conscious.

Then he opened his eyes and moved his head to look at me, wincing, it seemed with pain. 'Stay frosty, my friend,' he whispered.

'What the hell?' It was Shaz, at the door, surveying the scene. 'What's going on?'

'He dosed himself with his drug,' I said.

She was at my side, pulling back Davey's eyelids. 'BP?' she barked.

'Eighty on sixty-five.'

She banged the emergency buzzer with her fist. 'Code blue. Emergency procedure room,' sounded over the PA. 'Get an IV in,' she snapped as she pulled the crash trolley out of the corner and swung it around towards us, her two favourite boys. And then the thunder of feet running in our direction.

Ly (Natalie)

Má was already crazy before Dung gave himself his own medicine. Some days she was okay. Some days she was like she was before he went on TV with Charlie Cunningham: happy, or happy for Má. Other days she was crazy. The day Dung gave himself his own medicine, Má was crazy, even before the hospital called.

It was Sunday, my day off. Normally I sleep in, at least until nine. Then I go to the Victoria Cake Shop with Má to buy chiffon cake. When we get home, I watch *Paris by Night* with her while she eats her cake and drinks her tea. In the afternoon, I go shopping at Highpoint with my friend Bich. Sometimes we catch a movie there.

The day Dung got sick, Má woke me up before it was even light. 'Ly! Ly! Get up.' She shook me hard. *Đi ra công viên.* Come to park.

'Go away,' I said.

Má pulled the doona off me. 'Get up. You lazy,' she shouted.

What was her problem? It had been all good the night before. Dung had come for supper. He'd been away, on a trip to America, and I hadn't seen him since he'd been back. He picked me up from my salon, drove me home and stayed to eat *canh chua* with me and Má. Abigail wasn't with him, so Má didn't have to cook something just for her. Má didn't have to listen to Abigail say it's wrong to eat fish, that it's bad for the ocean. Dung and I didn't have to listen to Má tell Abigail: 'Plenty of fish in the sea, okay to eat a couple.' Abigail was out of town, Dung said, so no problem for Má.

And Dung was happy. He'd been sad, and sometimes angry with Má, ever since he went on TV with Charlie Cunningham and Má had to tell him the secret. But the night before the hospital called, it was all good. Hands wouldn't bother us anymore, so Dung and Má were both happy. When Dung left, he put his arms around Má. 'Love you,' he said.

Our family doesn't say that. 'Love you,' my clients say to their hubbies when they call them on the phone from my salon. 'I'll be home soon. Love you.' Or, 'Put the chicken in the oven, will you, darl. Love you.' Our family doesn't talk like that. But when Dung left, and I walked out to his car with him, he said 'Love you,' to me too.

Má already had her pink tracksuit on, ready for her walk, when she woke me up. I got out of bed. She would only have gotten crazier if I hadn't. *Con gái tôi là người thế nào?* What sort of daughter do I have? she would wail. *Một đứa con gái coi má nó không ra gì.* A daughter with no respect for her Má.

I looked out the window. No clouds. Only seven o'clock and already hot. I pulled on shorts and a tank top. Má would not be happy. She would tell me I looked cheap. And that people would see my fat legs. Well, too bad.

We walked to the park. Má walked fast, like a beach crab. I followed, but not fast enough for her. She stopped at the corner of our street and turned around. 'Pss,' she hissed at me, '*Sao con đi chậm vậy?*' Why are you so slow?

When we got to the park, Má did her warm-up exercises on the concrete around the flagpole, walking like she was on a treadmill, waving her arms like she was a windmill, slapping herself like she was crazy. If there'd been other people in the park it would have been embarrassing, but there was only me, sitting on a bench near the flagpole, watching Má.

Then Auntie arrived. Uncle too. He was carrying the boom box for the tai chi music. Má was better, not so crazy, after she did tai chi with Auntie and Uncle. Má and I got to Victoria Cake Shop before it was open, but we didn't have to wait long. Má got her favourite: durian chiffon, nice and fresh, lots of cream, just the way she likes it, and when we walked home, she held my hand. That's another thing my family doesn't do.

I was getting ready for Highpoint when the hospital called. Má was still watching *Paris by Night*. Dung had brought her back a DVD from America with new episodes, but Má was watching her favourite, number forty.

The lady from the hospital said she had tried to call Abigail, but Abigail hadn't answered, so the lady left a message on her mobile and called me. 'Dr Tran is very sick,' she said. 'You should come to the hospital.'

Sick? 'What's happened?' I asked. 'My brother was okay last night. He was good,' I told her. Had there been an accident?

No. No accident. 'Don't worry,' the hospital lady said, 'but come as quick as you can.'

Don't worry, but come quick? What was going on? But I didn't ask any more questions. I didn't want the lady to think Dung had a stupid sister.

The bus would not be quick, so I called a taxi. I told Má we had to go to Dung as quick as we could. 'Con không thể đến bệnh viện anh Dung ăn mặc như vậy. Con sẽ làm mất mặt ảnh,' Má said. You cannot go to Dung's hospital dressed like that. You will shame him.

I knew Dung would not be shamed and, anyway, I didn't want to waste time getting changed.

At the hospital, the nurses asked us if we'd like tea. First the nurse who was a friend of Dung's. 'I'm Sharon, but your brother calls me Shaz,' she said. 'He's such a sweetheart.' Shaz sounded sad. 'Let's get you and your Ma a cuppa.'

Then the nurse from Intensive Care, where Dung was. 'What about a cup of tea?' she asked.

'We just want to see my brother,' I said.

Then the Intensive Care nurse told us what Dung had done. 'Do you know why he would do that?' she asked.

'No,' I told her. 'And what you say he did can't be true. The medicine my brother discovered wouldn't make him sick.' Dung was smart. He wouldn't make a mistake like that.

The Intensive Care nurse took us to the room where Dung was lying. He was very still, strapped to the bed. He couldn't have moved even if he wanted to. His arms were bare, and everybody could see the scars on his wrists that Dung always covered up. He wouldn't like that. There were tubes coming out of him, one out of his mouth – to help him breathe, the nurse said – one out of his arm and one from under the sheet. All connected to machines.

Má started to cry. She didn't make a noise, but tears were running down her face.

'You can hold his hand. You can speak to him,' the nurse said. 'He's not conscious, but he might hear you. It might help him.'

Má didn't understand. '*Má, nói chuyện với ảnh di,*' I told her. Talk to him.

I held Má's hand. I took her up close to Dung. '*Má thành thật xin lỗi,*' Má whispered. I am sorry. '*Má thành thật xin lỗi con Dung ā.*' I am so very sorry, Dung.

By the time Abigail arrived we'd been at the hospital for many hours. It was already dark outside. I was holding Dung's hand and Má was squatting on the floor, like she was peeing. She was crying and moaning, saying *Má thành thật xin lỗi* over and over, but the nurse said it wasn't a problem. Má was not disturbing anyone.

Abigail looked at Má, then at me. She moved her lips like she was going to say something, then she must have changed her mind. I let go of Dung's hand and Abigail took my place. 'I'm sorry, I'm so sorry,' Abigail said to Dung. 'This is my fault.'

My brother. Very still. Má and Abigail. Both very sorry. Both thinking what had happened to Dung was their fault.

I thought I knew why Má was sorry. But Abigail – why was she sorry? Why did she think it was her fault Dung was sick?

'I'm sorry,' Abigail said again.

'*Má thành thật xin lỗi, Má thành thật xin lỗi,*' Má moaned.

I don't think my brother heard them.

Miles

When a Code Blue sounds at the Oxford, a medical emergency team sets aside whatever they're doing and runs to the site of the call. On the morning of Sunday 26th of November there were five on the team: two doctors (a medical registrar and an anaesthetics registrar), two nurses (an ICU specialist and a coordinator for the team) and an orderly. All, apart from the orderly, were women, and all, including the orderly, had their hair tied back in ponytails – a ridiculous detail I'm ashamed to say I noticed during the brief time the coordinator permitted me to stay in the procedure room and observe the team's work.

Hospital records show that they arrived one minute and five seconds after Shaz bashed the Code Blue buzzer, well within their five-minute target response time, one of the key performance indicators for the MET team, which is what the medical emergency team are called, despite the redundancy of the second 'team' – a grammatical observation, as irrelevant as the ponytails, that also occurred to me while I watched them struggle to resuscitate Davey.

The MET team had been regrouping in Emergency's lunchroom, fifty metres away, after a false alarm. A first-year nurse had called a Code Blue in response to a patient's chest pain, which had turned out to be indigestion.

For me, the one minute and five seconds had passed in a flash, during which I'd failed to do as Shaz instructed. I hadn't managed to get an IV in, despite digging around determinedly in Davey's right forearm, searching for his median cubital vein.

Shaz, though, had turned pro, outwardly putting aside her shock. She'd assessed Davey's clinical state, which was deteriorating rapidly. She'd called his name, trying to get a response, and failed. His breathing was shallow and desperate. Respiratory failure was imminent. He needed to be intubated and ventilated, but when she put a finger in his mouth and attempted to push his tongue aside, he resisted.

'They'll need sux,' she said. She turned to the crash trolley and selected a syringe of suxamethonium, the muscle relaxant that would enable the MET team to insert a garden-hose lookalike into my buddy's mouth and down his trachea. But to give suxamethonium, you need an IV line.

The door opened and the five members of the MET team arrived, simultaneously it seemed.

Shaz spoke before any of them could suss out the scene and express the horror she knew they'd feel. 'It's Dave Tran,' she said, addressing Phillipa, the med reg who I'd interned for the previous year. On day one of that rotation, Pip had told me that she had interned for Dave, whom she knew was my friend, a few years previously. She'd learned all she knew from him. Now Shaz told her that Dave had administered the drug he'd discovered to himself.

'You saw him do it?' Pip asked, her incredulity mirrored in the faces of the other four MET team members.

'No. Miles did,' Shaz said.

The five newly arrived, now-stunned, heads swivelled in my direction. Pip raised her arms, palms up, in a silent 'what the fuck'.

Shaz's top-line briefing had taken ten valuable seconds. 'Pip. Forget the "whys",' Shaz said, 'let's move. We need an IO line in, stat.'

Given my failure to find a vein in Davey's arm, the next step was an intra-osseus line. They would have to drill through his bone to access his bloodstream via his bone marrow. The ICU nurse had already intuited as much. She'd retrieved the IO kit from the bag of tricks she totes to the team's gigs, and had passed it to the anaesthetist, who took out the drill and without hesitation bored a hole through the top of Davey's right tibia. They had a line. They could now give Davey fluids – like the normal saline he'd mentioned to me an hour and a half previously – to shore up his plummeting blood pressure, and drugs – like the sux that Shaz had ready.

But Pip needed to make her own assessment of Davey first. 'I don't think it's anaphylaxis,' she said. We could all see that. Neither his eyelids nor his lips were swollen. 'BP?' she asked the anaesthetist.

At Shaz's urging, the team had snapped into full-on business mode. While the anaesthetist drilled into Davey's leg, the ICU nurse had stuck defibrillator pads on his chest and hooked him up to a vital-signs monitor. Once the IO line was in, they'd swapped places in a smooth, linedancing-style move. The anaesthetist was now checking Davey's read-outs on the screens. The nurse was pouring in the saline via the IO line.

It wasn't working. 'I'm not seeing a BP,' the anaesthetist said. They were losing him. She turned to Davey, pried his mouth open, the endotracheal tube ready to pass. But his tongue still wasn't completely flaccid. 'I am going to need the sux,' she said to Pip.

'Okay.' Pip nodded to the nurse.

Thirty seconds later the anaesthetist passed the tube and started ventilating Davey. A minute after that the alarm sounded. 'VF,' the anaesthetist said. Ventricular fibrillation. Pip had known it was a gamble. Suxamethonium drops your blood pressure, and when that blood pressure is already low the further drop can be fatal. Davey was now pulseless. His heart rhythm was incompatible with life. But it was a shockable rhythm.

'Stand clear,' Pip yelled.

The coordinator took my arm and pulled me away from the gurney, where I was in the way. It was her job to sort what needed to be sorted, and in this case that was me. 'He doesn't have a wrist band, and there's no UR number on his charts,' she said.

Jesus. Her colleagues were trying to resuscitate their beloved former colleague and that's what she was worried about? But a dummy spit from my court wasn't going to help anyone. 'No. He's not an admitted patient,' I told her, never taking my eyes off his body on the gurney.

The first shock didn't work. Pip was trying again. 'Clear,' she shouted.

I moved to the crash trolley. *You'll need some adrenaline if I have a reaction*, Davey had said. If the shock didn't work, they would. I rummaged through the drugs. The coordinator had followed me. 'There's no adrenaline,' I told her.

'Don't worry, we've got some,' she said, putting her hand on my elbow. I'd seen her before, at the last Emergency Department karaoke night. She'd been an enthusiastic chair dancer, lip syncing along with the singers, consistently a half-beat behind, totally unco. Enid. Was that her name? Or Claris?

'I'm going to have to ask you to wait outside,' maybe-Enid, maybe-Claris, said. 'I'm calling in the Medical Director and the Director of Nursing, as well as the ICU Director,' she said, her grip on my arm tightening a little, 'and, just so you know, I'll be suggesting they call the police.'

Abigail

If I'd got to the hospital earlier I might have been able to reach him, communicate with him. The doctors say that's extremely unlikely, but I've never been convinced.

'They're waiting for you,' the nurse who came to let me into ICU said. She touched my arm above the elbow and gave it a little caress. I was already a widow in her eyes.

She took me to a small room off the corridor that I could see led to the ward, to David. Five men, all old enough to be the nurse's father, were seated around a table meant for fewer people. Unlike the nurse, their faces were implacable. They'd done this before. They stood and introduced themselves. The Director of Intensive Care: 'Call me Fred.' The Medical Director: Geoff, something. David's mentor, Prof Patterson, who I knew already. He didn't invite me to call him Ian. And two policemen. They must have said their names.

'I want to see David first,' I told them.

'Of course,' Fred said, and he led the way down the long corridor, leaving the other four men to wait some more.

All the evidence pointed to the person in the bed being David. The sign on the bedhead said *Patient: David Tran.* Natalie was there, holding his hand, and Mai was squatting on her haunches, rocking and moaning. But the body didn't look like David. In the forty-eight hours since I'd last seen him he'd become a bloated object, his stomach so swollen he looked pregnant. His head had tripled in size.

Fred stood beside me, explaining that David was intubated because he couldn't breathe and catheterised because he couldn't pass urine. They'd inserted a 'central line', a tube, in his neck so that they could give him drugs more easily. A monitor played his heartbeat: *beep-beep*, pause, *beep-beep*, pause. It sounded normal, but I didn't feel reassured.

Natalie moved away from the bed and I took David's cool, limp hand. I knew then that he was going to die. My life was over too, but I would have to carry on, reliving our last argument every day of my life. David was the lucky one.

Fred escorted me back to the four other men who again stood, but perhaps more reluctantly this time. We sat, and the talking that they'd been waiting to do, perhaps impatiently, started. Fred went first. He seemed to weigh his words, which exited his mouth in a slow, marginally comprehensible sequence. He finished each sentence, paused, repeated the last phrase, waited for me to nod my understanding, then moved on to the next piece of information he needed to impart.

In this excruciating way, I learned that David's heart had essentially stopped, shortly after he collapsed. Not for long. They'd got it beating regularly within a couple of minutes. They hoped there wouldn't be brain damage. It would be a few days before they knew for sure. For now, he was in a medically-induced coma. If he woke up – Fred paused, corrected himself – *when* he woke up, he would be distressed by the tube in his throat that was helping him breathe, which was why the sedation, the induced coma, was necessary.

There was a box of tissues on the meeting table. Fred slid it closer to me and continued talking. He had great admiration and affection for David, he said, and had rushed into the hospital, even though he wasn't on duty, when the coordinator of the team who'd resuscitated David phoned him. The coordinator had told Fred what Miles claimed David had done. Fred had personally spoken to Miles to confirm, then called Prof Patterson – they'd been interns together many years ago – who had also rushed in.

Unlike me, who'd taken her sweet time, arriving twelve hours after David collapsed. A full half-day.

I'd been in Gippsland, at a demonstration against the logging of the remnant old growth forest at Marble Mountain. I went down there early on the Saturday with a Friends of the Forests group. It seemed important at the time.

There were about twenty of us, and, with the help of a like-minded carpenter whom we'd pressed into service, we built a thirty-metre-high tripod-type structure to block the logging trucks that were expected on Monday. Then a cherry picker deposited a protestor at the top of the tripod to sit it out. We set up camp at the base and sang songs to support him. On the Sunday we stood around chanting, 'Stop the damage to our state forest', waiting for TV crews to arrive, which they didn't.

I hadn't enjoyed the weekend. My fellow protesters were uni students, a decade younger than I was, the boys only just on the cusp of daily shaving. I sensed they regarded me as weird rather than wise, and I wished I'd chosen to hand out how-to-vote cards for the Greens at Saturday's election, instead of going to the demo. But, worse, I was out of mobile range, so I hadn't spoken to David since Friday night, when we'd had a major blow-up. Our argument had niggled at me all weekend.

I left the protest at about three on the Sunday afternoon, to carpool home with two of the boys. When we reached Traralgon, my mobile bleeped three voicemail messages: the first from the hospital, the second from Natalie, the third from Prof Patterson. None from David.

My companions could hear the messages as I played them. Without me asking, they abandoned their plan to stop at McDonald's for an early dinner. The kid driving broke multiple speed limits getting me to the hospital. Still, I was the last to arrive. I was mortified.

While I was incommunicado, the doctors had put David on life support, but they hadn't worked out what the problem was. Now Fred and his team needed to rectify that. They needed to understand what they were dealing with, urgently. It looked like an immune system reaction. Not an allergic reaction, and not an anaphylactic reaction. Something different. An immune system meltdown. Fred needed to draw on Prof Patterson's expertise to be more confident, so he'd shared some details of David's condition with him. He hoped I didn't mind. I nodded. I didn't.

Despite my defeatism about David's prognosis, I willed myself to concentrate on Fred's words, which surely held the key to David's recovery. It was possible, he said, that the contents of the vial David had injected were contaminated, that David got infected from the contamination. Certain bacteria, like staph, can cause immune-system meltdowns. In which case, what David needed was antibiotics. More likely though, the vial wasn't contaminated, and the immune-system meltdown was a bizarre, severe reaction to David's drug. In which case, what David needed was steroids. Specifically, a large dose of hydrocortisone. But if they gave David the hydrocortisone and he was suffering an infection, that would probably make his condition worse. So, they had a dilemma, and it needed to be resolved urgently. Prof Patterson had already been in touch with his contacts at the government labs, and they'd agreed to prioritise testing the remaining contents of the vial David had used. But the tests would still take forty-eight hours. Fred and his team needed to act before that.

They were playing Russian roulette, and they'd delayed pulling the trigger until I arrived. 'Give the hydrocortisone?' I suggested, and Fred said that was currently their preferred option.

Then the police took over. They had nothing to tell me. Just one question, said the older policeman, who took the lead. One question that he didn't need to repeat.

'Abigail,' the policeman said, quite gently, 'do you know why David did this?'

Foxy

I got the call just before six pm on the Sunday, the day of the incident. Edwina and I were in the car, heading back to town from Merricks. Our weekend had been low-key. The election had been duly run – a lay-down misère for Labor so there'd been no parties, scheduled or impromptu. I'd played eighteen holes on Saturday, nine that morning. I was feeling relaxed.

It was CC on the phone. His greeting itself was a heads-up: 'Harry. You alone? Can you talk?' He was normally more upbeat. *Foxy! How's my fix-it man?* was CC's usual opener.

It was coming up to seven months since I'd seen his son on TV, and now my prophecy had come to pass. I didn't try to hide my concern while he filled me in on Charlie's shenanigans. I didn't tell him it was going to be an easy recovery. CC didn't appreciate glib reassurance. Nor did I exaggerate the gravity of the situation to make myself look good when I pulled off the save, as I anticipated doing at that stage. I didn't have to. Charlie was in trouble. CC knew it.

Tragedy was looming – that was plain as day – and I knew my assignment would be challenging, but I felt quite buzzed up, almost like I'd thrown back a couple of respectably aged single malts. Charlie's shit had hit the fan, and CC had called *me*. One of my oldest clients was walking the satisfied customer talk. I had no idea what a poisoned chalice I was being handed.

CC wanted me to meet with Charlie that evening at my office. He wouldn't join us – he was down at the farm – but Joe Unger would.

'We're about forty minutes from town,' I told CC. 'I can meet them in an hour.'

In fact, we were only five minutes from home, but while listening to CC I'd decided to stop and have some scrambled eggs before heading on in to the city. My gastritis was giving me grief, and the Losec didn't seem to be holding it at bay. Eggs would coat my stomach, soothing it in preparation for what I anticipated would be a long, arduous evening. I was already running scenarios in my mind. 'And Tran … is he going to pull through?' I asked.

CC said the doctors had resuscitated the young doctor, but he hadn't regained consciousness and was now on life support. That information came from the Professor, who'd been in touch with CC as soon as he heard the news from the head honcho of Intensive Care, one of his cronies. The Professor was at the hospital now, with Abigail, acting as a conduit between her and the medical boffins. Good. The outlook for Tran seemed grim, but we had a man in the tent who was reporting back.

Cunningham Junior was an hour late. Joe backgrounded me a little while we waited for the boy. We stood at my office window, enjoying the late sunset courtesy of daylight saving. Well, *I* enjoyed it at least – I doubt Joe has a sentimental bone in his bean-counter body. It was a magnificent show, sunset that night. We were only a few weeks from the summer solstice, and the sky was streaked with clouds. As the sun slipped away, turning those clouds a really quite gorgeous pink, a flash of light from across the road caught my eye. Charlie. The last light of day gave his yellow Lamborghini – a Diablo, no less – the aura of a golden chariot. That car was a gift from CC, bestowed to celebrate Charlie's last jaw-dropping achievement: surviving until his thirtieth birthday.

My new charge steered his wheels into a 'No Parking' spot. If Joe hadn't been at my side I might well have called the authorities to have the car towed, but, interestingly, he and I were on the same page. 'Almost fifteen thousand dollars we've paid, year-to-date, in parking fines for the young prince down there,' Joe said, shaking his head in disbelief. It appeared that the rules of the road were for mere mortals. They did not apply to, or interest, young Charlie.

'Can you believe it?' Joe continued. 'Fifteen k!' One would almost have thought he'd had to stump up the dough himself. I could feel Joe's pain though. And I knew I simply had to get into a better frame of mind – Charlie was the future – but I was struggling.

Charlie, always pale, was positively pasty that night. He seemed anxious too, bereft of his usual swagger. Beads of sweat had formed on his upper lip, although it was quite a mild evening for November. Joe had told me the boy now had a serious drug habit. Perhaps that, rather than the business with Tran, explained his agitation.

Charlie also looked like he'd packed on a few kilos since our paths had last crossed. In fact, he was well on the way to sporting a spare tyre. Rather precocious of him, I thought: a paunch is one of the privileges of middle age. And it didn't fit with the cocaine Joe said our young prince was now so fond of. The possibility that Joe was embroidering the truth crossed my mind. Perhaps he was throwing a little extra into the mix, giving the boy's downfall a wee nudge.

Charlie sat on my white leather couch. He seemed embarrassed. Tears welled. Both were out of character – the weepiness, the contrition. Then he hung his head, cradling it in his hands.

'Tell us the whole story,' I said.

Joe frowned, emphasising his disapproval. He's still a lawyer at heart. His profession's modus operandi – tell 'em what they need to know, no more, no less – is deeply ingrained. Well, bugger Joe, I thought. I was sure he knew a hell of a lot more than the headlines he'd shared with me before Charlie graced us with his presence.

Christ, it suddenly occurred to me that the whole debacle might have been a set-up by Joe to jangle CC's succession plans. Joe and CC shared an abiding passion – money – and a long history – making bucketloads of it. According to Joe, they also shared a firm commitment to ensuring that Charlie and his sister didn't piss all the Cunningham money away. Quite frankly, I was never so sure about that pact. CC doted on his kids. If it came to a showdown between Joe and one of the Cunningham brood, I would not have bet on Joe. Still, he had the obvious bases covered. There was a trust fund, of course, and Joe had a strategy to deal with the two children's significant others. When Charlie tied the knot with that model, Mercedes something or other, Joe signed her up to a watertight pre-nup – or so he bragged to me at the wedding, in a version of 'Oh what a beautiful bride' unique to Joe Unger.

But whether this was a stuff-up or a conspiracy, I had to insist that Charlie confess. *Seek first to understand:* it's always been my motto. The more I knew, the easier my job. By the next day, Charlie's watery contrition would have iced over to defensiveness. I'd given up a comfy night at home with Edwina watching *Poirot* on the box. I'd had the foresight to eat before I ran to the rescue. Charlie boy could spit it all out.

He started talking. One minute waxing lyrical about his machinations – boasting, not to put too fine a point on it, about his business acumen. The next minute waning into despondent self-pity, wallowing in the unfairness of it all. I wondered if it *was* the drugs talking. Had the boy's dabbling tipped over into something quite serious, as Joe claimed?

But whether or not there was a chemical explanation for Charlie's bizarre performance, I decided that Joe had not orchestrated this saga. With Charlie in charge of both Capella and SuperMab, Joe had lost control of the money. If news of the consequences got out, it would be hard for him to avoid looking worse than ordinary, even with my best efforts brought to bear, and that's not a position Joe Unger would ever risk putting himself in.

No, this was young Charlie's doing.

He'd taken initiative, I'll give him that. He was no doubt trying to follow in CC's footsteps, and who could blame him? He'd managed to get two deals on the table. The first was quite unrelated to this Tran business. It had gone spectacularly wrong, and, sadly, CC, as well as Charlie, had a case to answer there. Like a dog with a ball, Charlie had brought an exciting opportunity to his father. CC, believing his black-sheep son had at last developed the chops for business, had let down his guard.

Some Greek chap, purporting to be a software engineer, had been pedalling what Charlie referred to as 'algorithms', algorithms that could supposedly manipulate videos in some clever way. 'What are these "algorithms"?' I asked. Equations, I was told. The boy, and his normally savvy father, had made a down payment on some equations that had turned out to be fake. Goodness me!

The Greek had shown them a video he'd tricked up of George W Bush shirt-fronting Kim Jong-il. 'CC was impressed,' Joe said, perhaps trying to mitigate his boss's foolishness. 'Obviously there was money to be made if the technology was legit, and CC thought there was influence to be gained too,' Joe continued.

'How so?' I asked. Charlie, perhaps anticipating the further embarrassing details Joe was about to share with me, got up and moved to the window, where he stood, perhaps gazing at his wheels wishing they could transport him to some more pleasurable gathering.

Joe scoffed. 'Think about it, Foxy. A day out from an election we could make a fake video of some Labor apparatchik saying they would remove negative gearing on investment properties if elected. We'd run it on TV and all the mortgaged-up fence-sitters would vote for our people. It'd be a shoo-in.'

'So you were on board with buying these algorithms?' I asked, confused.

Joe bared his teeth in a grimace. 'No, of course I wasn't. I wasn't in the meeting. By the time I heard about it CC had already agreed to give the Greek the half-mill purchase option fee. CC asked me to organise the due diligence before Capella took up the option and bought the ... technology.'

'And?'

'Well, it was a bit late. The algorithm world's rife with scams. They "work" on the crook's equipment but not on anyone else's. So I insisted on seeing a demonstration on one of the CFO's computers.'

'And?'

'Faced with that request, the Greek skipped the country. He's in Buenos Aires, we believe,' Joe said.

'Do we have an extradition treaty with Argentina?' I asked, mischievously. Joe grunted. He knew that I knew CC would not want this getting out. He would rather lose five hundred thousand dollars than compromise his reputation as a whip-smart businessman.

Perhaps sensing that my to and fro with Joe had run its course, Charlie had ambled back to resume his position on the couch, head bowed in a *mea culpa* pose. 'Well, it's only five hundred thousand,' I said, and I like to think I observed Charlie shift uncomfortably. But perhaps it's only the bright light of hindsight illuminating that memory. 'Surely nothing you can't handle, Joe,' I said.

'No,' he agreed. 'I was working on it.'

But while Joe contemplated which nifty accounting move was most appropriate, Charlie had come up with his own fix. It involved SuperMab and was an impressive-sounding deal, I must say, although perhaps a bit too good to be true. We never got the chance to find out, because Charlie decided to play the role of his own worst enemy. He'd shared the details with Tran – boasted about it, I'm guessing – and Tran had gone off like a loose cannon. So there we were, Charlie, Joe and *moi*, chewing the fat on a balmy Sunday evening, contemplating the sad reality that before Capella had won on any of its bets, we had two duds: spectacular ones.

Joe ran through the Q&A again with Charlie, seeing if his story held up, while I weighed the options. There were gaps in the young prince's version of events. I could see why Tran would be livid, but I didn't understand how giving himself his drug would help the situation, for anybody. Had he intentionally taken a massive dose to land himself in hospital, as a matter of honour? That sounded extreme. Or was the drug toxic, the reaction one of those unpredictable occurrences that everyone except Joe's zealous biz dev boys pretends will never happen? Or had Tran taken something else, *not* his mAb like we'd been told?

More importantly, who else knew what Charlie had been up to? That was information I needed urgently. *Seek first to understand.* I needed to walk that talk.

Who else knew what Charlie had so precipitously told Tran? Who else had *Tran* shared that information with? At the hospital, Abigail had told the police why she believed her beloved tested his wonder drug on himself. The Professor had relayed her thoughts to CC, who'd relayed them to me. Cockamamie, muddled in the retelling, I thought. But at least she hadn't mentioned what Charlie had told Tran. Still, I had to keep her close and check her story. And there was a girl at SuperMab who might be in the know, a science girl. There was a receptionist too, but she was just eye candy from the Cunningham Family Office. Joe had installed this one in Charlie's lair to keep tabs on the young prince. And look how well that had turned out. But if she'd stopped preening long enough to cast her no-doubt doe-like eyes about, well, she might know something. We had to pick her brain.

I didn't have the luxury of time. We would not be able to keep this quiet. Hospitals leak like sieves. Tran had trained at the Oxford and he'd still be well known around the traps. He'd have both friends and foes. If one of his friends didn't put the story out to right some perceived wrong against him, then a foe would probably try to even a score. More likely though, one of the nurses would flog the story to *The Times*, or maybe *The Daily*. Nurses are paid a pittance so you can't blame them. They might get a couple of grand for a story like this. No, it would definitely come out. And we had to make sure that the breaking news was a story that worked for us: for the Cunninghams, and for the Capella investors.

I decided to go negative. It's never my strategy of choice, but in these circumstances – well, I decided it was the right move. It sounded like Tran was not long for this world. But on the other hand, he might live. We needed a narrative that would fit both scenarios. We needed to avoid having to make awkward, embarrassing retractions if Tran rose from the dead, so to speak. I scribbled down a few words as an *aide-mémoire* for the call I would make to a friendly journalist once Charlie left.

I made a mental checklist.

The gaping holes in Charlie's story? The Professor

was in our corner. He would help me clarify some of the discrepancies in this unedifying narrative. He could sound out the science girl.

A scapegoat. With a stuff-up this big, someone's head had to roll. I had to find a whipping boy, or girl.

Then there was Charlie. He could do more damage. I had to get him out of the picture, convince his doting dad that was the best plan.

And doting dad? I had to manage CC's expectations. He was no fool. He knew this was a shitstorm. But he would still expect it to be sorted. I had to under-promise and cross my fingers I could over-deliver.

'Is there any blood test that could confirm Dr Tran took EIGHT and not something else?' Joe was asking Charlie as I refocused on his interrogation of the boy.

'Like I would know,' Charlie said.

Truer words had never been spoken. My new charge did not have a fucking clue, but at least Joe – good man – and I were on the same page.

'Are we done? I need to get straightened out,' Charlie said.

'Yes, I think we are done,' I said to my new client. 'You've been very helpful, Charlie. Thanks for sitting with us.'

Joe shot me a look. Was he surprised at my fawning? Surely not. He'd seen me turn on the charm for all sorts of riffraff.

'We'll be able to sort this out,' I told Charlie. 'I'm here to help, don't ever forget that. You go home, get some rest. And why don't you think about where you might like to take a break, probably just for a few weeks. I think it's best if we get you out of the line of fire.'

Of course, now I realise that I should have kept Charlie close. But I wasn't to know what he would get up to once we got him out of the country.

A thought struck me as I watched Charlie lever himself up from the couch and slouch towards the door, presumably on a mission to rustle up some consoling white powder. 'You said someone was with Tran at the hospital, in the Emergency Department. A school friend?'

'Yeah, so?' my client replied.

'And who might that have been?'

'What does it matter? His mate just watched.'

Goodness, was the young fellow under the misapprehension that *I* was the enemy? 'Humour me,' I said, mentally doubling my fee in compensation for the pain and suffering inflicted by this dissolute charmer.

'It was Southcott. Miles Southcott,' Charlie said finally.

Rosa

I heard the news from Jude, who runs the BEST grapevine as well as the mAb manufacturing lab. I was on the train, on my way to work, on my way to meet him – Golden Boy – when I got her text. I was still Dave's right-hand girl, so you might have thought someone – someone like Prof – might have said, 'We should call Rosa.' But no, it fell to Jude, who read about it in the paper, to fill me in.

The Times. p4. Golden Boy. WTF? her message said.

I hadn't bought a paper that day. I was totally skint. The previous week, Dave and I'd had a massive falling out. I'd thought I was going to lose my job. Now, even though it looked like he would give me a second chance, I was still in super-frugal mode.

The woman sitting opposite me on the train had a paper sticking out of her bag. I pointed, she passed it over, and there it was on page four:

Scientist critically ill

Dr David Tran, the co-founder of the biotechnology company SuperMab, was admitted to the Intensive Care Unit of the Oxford Hospital yesterday morning in a serious condition. Sources say

Dr Tran collapsed in the hospital's Emergency Department after injecting himself with an as-yet-unidentified substance.

Professor Ian Patterson, a SuperMab board member and its spokesman, said that Dr Tran had been under considerable stress in the lead-up to the first clinical trial of the company's new drug. Professor Patterson said the trial will be delayed until Dr Tran recovers.

I'd like to be able to say I was stricken with concern after reading those two paragraphs. My boss, my saviour, now apparently laid up in Intensive Care. But I wasn't. *This is not good news for me* – that's what I thought. I know, it sounds heartless, and it was.

Here's my defence: I was on my way to meet him, Dave, for what I hoped would be a reconciliation – a professional one. There was never anything going on relationship-wise between me and Golden Boy, although Jude had told me there'd been rumours. I was taking my A game to that meeting. And now he'd injected himself with 'an as-yet-unidentified substance'. What was that about? The injecting himself. The unidentified substance. I replayed my last conversation with him. He'd been conciliatory – nice Dave. He'd called to set up the meeting I was heading to. Then, a thought struck me. Could the unidentified substance be EIGHT? He'd — what? — done some weird self-experiment? No. Dave played by the rules. I couldn't see him going rogue. So, what was going on? I was clueless. But it was obvious that now our make-up meeting wasn't going to happen. I wasn't happy.

'Anything wrong, luv?' the newspaper's owner asked me.

I passed her paper back. 'No. Fine. Thanks,' I said.

Train lady looked at the page I'd been reading. 'I feel for their parents,' she said.

Their parents? What was she on about? But whatever. I nodded.

She knew I was faking it. Train lady pointed to the article above the one about Dave: 'The Bali Nine'. Nine Australians had been convicted of drug trafficking in Indonesia the year before. Some got the death penalty. The appeals, the haggling between the Indonesian and Australian governments, were still going on.

'It says they'll get the firing squad,' she said. 'I don't think that's right. Mind you, what they did was wrong … I'm totally against drugs … but the firing squad …' She shuddered. 'What do you think, luv?'

I agreed. It wasn't right. I looked out the window, shut her down. The train streaked its way to the city. The bush segued to the 'burbs. Row after row of backyards, their owners' crap, life's detritus, displayed for my viewing pleasure. The train slipped into a tunnel. The window became a mirror. A girl with an insomniac's dark-rimmed eyes stared back at me. There was dog dribble on her T-shirt. Closer to town, as the 'burbs got grimier – or edgier, depending on your point of view – I scanned the graffiti for a fun tag, something to cheer me up. *Niente*.

I looked at my phone again, at Jude's text. Pressed reply. Tapped out *OMG, WTF?* My solicitation whooshed away, into the ether.

I got off the train at North Melbourne and pedalled towards the SuperMab office. Dave had told me to meet him there first thing Monday. Given the news, I could have gone to the lab at BEST instead. Magical thinking kept me en route to SuperMab. If I did as Golden Boy had said, maybe he *would* be there, out of hospital, waiting for me.

Rubbish thinking, that was. At SuperMab there was only our trusty admin, Yvette, who was on the phone. She made a shitload of calls and used a headpiece so that she could multi-task while she gabbed on: admire her nails, check her mobile, play solitaire on her computer. I wheeled my bike past her. As well as no labs, the SuperMab office had no bike racks. Yvette frowned and shook her head at me. Your bike's dirty and it lowers the tone of the workplace, she'd told me previously.

I ducked into the research office. I'd been off work the week before, at Dave's insistence. A leave form was on my desk, as Dave said it would be, and he'd signed it. I did the same and walked back to Yvette.

She was still working the phone. 'There *are* seats on the afternoon Hong Kong flight, Mr Unger, but I couldn't get him First.' Twirling her hair. Holding out her hand for my form. 'Yes, I have got him waitlisted. Elite Travel aren't hopeful that there'll be any cancellations though.' Looking at the form. An incredulous rise of her eyebrows. 'The best I can do is a nice seat in the upper cabin of Business, but Charlie's not happy. Not happy at all.' Turning away from me. 'Yes, Mr Unger. It is only one seat we're talking about. Charlie says his wife isn't travelling with him.' Drumming her black-shellacked nails on the desk. 'Certainly, Mr Unger. I can try PrivateJet. I'll see if they have an empty leg flight to Hong Kong tonight. I'll get right on to it.'

Weird. Dave was in hospital, but Charlie was off to Hong Kong.

'How's Dave?' I asked before Yvette could turn her attention to the crucial task she'd just been assigned.

'Oh, not good, I'm sorry to say. He's on a ventilator. His kidneys have … stopped … too.' She pulled a pained face, maybe trying to channel renal failure.

'What happened? He was fine Friday,' I said. 'He called me. We talked on the phone.' For some reason I felt the need to make it clear to Yvette that Golden Boy had *called me* – that *we talked on the phone.* Me. What a loser.

'I have no idea what happened, Rosa. I only know what was in the paper.' An internal switch flipped, a seamless segue to administrator mode. Yvette was done with the caring and sharing. But I stayed put. I knew she knew more than 'what was in the paper'.

'I'm sending flowers,' Yvette said.

What was the right response? Lilies would be nice?

Yvette. Prepped for men to tumble before her, frocked up in her Monday outfit, the above-the-knee red shift dress, the red-and-white scarf artfully knotted at the neck, the black ankle boots. Me. Dressed for comfort. Elastic-waisted pants and my dog-slobber-enhanced T-shirt. Out of my depth. Sinking fast. Knowing it.

'No need to chip in, the Cunningham Family Office will cover it,' Yvette said.

Dismissed. But I was apparently glued to the floor.

'Well, if there's nothing more, time tick-eth.' Yvette waved her forefinger like a metronome. 'I'm arranging Charlie's travel.'

On your bike, girl.

Yvette was back on the phone before I reached the door, but not to PrivateJet. 'He didn't fit into the Cunningham culture,' she was saying. Maybe she'd had a friend on hold while she dealt with Mr Unger and then pesky me. 'He was an academic to the core. Yes. Yes, I know. They live in another world. They're completely unsuited to corporate life.'

Dave. She was talking about Dave.

'Yes, Asian. Vietnamese,' she said. 'Well, exactly, they don't fit in everywhere. He was like a fish out of water here.'

I wheeled my bike to the lift. Swap out 'Vietnamese' for 'Italian' and 'he' for 'she', and Yvette could have been dissing me! But, wait. 'He *didn't* fit in?', 'He *was* an academic?' What was it with the past tense?

At BEST the labs were deserted. Apart from the IT guys in the nerd bowl, tapping away at their keyboards and nodding their heads in time to whatever was blasting through their earbuds, everyone else was at Prof's attendance-mandatory Monday-morning meeting.

So. Me. Twiddling my thumbs. Wondering what to do. I called Jude. 'I'm working the grapevine. I'll swing by around three,' she said. Judith Winstanley is that person who not only fronts to events billed as 'networking opportunities', but is not embarrassed to admit it. That day, that was okay.

Hours to fill in until Jude surfaced with more news, and no actual work to do. Everything was on hold until I had my planned meeting with Dave.

I needed a distraction. Email. I trawled it. An invitation to a pipetting workshop. 'Learn how to reduce RSI.' I expected to be spending at least a few more years at the bench, pipetting. Not just boring-as, but apparently a cause of RSI. I signed up.

Laycock Lab were emailing threats, trying to smoke out the thief who'd nicked an assay kit from their stash. Those kits cost over four thousand bucks a pop. My Laycock Lab co-workers weren't happy. It looked like someone had been rooting around in my lab too. The door of one of the cupboards was slightly ajar, its contents misaligned. Someone had probably been trying to sniff out a piece of equipment they wanted to 'borrow'. But I couldn't see anything missing.

I decided to call Margaret, Prof's long-serving, long-suffering PA. If *The Times* was right then Prof knew what was going on with Dave. He would probably have told Margaret, to whom he outsources almost all human interaction. She probably had a call list of people who needed to be kept in the know. I might even be on it. I dialled. Straight to voicemail. I hadn't prepared recording-ready remarks. I hung up.

Midday came. I decided to eat lunch in the cafeteria, hoping to get some goss. Jude wasn't the only nosy parker at BEST, she was just the best.

The cafeteria was totally BYO as far as actual food went, but it had a food-court vibe courtesy of the leftovers people brought in. Microwaved samosa funk, essence of pad thai, aerosolised fat pong, the stink of the dieters' tuna salads – all intermingled for your smelling pleasure. Most days I ate my bull-boar-salami panino in the lab, at the bench. Against the rules, but what were the admin mafia going to do? Arrest me for eating a sandwich?

I sat with Kenny and a couple of new post docs he'd taken under his wing. By November 2006, Kenny and I were the only two members of our PhD cohort who hadn't submitted our theses. Kenny, a slow writer, was still sweating the word count. The others were out in the real world. Georgina: a post doc in London. Dunstan: not sure science was his thing, now that he'd got the gong. On a gap year, travelling around the country in a campervan, loving it. Nico, my ex: doing his post doc in Seattle, happily disentangled from me and my not-so-brilliant career.

'Word is Tran shot up in the Oxford's ED,' Kenny said, 'with something weird. Some poison, I heard.'

'This Tran is the person you introduced me to last week?' one of the post docs, a Sri Lankan guy, asked Kenny. 'The one who was pulling the all-nighters?'

'He's the one, yep. But, Jeeves, mate, no way was Tran working. He doesn't have to. He's a big shot. Rosie here's his bench bitch.'

'What day was that?' I asked.

Jeeves seemed embarrassed, by Kenny I hoped. Bench bitch? Come on.

'Wednesday. It was Wednesday,' Jeeves said. 'And I saw him Thursday too. About seven in the morning. I was arriving. He was leaving.'

'Trouble with his woman, I reckon,' Kenny said. 'She probably kicked him out and he had to crash here. She's some animal rights nutter, isn't she, Rosie?'

I met her once – Abigail, Dave's 'woman' – at a Cunningham party. My invitation was a mistake. Had to be. A professional-staff mailing list, some hapless party planner hits send, and *presto*, I was one of the rent-a-crowd, sipping mojitos.

Not quite one of the beautiful people though. I hadn't understood what 'Christmas in July' meant. I'd worn my best sweater and warmest woollen pants, but the Cunninghams had their central heating pumping, emulating a typical sweltering 25th of December. And worse, I arrived clutching a jar of dark sticky stuff. Honey, and not just any honey either. Bundy honey. I dissed the trees of Strangeways unfairly. Box-ironbarks aren't all wimps. That year the *Eucaylptus goniocalyx*, aka the Bundy, had flowered, something it does only every seven years. Beautiful cream flowers, not dissimilar to dandelions, that attract white butterflies. Pep moved his beehives close and *voila*, Bundy honey, the colour of rum and a valuable trade for the occasional rabbit – Pep could no longer see well enough to shoot the little buggers – or a bottle of our neighbours' Nebbiolo, or in this case a gift for the party hostess. I guess she was one of the glamorous ladies in caftans, whom I didn't meet and felt too stupid to approach.

I tried to palm the gift off on Abigail. 'Some honey for you, from home,' I said when Dave introduced us, holding the jar out to her.

Abigail's arms never left her side. 'I'm vegan. We don't eat honey. Bees make honey for themselves, not for humans,' she said.

Ouch! But although Abigail and I hadn't hit it off, I still had to push back against Kenny. Dave shooting up with some poison? 'I can't believe Dave would OD,' I said. I knew I sounded *agitato*. 'That can't be right. He's not the type.' I breathed deep, slowing my words right down.

'Didn't you read the paper?' Kenny said. *Dr David Tran had been under considerable stress.* What do you think "under considerable stress" means?'

I pushed back again. 'I'm stressed too. The trial, our phase one, it's starting next week.'

'*Was* starting next week. Now it's "on hold" because of Dave,' Kenny said. 'My cousin signed up for it, remember? He's going to be bummed. He really needs the cash. But what I'm trying to tell you is that "under considerable stress" is code. Code for "tried to top himself".' Kenny paused for effect. 'You'll have to face it, Rosie. Golden Boy's finally hit the wall. He looked ratshit last week too. Totally rooted.'

Jude didn't show. It was after four-thirty when I called it a day. I'd probably miss the five-ten train and have to catch the five-fifty. Transportation. My obsession. The five-fifty was always chockers. I'd probably have to sit on the floor.

I'd strapped on my bike helmet, decided to push it and take a shot at the five-ten. I was at the lab door, pumped for my sprint, when I heard Prof's voice. He'd stepped out of the lift. He was walking towards me. *He* was the one sprinting. He was always in a hurry, but ...

'Rosa. Wait. Wait up,' he called out.

What was he doing here? When I'd flamed out of the PhD program Prof had acquiesced to the deal Dave put forward, but he hadn't spoken to me since. Radio silence. Rosa Giannini: redacted. What's more, Prof never visited the BEST boys and girls *in situ*. On rare occasions he would escort some visiting dignitary through the labs. Prof, the benevolent potentate, moving amongst his subjects. But management by walking around was not his style.

Yet there he was, outside the lab, telling me to wait up. He stumbled to a halt. For a moment he seemed as surprised as me that he was there, that he was about to speak – and to Rosa Giannini.

Then he got a grip. 'It's about David,' the mAb Meister said.

Foxy

I needn't have pressed Charlie to reveal the identity of Tran's hospital accomplice. Kip Southcott had left a message on the mobile during my sit-down with the young prince, and I got on the blower to him when I got home from my office that night. Miles was already at Kip and Sally's. He's got his own pad of course, but young people, 'Gen X', when trouble strikes, they're homing pigeons. I told Kip to keep him there – I'd pop over the next morning.

At my crisis meet with Charlie and Joe, I'd discovered that Charlie was going to flip SuperMab. A trade sale of the company before the phase one trial started, a simple, tidy transaction – that was Charlie's way out of the hole that his ill-judged enthusiasm for algorithms, his father's desperate wish for him to succeed and a Greek fraudster had managed to dig for Capella.

Charlie had a buyer signed up. Mervatis. A Big Pharma. Mervatis had done their due diligence. The heads of agreement were in place. It was pretty much done and dusted. Mervatis would pay an upfront just south of twenty mill. In return, Capella would hand over the patent for Tran's super mAb and all the data. There would be a royalty stream too, a small one, once Tran's drug made it to market. But that was a long way off, if indeed it ever came to pass.

When Charlie recounted the details to Joe and me, I admit, I was fleetingly impressed. He'd lost on one deal, now he would win on one. The price he'd negotiated for SuperMab would make his half-a-mill loss on the algorithms pale into insignificance, if, God forbid, it ever came to light. Admittedly, the sale price would have been higher, probably double, with a successful phase one trial under our belt, but if the trial went belly-up SuperMab would be worth nothing. Selling wasn't a *bad* move – even Joe had grudgingly admitted that. A somewhat conservative move, yes, but possibly good business.

That happy thought was short-lived. Charlie is a braggart, though at least he had the grace to hang his head when he got to the turning point in the sorry saga I forced him to tell. There was no need whatsoever for Tran to know, but Charlie was born a peacock. On their trip to the States, while Tran was making a splash at some conference, Charlie fine-tuned the deal with Mervatis. He met up with Tran in LA before they both got on the plane for home, Charlie to get the Capella board's sign-off, Tran to finish prepping for the trial he didn't yet know wasn't going to happen – or at least not on his watch. Charlie, presumably after a few lemonades, could not help himself. He spilled the beans. And I suspect his delivery of the news would have been bereft of any sensitivity. Tran went ballistic.

Miles was doing the same when I arrived at the Southcotts' the morning after my call with Kip. 'Charlie's a cunt,' he said by way of greeting, 'a fucking cunt. And this story in *The Times* ...

it's bullshit! It makes it sound like Davey tried to top himself. Where did these lies come from? That's what I want to know. There's not even a by-line. Who freaking wrote it?'

I'm not a hugger of men. I find it a tad distasteful to even *watch* chaps embracing, but I hugged the boy. 'Miles, I'm sure the truth will come out,' I said. 'Let's calmly talk through what happened so that we're all on the same page. Before we start though, tell me, how's David? Any news?'

Miles looked away. Was he tearing up? Charlie the weepy one the night before, now Miles? These young fellows needed to – what's the saying? – 'man up'. Yes, man up, and quick smart.

Sally answered for Miles. 'Poor Davey's no better, perhaps a bit worse, if anything. It's hard to get straight answers from these ...' She looked at Miles apologetically. Did she mean doctors? 'They think it may be something to do with the immune system, some terrible, completely unexpected reaction to his drug. Milesy, can you explain it to Foxy, darling?'

Miles had stemmed the tears. He gave me an explanation that, frankly, was so garbled I was none the wiser when he finished. I didn't try to hide my confusion, and Miles, rather surprisingly given his angst, was perceptive enough to see it.

'Look, immunology's not my strong suit,' he said.

Quite. I was just glad that I wasn't one of Tran's loved ones, and that Miles wasn't Tran's physician filling me in on what was going on.

'Is there any treatment? Do you know, Miles?' I asked.

'Yeah. The Intensive Care guys are trying to get hold of some from America. It's a mAb, like Davey's drug. Which is sort of weird.'

Indeed. Weird. And although I wasn't sure how much credibility I should ascribe to Miles's sketchy description of the proposed treatment regime, it did look like my attempt to obfuscate the story that Tran had given himself his own drug was going to be short-lived.

We sat on the terrace overlooking the Southcotts' pool. They're in South Yarra, only a block from the Botanic Gardens, and Sally borrowed heavily from its layouts for her own garden design. It's a restful setting, and that day there was an abundance of flowers: azaleas, gardenias, even a magnolia. She brought out a tray with coffee and muffins – pear and chocolate that I knew came from Grenier, although she'd taken off the wrapping that would have given her away.

Sally had cleared her calendar for the day. She was going to visit 'Davey'. He was still unconscious, but she thought he might sense her presence. They had a very special bond, Sally reminded me. Although only family was permitted bedside, she regarded herself as family – and of course *he* regarded her as family too, his second mother in fact. Of course, she wasn't going to make a fuss. But she would go to the hospital and she was quite sure Davey's 'Ma' would welcome her presence. Sally had cancelled Pilates, the massage she and Suzie Hollows had scheduled for after the class, and her luncheon at Royal South Yarra with Roz Giles. Sustaining focus on Sally's prattling was proving challenging. But the pertinent point was that Sally was heading off to the hospital. Or was she? She wondered aloud whether she should sit in on our little chat first.

Kip told her this was nothing we couldn't handle. She didn't argue, thank Christ. She told me how grateful she and Kip were that I was there to help and squeezed my shoulder. Sally was a beauty in days gone by, and she's still an attractive woman, but she needs to retire the flirtiness from her repertoire. It's become rather embarrassing. 'Bye, Milesy darling,' she said, blowing her son a kiss as she prepared to tootle off.

I had decided to play dumb. Until the day before, I had been completely in the dark about Charlie's machinations in relation to both the algorithm debacle and Mervatis. So all I had to do was dial back the clock in my head.

Miles started to fill us in. Tran had told him about the planned sale of SuperMab. That was bad news. The cat was out of the bag. But at least the summary Miles gave me and Kip of the transaction Charlie had been finessing did correspond with Charlie's version. My new client had been reasonably straight with me. That was good news.

'Why was an acquisition a bad thing, Miles?' I asked. 'Surely David would have done well financially. And this company ... Mervatis, I think you said, yes?' Miles nodded, calmer now. 'Mervatis would surely have done a good job developing the drug. And with these sorts of deals there's usually a royalty stream for the inventor. It sounds like a win-win to me, a windfall even.' I was being disingenuous, trying to smoke Miles out.

'Yeah, I thought that too. I asked Davey the same thing,' Miles said.

'So, you asked him this yesterday, when he came to the hospital?'

'No ... when we set the whole thing up. The day before ... Saturday,' Miles said. 'Why? Is that a problem?'

He'd seen me look at Kip and raise my eyebrows. Like me, Kip's been round the block and back a few times. He understood my signal, understood the complication this advance meeting might pose.

'Let's get back to the story,' I said, 'what would have been the problem if SuperMab were sold?'

'The problem was ... the problem *is* ... Charlie's a fucking arsehole.'

Miles sounded more resigned now, notwithstanding his harsh words.

'Charlie. Capella. They stitched him up. Davey had some stock options. There were a few tranches. Each one vested when one of his mAb's trials was done. The phase one, the phase two, the phase whatever ... look, I don't know how many freaking phases there are. But Davey only got his dough if Capella still owned SuperMab when the trials took place. Otherwise, nothing. By selling now, before even the first trial, Cunningham was totally screwing him.'

I felt a weight descend on me. Perhaps I was getting too old for this game. I was struggling to maintain my facade of ignorance. And now I had to face an additional challenge: Tran had spread quite a chunk of information around – to Miles, and who knew who else.

When Joe acknowledged at our meeting with Charlie the night before that, no, Tran would not have benefited from

Charlie's transaction if it had gone ahead, I was unimpressed. It would not be a good look for Capella, or the Cunningham family, if it came to light. Many would see it as greedy and, quite frankly, that was my thought too. After the Professor's misstep with the American chap, no one could blame him for ensuring that Tran had no share in the patent for the antibody that SuperMab licensed from BEST, this EIGHT. *Fool me once, shame on you. Fool me twice, shame on me*, I say. But Capella had to give Tran *something* to get him on board. A joining fee and generous stock options were Joe's solution. I hadn't been aware of the stipulation – the fine print, the little sting, call it what you will – about Capella's ownership of SuperMab at the time of the options vesting, but then it's not my business to know such things.

'I had no idea a sale of SuperMab would be mooted so soon. After the phase one, yes, but not before,' Joe had said the previous night, by way of explanation, but without a skerrick of regret, let alone shame. And, in fact, that was probably true. Quite possibly it was an unintentional blow, as Joe maintained. But in my opinion it was a mistake to make Tran a victim. My modus operandi is to always leave something on the table for the other side. In this instance, that was not done. A mistake was made.

But now it was history, a given. We had to move forward.

Kip had been looking increasingly uncomfortable. He'd ignored a call on his mobile. He'd eaten a second muffin. He'd gone inside, reheated the coffee in the microwave, pronounced it burned and called for the housekeeper to prepare a fresh pot.

'Miles,' I said, 'if what you say is true, I can appreciate that the proposed sale was a disappointment for David …'

'A disappointment! A freaking disappointment! The super juice … it was Davey's. He'd busted his guts, he'd …'

I raised my hand to halt the tirade. 'Please, Miles, hear me out. I'm not the enemy, you know. As I was saying … it would have been very disappointing for David, I understand that, but what I can't understand is how giving himself his mAb, if that's what he did give himself …'

Miles interrupted. 'Of course it was.'

'Yes, I'm sure you're right, and I'm sure it will be investigated and confirmed in due course. But how was giving himself EIGHT going to help? What on earth was he thinking?'

I'd asked Charlie boy the same question the night before. Charlie said he didn't know. He didn't know why Tran had done it. There were no tells when Charlie gave me this response, so I was inclined to believe him and conclude it was another of the many important details the Cunningham son and heir really didn't know. But the explanation Miles proceeded to give Kip and me – the strategy he claimed Tran was pursuing – I thought entirely farfetched. Admittedly, I'm no expert on Pharma transactions, but still, the yarn Tran had spun Miles didn't gel. And it was a completely different explanation from the one Abigail had given the police in the Professor's hearing. I'd called the Professor that morning and he'd confirmed again that, no, Abigail hadn't mentioned a possible sale of SuperMab in the very odd account she gave of what Tran was thinking before the incident. I decided it wasn't the moment to share her story with Miles, but his version of events made no more sense than hers. Quite frankly, I was mystified.

By this stage of our powwow, Kip knew that his boy was up shit creek and that he and old Foxy would have to provide the paddle. If Tran kicked the bucket, Miles could be looking at a charge. Manslaughter, perhaps – I wasn't sure. In due course, more astute minds than mine would be put to work on the matter. But his meeting with Tran the day before the incident: that would not help his case. It smacked of premeditation.

Sadly, though, the penny had not yet dropped for Miles. He was sitting there like the innocent abroad he still appeared to be. He still had some growing up to do, I thought. But, no matter, I expected it would make my job easier.

It was also glaringly obvious that Miles didn't know that his father was one of Capella's founding investors.

Oh, yes.

Kip Southcott was one of the first chaps I tapped. I reasoned that he'd be keen to finally get a return on all the cash he'd coughed up for Tran's education. And I was right. Kip didn't hesitate. He wrote his cheque with brio, a two-mill stake from his family trust.

Now someone had to bring Miles up to speed. Someone had to tell him that he could be facing a serious charge – worst-case scenario, jail time. Someone had to tell him that his family, his father – hell's bells, Miles himself through their trust – were major investors in Capella. Miles had stood to gain at Tran's expense. Miles had to be appraised of these home truths because he had to be persuaded to keep quiet while I did my job. *Seek first to understand.* I had to determine whether anyone else out and about on the streets knew of Charlie's plan to sell SuperMab, and whether Tran had broadcast his side of the saga to anyone apart from Miles. And I had to find out whether Tran's purported counter move to Charlie's deal was real. It was crucial to ascertain that, and ASAP. Once I determined who knew what, I had to work out what it would take to bring them on board. Until then, I needed Miles to stay mum.

Fear. Fear, and loyalty, would silence him. Fear for himself and loyalty to his family. Someone had to push his buttons though. Push them hard enough to activate those emotions. *Moi?* Yes, I was afraid that someone would have to be me. But it was really a father's role.

Kip cleared his throat. 'Miles,' he began, 'Milesy …'

Good. I was going to be spared.

Abigail

The first I heard of the notion that David self-injected 'an unidentified substance', not his own drug, was when I read Prof Patterson's quote in *The Times*. I never trusted the Prof after that. Nobody said 'suicide' in my hearing, but friends who called to offer support in the days that followed did broach the subject of David's stress levels, which Prof Patterson had chosen to describe as 'considerable'. Did I see the warning signs? I mustn't feel bad, and certainly not guilty, if I hadn't.

From the moment I saw David in ICU I was stricken by a fierce, unremitting headache, as if someone had secured a metal band around my skull and was tightening the screws. Many thoughts of the guilty variety crammed my pained brain. Not monitoring his stress levels well enough wasn't one of them.

What I did in Rwanda was. I wasn't faithful. At the time I told myself David and I were no longer in a relationship, but that wasn't quite true. We never officially broke up, and we were in touch, often, usually by Skype. Always the gallant one, David was especially thoughtful, always interested in what I was doing, supportive and admiring. But Kigali, where I was based, wasn't conducive to monogamy. A decade after the genocide, Rwanda's capital was teeming with aid organisations keen to expiate *their* guilt for either not doing more, or not doing anything. The NGO workers on assignment, the UN workers on mission and the journalists passing through all formed a heavy-drinking expat community, of which I was an active member. The consensus view was that vows of fidelity were non-binding on African soil. I had a series of affairs, some intense. I don't know if David had expected me to be faithful, but now I couldn't forget my betrayals.

We started living together when I came back to Australia. What should have been a joyful step was flat from the start, possibly because I was the one who suggested it. The fact that I was a reluctant returnee, and that my time in Rwanda ended badly, may also have contributed.

In contrast, David's career was going spectacularly well. His big idea about fixing the immune system appeared to be right. He'd done the animal experiments with EIGHT while I was away. Conveniently, I'd been able to pretend they weren't happening while I was living on another continent. He and Prof Patterson had lined up the investors who would fund the drug's development. David would get a joining fee, a 'golden hello', he called it. At last he would be able to realise his dream of buying a house. For Mai and Natalie, not us.

He bought them the house that they'd rented ever since they came to Australia. He had a lawyer make some enquiries, found the owner was willing to sell for the right price, and paid cash. He kept it quiet, saying it was best if Mai and Natalie's neighbours didn't know.

We moved into a one-bedroom third-storey walk-up in

Brunswick. David signed the lease before I came back. We couldn't afford anything closer to the city. There was nothing wrong with the apartment, it just wasn't the homecoming I would have liked.

The thirteen months that followed were rocky. I can't pinpoint when things started to really unravel. It wasn't when he told me that Charlie Cunningham would be running SuperMab. Charlie was one of the knife pranksters from my college waitressing days, so David probably expected me to disapprove. 'Hopefully he's matured since college,' was all I said, and David eagerly assured me that Charlie had.

But by the time we went to the Cunninghams' ridiculous 'Christmas in July' party we were bickering about nothing and everything. Was it me, or him, or both of us? I don't know, but I think David was different, much less sanguine, after the appalling promotional video he did with Charlie. He came across as Charlie's minion.

David was accustomed to people using him, but everyone has their limits. Perhaps he reached his and took it out on me. Or perhaps he'd got used to being without me, handling things without me, while I was in Rwanda. Perhaps he didn't need me any more but was too kind to tell me. I don't know.

I do know that by the time of the party I was disinclined to play the supportive partner. The heating at the Cunninghams' was turned up to tropical, and the female guests were given flower garlands to wear as necklaces. Carnations, which were out of season. The party included optional pre-lunch golf. When one of the society matrons came over to chat and asked if we had played (neither David nor I had, ever) I told her I thought golf courses should be converted to artificial grass, because watering their vast expanses verged on a criminal waste of a precious resource. Otherwise, the game should be banned. I also tore strips off David's research assistant, Rosa, who tried to gift me a jar of honey. I knew I was behaving badly.

It didn't help that during our last year together, Mai's health deteriorated. Her memory became erratic, her gait unsteady. One Sunday she stumbled and fell during her regular walk with Natalie. In the weeks that followed, David took her for multiple appointments and tests to investigate what he was sure was an emerging medical condition rather than an accident. He was right, but at the time I thought he was overdoing it.

David seemed to catch her forgetfulness. Mostly trivial stuff. Where were his keys? Yes, he would buy the bread on his way home, but didn't. Once, though, he failed to arrive at a friend's daughter's birthday party where we'd planned to meet. When I got home he was sitting on the couch, watching the hockey on TV. He had zero interest in sports.

Then, in August, the first of two major quarrels. It was about apologies. The prime minister, John Howard, apologised to Vietnam vets who weren't welcomed back to Australia as heroes after the war. Fine, they probably deserved an apology, but Howard was still refusing to apologise to Indigenous people over the Stolen Generations. For sixty years, our governments had forcibly separated Indigenous children from their families, an act surely as worthy of apology as the disrespect shown to servicemen and women returning from

Vietnam. I decided to make a statement, so I drafted a new footer for my emails:

Abigail Banks
I live on the land of the Kulin people and I pay my respects to their elders, past, present and emerging.

I showed it to David. 'What does that even mean, Abigail?' he asked. 'You don't even know any Aboriginal people. What are you going to do? Invite a random mob to move in with us? How are you going to "live by your principles" on this one?' It was the only time he ever spoke unkindly to me.

Our second argument, two days before his fatal self-experiment, I was the unkind one. So, while he lay unconscious in ICU and the government's lab examined the dregs of the vial he used, I almost hoped their tests would show that the 'unidentified substance' it contained *wasn't* EIGHT. Then I wouldn't have to feel so guilty about that last argument. How ashamed I am of that hope.

Of course the lab confirmed that the vial contained David's mAb. The doctors had already given him the hydrocortisone by this stage anyway. It was the right decision, because he didn't have an infection. The contents of the vial weren't contaminated.

Once we had the results, I asked the Medical Director, Geoff Kuhn, to put out a press release to quash the rumour that David had tried to take his own life. *The Times* ran a story paraphrasing the release. It included a quote from Geoff: 'We believe that Dr Tran administered a dose of the investigational monoclonal antibody SMB1412 to himself, in what was essentially an "N-of-1 trial", and that his subsequent clinical course represents an unanticipated severe adverse reaction to the product.'

Now the tone of my well-wishers' calls changed. How brave, how like David to do something so noble: to run a trial on himself rather than put the lives of the men who'd volunteered for the trial at risk. What David did was brave, and noble, but it was more complicated than people thought.

I'd told the police why he'd done it. I'd told his doctors, Natalie, Miles and Sally Southcott too. I'd seen the disbelief, then horror, in their eyes. I wasn't ready to tell my well-wishers and spread the story around further.

Meanwhile, I was spending my days at the hospital, getting twice-daily updates from Fred, the director of Intensive Care, who continued to personally supervise David's treatment. Despite that care, David was getting worse. He had renal failure, so he was on dialysis. He was still being ventilated. His toes had gone black. His fingertips too. Gangrene. 'When David recovers, he'll need surgery,' Fred said. David's gangrenous digits would have to be amputated. 'When he recovers.' Fred definitely said that, but it was one of the few phrases he didn't repeat.

Blood tests showed that David's body had released dozens of proteins called cytokines. Fred said the cytokine release was a response to the dose of EIGHT he'd given himself. In the large quantities now circulating in David's bloodstream, these cytokines cause severe inflammation. That inflammation led to the multiple organ failure he now had. What David was suffering was called a 'cytokine storm'. I'd heard those words before.

Miles

It was a relief to know for certain that Davey *had* shot up with his mAb, the not-so-lucky EIGHT. At least that part of his last I-need-a-favour pitch was true. And the confirmation that his immune system was melting down, that he was suffering this cytokine storm thing, gave my obsessive Googling a new search term.

I'd been hitting Google hard in the five days since 'the incident', which is what Foxy had started calling Davey's self-experiment. I was confined to quarters, so I had time on my hands. The Oxford was now a no-go zone for me.

'What the fuck were you boys thinking?' Geoff, the Medical Director, asked when he arrived in Emergency that Sunday, after being summoned by the MET team coordinator.

I didn't think I had anything to hide, or that what I'd done – watch Davey – was wrong, but some self-preserving instinct kicked in. I 'took the fifth' as my old man and Foxy subsequently encouraged me to keep doing. 'Davey said he had to test EIGHT on himself because he needed the data,' I told Geoff.

'That's it? That's all you've got to say for yourself?'

'Basically, yeah.'

'Not good enough, Miles. I don't know what this is about, and until I do you're not to put a foot inside this hospital.'

So, while Davey lay comatose at the Oxford, I sat home alone. Foxy thought it wouldn't be a good look for me to be out and about socialising, given the seriousness of Davey's condition. The old man and Mother agreed. I didn't need to be pursuaded. I didn't feel like socialising. And I didn't need to be told that it would have been bad form, even if I had felt like it. I mean, Jesus Christ, who did they think I was?

I spent serious chunks of time staring out the floor-to-ceiling windows at what the agent who sold me my apartment described as a 'million-dollar view' of Port Phillip Bay. I learned that kitesurfing is hard. Each day at about 6 pm a drove of dudes rocked up to give it a shot. Not one managed to fly.

I listened, as patiently as I could, to Mother's updates, which she alternately phoned in or delivered in person, along with the chicken soup she thought I might need. She was visiting the hospital every other day, sitting with Ma and Natalie and Abigail, who of course were there every day. She thought they appreciated her company.

Mother's reports were very top-line. Davey was 'fighting for his life'. The doctors had put him on a machine 'that was letting his heart and lungs rest'. That would be an ECMO machine. It would be draining out Davey's blood, removing carbon dioxide, adding oxygen, and pumping it back into him. His need for ECMO was a bad sign.

Worse, the next day, Mother reported that Davey's liver was failing. I tried to get more details from my fellow docs, but none picked up when I called.

With nothing better to do, I replayed – *ad nauseam* – my heart-to-heart with Davey in the caf the day before the so-called incident, trying to figure out what I'd missed. Because by now it was clear that not everything my buddy told me that day was true.

Charlie Cunningham *was* shafting him. That was true and no surprise. Charlie was selling SuperMab. All he needed was the Capella board's tick of approval for the deal. Davey said Cunningham had that covered. It was just a formality. Once the board signed on the dotted line, it was done. Davey would be out of a job, and out of the money.

The job wasn't such a big deal. Davey could get a new job. He could go back to being a doc, or saddle up at another biotech company somewhere, maybe in the States. He would have choices. The money, though, *was* a big deal. Davey's stock options wouldn't vest if SuperMab was sold before the first trial of his super juice. For Davey that was a *very* big deal.

But my buddy had finessed a countermove. He'd found a saviour: Sino YingTech, a Chinese company. Davey said they were cashed up and looking for investments. 'My yellow knight' he called them when he pitched his plan to me in the hospital caf. Sino YingTech were willing to take a stake in SuperMab rather than buy it outright and, added bonus, their deal was conditional on Davey staying put at the company. Sino YingTech wanted to fund the full development of EIGHT. When his super juice finally made it all the way to some lucky patient's bedside, Davey would be there to feel the warm inner glow, enjoy the kudos and collect the big bucks.

There was a catch. Sino YingTech needed some human data before they signed on the dotted line. EIGHT had to have been given successfully to at least one person. Davey decided to be that person.

I'd always had complete faith in Davey. I'd never seen him be wrong about anything. But testing his invention on himself? Wasn't that a bit risky? And weird? 'Why not just bring the trial forward?' I'd asked him in the caf. 'Let the dudes who've signed up for it do their job?'

'I can't,' Davey said. 'The trial's being run by a contract research organisation, ClinHelp. Remember Gigi, one of the women you saw when you dropped by my office? She's in charge. The trial's scheduled for mid-December. No way will they change that plan without me telling them why, and if I tell them why Charlie will hear about it. And if Charlie hears about it ...'

'Okay. Got it.'

'Anyway, it's the right thing to do. There's always a risk that something might go wrong in a first-human trial. Why should others risk their lives if I'm not willing to?'

So Davey had decided to 'do a Barry', Barry being Barry Marshall. He's an Aussie doctor, a gastroenterologist, who bagged the Nobel Prize for working out what causes stomach ulcers. Even I'd heard of him. Barry thought that a bacterium named *Helicobacter pylori* was to blame. Conventional wisdom said it wasn't. The medical establishment view was that ulcers were all about stomach acid, too much of it. Stress, spicy food, booze – they all dialled up the acid level, and eventually created an ulcer.

Barry couldn't turn that view around, so he chugged a *Helicobacter* cocktail, aiming to prove the doubting Thomases wrong. Which he did. Barry got gastritis, the precursor of stomach ulcers, and bad breath from the bunch of nasty

Helicobacter roiling in his stomach. After a course of antibiotics, he was fine.

But if 'doing a Barry' and 'going first' like Davey planned had become a thing, it was news to me – not that that meant much. 'Okay. So you're doing a Barry. Cool,' I said. 'You'll win the big prize too. You deserve it, buddy, but I still don't get why the Capella board will go with your deal, not Cunningham's?'

'Prof Patterson, that's why. He's on my side,' Davey said. 'If I satisfy YingTech, if they're in, Prof will back me. He's given me his word. He wants to take EIGHT all the way to market as much as I do. If there's a viable alternative to Charlie's sale, he's confident he can persuade the board.'

Cunningham was an arsehole, but Davey had sorted it. That's what he said, and I believed him. I wasted no further time or brainpower workshopping his plan.

But it turned out there was a gaping hole in Davey's story. I was the only non-comatose person who'd ever heard of Sino YingTech.

Cunningham *was* planning to sell SuperMab. Foxy even came close to admitting it. The day after my confab with him and my old man, Foxy buzzed the intercom at my apartment. 'Let's walk and talk,' he said. I came down, climbed into his mustard-yellow Triumph Stag and we motored up to the Botanic Gardens for a power walk around the Tan. Just the two of us. A cheeky man date. 'Look, I believe there was some talk of a sale, Miles,' Foxy said as a flock of blonde Toorak skeletons jogged past us like we were standing still. 'Something was in the wind, I'm told, although I'm not sure if there'd been real negotiations.'

It would have been futile for Foxy to deny that there was a Mervatis. As an intern I'd written scripts for their drugs every day. And they sponsored the residents' Christmas do. 'But I'm afraid that story about another interested party, another bidder, Sino YingTech you said the company was called, it just doesn't check out,' Foxy said. He insisted there was no white knight, let alone a yellow one. Davey's claim that he'd found a saviour, that Sino YingTech were galloping gallantly to the rescue? Not true.

I didn't want to believe Foxy. I didn't want to believe Google either. How was YingTech spelled? Yengtek? Or maybe Davey said Yangtech? Nothing came up when I searched those versions of what I thought my buddy said, and I even tabbed past the first results page. So – what – Davey had lied to me? Maybe on the day Davey did his self-experiment, he was about to tell me what the real deal was, before I rushed off to attend to skateboard boy and his helicopter olds. Perhaps that was what he was suddenly so keen to 'share'? Perhaps his white knight was Russian, not Chinese?

But at least it was confirmed that Davey had given himself EIGHT. That was something. Something definite. And what he was suffering had a name: 'a cytokine storm'. I needed to understand what that meant. I needed to supplement Mother's bulletins.

Dr Google brought more bad news. Cytokine storms are an exaggerated response when the immune system encounters an invader, it told me.

Davey's EIGHT wasn't the first drug to cause this exaggerated response, but mostly the invaders are pathogens – bacteria, like staphylococcus, or viruses, like influenza. Flu. That crappy, headachy, aching-all-over, feverish feeling you get when you've got the flu? That's a cytokine storm. I mean, who knew?

But not all flus, and not all cytokine storms, are created equal. Mostly, people recover from the flu, but sometimes they don't. Back in 1918, a virulent flu strain killed more than fifty million people. The Spanish influenza pandemic. For some – the lucky ones, I started to think – death came quickly. One minute fine, the next they were falling off their horses or collapsing on the footpath, dead. But most of the fifty million deaths weren't like that. Most deaths were horrible. Dark spots, from lack of oxygen, would form on victims' faces, and when the spots spread, those victims turned black. It was like they had the plague. Others got subcutaneous emphysema – pockets of air just beneath the skin. They crackled when nurses rolled them over. The pain was excruciating.

But, good news if it happens again. There's a treatment. It's a mAb – the mAb that Prof Patterson discovered, or kind of discovered. The one that some other dude took the kudos for. Pandaid. It blocks the immune system's exaggerated response and quells the storm. The mAb that I'd heard the Intensive Care docs were trying to get hold of? Pandaid.

Then another Mother bulletin: Pandaid didn't work for Davey. His immune system's exaggerated response to EIGHT wasn't the same as the exaggerated response that a severe flu virus sets off.

'Davey's doctors are worried,' she said, 'His lactate is ten. Do you know what that means, Milesy?'

I did. A lactate of ten meant my colleagues' efforts to prop up Davey's failing organs and normalise his blood pressure weren't working. It meant that his tissues weren't getting enough oxygen. A lactate of ten meant my buddy was cactus.

Rosa

The flyers for the vigil were posted up around BEST sometime during the morning. They weren't there when I arrived, but they were in the lift, on the noticeboard, by the water cooler and in the loo by the time I emerged from the lab at lunchtime. An email from Margaret, with the hospital's update on Dave's condition attached, had greeted me and the other BEST boys and girls that morning. The email's news presumably prompted the vigil, which would take place in Princes Park that night. Beer, wine, pizza, and the opportunity to collectively send love and get-well thoughts over the ether to Dave. The plan was to assemble at six in the foyer and walk across the road to the park en masse. Kenny was the organiser. He was atoning for his previously voiced view that Dave had 'tried to top himself'.

The vigil sounded a bit New-Agey. But thus far I'd spent the day staring into space, digesting the news that Dave had given himself EIGHT, wondering what to do next. I decided to go to the vigil. I wouldn't put myself under the pump to catch the last train home. I'd crash at Jude's. She'd said I was welcome any time, and I'd taken her offer up a couple of Friday nights. I'd felt every spring in the sofa bed I was assigned, and the three junior Winstanleys got up early, and noisily, on Saturdays for their roster of activities, which included synchronised swimming, little athletics and expressive cello. But I'd felt welcome.

'Mmm. You might want to rethink the vigil,' Jude said when I called to book the sofa bed. 'You might feel uncomfortable.'

'I'll be fine,' I said. 'I mean it's sad, it's awful, but I'll be okay. I'd like to be there.'

'No, seriously, Rosa, people are saying the cytokine storm was sort of predictable. Foreseeable, at least. They're saying you should have known it was a possibility.'

Someone, Jude said, had remembered that EIGHT wasn't the first mAb to cause a cytokine storm. 'Someone' was right. A few mAbs do. And someone had also remembered that a particular mAb called OKT3 does. Someone was right about that too. OKT3 was the first mAb used to treat patients, the mAb that featured in Prof's 'A Potted History of the Miraculous mAbs' lecture. And although it does prevent rejection of kidney transplants, it has a downside. Fevers, chills, shortness of breath: a cytokine storm. Not as severe as the storm Dave was apparently suffering, but, still, a cytokine storm.

Rumours sweep BEST like Mexican waves. Someone shouts out the latest goss and away it ripples until everyone has either echoed the initiator's opinion or swapped it out for their own further embellished version. My nameless co-worker's recollection had circled BEST. Everyone now realised that EIGHT was similar to OKT3, similar in ways that meant that because OKT3 causes a cytokine storm EIGHT might too. 'They're saying you should have warned Dave,' Jude said.

When I left the lab at lunchtime, the 'Capella the Star' printout that had been taped to the door by my anonymous well-wisher had been removed. The honour, wealth and renown it had predicted were no longer on my horizon.

It wasn't fair, because I *had* warned Dave. Months previously, all the material on EIGHT read, the data dutifully pored over, I saw there was a possibility that his super mAb would cause a cytokine storm. I wasn't certain it would happen – I couldn't be certain, no one could be – but there was a risk that when EIGHT was given to the men who'd volunteered for the trial, a cytokine release would follow, possibly a massive one.

So, me and Golden Boy, in the lab, just the two of us. Me to Dave: 'What about a cytokine storm? Don't you think there's a risk that EIGHT might cause it?' A total blurt, rather than the reasoned words I'd rehearsed.

'What? What are you talking about?' he said.

'Cytokine storm. It's when …'

'I know what it is,' Dave said. Unimpressed, annoyed, angry even. 'Of course I know about cytokine storms. So … come on, Rosa, what? What's it got to do with EIGHT?'

Dave was *brusco*, verging on rude. Where was nice-Dave who'd listened patiently to me rabbit on about Sicily, Strangeways, bees, and chooks without heads? The Dave who'd taken pity, given me a job, made the resurrection of my PhD a possibility? My mouth-dump. Totally out of the blue, I'd challenged his project, his baby. Good one, Rosa. Pissed off your new boss. Or, maybe it wasn't me. Maybe it was him. Maybe Dave was a street-angel home-devil, and the lab was home, where he could show his true colours.

Whatever. I pressed on. I told him why I thought EIGHT might cause a cytokine storm. Suffice to say that OKT3's target molecule and EIGHT's target molecule are neighbours on the blood cell where they live, like-minded neighbours that act the same and often work together. If a mAb that stimulates one of these molecules causes a cytokine release, it was possible, likely even, that a mAb that stimulates the neighbouring molecule would too.

Dave wasn't having a bar of it. 'Nice theory, Rosa, but it doesn't happen,' he said. 'We didn't see it in any of our animal studies.'

'But you didn't really look for it,' I said. He – they, Dave and Prof – hadn't. In their rat study they didn't test for cytokines until a week after they gave the animals EIGHT. The rats could have had a cytokine storm, a mild one, and been over it by the time Dave did the assays.

Dave looked at me and raised his eyebrows. *You, you loser, you're challenging me, Dave Tran, superstar?* those eyebrows said.

Then a quick segue to nice-Dave. 'Maybe you have a point,' he said, 'but we've done the primate work, and we didn't see any toxicity. You know that. There was no cytokine release in the monkeys. You re-did the last experiment yourself. And Safe Medicines is reviewing our file. So far they haven't raised any concerns. It looks like they'll approve the trial, and then we're good to go. There's nothing to worry about.'

There is something to worry about. That's what I should have said. I should have pushed back. I had another point to make, more cytokine storm intel to share. But I didn't make that point. A crisis of confidence. Why hadn't anyone else seen the similarity between the two mAbs, understood the risk and raised the alarm? Maybe because there was no risk. Maybe I was the loser Dave saw. Then again, maybe not. Golden Boy and the mAb Meister were emperors, absolutely. Maybe people like me, people who shared my suspicions about EIGHT's safety, were too awestruck to tell Dave and Prof they were stark-naked.

Or maybe I was an idiot. I wussed out. My face was hot. Red as a beetroot most likely. Golden Boy, sitting beside me at the lab bench, was faking sweetness and light while no doubt wondering how such a dud had washed up as his research assistant.

'Thanks for your input, Rosa,' he said. 'But don't worry. It's not your problem. If anything goes wrong, it's on me.'

And now it was on him. Mother Nature had been a nasty bitch, and it was on Dave. So, what should I do? Tell Jude? Tell Kenny? Post another flyer telling the BEST boys and girls all about my warning? How desperate would that look. No, Dave could tell them himself, when he got better, which he would, soon.

Jude was still on the line. 'Rosie, I know it's not fair that people are putting this on you. Making you the scapegoat. I mean, Dave should have known. Prof should have known. They were the grown-ups in the room.'

'Thanks very much,' I said.

'You know what I mean. It isn't fair. But you know what I say.'

'I've forgotten. Tell me again.'

'Fair's a hair colour.'

Ly (Natalie)

We went to the hospital every day. Má, Abigail and me. Some days Auntie came with us. Some days Mrs Southcott also came and sat with us around Dung's bed. The doctors wouldn't let Má stay all night like she wanted, so every day we had to leave when visiting hours finished and come back the next morning.

Even though nurse Shaz didn't work in Intensive Care, she still came to talk with us every day. It was Shaz who told us that Dung's doctors would soon turn off the machines that were keeping him alive. They had done X-rays of his brain and found that it had been without oxygen too long on the day he gave himself his own medicine. He would never get better.

We had to prepare for Dung's passing, so Auntie asked Abbot Thay Phuoc Quang from her temple to come and chant for him. Má was happy that Abbot Quang agreed to do the chanting for Dung. Má is not devout like Auntie, but when my brother died she wanted to do everything right. She wanted Dung to have merit in the eyes of the Buddha, so that he would make Dung's next life beautiful.

Má and Abigail became close when Dung died. Abigail felt bad because she and Dung had argued, and she didn't see him again until after he became sick. I told Abigail it wasn't her fault, but she still felt guilty. I think that was why she was so kind to Má. Perhaps it was also because of what Abbot Quang said to us: 'You are sad that someone close to you has gone away. So then, care about the people who are here with you now. Be happy with them, because one day they will go away too.' I think his words helped Má and Abigail, but they didn't help me.

Abigail is okay. I like her. I hope Dung said *love you* to her after they had the argument just like he said *love you* to me and to Má. And of course I care about Má. I don't blame her for what she did.

But I always cared about Dung more than I cared about Má, or Abigail. So no matter what Abbot Quang said, I was sad my brother was gone.

Shaz said there would have to be an autopsy. I tried to explain this to Má, but she didn't understand. '*Tại sao họ khám nghiệm tử thi?*' she asked. Why will they cut up his body? '*Chẳng lẽ họ nghĩ ảnh làm điều gì sai lầm?*' What do they think he did wrong?'

Shaz said it was the law. A government person called the coroner had to work out exactly how Dung died. Má didn't understand, or didn't want to. She got angry with Shaz, even though it wasn't her fault. When that happened, I asked Mrs Southcott if her son could help, but she said he was in trouble. The hospital thought he should have stopped Dung giving himself his own medicine, and now Miles might lose his job. He couldn't help us.

In our culture we don't touch a person after they've died. We let their body rest for eight hours. Death is painful. You must not torture your loved one any more by touching them. Their nerves can still feel pain. You must not cry near them. They might hear you. Do not disturb them. It will make the pain of dying worse.

It was important for Dung that we let his body rest, because he must have had a lot of pain. His head was so swollen. 'He looks like the elephant man,' I heard one of the nurses say. She must have heard me speak Vietnamese to Má and thought I didn't speak good English.

Abigail said there was nothing she could do about the autopsy, but she arranged with Shaz that no one would disturb Dung's body when he passed. We could sit with him in Intensive Care for five hours. That was the best Abigail and Shaz could do. Then the government would collect Dung's body.

Auntie and two of her friends did the chanting. *Nam Mô A Di Đà Phật*, they chanted very softly, over and over for the five hours. *A Di Đà Phật* is Amitabha Buddha. Auntie says that if you chant his name many times, Amitabha Buddha will hear you; he will take your loved one to paradise, to the Pure Land.

We sat beside Dung's body. Me, Má, Abigail and Mrs Southcott, all very quiet, while Auntie and her friends took turns to chant *Nam Mô A Di Đà Phật*, over and over. I prayed that five hours was long enough for Amitabha Buddha to hear us. And I prayed that Auntie was right about what Amitabha Buddha would do when he heard his name.

Miles

Watch the news and more nights than not you'll see the anchor strike a pose, turn to camera three and wrap a tearjerker with solemn words: 'The family of the dead man have been offered counselling,' she – because it's the girls who read the sob stories – might say. A tragic accident, and: 'Workers at the mine have been offered counselling.' A vicious crime, and: 'The witnesses have been offered counselling.'

I could never imagine spilling my guts to some stranger if tragedy struck. I couldn't imagine tragedy striking. So I never saw myself joining the burgeoning ranks of those 'offered counselling', let alone being one of the punters who took up the offer. But there I was, three days after Davey died, 'meeting with' – her term – Veronica, my psychologist.

When Mother told me Davey's doctors were turning off his life support, I'd rocked up to the hospital. My place was with the chanters. The ICU staff didn't think so. They called the medical director, who agreed with them. My presence was inappropriate. Let's just say I chucked a wobbly. Security was called. So now my return to hospital duties was contingent upon participation in a counselling program, amongst other things.

Foxy hooked me up with Veronica. 'I'm here to help,' I imagine he said when the old man told him I needed a psychologist. It's Harry Renard's mantra. When I saw the movie, *Harry, He's Here to Help*, I wondered if Foxy might rebrand – movie-Harry is a serial killer – but I guess Foxy's not an arthouse film fan.

I met Foxy at the club for lunch before my first session with Veronica, the club being a 'safe place' for me to appear in public, despite my buddy's recent death. It being Thursday, the old man and two of his and Foxy's closest cronies – Thos and Rich – joined us. The foursome has a set-in-stone lunch date: 12.30 every Thursday. Only two excuses are accepted for a no-show: a trip overseas, or illness. An interstate meeting? No. It's poor form to beg off lunch when you're only going to Sydney. Can't your secretary manage your calendar better? Illness? Fair enough, but only if it requires hospitalisation – your own. A family member? Our condolences, but visiting hours are after the lunch service. And a good feed will brace you to sit by the sick bed, old chap.

'We take turns to provide the beverage, Miles,' Foxy said when we were seated 'at table', 'and I'm delighted to say that today it's mine.' The foursome all put their wine down at the club, where the cellar is a real one, underground. 'A Léoville-Las Cases,' Foxy announced. 'The 1982.' He only had four bottles left and he was delighted to share them with three of his closest chums and one chum's errant son. 'Well, I think the sun's over the yardarm, don't you agree, gentlemen?' he said.

At that prompt, the four gentlemen pounded the table with fisted hands and the waiter approached at a clip with the first decanted bottle. He'd seen this pantomime before.

It felt like a lifetime since my last meal at the club. In the meantime, the food had gone upmarket. Now there was a menu du jour, courtesy of a new French chef. It was a far cry from the over-roasted lamb and practically salt-cured three veg served up in my youth, when we were brought along for family bashes – the old man's birthday and the like. Davey's was the only non-white face in the dining room on those occasions, and his presence did not go unnoticed. After his debut visit, I overheard the old man tell Mother that the club president had suggested we might be more comfortable at a restaurant the next time we wished to dine with that particular guest.

Mother told the old man where the president could stick it, and, for good measure, chose the club, rather than the more fashionable venues she preferred, for a dinner to celebrate her next birthday. And, no, thank you very much, she didn't want a private room. A nice table in the centre of the main dining room would be super.

Two decades later, the booze-ravaged faces in the dining room bore testimony to a sad truth: Mother's attempt to diversify the club demographics hadn't gained traction. Nothing but the food had changed. Her Maj still hung on the south wall, casting her 'we are not amused' gaze over the old codgers, but otherwise no female faces. Women are tolerated at dinner but have never been admitted for lunch, and that would only change 'over my dead body', Foxy had assured me while we ate our entrée of lambs' brains. Jews could now join, in theory, but no member of the luncheon foursome could think of any who'd been nominated.

That day only white men – lawyers, retired doctors, business moguls, and their wealth managers – were tucking enthusiastically into their mains: Wagyu eye fillet, grilled to their liking; potato rosti; steamed asparagus and a beetroot relish side. It was a meal Davey would have enjoyed, his fillet served rare, just like the slab of meat in front of me.

My appetite vanished and I focused on the booze.

We were into the last of Foxy's precious bottles and the talk had turned bolshie. Golf scores covered off, the four old boys were riffing on their favourite theme: the country's going to hell in a handbasket. *That Labor chap got a third term. Unbelievable! Do you know anyone who voted for him?* None of them did, or would admit to it. *Thank Christ we've at least got little Johnny Howard looking out for us in Canberra.* And so on.

Foxy caught me surveying the dining room and lassoed me back into the conversation. 'So what's next for you, Miles?' he asked. 'I'm sure this unfortunate business will be resolved soon and you'll be back at the hospital in no time at all, doing good work. Any thoughts about your career? I'm here to help, remember.'

Foxy permitted himself a slight upturn of the lips at his own drollery but didn't show his teeth, thank Christ. They'd been way over-whitened. Thos, Rich and the old man smiled good-humouredly.

I hoped it was Foxy's catchphrase that they found amusing, because I didn't find his remarks funny. Unfortunate business? Davey was dead. *Unfortunate*, that. The last two weeks of his life? Hooked up to a bunch of machines. Very *unfortunate*, to die that way. Nobody, not Davey's Ma, or Natalie, or Abigail, and none of the Oxford docs, got to talk with Davey after he collapsed in Emergency. Davey spoke his last words to me from the procedure room floor: *Stay frosty, my friend.* Jesus Christ. Couldn't he at least have said something profound?

Now, the coroner was investigating. There wouldn't be a funeral, or even a memorial service, until the coroner released his body. Until then, we all had to wait for what Mother had already started to refer to as 'closure'. And my return to the Oxford, as well as being contingent on the counselling, depended on the coroner exonerating me from any wrongdoing. Yes, *unfortunate*, the whole freaking business.

Foxy's smooth. He picked up on his faux pas before I could vent. 'Tragic, it's a tragic business,' he said. 'I'm sorry, Miles, I misspoke. Do forgive me. But let's focus on the future. Any thoughts?'

I didn't have the energy to go another set. 'Yeah, I'm not sure,' I said.

'Could we perhaps tempt you into the biotech area? There's lots going on, plenty of opportunities. One has to run hard, but the rewards are there,' he said.

What was he on about? I'm no scientist, no Davey. It sounded like Foxy was losing it – he was pushing seventy.

He threw out a qualification. 'Marketing or business development, they might be good slots for you, Miles.'

Great. I could spend my days hanging with arseholes like Charlie Cunningham, who hadn't let Davey's imminent death curb his globetrotting. He was in Hong Kong, partying hard, telling the young ladies at those parties that he and Mercedes were over, according to Rupert Stone, who'd texted me that update the previous week.

'Thanks, Foxy,' I said, 'but I'm thinking I'll specialise. I'm thinking derm. But the training program's as good as a closed shop.'

Foxy looked relieved. He was off the hook. 'Dermatology?' he asked.

I nodded.

'I like that line of thought, Miles. Good for the cashflow and no nasty out-of-hours call-outs.'

Which were my thoughts exactly. Dermatology would be a good resting place for a Mickey Mouse doc like me. Thos and Rich approved too, and the old man did a little basking in the reflected glory of his son's brilliant career planning. Tales of how well various chums had done in dermatology were told. One had a big yacht. A forty-two-footer, was it? Thos thought so. That big? He couldn't be sure, but it was certainly impressive, and big. Another successful 'skin-man' took weekend trips, every month, to Singapore for brunch at Raffles.

Good thinking, Miles, was the consensus. Foxy insisted I have the last half-glass of Las Cases, and they started workshopping a plan to get me trained as a boat-owning, weekend-tripping dermatologist. Foxy knew someone, of course. He would have a word. Yes, he understood that there were devilishly few places on offer in the training program, but there was always a spot for the right man.

Luncheon concluded, Foxy and I kicked on to Tryst, his preferred venue for a postprandial sobering espresso. A pre-counselling briefing came with the coffee. 'Veronica's clients are mostly lawyers,' Foxy told me. 'The law is such a stressful profession, and Veronica is very good. I've backgrounded her on the situation, and I'm sure she'll be able to help.' He sounded like he was pimping her.

We were sitting on stools outside the cafe. 'Isn't this laneway scene simply marvellous?' my self-appointed patron said. Foxy had gone to seed. There'd been too many liquid lunches, too much time in the golf buggy rather than walking the course. But even in his prime, the stool would have been way too small, way too low. With his oldster's gut he looked like Big Bird balancing on a budgie's perch.

'Do you know what inspired the naming of this little establishment?' he asked.

Tryst? I did. Foxy had been my informant, but I let him play the raconteur again.

He pointed across the lane to the red door in the club's brick wall. 'Chaps used to have girls brought in through that door for a little socialising. It opens onto the garden, and in the corner there's a wee staircase leading to the first floor. This was before wives were permitted as dinner guests of course.' He chuckled. 'Fun and games, eh.'

Ten minutes later, I could see the crown of the club's Moreton Bay fig from my chair in Veronica's office. She didn't have a couch. I felt cheated by that. Admittedly, though, my expectations were based on movies rather than my time as a doc, so maybe the couch was never gonna happen. My only personal experience in any vaguely similar setting was the psych rotation I did at a mental hospital when I was a medical student. I was assigned the management of pinheads who'd smoked too much dope and tripped over into psychosis. The meds don't touch those dudes. As for a talking cure, forget it. You're talking to the hand. They certainly don't get a couch. Sedation, sedation, sedation – that's the management plan. If that doesn't work? Ramp up the sedation.

And at the Oxford only rellies of a deceased get counselling. A patient flatlines, and social workers shepherd the family away for the cup of tea. Who knows what they say.

'So, this is where you help people,' I said to my counsellor.

Veronica had a soothing voice. I guess you would say she was warm. 'I can imagine how difficult all this must be for you,' she said.

Veronica seemed kind. If she's a mother I bet she's a good one. But how difficult 'all this' was for me? Jesus Christ. She didn't have a freaking clue.

I leaned forward, buried my head in my hands and moaned. Actually, and I'm ashamed to admit it, I howled. Davey. My buddy. Dead at thirty-three.

Veronica's office was on the fifth floor. Only the birds could see in, and there were precious few flying past. Still, she got up from her chair and pulled down the blind. 'It's okay. Take your time,' she said. 'Let your grief speak.'

Rosa

I spent the time between hearing that Dave had done a personal 'N-of-1' trial and his eventual death in a kind of limbo. There was no more prepping to be done for a trial that was never going to happen. Any further editing of the trial documents I'd been assigned to write would have been a waste of time. I spent that time cleaning out the freezer, chucking the out-of-date reagents, stacking the boxes of pipettes neatly. Busy work. I sent magical thoughts Dave's way. *Get better. Tell me, and everyone else, what this is all about.* And I spent that time worrying about my future.

But I wasn't worrying that my BEST co-workers were right, that 'the incident', as they were calling what happened, was my fault. I wasn't thinking that, if I'd been more persuasive, if I'd shared my further intel about the risk of cytokine storm, Dave wouldn't be fighting for his life. Because the week before his self-experiment, Dave looked at all the EIGHT data again. And when he called me on the Friday, when we 'talked on the phone', as I so awkwardly told Yvette the day after the incident, he'd worked it out. And he'd acknowledged the inconvenient truth to me. There was a risk that EIGHT would cause a cytokine storm.

'You're right,' he said.

Awesome. It was nearly six months since I'd raised the red flag, but still, awesome. Nice-guy Dave was back, and he agreed with me – and not just because of EIGHT's similarity to OKT3, either. The Friday before the incident, Dave told me what I already knew. The fact that there'd been no cytokine release in his monkey tests meant nothing.

He'd looked at the data closely, like I had, and seen that in monkeys EIGHT didn't produce those sought-after regulatory T cells, the TREGS that had earned EIGHT its reputation as a super mAb. EIGHT wasn't effective in monkeys. It was effective in rats, yes, but not monkeys. So, how could it be reassuring that it didn't cause toxicity in monkeys? It wasn't reassuring. The absence of evidence is not evidence of absence. 'I used the wrong primate model,' Dave said. So now he had a new plan. It wasn't to test EIGHT on himself.

The day after the incident, the day I was meant to be helping Dave work out how to implement his new plan, I told Prof what that plan was.

Prof, waylaying me at the lab door: 'When did you last speak to David?'

Me, en route to my train: 'Friday.'

Prof: 'Did he say anything about putting the trial on hold?'

Me: 'Yes. He said he wanted to test EIGHT on chimpanzees first. We were going to talk about a chimp study today. The design. The logistics.'

'That makes sense,' Prof said and nodded sagely, as if he knew about it – maybe as if Dave had discussed it with him.

The next time Prof and I spoke was the day after Dave died. Margaret summoned me to Prof's office and I sat with the mAb Meister at his meeting table. 'I don't think there'll be an inquest,' Prof said. 'The coroner is investigating of course, but an inquest would be unnecessary, and time-consuming. I think we need closure.' He was speaking slowly, as if I were a simpleton, and looking at me intently.

I didn't have an opinion about an inquest. Either there would be one or there wouldn't, it didn't matter what I thought. Closure? Dave had died yesterday, my parents eighteen years before. I could totally guarantee Prof that closure regarding Golden Boy's death wasn't coming anytime soon.

'The coroner's police will interview you,' Prof continued.

'Me? Why?'

'Because David told you what he planned to do,' he said. 'Don't be worried. Just tell them what you told me when we talked the day after the incident.'

But I *was* worried. Because when I talked with Prof the day after the incident, I didn't know Dave had injected himself with EIGHT. We were still in 'unidentified substance' territory. I'd answered Prof's question – yes, Dave had told me he was putting the trial on hold – but I didn't tell him other fun facts. Like, I'd warned Dave about the risk of a cytokine storm with EIGHT. There was that, and more, that I could tell Prof – maybe should tell Prof, and maybe the police too – now that Dave's test with EIGHT had turned out to be fatal. But where should I start?

'And you don't need to worry about your PhD,' Prof said. 'I'm sure we can sort something out once this business with the coroner is resolved.'

Relief. I didn't have to raise the subject at such an awkward time. 'Okay. Thank you,' I said. 'But do you know why Dave tested EIGHT on himself? Why didn't he wait to test it on chimps like he told me he was going to?'

Abigail

I first heard the words 'cytokine storm' two days before David tested his drug on himself. We'd had a rough week. He'd got back from a trip to the US on the Monday and jet lag hit him hard. Struggling to sleep, he'd been heading into the lab at night, getting home around four or five in the morning, disturbing my sleep too. Friday night we were eating Indian takeaway on our balcony, trying to talk above the revellers at the bar across the road.

I was looking forward to getting out of town the next day for the logging demo. I love being in the forest: the stars, not the streetlights, illuminating the night, and the birds waking me in the morning. I did feel bad about going away so soon after David's return, but not bad enough not to do it. I'd added the masala curry David liked to our takeaway order to make up for my impending absence.

David picked at the beef. 'I've got something to tell you,' he said. 'You're not going to like it.'

I thought he was breaking up with me. Our time together started clicking through my brain like slides in an old projector. It jammed on our fight over my email signature acknowledging traditional landowners: David, pointing his finger at me, yelling, *Live by your principles*. Because he had yelled. Just like the drinkers across the road were now yelling, 'Skoll!' David's words, his yelling, hadn't persuaded me to delete the signature. But surely we weren't going to break up over it?

It was probably something else. He hadn't seemed happy for a while. Six months, perhaps. That was a long time to be unhappy. I knew we needed to have a conversation about what wasn't right between us.

'I need to do some more tests on EIGHT, before the human trial,' David said.

We weren't breaking up. But I wasn't sure if I was relieved.

David now believed there was a risk of a cytokine storm with EIGHT. Rosa, his assistant, whom I'd insulted at the Cunningham party, had warned him months ago, but he'd underestimated her judgement and dismissed her assessment. Now he'd decided she was right. It was far from certain that his mAb would cause a cytokine storm, but it might. Believing that, he couldn't allow it to be tested on the men who'd volunteered for the trial. He couldn't put eight lives at risk.

'I'm going to test EIGHT on chimpanzees,' he said, forking a chunk of dead cow into his mouth.

Of all our animal cousins, chimpanzees' DNA is the most similar to humans. Ninety-eight per cent similar, David said. And their immune system is virtually identical. That was his rationale. If EIGHT didn't cause a cytokine storm in chimpanzees, he would feel comfortable testing it on humans. 'I know you won't like it, but they're only animals, Abigail,' he said.

'You won't like it.' I doubt truer words have ever been spoken. The idea of anyone, let alone David, experimenting on any ape, but especially chimpanzees, enraged me. David knew that.

He knew how distressed I'd been when I read about the experiments on monkeys to investigate whether nerve regeneration could be 'forced'. Their scientist 'owner's' hypothesis was that limb function isn't irretrievably lost when the nerves are cut. He severed the monkeys' spinal cords so that the nerve connections to one of their arms were lost. Forcing also meant strapping the monkey's good arm into a straightjacket, and, if that didn't work, administering electric shocks until the monkey moved its numbed arm. The forcing worked but drove the monkeys crazy. They chewed off their own fingers.

At the time, such mistreatment of animals in the science world wasn't isolated. Experiments with baboons, aimed at understanding car-accident-induced head trauma, were worse. A pressurised piston was slammed against each baboon's helmeted head. Shamelessly, the researchers documented the outcomes on video, posing the dazed, brain-damaged, sometimes crippled and quivering animals for the camera, laughing at them, mocking their desperation.

'What do you mean "tests"?' I asked David. 'How, exactly, are you going to "test" EIGHT on chimpanzees?'

He would only be doing safety tests, he said. He agreed, the nerve-severing and head-trauma experiments were shocking. Inexcusable. Cruel. What he was planning wasn't like that. He wouldn't be making the chimpanzees sick like he'd done with rats, who'd been given the arthritis that EIGHT was designed to treat. He'd just give the chimpanzees a test dose of EIGHT and observe them. Take blood samples. Watch and wait. If the animals didn't experience a cytokine storm, the human trial would be back on the agenda.

'And if they *do* experience a cytokine storm?' I asked.

He would have to sacrifice the animals, humanely of course.

Humanely or not, they would still be dead.

David knew that chimpanzees had been my life in Rwanda. They're an endangered species, already extinct in some African countries, their numbers way down in others. Capture of infants and juveniles for scientific experiments and for use as pets, shooting by poachers for bush meat, deforestation and diseases like Ebola had all contributed to the fall.

In response, reserves had been created where wild 'chimpans', as the Rwandans call them, could live undisturbed by humans, who observed the animals' lives at a respectful distance. I volunteered at one such reserve: the Buranda Chimpanzee Project, in the rainforest south-west of Kigali. Every day we would hike out in teams to find our allocated group of chimpanzees – easy if we knew where they'd built their nests the night before, arduous if we didn't. Then we would watch our chimpans, recording everything they did.

I didn't doubt David's claim that chimpanzees' DNA is strikingly similar to ours. They're like us in so many ways. They love hanging out together, and I grew to love hanging out with them, especially Quintana and Tike. Quintana was a female chimp, the same age as me. She'd raised four children and was in the process of raising her fifth – Tike – but she still had love to spare and share. She took to grooming me, just as she groomed Tike, inspecting and cleaning my ears, studying the lines of my hands like the most conscientious palm reader, flicking off the tiniest specks of grit.

Quintana and Tike were from a colony that lived halfway between Kigali and Buranda. I rarely saw them more than once a month, but they gave a good impression of not just remembering me, but of looking forward to my visits. Especially Tike, who would leap from her tree into my arms, wrapping her arms around my neck, kissing me. Unconditional love.

Now David was going to test the drug he'd invented on Tike and Quintana's kin, rather than risk eight human lives.

Not if I could help it. 'If there's a chance of something bad happening, then have some guts,' I told him. 'Try your bloody drug on yourself.' I got up from the table and went inside. I may have slammed the door.

I got undressed, brushed my teeth and went to the bedroom door. David was still on the balcony. He was on his phone. 'Hey, Miles, my friend. How's it going?' he was saying. The last words I heard him speak.

'Try your bloody drug on yourself.' The last words I spoke to him.

Foxy

Once we knew Tran's life support would be turned off, we could spin the incident however we wanted. He wasn't going to argue. The Professor and Joe hadn't spoken since Tran's self-experiment, so I organised a little get-together for the three of us after his death. We needed to all be on the same page.

I wanted to make our meeting convivial, to head off the possibility that Joe would be so crass as to say, 'I told you so' to the Professor. Because I was sure that's what he was thinking. Christmas was fast approaching, and the weather pleasant, so late-afternoon drinks in the club's courtyard would have been my choice. But that would not have suited Joe. The club hadn't accepted membership nominations for his tribe until very recently, and he couldn't let bygones be. Privacy was paramount, so it had to be my office. My secretary, Deidre, got in a nice bottle of Sullivans Cove, the single malt, and a platter of Le Traiteur's chicken sandwiches. We were all set.

The Professor spoke first, no doubt perceiving it as his right. I was happy to give him that, and Joe didn't appear troubled. Joe's a whisky connoisseur, so I'd expected the Sullivans would please him, but, surprisingly, he seemed equally interested in the sandwiches. When meetings are scheduled at mealtimes, Joe's modus operandi is to eat beforehand, to avoid being distracted by hunger if the food's not to his liking, or the need to chew if it is.

The Professor summarised what we already knew. Tran had told his assistant that he intended to experiment on chimpanzees before going ahead with the phase one trial. Then, inexplicably, he'd shared his plan with the fair Abigail, who leaped to the animals' defence, insisting that her beloved test the bloody drug on himself.

'Foxy, I'm wondering if this could be a set-up?' Joe asked, swallowing the last bite of his third sandwich.

'Go on,' I said.

'I'm sure you both know what I'm getting at,' Joe said, looking at the Professor for the first time. 'I mean, testing a drug on yourself to save a few monkey-type animals? Only a fucking idiot would do that, and I don't think Tran was an idiot.'

I have to say that I agreed with Joe. It did seem idiotic. Yet it was also an explanation that happened to be very convenient for us.

'There's actually a historical context to what David did,' the Professor said, looking pleased with himself – perhaps because he now had the opportunity to lecture me and Joe, whom he no doubt regarded as philistines.

The Professor explained that it had once been *de rigueur* for scientists to experiment on themselves. If a doctor wasn't confident that the medicine they'd discovered would 'do no harm', as the Hippocratic oath urges, they tried it on themselves before they tried it on others. Once upon a time, the honourable course was to 'go first'.

How bizarre that sounded. Oh I knew about Barry Marshall,

of course, the doctor chap from Perth who swallowed some bacteria or other to prove his point about stomach ulcers, but, according to the Professor, there was a veritable raft of other fellows who'd done similar things.

Some chaps from St Louis in the US, for example, who'd injected themselves with blood from patients afflicted by rare blood disorders, aiming to prove that leukaemia was a transmissible disease. And scientists at a Danish pharmaceutical company who'd tested the new drugs they were developing on themselves. The Professor told us that the St Louis doctors' workplace became known as the Kamikaze School of Medicine when one chap nearly died after injecting himself with blood from a patient with some terrible condition called aplastic anaemia. Fascinating. And, amusingly, the Danish Pharma even had an incentive scheme for their staff: the most prolific self-experimenter was honoured at the annual dinner dance with a prize – a plastic skeleton named Jacob.

But how did the Professor think this 'context' would help us, I was wondering. Joe was obviously wondering too. 'If we put a historic spin on the incident, won't there be blowback?' he asked. 'Won't your scientists be under pressure to start testing their own bright ideas on themselves?'

'No. Ethics committees wouldn't allow it these days,' the Professor said. 'A young lab technician at Johns Hopkins died just a few years ago after she participated in one of the university's studies.'

'That's going to be a complicated "historical context" to pitch then, don't you think?' Joe said, rightly, scoring a point off the Professor.

I decided to close the discussion down. 'Professor, I agree with Joe,' I said. 'I'd suggest we don't open that can of worms. I think it's simplest if we go with the animal welfare story. Agreed?'

The Professor nodded, perhaps reluctantly.

So that just left a couple of loose ends to tie up. 'What about Mervatis, Joe?' I asked. 'Can we count on them keeping quiet about the fact that there was a deal on the table?'

'Won't be a problem. I mean who'd want it known that they were about to buy what turned out to be a crock of shit?' he said, looking pointedly at the Professor, who stared back poker-faced, either too thick-skinned to be phased by Joe's barb or too self-possessed to display his hurt. 'But don't worry, Foxy, I'll cover them off. I'll have a quiet word with the bloke Charlie was dealing with,' he said.

Jolly good. That just left Miles. He seemed to have accepted that Tran's 'white knight' alternative to Mervatis was a fiction, but he was hanging on for dear life to the true part of the fairytale Tran had spun him: Charlie was going to sell SuperMab to Mervatis. If we could talk Miles into staying mum about that plan, the disappointing financial consequences that Tran would have experienced as a result of the sale wouldn't come to light. We would avoid awkward questions about Tran's state of mind at the time of the incident, not to mention the Cunninghams' business practices. There wouldn't be an inquest, something we very much wanted to avoid.

'Professor,' I said, 'I might call on you to assist me with young Miles Southcott. We need to get him on board. I'm wondering if you'd be kind enough to have a word with him, doctor to doctor?'

'Yes. Happy to do that,' the Professor said. But he didn't look happy. He took a slug of whisky and grimaced.

'Let me cut it with some ice,' I said, reaching for the bucket Deidre had thoughtfully provided.

'No, it's fine thanks, Foxy,' he said. 'It's good.' He raised the glass and looked at the ochre liquid, quizzically perhaps.

'There's something else we need to discuss,' he said. 'Gigi Johansen came to see me. She's the local manager of ClinHelp, the company that was going to run the trial.'

'Pretty name for a scientist. Gigi,' Joe said.

'She's concerned,' the Professor said, ignoring Joe, who was starting to get on my nerves too. 'The protocol for the trial specified that the eight volunteers each receive their dose of David's mAb ten minutes apart.' He paused, then continued, correctly observing that he needed to spell out for us what was wrong with that, what she was concerned about. 'All eight of them would have got their dose before the first volunteer got sick,' he said. Another pause. 'They could all have died.'

We sat silently. The sandwiches had been consumed, the whisky bottle was close to dead. Christ. Eight lives almost lost.

Joe cleared his throat and spoke. 'So whose bright idea was that?'

'Gigi claims it was Charlie's,' the Professor said. With this slam-bam schedule, the volunteers wouldn't have had to stay in the dosing facility for so long, he explained, and staff costs would be lower. According to Gigi, Charlie had been insistent the trial come in on budget. So that was the solution.

Charlie's solution? Her solution? Gigi claimed it was Charlie's. She'd told the Professor she was pressured by Charlie to specify that dosing timetable in the trial protocol, as a cost-saving exercise. It wouldn't have surprised me if that was true, but at least he'd had enough sense not to put his request – or, more likely, demand – in writing.

But we weren't quite off the hook. The Professor informed us that the police had a copy of the protocol. So, assuming someone in the coroner's office could understand it, the silly dosing plan would come out. And Gigi, the Professor said, was determined not to see her promising career go up in smoke. If that looked like happening, she wouldn't be burning at the stake alone.

'The regulator, Safe Medicines, approved the trial, didn't they?' Joe asked.

The Professor nodded.

Joe turned to me. 'There's our scapegoat, Foxy. We blame them,' he said.

He was right. Safe Medicines was the perfect scapegoat. Even a science dunce like me could see, now that it had been pointed out, that it was madness for eight hapless chaps to be given Tran's drug essentially at the same time. In approving the trial, Safe Medicines had made a mistake.

It would be easy to focus the blame on them, but we also needed to minimise the chance of the police or the coroner having long conversations with Gigi. She could easily panic and start dumping Charlie in the *merde*. We needed to get her out of the country as well as Charlie. Oh, of course the authorities could still call her on the phone – even arrange a video conference – but if we got on the front foot with the blame game, we would deflect any interest in her. People are lazy. If she was far away, then the different time zones, and the complexity and cost of getting in touch with her, would work in our favour. If there was no obvious need to talk to her, the police probably wouldn't bother.

'ClinHelp's a big international outfit, isn't it?' I asked Joe.

'Yep. Headquartered in North Carolina,' he said.

'I'll get her boss on the phone,' I said. I was sure he wouldn't want one of his employees embroiled in a public debate with a client over who said what. Her boss would be keen to protect his company's reputation. I expected there would be some distant outpost to which the prettily named Gigi could be promoted.

I stood up. 'Well, I think we're done here,' I said to the Professor. I'll be in touch about Miles, but otherwise I think Joe and I can sort this.'

The Professor despatched, Joe and I settled back to enjoy the last of the Sullivans. 'You're chipper today,' I said. It was an understatement. Chronically dour, that day Joe was positively buoyant. 'What's the story?' I asked him.

Joe hesitated, I expect deciding whether to confide. 'It's Charlie.' Joe now seemed to be trying to suppress a smile. 'He made another payment to the Greek, after CC and I told him to hold off until we'd seen the algorithms perform on our own computer system.'

Oh dear, the equations had reared their ugly head once more. 'How much?' I asked.

'Two,' Joe said, looking grim now. 'Two mill.'

'Two and a half million dollars? Gone?' I asked.

'Actually, four and a half. Charlie kept raiding the coffers after he left for Honkers. He took another two million as a stake. He doubled down, hit the casinos, tried to win back what he lost.'

I sighed. Poor CC. The apple had indeed fallen far from the tree. But I was confused. Joe kept a tight rein on the finances. How had Charlie gotten away with this?

'He doctored the monthly reports he had to submit to me and CC,' Joe said, reading my mind. 'Gave Yvette a spreadsheet with fictional numbers to copy and paste into the report we saw. I only found out after Charlie left the country and Yvette used the actual bank statement to prepare this month's report.'

'So CC knows?'

Joe nodded. 'He's crushed, and livid. We had the motherfucker of phone calls with the young prince a couple of days ago.'

I could imagine.

'Charlie's been retired from the business for the foreseeable future,' Joe said, allowing himself a tight-lipped smile. 'Condemned to survive on his trust-fund cheques.'

Ah. Now I knew why Joe had been so chipper. But there was more. 'So, the Capella and the SuperMab bank accounts had a sole signatory? Charlie?' I asked.

Joe scoffed. 'Of course they didn't. CC, Charlie and I were all signatories, but any one of us could operate on the accounts.'

'But why did you set it up that way?' I asked, although I thought I knew.

'CC wanted to give Charlie responsibility. I merely actioned his wishes.' Joe sat, nodding his head like it was a rocking chair. Content.

CC had wanted to give Charlie the opportunity to make his

mark. Joe had removed the scrutiny that might have kept the son and heir in check. Now Joe needn't worry about Charlie taking over the Cunningham Family Office and becoming his boss. Joe's play hadn't come cheap – four and a half million dollars – but it was other people's money, not his own.

Ly (Natalie)

In our culture, funerals are usually held at a funeral parlour, but Auntie arranged for Dung's to be at the temple, which was an honour. We had to wait for the autopsy to be finished, then my brother's body would be prepared for the viewing.

Abigail, Auntie and I tried to do everything the way Má wanted after Dung died. When we got back to our house from the hospital, after his body was taken away, Má wanted to set up the altar in the living room. I got the box of photos down from the shelf in my wardrobe and picked two for Má to choose. I liked the one of Dung at the mountain the best. Soon after we arrived in Australia, the Aussies who look after refugees took the Vietnamese kids there on a bus so that we could see snow for the first time. The leader of the trip took a photo of Dung sliding down the mountain on a black plastic rubbish bag. He looked so happy. But for the altar, Má chose the photo of Dung in his private-school uniform.

People came to our house and paid their respects to Dung. Auntie and Uncle, Trà My and Trà My's mum, Kim, came. The number-eight Nguyens, the number-fourteen Nguyens, all our neighbours. They lit incense sticks and placed them on the altar. They offered rice and tea to Dung.

Miles and Mrs Southcott were the only Westerners who came. None of Dung's other Aussie friends, not even Shaz, came. The potato-head Charlie Cunningham didn't come either. Abigail said not to be offended. Westerners don't visit when someone dies. Dung's friends and colleagues would pay their respects at his funeral.

Abigail became like a daughter to Má after Dung passed, but Má didn't even like her before he got sick.

Dung met Abigail when he was at uni. He was still helping Miles, so that Miles could become a doctor as well as Dung, but when Dung went to live in college with Miles, Mrs Southcott said she wouldn't pay Má anymore. The Southcotts paid the money to Dung instead. It was an allowance, just like the one they gave their own son. So Má had to get the money for Hands from Dung.

That made my brother mad. I suppose he could forget about the money Mrs Southcott was giving Má when he didn't see it. He could forget that Hands was visiting Má and me every month to collect the money. But it wasn't so easy to forget when he had to pay it himself.

So Dung said no. Má shouldn't pay Hands anymore. The government wouldn't send him back to Vietnam just because Má had lied about being his mother. That was a long time ago. We'd been in Australia for more than ten years, and now he had many Aussie friends who respected him. They would help us with the government. Má wouldn't go to jail like she feared. No way.

Then Dung told Má about Abigail. She was one of the Aussies who would help my brother sort it out so that Hands wouldn't bother us anymore. She lived in college with Dung, and she'd helped a girl who was in trouble. She knew how the government worked. She would help sort it out.

Then it was Má's turn to be mad. *'Bây giờ con học đại học, Má con không lo đủ cho con hay sao?'* she said. I'm not good enough for you, now you're at uni? *'Bao nhiêu năm nay má lo cho con tận sức? Bây giờ con Úc đó nó lo cho con?'* I've looked after you all these years. Done my best. And now some Aussie girl is looking after you?

That was why Má didn't like Abigail, even before she met her. Dung told Má she was being silly. This wasn't about Má not being good enough. He wanted to get rid of Hands from our life, that was all. He could do it with Abigail's help.

There'd been many chances for Má to tell me that Hands was not my Pa. When he hit Dung was one of the chances. When I helped Má with English so she could ask Mrs Southcott for money was another. All the Mondays I waited with her for Hands to collect the money were also chances. 'He's not your Pa, Ly,' Má could have said. And I would have been happy to know that dickhead Hands was not my Pa, even though I would not have been happy to know who my real Pa was.

Má didn't use any of those chances to tell me. I didn't find out until she wanted to stop Dung telling Abigail that she wasn't his Má. Má said that if he did that, Hands would not just report her to the government for lying; he would also tell people, everyone Má knew, that he wasn't my father. He would tell them that my father was a pirate who raped her. It still shamed her, that she'd been raped.

Of course Dung didn't want to shame Má, so he did what she wanted. Every month while he was at uni, and every month while he worked at the hospital and at the company that was making the medicine he discovered, Dung gave Má the money for Hands. Má thought she had sorted it out. She thought it was all good. Then Dung went on TV with Charlie Cunningham and Hands wanted more money.

Miles drove Mrs Southcott to our house when they came to offer condolences. 'How are you holding up?' Mrs Southcott asked Má. 'You must tell us if we can do anything to help, anything at all.' It was not Miles who offered to help. Dung's friend was very pale. He didn't look like he could help, even if he wanted to.

But still I did what Dung wanted. The night before Dung took his own medicine, after he ate *canh chua* with me and Má, after he hugged Má and said, 'Love you,' I walked outside with him to his car. Dung opened the passenger door and took out a parcel wrapped in shiny purple paper and tied with a gold ribbon. 'Love you, Ly,' Dung said, and gave me the gift.

It wasn't my birthday. 'It's to celebrate the anniversary of your salon,' Dung said. But it was two weeks until the anniversary of my salon. 'I'll be busy with work for a while,' he said. 'So I'm giving it to you now.'

I went to open the gift, but Dung stopped me. 'No. Wait. Wait until the anniversary.'

I didn't wait like Dung told me. The 11th of December is the anniversary of my salon. That was the day Dung died. I opened his present when Shaz told us that Dung would pass soon.

Dung hadn't given me the Juniper Sling perfume he knew I liked. Inside the beautiful parcel there were only papers and a small envelope.

When Miles and Mrs Southcott came to offer condolences, they drank tea that Má had prepared and sat looking at the altar in the lounge room with all the neighbours' offerings. When they got up to leave, once more Mrs Southcott said to Má, 'You must tell us if we can do anything to help, anything at all.'

I walked with Miles and Mrs Southcott out to Miles's little red car, just like I'd done with Dung the night before he gave himself his own medicine. I waited while Miles opened the door for Mrs Southcott and she got inside. When Miles walked to his side of the car, I did what Dung had told me to do in the letter that was inside the beautifully wrapped parcel. I pressed the small envelope from the parcel into the hand of his friend. 'To remind you of Dung,' I said.

Miles

The cops interviewed me a couple of days after the incident. Two detectives. Mr Plods.

'Dr Southcott, did you assist Dr David Tran in administering a substance to himself?' one asked, while the other stood, pencil in hand, poised to write down what they seemed to be anticipating would be my confession.

'It wasn't "a substance", it was the drug he invented. And, no, I just watched,' I said.

'Thank you for your time, Dr Southcott.'

My next interview was to be with the coroner's police and, Foxy predicted, would not be a repeat of my exchange with the Plods. 'We can't count on the next officers being so low-key,' he said. And their go-to question would be: what did Davey tell me, his hand-picked observer, about the thinking behind his brilliant plan to experiment on himself?

The interview was likely to be early in the New Year, so, the week before Christmas, Foxy set up face-time for me and Prof Patterson. Foxy thought it important that Patterson and I get together and 'sort this business out'. Foxy's such a pompous old prick.

Thursday night I was to drive to Patterson's home, where

he would be meeting with his students. A last-minute addition to the schedule, I got the eleven pm slot. Thursday night, eleven pm. Jesus Christ, I knew there was a reason I hadn't gone into research – apart from my total lack of interest and ability.

Patterson gave a guest lecture when I was doing med. I can remember the beginning, but not the end. A nap? An early exit? One or the other.

He was still busy with his ten-thirty when I rocked up to his home a decade later. There was a line of chairs for his students in the hall, where perhaps Davey had sat waiting his turn, not that long ago. But Patterson's wife, Jeanette, who seemed happy to be playing Ruby Receptionist for her man, invited me into the family room.

She was a massive tennis fan, and just happened to be replaying the Baghdatis–Federer final from the Open almost a year ago. She said she felt sorry for them, Baghdatis especially – it must have been awful to have to keep playing in that heat. I agreed with my hostess – yeah, they *should* close the roof at Rod Laver when the temperature's north of forty – although now that I'm out of the game, I actually don't mind kicking back, an ice-cold in hand, watching my former opponents melt while they chase a fluffy ball.

Jeanette offered tea. Herbal or Lady Grey. I would have preferred something stronger, but what the hell, I said yes to a chamomile infusion and sat with Patterson's wife feeling the Cypriot's pain as Federer trounced him.

When my turn came to enter the Prof's den, he didn't waste time with small talk. 'This is a terrible business, Miles,' he said. 'We don't want to make it any more hurtful than it already is for David's family. And we don't want to complicate things further, make things even more awkward, for the Cunninghams and Capella.'

Me? Of course I didn't want to make it any more hurtful than it already was for Davey's Ma and Natalie. Or for Abigail, who was in stiff-upper-lip mode when Mother and I visited, but had to be feeling like shit.

As for the Cunninghams and Capella: fuck them. Charlie hadn't even seen fit to cut short his R and R in Hong Kong when Davey died. According to another voicemail from Rupert Stone expressing condolences at Davey's passing, Charlie was 'still cruising the casinos and being a dick'. So, yeah, I was profoundly untroubled at the prospect of things getting 'even more awkward' for the Cunninghams and Capella, even though, as Foxy kept pointing out, I was technically one of their investors, which 'rather complicates matters'.

'Foxy's told you that this story of David's, that he'd lined up another buyer for SuperMab, isn't true, that it can't be true?' Patterson asked, although it wasn't a question.

'Davey was persuasive about Sino YingTech,' I said, although in fact Davey wasn't, and hadn't needed to be. I trusted Davey and he knew it. But Patterson did need to be persuasive. He was the big gun. His mission: reel in Southcott.

Patterson punctuated the facts with his version of a smile – a grotesque grin, the corners of his lips upturned, the rest of his face a mask. 'There is no Sino YingTech.' Smile. 'No company

of that name exists.' Smile. '*I* didn't hear of this so-called plan.'
He took a break from the smiling, repeated the word 'plan' this
time with a question-mark inflection. 'David didn't mention
anything of the sort to me. So of course I hadn't, couldn't have,
committed to supporting any such proposal at board level. In
any case, this *ab uno disce omnes* idea is ludicrous.'

I doubt that he expected a blocko like me to understand and
I didn't try faking comprehension.

'*Ab uno disce omnes*. From one, learn all.' Patterson looked
content. He'd said all that was needed. But I was no closer to
understanding. It must have shown.

'You say David said this Chinese company wanted data
from at least one human subject before they would invest. But
if a company needs the reassurance of human data to invest
in a new project, it's simply not plausible that they would be
satisfied with information from just one person,' my former
lecturer explained. Smile. Then he went in for the kill. 'No one
even peripherally involved in science … or medicine … could
possibly believe what you *think* David told you.'

Except me. Take a bow, Milesy, you star.

I'd been warned: 'The Professor can be a trifle blunt. He
doesn't suffer fools gladly,' Foxy had said.

'So … why …' I started to ask.

Patterson didn't wait for me to get the words out. 'Why did
David tell you this story … about his … *plan*?' He spat the word
that so offended him, and I copped a spray. Nor did he wait for
an answer from me. Not that I had one. Not that he had one
either. 'I've got no idea. But you know, Miles – Foxy's briefed
you – you know that David told Abigail what he was planning.'

I knew what Abigail was saying, although I didn't rub salt into the wound by asking her about it when Mother and I visited. She was admitting to essentially goading him into doing the self-experiment that killed him. 'The chimpanzees,' I said.

'Yes. Exactly. And he told his research assistant the same thing. David had some concerns that he hadn't used the right primate species for the pre-clinical studies. So, before the human trial went ahead, he was planning to do some further studies in chimpanzees.

'And that makes perfect sense. Chimps are the gold standard for nonhuman primate studies. But they're an endangered species, and Abigail felt very uncomfortable about the prospect of David experimenting on them. She's a very principled young woman. She persuaded him that the honourable course was for him to try EIGHT on himself, rather than subject chimpanzees to any risk. He came around to her way of thinking. Regrettably, in my opinion. But there was never any mention of a "white knight" or this Sino YingTech.'

Patterson seemed to be waiting for me to nod my agreement. To what though? Chimpanzees are special? Sino YingTech was a figment of Davey's imagination? I'm an idiot? Nah, I wasn't playing.

'Now I obviously can't, and won't, encourage you to lie to the police. That's not what I'm doing.'

And then, straight-faced, no shame, that's what he did: 'But, Miles, you must realise that what *you* say David told you, what you *think* he said, is not true. You may have misheard. It could be a misunderstanding on your part. So we're merely encouraging you to think carefully about whether it's even worth mentioning to the police, whether it's something that the coroner needs to hear. It could prove to be a distraction, an awkward and pointless distraction. Quite frankly, it will be a lot easier for everyone – you especially – if it's never mentioned. So we suggest that you say something like "David told me he needed the data". You didn't ask why, he didn't say.'

My audience with Prof Patterson was over, his final words like the conclusion of a one-on-one tutorial with a tiresome D-grade student: Here's what's on the exam, cretin.

So, okay, Davey lied to me. There was no Sino YingTech, no saviour of any colour. So, what the fuck was he up to then?

I'd been focused on our conversation the day before his self-experiment and that had got me nowhere. Now I started mining our chitchat the day *of* the incident for clues.

You'll need some adrenaline if I have a reaction. Plenty here. There was fuck all on the crash trolley when he collapsed and I reached for it. Okay, the MET team brought their own, but, still, it was another lie.

I want you to look after Ma and Natalie … and Abigail too … if this is my final act. Which it turns out it was. Things had gone more than pear-shaped. So, what was I up for now? What did 'looking after' my buddy's Ma and sister mean, in, like, practical terms? I decided to park that interesting question.

Rosa. The science chick. *She knows more about EIGHT than I do,* Davey also said before he shot himself up with the stuff. Talking with Rosa Giannini had to be my next move. She was the brains, and Prof Patterson said she was singing from the same song sheet as Abigail. *Davey was planning to experiment on some chimpanzees*, was the chorus.

I called her the next day. She said she was more than happy to meet for coffee. Later that afternoon would work for her. I hadn't expected such enthusiasm, but cool. She suggested Giorgio's. She wasn't to know it was an old haunt of Davey's and mine. Or was she? Maybe they *had* been close, Davey and his research assistant – so close there'd been pillow talk? He'd basically denied she was anything more than an employee, and I couldn't see him cheating on Abigail. It wasn't his style. But then, before the incident, I would have said lying wasn't his style.

Rosa Giannini said she'd be riding her bike to our meetup. Why she thought her mode of transportation would interest me, I have no idea, but okay. I waited for her outside Giorgio's. I picked her out of the crowd of punters huffing and puffing their way up Bourke Street. She bailed about fifty metres from where I stood. A commuter cyclist, I thought, not in it for the workout.

As she wheeled her transportation to our rendezvous, I saw that I'd been too quick to judge. Her bike was an old clunker, bereft of carbon fibre. She'd been pushing a barrow of bricks up the hill.

Davey's colleague mucked about locking her wheels to a lamppost and unhooking a pannier bag from the bike's rack. Eventually we made it inside.

She chose stools in front of the cake display that looked unchanged from the times Mother used to bring Davey and me after school for hot chocolates. Rosa Giannini ordered a cannoli – presumably an exclusive insider option which the waiter produced from under the counter – and an espresso. It was too late in the day for a legit Italian to drink café latte, she explained.

Untroubled by that constraint, I went with a latte. Our server smirked. 'Just latte, or café latte?' he asked.

'*Certo che vuole il café*,' Davey's research assistant snapped back at the smartarse. 'I'm sorry about that,' she said to me.

I couldn't give a rat's about what some smarmy waiter thought of the way I ordered my coffee, but it was cute, the way she pulled that dude into line, and sweet, the way she apologised for one of her clan.

But despite convincingly sorting my coffee, Rosa Giannini looked uneasy. Was she tossing up whether to roll with the 'I'm sorry' riff and express her condolences about my buddy's death? Or was she holding back because she thought there was something dodgy about the whole incident and I, the surviving one, was somehow guilty of dodginess by association? In the immediate aftermath of the incident I sensed that same dilemma permeating my now rare social interactions.

Rosa had propped the bulging pannier bag under her stool. It toppled over, obstructing oncoming, latte-seeking foot traffic. She stood up to retrieve it, knocking her espresso over with her elbow.

'I'm sorry,' she said, resuming her position.

I held my finger up to our server to signal my companion's need for another espresso. I needed to move the conversation along.

Rosa

Miles Southcott is as cute up-close as he looked on the cover of *People* magazine in his tennis-playing days. And he's a total charm bomb.

I met him the Friday before Christmas. Dave's death hadn't put the kibosh on the seasonal piss-ups, but I'd decided to give that year's celebrations a miss. Was I worried I'd be the wallflower? That the two-buck-chuck-fuelled jollity wouldn't trump the cold shoulder my co-workers were still giving me? Or did I anticipate the customary conversation-starter at such occasions – *How's your year been?* – and the awkward silence that would follow if I told the truth – *Awesome. Won the trifecta. Flunked out of my PhD, split with my fella and killed my boss?* Meh. That question would not have been posed. Only peeps who'd been living under a rock would be in the dark about how my year had been.

And worse, I was now being blamed for eight deaths that didn't happen, not just one that did. Some BEST boy or girl had got hold of the trial protocol. The latest Mexican wave of gossip sweeping the labs related to the stupidity of giving the healthies their doses ten minutes apart, of treating the trial subjects as a virtual assembly line of arms. All eight of them, Kenny's cousin included, would probably have lost their lives. But I didn't write the protocol. It was Gigi, not me, who included the ten-minutes-apart dosing plan, so that the trial would come in on budget. It was Charlie, not me, who'd issued the come-in-on-budget edict in the first place. And it was Safe Medicines, not me, who approved the protocol.

But everyone else embroiled in this sorry saga had gone to ground. Yvette: happily back in the real world, aka the Cunningham Family Office. Charlie: still in Hong Kong as far as I knew. And Gigi: transferred to Poland. So, sure, why not blame me!

I was strongly tempted to just stop turning up to BEST, but what else would I do all day? Hanging around Strangeways wasn't an appealing option. The summer was shaping up to be a shocker. Parched of spring rain, the grass hadn't grown, totally stuffing the food chain. Starving mice had descended on the house in plague proportions. Frankie had packed the pantry contents in plastic, but the little buggers were eating through it. And they'd brought snakes with them. Pep had killed a brown, coiled up with a mouse in its mouth underneath the clothesline. The mouse got away, but Pep's kelpie wasn't so lucky. Pep didn't see the snake this time, but when the dog started foaming at the mouth, Pep knew what had happened. He didn't bother with the vet. He couldn't afford three thousand dollars for an injection of antivenin. He shot the dog.

To keep busy, and earn some moolah, I'd picked up barista work at a Brunswick Street cafe. Considering where my science career was at, I felt it would be prudent to add 'recent employment making coffee' to my CV. Before I started my shifts, I came in to BEST, set out some test tubes, lined up a few pipettes, opened a binder at an assay protocol page and slung a hoodie over the back of my stool. I doubt anyone noticed I was missing in action. The day Miles called, I'd pulled a couple of hundred acceptable espresso shots, then swung by BEST to tidy away the stuff I'd set out in the morning. An early train home was in my sights. I had no problem swapping out that plan for the coffee date he suggested.

He was waiting for me outside Giorgio's. 'Thanks for coming,' he said, 'thanks so much.' I was wheeling my bike and struggling to balance it. Miles seemed to intuit that a handshake would have been challenging and, in lieu, gave my back a little rub. Tragically, I may have blushed. And when I tried to lock my bike to a post, I segued to a total fumble-fingers. Miles crouched down. 'Can I help?' he asked.

'Davey claimed you knew more about EIGHT than he did,' Miles said when we were inside with our coffees, 'so I've come to talk with the expert.' Like I said, charm bomb.

'All Davey told me was that he was testing EIGHT on himself because he needed the data,' Miles continued. 'And I just rolled with that, because Davey was super smart, so why wouldn't he know what he was doing? Now I hear that he was going to test his super juice on chimps, but Abigail talked him out of it.' Miles paused, frowned. 'I just don't get it. What was the big deal? I mean, don't you do experiments on monkeys all the time?'

Prof had cautioned me: 'Until the coroner's deliberations are complete, don't speak to anyone about your last conversation with David. And don't discuss his change of heart about the chimpanzee experiments with anyone, inside or outside BEST.' Fair enough. Or maybe not. Because how long was this new chummy mode of Prof's going to last? The memory of how he treated me after my PhD stuff-up was still fresh. Rosa Giannini: redacted. Anyway, what right did Prof have to tell me who to talk to? And Miles seemed to have most of the story already. He knew about the chimpanzee plan. He knew that it had segued under domestic pressure to 'better not study chimpanzees'.

'For a start, chimpanzees aren't monkeys,' I told him. 'They're more intelligent than monkeys, and they're more like humans than monkeys. They can be taught to do a bunch of human stuff too, even to sign ...'

I was talking too fast. Miles looked confused. 'Sign?' he asked.

'To communicate with sign language.'

'I may have known that,' he said.

'And, as well as being almost human, they're close to extinct. So, I doubt that it's easy to get permission to experiment on them. We would have had to jump through a bunch of hoops to get a chimp study done. High hoops, I expect.'

'You *doubt* it's easy? You *expect* the hoops would be high?'

'I've never done a chimp study.'

'But Davey had, yeah?'

'No. No one at BEST has, as far as I know, anyway. We don't have a chimpanzee colony in Australia.'

'I'm confused,' Miles said.

'There are no chimpanzees in Australia that can be used in medical experiments, or for testing drugs.'

'So, what am I missing here? How were you, how was *Davey*, going to test his super juice on these almost-human, hard-to-find animals, then?'

'I don't know. He only told me about the idea on the Friday before the incident. Scientifically it made sense, but we were going to talk about the logistics on Monday. Maybe Dave had ideas. There are chimp colonies in the US. Maybe he was going to take some EIGHT over. Do the study there.'

'You think?' Miles asked. 'I mean, people do that?'

'I've never heard of it. But I just don't know. It's above my pay grade. I don't know what he was planning. What he was thinking.'

Miles was shaking his head. He got up abruptly. 'We should keep in touch,' he said. Another back rub, and he was gone, sticking me with the bill.

Was the chimp study a possibility? It was a big ask, for sure, but, like his friend Miles said: 'Davey was super smart.' So maybe Golden Boy did have a plan.

What I didn't believe was the 'I-love-animals' about-turn. Dave? The Dave who I'd watched sacrifice a monkey at the end of a toxicology study? No drama. He anaesthetised that animal, stuck a needle into its chest, hit the heart and bled it out without so much as a butterfly flutter of his Golden-Boy eyelashes.

That same Dave, Prof said, had been persuaded by Abigail to put his life on the line for a couple of chimpanzees. And this had happened between Friday, when he came up with his let's-study-chimps plan, and Sunday, when he did his self-experiment?

No. I didn't think so.

Miles said he didn't get it. No wonder: it didn't add up. And then it struck me. I thought I knew what super-smart Dave had done. When you work something out you wonder why it took so long. But what I worked out was big, and shocking, so big and so shocking that I couldn't say it out loud until I had proof.

Miles

My counsellor said I was blocked. Veronica believed I needed to find a narrative for the incident, a story that would help me transition to acceptance, a story that would reconcile me to Davey's death. She would normally have recommended morning pages. The blockee writes three pages (no more, no less) every day when they wake. The subconscious, one's innermost thoughts, are translated onto the page. It's a tool creatives use to prompt – who could have guessed – creativity. And, in my psychologist's experience, writing morning pages also prompts resolution and acceptance, when these are what a client needs.

But even though morning pages were a cornerstone of Veronica's counselling toolkit, somehow, she doubted the written word was my natural medium. Yeah, she is one perceptive lady.

Something physical might work though, some activity that reflected the inner Miles. Perhaps hitting tennis balls, hard, might do the trick – perhaps with one of those machines. 'What *are* those machines called?' she asked me.

'Lobsters,' I told her.

I doubt drinking was the activity she had in mind as she tried to move me towards resolution of my confusion (why did

Davey do it?) and angst (what the fuck am I supposed to do now?). Not that I ever shared the specifics of my turmoil with her. For all I knew she was reporting back to Foxy. But she could see I was troubled, and she could imagine how I felt – or so she said every time we 'met'.

Elite athletes are spectacular boozers. The event's over and we get completely legless. Booze, and doping: the sports world's dirty secrets. Although these days, not so much. Now that every phone has a camera, any punter so inclined can publicise the extracurricular activities of the stars.

I've never been into drugs. That's not just a pro forma denial. Why would I do such a self-destructive, not to mention illegal, thing? Scout's honour, I've never done drugs. Booze? Totally another story. Vodka's my tipple, Grey Goose my brand. I like to think I would have got there on my own, but I have to admit that, when it came to solving the mystery of Davey's death, it was the Goose that brought it home.

She knows more about EIGHT than I do, Davey had said, about Rosa Giannini. Yet she didn't have a clue how he was going to pull off these chimp tests that he hadn't thought to mention to me. So – what? He'd been bullshitting me about his research assistant? I didn't think so. He *had* been bullshitting me, but not about Rosa Giannini.

My buddy not only lied to me, he'd lied to her and to Abigail too.

Abigail's planning a re-education program for me, Davey had said, apropos his animal lib reading material. Right, and I was spotting him for the compulsory practical exercise of that program: *Davey, now try your freaking super mAb on yourself.*

Nah. Davey had let Abigail talk him out of something that was never gonna happen.

I don't normally drink alone, but my sunset curfew had been in place for a month, and I'd started cutting myself some slack. Mostly, I'd been pacing it – a half-bottle a night, max – but after my Friday coffee date with Rosa, on the heels of the fall-into-line-Miles private tutorial by Patterson, I had to face reality: Davey *had* been up to something dodgy. That realisation left me feeling like a dick. I needed more slack. I finished the bottle.

I normally sleep like a sleep-trained baby, but I woke at four. My blood vodka level was plummeting. I got out of bed and stumbled into the living room. I needed paracetamol, or more booze. Probably both.

And there was Davey. In pictorial form. There'd been a photo in the envelope Natalie presented to me at the conclusion of Mother's and my visit to the Trans. *To remind you of Dung*, Natalie had said. Sweet. I'd chucked it on my dining table, where it still sat, two weeks later, a growing collection of unwashed coffee mugs keeping it company.

My mother, my father, me, Davey had said proudly, the first time he showed me that happy snap, twenty-something years ago. Now, there the threesome were: Davey; his mother, Madame Pham; and his father, Yew Pham.

I picked up the creased-to-buggery pic and gave it serious attention. Davey junior, a little tyke, only just standing, was holding his mother's hand, looking up into her eyes as she looked down into his. He was wearing some ridiculous dress sort of thing, but few people looking at the pic would have noticed. His mother was the star, her glossy back hair secured in a bun at the nape of her neck (a 'chignon', Davey had proudly told me) her figure-hugging dress (a cheongsam, her son had said) a startling sapphire blue. Davey's father, in a double-breasted pinstripe suit looked straight into the camera, borderline smug. *My family. Pretty cool, eh?* his expression said.

I propped the photo back up against a mug and sat down at the table to eyeball it from a slight distance. *To remind you of Dung.* I'd taken the photo out of the envelope while Natalie and I stood at the kerb, beside my car. I'd looked from it to Natalie. *He wanted me to give it to you*, she'd said, and walked away, back into the house and the altar they'd set-up to honour her brother, my buddy.

I'd been preoccupied with my own grief. If I'd wondered how she knew he wanted her to give it to me, it was only fleetingly. Now, I pondered that question a bit more energetically. And at long freaking last, I got it. I knew who had pushed Davey to do what he did.

When I saw him for the last time, in Emergency, he'd wanted to tell me some stuff – *You know, 'share'*, he'd said, before I blew him off and went to sort skateboard boy. Now I got it. Because my first viewing of the family-of-origin pic that I was now staring at coincided with some serious sharing by Davey about his erstwhile stepdad. Natalie's Pa. Kevin Tran. Hands.

I should have known the incident was the next instalment in the Hands saga when I opened the procedure room door and saw Davey lying in his own vomit, the three-inch scar

emblazoned on his forehead. Hands's calling card. Perhaps –
and here's a sucky shout-out to Veronica – that knowledge was
just buried deep in my subconscious.

But it was the vodka that brought it home. At four am, my
brain cells one shot shy of pickled, I finally got it. Davey hadn't
left anything to chance. The happy snap was Davey's prompt to
me: *It's about Hands, Milesy.*

Davey's 'sharing' about Hands happened during his
recuperation from injuries inflicted by that lowlife, injuries
sustained after one of the Trans' nosy parker neighbours saw
Mother and me drop him home from school one day. Word
spread on the Viet grapevine: Dung had traded up. Hands
sniffed money in the wind. Davey and his Ma were living a lie,
and Hands knew their secret.

A couple of days after our visit, Davey turned up at school
in a bad way. He hadn't moved in with us then, but it was one
of his sleepover nights, and therefore one of Mother's pick-up-
the-boys-from-school days. My sports kit wouldn't fit in her
450SL, so she'd rock up in the Range Rover, double-park, then
hover near the gate, posing in one of her casual I'm-a-good-
mother-but-a-woman-too outfits: a cashmere sweater casually
slung over her shoulders and porn-star sunnies were usually
involved.

When Davey limped out that day, his right eye swollen shut,
the gash on his forehead inexpertly bandaged – by me – her
meltdown was spectacular. Woe betide the lad responsible. His
expulsion was a given. The perpetrator's family? It was going to
be lawyers at ten paces. The child's parents needed to face the
consequences of raising a delinquent. He – and one of her two

boys better give him, the culprit, up quick smart – was obviously a budding psychopath who had to be set straight. Were there still reform schools?

When I'd first seen Davey at school that morning I had no idea who'd beaten him up, or why, but I'd anticipated a strong reaction from Mother and I'd suggested to Davey that he have an explanation ready, an explanation involving a door. I've never been an imaginative liar. But, back then, Davey's English was ninety per cent spot-on, ten per cent bizarre. *A door hit me*, he told his protector.

He stuck to the door story, even after sustained interrogation, even after his aching wrist was diagnosed as a fractured scaphoid. It's a classic injury when you trip, or you're pushed. It's instinctive: your arm shoots out to break the fall and *snap*, broken wrist. It's rarely inflicted by a door.

Davey's scaphoid healed. It was his left wrist, a clean break. Four months later, his cast came off. It didn't give him any pain after that, or none he complained about.

The injury to his forehead didn't fare so well. It was more than a gash. Mother got a plastic surgeon onto it – one of the top men in town, naturally. But the damage done by a knuckleduster-style ring planted just above the eyebrow proved a challenge even for the Toorak set's go-to guy. It was an ugly Y-shaped wound. The star surgeon's first shot – a subcuticular set of sutures, a nice mend worthy of his regular ladies-who-lunch clientele – broke down. The delay between the assault and surgery hadn't helped. Mother's man closed the wound again, the second time with superficial stitches, fourteen of them, which freaked his patient out. (Fourteen is a very unlucky number.) Despite the expert sewing skills brought to bear, the result was poor, the scar obvious.

So, at last, I got it. The happy snap wasn't to remind me of Dung. It was to remind me of Hands. I'd been focused on one arsehole – Charlie – and, yeah, he had a case to answer, as my lawyer mates would say. But first I had to focus on another arsehole.

Rosa

It was a sunny June morning when I saw my parents for the last time. They left me with Frankie and drove away, Mama wearing her flowery dress with the pink buttons down the front, Papa in a grey suit, his thick black hair slicked back, his shoes as shiny as his hair. They were going to work.

Mama kissed me on my right cheek. '*Ci vediamo stasera mia bella,*' We'll see you tonight, my beautiful.

Then Papa kissed me on my left cheek. '*Sii buono.*' Be good.

That was our ritual. Every morning when they left me with my aunt, the same words, the same kissing deal. Frankie in her apron, in my memory old even then, watching, waiting to play her part. '*Mi prenderò cura di lei.*' I will look after her. '*Non si preoccupi.*' Don't worry.

Then my parents would get into their car. Papa opening the door for Mama. Mama turning to wave at me, watching from the window. Then Papa would shut the door and bang the roof of the car with the palm of his hand.

When their car disappeared from view, I would run to the bathroom, stand on the stool and look in the mirror at the mark my mother's red lipstick had left on my cheek. When her kiss left a perfect imprint, I was thrilled.

Was it perfect the day they didn't come back? I don't know. I can't remember the impression of my mother's last kiss, yet I can remember every detail of the last time I saw Golden Boy. *Non è giusto.* Not fair.

Thanks for your input, Rosa. I can still hear Dave's voice dismissing my warning about the risk of a cytokine storm with EIGHT. Thanks for your input, Rosa, but we'll continue on our merry way. It's business as usual, because what would Rosa Giannini, who doesn't even realise when her own hybridoma's carked it, know? A few things, actually. So, snap decision. I would test my hypothesis. I would do some experiments. I would have to do them in secret though. So I did. I went rogue.

The obvious experiment would have been another primate study. But testing EIGHT on any primates – not just the elusive chimpanzees but any monkey species – was impossible for me. To get into a primate facility and even touch one of the residents you need approval from an ethics committee. Golden Boy would have had to sign off on the ethics application. As if.

I had to be resourceful. My thinking: try to recreate the conditions EIGHT would encounter in the body. Try to mimic those *in vivo* conditions *in vitro* – in the lab, at the lab bench. What about simply adding EIGHT to human blood and testing the mix for cytokines? Golden Boy had already done that. There was no cytokine release. But that experiment didn't reflect the conditions EIGHT would encounter in the body. When you inject a mAb, the bloodstream quickly distributes it. The mAb settles in the body's tissues within a minute or so.

In those tissues, blood cells aren't moving so fast. The mAb can latch onto its target molecule, on the target blood cell, and do its thing.

So, I needed to turn the tables on the blood cells. I had to keep EIGHT stationary to give it and its target molecule a better chance of getting together, of reacting. I got a plastic petri dish – which is essentially a saucer – to stand in for the body's tissues, and I basically stuck EIGHT to the plastic. In immunologist's jargon, I immobilised it.

It sounds easy. It wasn't. I tried a couple of different methods that didn't work. Some mAb stuck, but not enough. Fast-forward to my fix. A cooking analogy, courtesy of Frankie, again. Quince jelly this time. To make it, you cook up quinces, strain off the liquid, add sugar to that liquid, then boil it down. *Voila!* – sticky jelly. I did something similar with EIGHT. I borrowed a hair dryer from the BEST girls' bathroom and blew warm air onto a solution of EIGHT. Woo-hoo! – it worked. Enough of the liquid evaporated for EIGHT to stick to the plate. The first step in my method sorted. Go, me!

The week before the incident, precisely one week before I got Jude's WTF text on the train, Dave caught me out.

He'd been at some conference in the US, telling the immunology glitterati all about EIGHT. I knew he was getting back that day, but I was still surprised when I got to BEST and found him waiting for me.

His roll-along was on the floor, his suit pack chucked on top of it. It looked like he'd come straight from the airport. I watched him from the door. He was swivelling in my chair at the lab bench. Three-sixty-degree swivels. Why was he there? He mostly hung out at the SuperMab office. The lab at BEST was my turf, not his.

He ignored me on his first swivel past.

'Good trip?' I asked the next time I entered his line of sight.

He stuck his foot out and stopped, facing me. 'All the EIGHT's gone,' he snapped. 'There's none in the fridge. What's going on?'

A drop of sweat formed under my armpit and rolled down my side. I could smell it.

'There's more coming, from Switzerland,' I said. Jude's lab at BEST wasn't accredited to make mAbs for human use, so Gigi had contracted a Swiss company to manufacture the EIGHT for the trial. 'It should arrive today.' It wasn't arriving that day. Later that week was more likely.

Golden Boy wasn't going to be fobbed off. 'That's not what I asked,' he snarled.

What could I say? No one could have nicked our stock of EIGHT. We kept it in a locked container in the fridge. Maybe I'd dropped the flask? Oh, clumsy me! So sorry, Golden Boy, I dropped your precious super mAb.

'Come on, Rosa. What have you done with it?' He'd started out irritated, segued to mad. Fury loomed.

I was busted. I had no choice but to 'fess up. So I came clean. Full disclosure: my idea of getting EIGHT to stick to a petri dish, my hair-dryer innovation, the whole Rosa-goes-rogue story.

Dave stopped his swivelling. He listened. I not only had his attention, but the living, breathing Golden Boy looked at me with respect. A bit late, but respect from Dave Tran? I was taking that any day.

I pressed on. I explained my next step. I needed what scientists call a 'positive control'. I needed a mAb that causes both a cytokine storm in people and a cytokine release in my lab test system – aka sticking it to a petri dish and adding blood. The mAb known as OKT3 causes a storm in humans. So if I air-dried OKT3 onto a dish, added some blood cells and got a cytokine release, then I had my positive control. After that, I could do the same with EIGHT. If EIGHT gave a cytokine release under the same conditions, it would probably cause a cytokine storm in humans, like OKT3 does. It would have been a red light for the trial. It would have demonstrated that there was a risk that could not be ignored.

That's when Dave snapped. The respect. Gone. Okay, he knew the positive control drill. He probably thought I was telling him how to suck eggs. Or was it my mention of OKT3 that set him off? Was he remembering our little bench-side chat, when I'd compared OKT3 to his precious EIGHT?

'Show me your notebook,' he said.

Fuck. My lab notebook. Like a good BEST girl, I'd recorded all my experiments, all the data I'd generated, in that book.

'Your notebook!' He was yelling. I pulled it out of my pannier bag.

He took the book, swivelled back to the bench, flipped the pages. I stood motionless, still at the lab door, facing his back. I thought about doing a runner. 'Remember Rosa Giannini?' the BEST boys and girls would say. 'One day she just left the building, walked away, didn't look back.'

I focused on the clock instead. Seven minutes and twenty-nine seconds later, Golden Boy spun back to face me. I'd worked those experiments in secret for almost six months, off and on, whenever I'd had the chance, whenever the coast was clear. I even had to take my own blood for them. Super awkward, but I did it. And the cytokine assays – what a bummer they were. I stayed late to run them. Caught the last train home. All that effort, all that subterfuge, and it took Dave Tran less than eight minutes to read all about it.

Finally, Golden Boy's pronouncement: 'This is grounds for dismissal.'

The next experiment is the crucial one. That's what I wanted to say. OKT3 *had* caused a cytokine release in my bench model. I had a positive control. Dave must have seen that in my notebook. But I didn't, couldn't, get the words out.

He was back looking at my book. I was toast. And if that was how it was, I wanted out of there, and ASAP. The standing around, the looking at Golden Boy's back, was getting old. I had to cut it. 'I'll clear my desk,' I told him. I wanted the photo of Frankie and my mother on the beach in Cefalù. That's all. The rest of my stuff I could lose, leave behind, *nessun problema*.

But I couldn't reach my desk without hurdling Dave's luggage. I stayed put at the door. 'I'll clear my desk,' I said again, like I meant it.

He didn't sack me. He stood me down. 'You're off work for the rest of the week,' he said. 'I'm going to reflect on this. I'll call you Friday.'

'What do you mean, reflect on it?' I said. I'd been busted, totally owned, but I squeezed out that *piccolo* pushback.

Another full-circle swivel on my chair. Again, Dave put his foot out to stop. 'Go ... I ... will ... call ... you ... Friday,' he said.

He wouldn't. There'd be no call. I knew that. An email, that's what I'd get, or a letter. Whatever. It didn't matter. I was going to be terminated at the end of the week.

'It's like you're sending me to purgatory,' I said.

'You're breaking my heart. Find a priest. Confess your sins. Repent,' Dave Tran said.

I didn't do any of those things. I spent the next week at Strangeways, tossing and turning until the wee hours, then sleeping in and spending the shortened days tidying my sock drawer and weeding the veggie garden for Frankie. Worrying about my future.

What was Dave doing that week? Finishing my experiments, I was sure of it. Unlike my parents, who drove away from Frankie and me, oblivious to their fate, Golden Boy knew he would die when he stuck a needle in his arm and pressed 'Start' on the syringe driver. I just had to prove it.

Miles

The day Davey told me his escape-from-Vietnam story, I was lounging on my bed watching 'the match', the McEnroe–Connors 1984 US Open semi. I had it on video and watched it *ad nauseam*, until the tape finally gave up the ghost. McEnroe was my man, my coach du jour's man: 'Miles, I want you to volley like Johnny Mac,' he'd taken to commanding. Mother, not a Johnny Mac fan, would counter: 'Milesy, don't you ever behave like that brat.'

Davey was hard at it, getting my homework sorted, despite his recent face surgery. He took a break from whatever he was excelling at on my behalf. 'Let me show you something, my friend,' he said, brandishing his slide rule. He was such a dork. He treasured that slide rule. It was a giveaway from the Red Cross and a teacher in the Hong Kong refo camp had taught him the moves. He could solve algebra way faster with his slide rule than the other maths nerds could with their calculators. His treasure should have been handy here in his new country, but he'd been banned from using it. The movement of the slider strip back and forth was noisy; some of the lads at school found it distracting, or so they'd complained after he aced the maths exam.

Davey was standing between Johnny Mac and me. 'Buddy, first, get out of my way, and, second, get with the program,' I said. 'Use the calculator Mother got you, not that slide rule thing.'

'No. I need your advice,' he said.

He flipped the contraption over, popped the back off, and took out the real treasure tucked snugly into its secret compartment. The photo, folded twice into perfect quarters. Davey's family. Now, twenty-something years later I could look at the threesome as often as I wanted. I still thought they were pretty cool.

But Davey's origin story, which he'd proceeded to tell me, wasn't cool. His father was in business. Although Davey told me he didn't know what that business was, I got the feeling he did know, and it was something dodgy. He said his father had been tight with the Yanks, and after Saigon fell to the communists, that qualified the Pham family for harassment, and worse. Davey's father was captured and executed. His mother decided to get out of town, where she was not just well known, but also a 'person of suspicion' because of her late husband's business dealings. Naturally, she took Ma, their cherished family retainer, along. Davey and his 'mothers' moved from village to village. They tried to stay below the radar, dressing and acting like yokels, not the prosperous city-dwellers they'd been. First, they headed North. The Chinese were encouraging Hoa to cross the border into the bosom of the 'Motherland'. Word filtered back from those who took the bait: China wasn't quite the Promised Land. So the trio turned back. Davey's mother settled on a new destination: Ba Tri. A river ran through it, and out to sea.

The exodus from Vietnam was in full swing, but my buddy's mother didn't want to buy three spaces on a big boat. She'd heard stories of escapees being double-crossed by boat owners. She sounded smart, strategic, like her son grew up to be. When she reached Ba Tri, she set herself up growing fruit and veg. She bought a boat and travelled up and down the river selling her produce. Once she'd prepped to her satisfaction, she changed up. Hong Kong was the next stopover on her itinerary.

One night, she and Mai loaded Dung into the little boat and packed it with water, the food she'd hoarded and the seaworthy engine she'd bought. They struck out for the river mouth.

Davey's mother had heard that pirates were doing their worst to the south. No problem, Hong Kong was north. All she had to do was make sure the sun kept rising starboard. How hard could that be?

Apart from the awesome 'beef steak' he was apparently fed, often, and which he talked about often too, Davey couldn't remember much about his days in Saigon. He could remember the first leg of his sea voyage though.

My go-to childhood memory is of the old man putting a tennis racquet in my hand. I struggled to hold it, but somehow managed to whack a ball into the net. Mother clapped.

Davey's touchstone memory was of pirates grabbing his mother and Mai. Six Thai pirates kitted out in sarongs, brandishing swords. They made his mothers strip. The pirates knew the escape-from-Vietnam drill. They slit the hem of Davey's mother's blouse and found her stash of diamonds. She had a roll of American dollars concealed in her belt. All of it went to new owners.

The pirates had tied their own boat to Davey's mother's. Diamonds and dollars collected, they man-handled the two women onto their own boat and below deck. My buddy heard screams, then moans, then silence. The sun rose twice before the pirates threw the two women back and sped off. His mother was dead.

Pirates, rape, murder. It was too much for my adolescent brain. It wasn't something that I could imagine happening to anyone I knew.

Davey had no memories of his sea voyage after that, but Mai had filled in the deets for him. Once she and little Dung miraculously reached Hong Kong and what should have been safety, Mai was just lucid enough not to protest when people assumed she was Davey's mother, after he called her 'Ma'. She told her inquisitors where she came from, but otherwise she was out of it, incoherent. The refugee controllers brought in a man from Saigon who said he'd recognised her when she and Davey were brought to the camp. They thought he might help them make sense of her rantings.

Mai and Davey were shit out of luck. The man was Kevin Tran. Hands. He'd been Davey's dad's driver in Vietnam. Given the course his life took in Australia, he may well have done Mr Pham's dirty work too, enforcing his dodgy dealings. But, that's just my speculation. The point is he knew Mai, and he knew Dung, and he knew Dung was not Mai's son. That knowledge had no value to him in a Hong Kong refugee camp. So he banked it. He convinced Mai that she didn't want Davey being an unaccompanied minor in that setting. So she stuck with the I'm-Dung's-mother story.

Kevin Tran needed to keep her close, so he proposed, or maybe insisted on, marriage. Mai accepted, or maybe complied. Then he bided his time. When the blended Tran family eventually reached Australia, Davey was an illegal. Now Mai and Davey's secret was tradeable.

Did I think my old man could help? Davey asked in my bedroom, twenty-something years ago when he first showed me his happy snap. Could my old man get them a lawyer, get it sorted so Hands had nothing on him and Ma? Maybe my old man *could* have helped. Back then I didn't think so. He'd just had Davey investigated by a private detective, who'd obviously done a crap job. My best guess was that, if my old man knew the truth, he would have had Davey sent back to where he came from. So I warned my buddy: don't tell anyone your secret. Don't tell the old man, don't tell Mother, tell no one. And, motivated by self-interest, I went a step further. Get your Ma to call Mother, I told Davey. Get her to suggest you live with us and that we pay her.

Davey moved in with us soon after. Hands got his hush money from us, the Southcotts, via Ma. Mother got her in-house refugee. I got the in-house tutor I needed. A triple win-win.

Davey had taken his beating. Fourteen stitches, transformed into twenty-eight giant white dots on his swollen-to-buggery head the last time I saw him, on the floor of the Emergency Department. Hands's calling card with his message: *You owe me, 'David Tran', and when you've got money, I'll collect. You'll pay what you owe.*

And Davey had paid, with his life. Charlie Cunningham had been shafting him, no question. Now I knew why it mattered so much. He needed money for Hands. That's what the freaking 'incident' was all about. Hands.

That epiphany gave me no comfort. I sat on my couch after my voddie binge, waiting for the paracetamol to kick in, staring at Davey's precious photo. If, when I first saw it, I'd told my old man his secret, my buddy would be alive. I knew it. What happened to him was on me. I'd always told Davey I owed him. He'd made my Plan B a reality. Now I owed him big-time. Now I had to pay back my debt.

Rosa

I needed to get back to my experiments. I needed to know if EIGHT would cause a cytokine release in my petri dish model. I believed that Dave had done the final experiment during the week I spent in purgatory at Strangeways. I needed to prove it.

To do that, I'd need some EIGHT. There was none. The three vials that I was expecting from Switzerland had arrived. They'd also disappeared. Obviously, Dave had used one for his self-experiment at the hospital, and he would have needed one for my final experiment, if he'd done what I suspected. But even then, there should have been one left. Maybe he'd chucked it out.

But Jude would have Dave's hybridoma tucked away in a freezer, and it would still be capable of pumping out EIGHT. I would put the hard word on her. I would need to explain why I wanted to experiment with a mAb that had turned out to be fatally toxic. Another confession: I went rogue, and why, and then I got caught. A deep breath. I called her.

She was at the supermarket checkout, and from the background noise – *Guacamole is disgusting! He always gets what he wants! It's not fair!* – accompanied by her offspring. She'd started her Christmas break early. Bummer. She, hubby and the junior Winstanleys were down at Dromana, at the beach house they rented every year.

'Come down. Spend New Year's with us,' she said. 'It'll be a quiet one, and you'll have to take the bottom bunk in Denzel's room,' she warned. Denzel was seven, and even his besotted mum described him as a terrorist. 'But I'd love to see you.'

The evening, as pitched, wasn't on my bucket list of ways to welcome in the New Year. Worse, Jude closed out her invitation with the news that she was 'worried about me'. A deep and meaningful on New Year's Eve about my once-brilliant career? Awesome. But apparently I didn't have a choice. We'd have a few chardonnays. I'd get to feel the sand between my toes and have a splash in the bay – which, Jude assured me, wasn't polluted at Dromana – and then I'd hit her up for some EIGHT.

The best-laid plans. 2007 didn't kick in as per mine. December 31st at Strangeways dawned hot as Hades. Frankie had just put the Moka on the stove for her umpteenth, and my first, coffee of the day when the music started up. *Boom, boom, boom.* Okay, not quite music. *Boom, boom, BOOM.* A hot gust of wind picked up the beat and whipped through the house.

'It's those bloody blow-ins,' Pep said. Except for Frankie and me, anyone who'd moved to Strangeways in the last hundred years was a blow-in. A quick segue to citizen detective, Pep grabbed his hat from the peg and hobbled outside to his ute. A cloud of dust followed him down the drive.

He was headed to the property next door, until recently a nudist retreat. Pep and Frankie hadn't socialised often with the retreat's owner, who Frankie ordered to cover up whenever he visited her *casa*. He was in a nursing home now, sadly *non compos mentis*, and his daughter had taken over his affairs, which no longer included hosting nudists. Some blow-ins were renting the cabins: three couples and assorted children of indeterminate parentage, Frankie said after she visited with a welcome plate of biscotti. Our new neighbours were ex-Byron Bay, where the cost of living had sky-rocketed. Reluctantly, they'd left that nirvana and, prompted by an ad on Gumtree, driven down the east coast to Strangeways, where fifty acres of bush, good for growing nothing much, beckoned.

But they were cash-strapped. An on-site New Year music festival had seemed the perfect solution. The prospect of boogying in the seclusion of Strangeways and crashing by a campfire had proved attractive to many city folks. The blow-ins had sold more than five hundred tickets at a hundred bucks a pop, Pep reported when he returned from his reccy.

The temperature was forecast to top forty. At ten am it was already thirty in the shade. A Total Fire Ban had been declared, but Pep's site visit suggested that if our neighbours got that memo, they'd decided it wasn't meant for them. The campfires had been set. Their fire plan if things got out of hand? They had a couple of buckets.

I phoned in my apologies to Jude. Pep and Frankie are stay-and-defend people when it comes to bushfires. Even if Pep hadn't been close to two years overdue for his hip replacement, no way was I evacuating to the beach.

We lugged the fire hoses into position, got the pump working and filled the ring main around the house with water from the dam. Then we turned on the sprinklers for a trial run. After nine years of drought, the ground was so parched our liquid offerings disappeared into a bottomless underground pit.

I scanned the horizon. The box-ironbarks, mangy on a good day, were like a forest of power poles since the cup moths had got to work over spring. Heat. Rising off the roof of the chook shed. You could've barbequed a chop on it. A sunburnt country? Absolutely. I wasn't loving it.

Then the smoke. A grass fire about five kilometres away. Maybe our neighbours saw it too. The soundtrack stopped. Now Pep turned on the sprinklers for real. A half-hour later they spluttered to a dribble. The dam was dry.

We turned to page two of the household fire plan. Pep switched the ring main's water supply over to the tanks we used for drinking and washing. I helped Frankie schlepp her treasures from the house to a little underground bunker Pep had dug, too small to house people. Photos of her parents, my grandparents, who I never met. The piano accordion her father had played but she couldn't. The two sets of rosary beads given to her and my mother the day of their confirmation. That task complete, there was nothing more to do but wait, listen to the fire trucks' sirens and, in Frankie's case, pray.

She still maintains it was her prayers that saved us. Maybe they did. Maybe God, not the fire authority, sent Elvis to Strangeways. Either way, that helicopter earned its keep. Thirty sorties, close to three-hundred tonnes of water on the flames, and by six pm the danger was over.

No more whirring chopper blades. Elvis had left the scene. No *boom, boom, BOOM* from next door. While the fire blazed, the police had set up a roadblock and turned would-be partygoers away. Silence. Frankie, Pep and I convened on the verandah and cracked a Prosecco.

Maybe it was the bubbly that cued Frankie's keening. The dam's main purpose was to water the veggie garden, the most important veggies being the tomatoes. Now Frankie's crop would die. *La catastrophe!*

As Frankie's glass emptied, her anxiety about the impending tomato famine escalated. Pep, who'd anticipated her meltdown, played his trump card. He would use the house tanks to water the wilting plants. We'd have to cut back on showers, but only wusses – blow-ins and the like – shower more than weekly anyway.

Awesome. Now I would stink. I fixed my eyes on the scrub down the hill, screening the now-useless dam. I could just make out two grey figures in the shadows. Kangaroos, both having a good scratch. Grooming complete, the bigger one gave his companion a quick whack to the back of the head. The attacked responded with a jab to his attacker's face and an I-mean-business, two-pawed follow-up shove to the chest. Big boy grabbed him around the neck, sprang back and, balancing on his tail, delivered a two-legged kick to the stomach. Gotcha! The smaller one fought back. An acrobatic kick. Take that! A scurry of tackling and pawing.

Were they having it out over a female? Was the big fella teaching the young one the tricks of the kangaroo trade? I have no idea. I'd lived in that sunburnt country almost all the life I could remember. The days in Strangeways I hadn't seen a kangaroo I could probably count on the fingers of one hand, but I'd never seen kangaroos box.

I turned to point them out to my family, but Frankie, reassured by Pep's commitment to the tomatoes, had shaken off her funk and was voicing her forecast for 2007. It would be a good year. Not only would the drought break, the New Year would herald an equally momentous event. It would be the year that her Rosa became a real doctor.

I looked away from Frankie's proud face. I searched the landscape for another glimpse of the boxing kangaroos. They'd gone, looking for a dam that wasn't dry was my bet. I shut my eyes. Is it possible to stem the flow of tears by squeezing your eyelids tight? No.

I'd dodged dismissal by Golden Boy, but the 2nd of January my luck ran out. Charlie Cunningham didn't even have the guts to sack me himself. It was Joseph Unger who threw me under the proverbial bus. An email from Mr Unger, who, as well as being the authoriser of Charlie's flight to Hong Kong, was apparently the Chief Executive Officer of the Cunningham Family Office. Mr Unger's email informed me that my services were no longer required. Nothing personal. My employment was being terminated because SuperMab, the company, no longer existed.

I had anticipated it. Plan B: return to barista world. But I also hadn't thought it would happen. So, what now? A stomach-roiling morning while I pondered that question. Then I visited Margaret.

'Don't worry, dear, I'm sure Prof's got something organised for you,' she said. But the post-New-Year beach-break had kicked in. Even Prof had retreated to his seaside shack for a couple of weeks.

Margaret was unwilling to disturb him to clarify my 'situation'. He was working. To emphasise that point, and get me out of her office, Margaret turned to her computer and got Prof's first email of 2007 up on her screen. To 'all BEST staff and students'. The mAb Meister did not wish them Happy New Year. BEST was facing a budget crisis. Reading between the email's lines, which I did over Margaret's shoulder, Prof had been counting on a financial reward once SuperMab completed its first clinical trial. Now that the reward was not going to happen, the BEST scientists' grant-writing efforts had to be ramped-up. If you'd been writing one grant before, now you were writing two; if you'd planned on applying for two, now you were putting in for three. Too bad if you were on vacation. You could work on vacation like Prof was doing. He would be returning to Melbourne on the 19th of January, and, starting that evening, the BEST boys and girls would be fronting up to review their grant proposals with the boss.

I wasn't on the email distribution list. I wasn't a BEST student or staff member. I wasn't writing any grants. I wouldn't have been a competitive applicant, because key sections of any grant I wrote would have looked worse than ordinary. Current employment: blank. Publications in the previous year: *niente*. Year the applicant gained their doctorate: not applicable. But I convinced Margaret to book me a slot with Prof on the 19th. 'Take a break until then, dear,' Margaret said. 'You look a little peaky. A couple of weeks at the beach would probably do you the world of good.'

A beach break wasn't what I needed. What I needed was some EIGHT and a place to work. Some money would help too. Mr Unger's email said I would receive the severance pay I was entitled to in 'due course'. How much severance pay and when I would receive it, Mr Unger didn't say.

I needed Jude's help. Like every lab head, she's got a slush fund. When, for example, she gets a discount on equipment or reagents, she siphons off the over-budget surplus to the slush fund, which is useful when, for example, a loyal former staff member needs a short-term job.

Another phone call. Jude was still beachside. But, 'No probs,' she said, 'the freezer needs cleaning out. I can cover you for at least a month on the casual-staff budget. I'm sure Prof will sort something for you by then.'

I wasn't so sure about that, but I *was* sure I could find EIGHT's hybridoma in the course of my summer cleaning job.

Ly (Natalie)

Auntie told Má she had to pray for forty-nine days if she wanted Dung's spirit to be reborn in the Pure Land, so Má went to the temple every Monday, every week for seven weeks. Even though Má was getting crazier, she was always dressed for the temple and not crazy when I came home early from my salon to take her.

I also prayed at the temple every week, because even before Dung died, even before I opened the parcel he gave me and read his letter, I knew he must have planned to take his own life. My brother was smart. If the medicine he discovered was going to kill him, he would have known that.

It's wrong to take your own life. I prayed that Amitahba Buddha would forget Dung did that. I wanted Amitahba Buddha to remember that Dung was kind and had done many good deeds. I prayed with Má and Auntie that Amitahba Buddha would take my brother's soul to the Pure Land.

Abigail visited us often after Dung passed. She was patient with Má, even though some days Má didn't remember who she was, and other days yelled 'Get out!' at her.

Abigail said she wanted to come for supper on Christmas

Eve, even though in our culture we don't celebrate Christmas. She brought Má and me a gift: a gingerbread house that she'd made herself. She'd baked biscuits for the walls and roof, piped on white icing to make it look like snow had fallen, then stuck smarties on the icing.

We were looking at the gingerbread house when Abigail told us that the police would interview Má and me in January about Dung's death. 'What? They think I do something wrong?' Má shouted at Abigail.

'No, Mai, they don't think you did anything wrong,' Abigail said. 'It's just something the government does when someone dies unexpectedly, like David did. They're going to interview me too. They don't think any of us did anything wrong. All we have to do is tell them the truth and it will be okay.'

Má is not good with the truth. She hadn't told me the truth about who Dung was and who my father was. 'It was a lie of omission,' Dung said when I found out my father was a pirate. 'She was only thinking of you, and what was best for you. Don't be angry with her.'

But Dung didn't say that when he went on TV with Charlie Cunningham and Má told him the truth about what happened on the boat from Vietnam. That truth was a lie of omission too. I could have said: *She was only thinking of you, what's best for you*. But Dung was too angry, and too sad, to listen.

'What the police want to know?' Má asked Abigail.

'I expect they'll ask when you saw David last, how he was when you saw him, what he said, and whether he told you he was going to test his drug on himself.' Abigail sounded like she was going to cry, but still she put her arm around Má and hugged her. 'You don't need to worry, Mai. Just answer their questions. Just tell them the truth.'

I was worried though, because if Má was crazy when the police came to interview her, which truth would she tell them? I was worried she would tell them the secret she'd kept for so many years. I was worried that she would tell them what she and Dung did on the boat.

And if Má did tell the police, would it help if I told them the truth about all the mean things Hands did when he came to pay me and Má visits? Should I tell them how he would come up behind me in the kitchen and stick his knees into the back of my knees so that I fell over? How he would stroke my cheek with the back of his hand so I could feel his ugly ring scraping my skin? How he once poured a glass of water over my head and another time cut off a piece of hair from my fringe, right in the middle? How sometimes he would make soft little circles in the palm of my hand with his finger while he made kissing noises with his lips? Should I tell them how I would puke when he left?

'Don't tell Dung,' Má would say when he left. And until the night Dung went on TV with Charlie Cunningham, I hadn't.

When I asked Dung what it was like living at the Southcotts, he said, 'It's not where I want to be, but I have to suck it up.' So I had to stay quiet and suck up what Hands did to me. Now, what part of that truth should I tell the police?

I looked at the gingerbread house. It was too beautiful to eat, and anyway there was too much of it for just me and Má and Abigail. It would be a waste to break it. So Abigail said that on Christmas Day she would give it to the people who have to live on the street because they don't have a house.

Miles

'At last, you call me,' Natalie said when I phoned on Boxing Day. 'Come tomorrow, at seven. I should have finished my clients by then.'

Her nail salon is in a cobbled lane, and little more than a cupboard: three massive barber-style chairs with footbaths on one side, a row of desks on the other where Natalie was still doing some high-tech procedure on a woman's fingernails when I arrived. A TV behind Natalie was playing a Mr Bean movie. The air was pure acetone. It's a wonder Davey's sister and her customer were conscious.

I sat in one of the barber chairs, feeling like a dick, while Natalie ran a machine that sounded like a dentist's tooth-polisher over the woman's nails. Procedure complete, the client tried to pay with a credit card. 'No, Wendy. Only cash,' Natalie told her. The woman made a show of checking her purse. She had the fifty bucks.

Natalie killed the lights, parted the curtain that led to a bed – 'for waxing,' she explained when I paused in front of it – and ushered me through another curtain to a tiny space where a table of the card variety was set up. We sat on stools, and Natalie grabbed a pack of cigarettes from a small filing cabinet. 'Want one?' she asked.

I shook my head. I suspected I'd choke if she started fagging away in the shoebox where we were now confined. Or die. I tried to remember if acetone was flammable.

I took out the photo she'd given me. 'Okay, what did Davey want me to do?' I asked.

Natalie lit up, took a drag, then jumped up and rummaged under the sink. She produced an ashtray, docked her cigarette, crouched down on the floor and rolled up what looked like a long-past-it bath mat to reveal a floor safe. Natalie twiddled its knob clockwise to a magic number, anticlockwise to another, then clockwise to a third. Open sesame. She stuck her hand into the safe's bowels and pulled out a plastic folder that held the bunch of papers Davey had left with her. She passed me the first document and smoked enthusiastically while I scanned it.

'Okay, I get that it's a mortgage. What else do I need to know?' I asked.

She started filling me in on the Hands saga. They'd been paying him ever since he assaulted Davey and I came up with the Southcott–Tran arrangement. First, from the money Mother and the old man gave his Ma. I knew that already, of course. But, conveniently I guess, it wasn't something I thought about often. Then they paid him from the allowance my old man gave Davey while we were in college, and, finally, from Davey's salary.

In May, Hands had increased his ask, big-time. He saw the bullshit promo on TV, with Charlie Cunningham bragging that SuperMab was a heartbeat away from landing a pot of gold and showed his no-doubt-ugly face, singing another verse of his you-owe-me song.

Natalie said Hands wasn't taking no for an answer after Charlie's boast about the billion dollars, and, more than ever, Davey couldn't risk the fact that he was an illegal immigrant coming out. How would it look? The superstar medical researcher: a refugee who wasn't who he said he was, who couldn't be trusted.

And what would Abigail say? He'd never told her his backstory, Natalie was as sure of that as I was. Then there was Mai. After more than twenty years in Oz, Ma was still scared shitless she would go to jail, or worse, for lying. Davey was not gonna let that happen.

A few years previously he'd apparently bought Natalie and Ma the house they'd lived in ever since I knew them. They owned it outright. Now Davey made a trip to the bank. He took out a five-hundred-thousand-dollar mortgage on the house. Half a mill? Is that all we were talking about? Shit, I would have lent him that. It would have been a big swallow, but I was pretty flush. Maybe I would even have given it to him.

But Davey didn't ask me for the money. He didn't ask for help until he rocked up to the Oxford with his own fix sorted. He must have thought I'd fail him again, like I did when he told me about Hands all those years ago. So he didn't ask me for the money and he didn't tell me what was really going down. If I'd been a better friend, maybe he would have.

'I can't make the payments to the bank,' Natalie said, 'I don't earn enough here.' She pointed in the direction of the torture bed. 'I need the insurance money.'

To pay down the mortgage, Davey was counting on his options vesting at the end of each trial. He must have had

an inkling that it might not play that way. Natalie passed me
another sheaf of papers. A policy insuring the life of Dr David
Tran for one million dollars. Natalie Tran was the beneficiary.
It covered her and Mai if things went belly-up.

'The insurance man has been here to meet with me,' Natalie
said. I tried to imagine an insurance assessor on the stool I
was sitting on. 'They won't pay until the government says Dung
didn't take his own life.'

'The government?'

'Yes. The government people who did the autopsy.'

'The coroner.'

'Yes. The coroner.

'The insurance man read in the paper that Dung injected
himself with something. It didn't say it was the medicine he
discovered. The insurance man says they won't pay unless the
coroner says Dung didn't take his own life.' She took another
drag on the second ciggie of our sit-down and stared at me,
defying me to say what we both knew: *But he did.*

I felt like I was still missing something. A gangster with
a bullshit name had walked away with half a million dollars,
not to mention the down payments he'd been collecting for
the previous twenty years. Davey had topped himself. And all
because some low-life had persuaded his nanny, a woman who
had miraculously delivered him to land and safety, to claim
him as her own? It didn't compute. I mean, there'd been other
options. When I'd told Davey to stay quiet about his origins, he
and I were barely out of short pants. By the time Hands upped
the ante and Charlie shafted him, Davey must have been able to
see my ancient advice for what it was: crap. He could have come

clean about his origins, hired a PR team, spun his own who-do-you-think-you-are story, become a legend.

'There's something else, isn't there?' I asked Natalie, who'd continued smoking doggedly while I ruminated.

She put her ciggie between her lips and parted her fringe.

The scar was healing well. The distinctive 'Y' shape that I'd seen on her brother was still visible, but it would fade. Of course it would. Davey had sewn her up himself, with the suture set I'd helpfully provided the night the Cunningham-SuperMab promo aired.

'I need some fresh air,' I told her.

I did a lap of the lane. It was a dead end. All the other businesses were closed. Tamsin and Guy's Hair and Make-up. Starr Immigration Law. Jimbo's, Australia's Headphone Store. All shuttered until the New Year.

On the second lap I got what I was missing. Hands had branded Natalie with his knuckleduster, just like he'd branded Davey. Who knows what else he'd done to her. No way would my buddy have voluntarily checked out, leaving his sister at the mercy of a low-life with that record.

As epiphanies go it was an obvious one. But a thunderbolt. Okay, my buddy had lied to me about Sino YingTech. He'd also used me as cover for his suicide. Now I had to face the fact that he was probably a murderer. Jesus Christ, what next? When I went back inside Natalie's beauty salon, was she – what? – going to pull back another curtain to reveal a Vietnamese gangster's body that she needed me to bury?

I walked over to the Starr Immigration Law shopfront. I rested my forehead on the metal grate that had possibly been installed to stop dissatisfied customers hurling bottles at the windows. I tried to remember a time when my life was cruisey. It wasn't that long ago, but the memory was gone-baby-gone.

I did another lap of the lane. I'm slow, but I get there. Davey told me the heart med was for his Ma. She had arrhythmias: atrial fibrillation, he said. The first-line meds hadn't worked. The cardiologist my buddy fixed her up with wanted to try flecainide. So, muggins here willingly nicked some for him from the Oxford pharmacy. Of course I'd helped. It was for Ma. Another Davey lie. He'd used the flecainide to eliminate Hands. Fuck. Just when I thought things couldn't get worse, I was an accessory to murder.

I lapped the neighbourhood a fourth time, then went back inside Natalie's den. She had the whisky out. Black Label. She poured two fingers for each of us and shot hers. Then she passed me a sheet of paper. 'He was never going to stop,' she said. 'Ma and I gave him the money from the mortgage, but then he wanted more. It was the only way.'

I scanned Davey's confession. He'd crushed up the flecainide tablets, mixed them with peanut butter and made sandwiches for Hands filled with the fatal concoction. Three tasty snacks on three consecutive days when my buddy's nemesis came to collect instalments of the payment he'd demanded from Davey. The confession exonerated Ma and Nat from any involvement or knowledge of his actions.

'What Dung wrote isn't true,' Natalie said. 'Má did it. Not Dung. Dung just told her what to do.'

'Why?'

'Because Má and I always gave him the money. If Dung had been there, he would have been suspicious.'

'So, you helped her?'

'No. They didn't tell me what they were doing.' She tilted her chin. 'I would have though. I wish I'd been the one to do it.' Defiant. Don't judge me. Don't judge Dung, or our Má. You don't know what our lives were like. She was right. I had no idea.

'So, how did it play? Where did he die?'

'At his house. His girlfriend found him. He'd already passed.'

If you haven't got a cardiac arrhythmia, flecainide gives you one. In his last hours, Hands's heart would have been beating like a drum. He would have had agonising chest pain. Not for long though. His blood pressure would have dropped so low he would have passed out. Not a pleasant death, but not as ugly as Davey's.

'So, what's with this?' I waved the confession. 'Has anyone been suspicious about how …' I wanted to say 'your Pa died' but stopped in time. Hands. Jesus Christ, what a father.

'No. Má heard from her friend that his doctor said it was a heart attack. I am to keep what Dung wrote in the safe though, just in case.'

'Okay. I'm getting it now. Except, after all that, why did Davey commit suicide?' Natalie wasn't going to admit that's what he did, but I was.

She lowered her eyes. 'Killing Hands was the only way,' she said. 'But Dung must have still felt bad. I suppose he couldn't live with himself.'

Rosa

Jude says you always learn something new about the deceased at their funeral. They liked hip-hop and a hot curry, or Beethoven and power walking. At Golden Boy's funeral, none of those hobbies, nor any others, were mentioned. But I did learn a couple of things about my late boss.

For a start, he wasn't Roman Catholic. *Confess your sins. Repent,* he'd said when he caught me out doing my rogue experiments. He had to be Catholic. But no, he was Buddhist, and his funeral was held in a Buddhist temple. The temple was actually just a hall, and, truth be told, totally kitschy. Surrounding it was a garden of bushes pruned into the shapes of deer, and statues of Buddhas – hundreds of them. In the temple, more Buddhas, including a ceiling-height female with flashing lights emanating from somewhere on her person. Buddha Disneyland.

I was back at BEST and went to the funeral with the BEST contingent. Prof had returned from holiday and I'd been all set to tell him about my experiments, which I'd finished. I'd found Dave's hybridoma in the freezer, extracted some EIGHT, immobilised it on a petri dish and added my own blood. When I tested the mix, I found it contained cytokines. My hypothesis:

proven. Not to big-note myself, but that made my model awesome. What it suggested about what Dave probably did: not so awesome. But Prof had higher priorities. A multitude of grant applications had to be reviewed with their authors. I was bumped.

In any case, Prof saw no particular reason to meet with me, Margaret said. I could have a casual research assistant position until Prof saw 'how the business with the coroner pans out'. And: 'Prof sends his apologies about your job. There was some sort of misunderstanding with the Cunningham Family Office. He hopes you had a good break.'

Margaret chartered three buses to get us all to the funeral, and Jude sent a group email urging us to wear lab coats. She didn't get any responses, for or against. We just didn't do it.

When we filed into the temple, Abigail and an oldish Vietnamese woman – Dave's mum, Mai, according to Jude – were standing at the front beside a table set up as an altar to honour Dave. Jude's intel came from the pamphlet that set out the order of service. A young Vietnamese woman, about my age, and an older, super-glam Australian woman stood on the other side of the altar – Dave's sister, Ly, and Sally Southcott, who was presumably Miles's mum. The four women stood with their hands clasped in prayer. Behind them, stands laden with wreaths of chrysanthemums and lilies. Behind the altar, Golden Boy's coffin. It was open. The pamphlet said we could file past, any time we wished.

Did I wish? I was trying to decide when a posse of non-BEST mourners swept into the temple. Three suited-up men: Miles Southcott and two companions, who hovered around him like a security detail. They broke formation and Miles lead them to the altar. Unlike the gauche BEST contingent, Miles Southcott's party knew the drill. They clasped their hands in prayer too and bowed to the picture of a young, smiling Golden Boy. My late boss's womenfolk returned their bows.

Yvette and another man in a suit were the next to arrive. The Cunningham Family Office contingent? Mr Joseph Unger, author of the your-services are-no-longer-required email perhaps? But no Charlie. Too gutless to sack me himself, and so disrespectful he couldn't manage to turn up to his business partner's funeral.

Abigail gave the eulogy. She was a ghost, frocked up in a bride's white, not a widow's black. Dark circles ringed her eyes, but her voice was strong and clear. She stood still, only her eyes moving, sweeping the temple, focusing on a new mourner with each fresh sentence. And she 'fessed up. She told us all what happened between Friday, when Dave phoned in his let's-study-chimps plan to me, and Sunday, when he went to the Oxford and, watched by his bestie – now seated five rows in front of me across the aisle – gave himself a fatal dose of EIGHT. She owned the role she played in her beloved's death. Then she turned to face his photo on the altar. 'You were so brave,' she told him, 'you'll soon be in a better place.'

It was a top performance, but I wasn't buying it. The David she honoured wasn't the Dave I knew. Dave set her up. She scuttled the let's-test-EIGHT-on-chimpanzees plan, like Dave surely knew she would. Golden Boy gave her a story she could roll with.

I looked across the aisle at Miles Southcott. He was shaking his head, and not in agreement. He didn't buy her story either. Golden Boy's bestie and I were on the same page.

319

Miles

My old man's and Foxy's efforts had been persuasive, and, yeah, Prof Patterson's too. If I told the coroner's cops about Charlie's plan to sell SuperMab, and that story became public, it would be awkward for my family, with us being Capella investors. And I'd look like a complete dick for believing Davey's I've-found-a-saviour shtick, when, as Patterson had so sensitively pointed out: 'No one even peripherally involved in science … or medicine … could possibly believe what you *think* David told you.' If a Pharma's investment in a new project were contingent on human data, experience with a single person wouldn't cut it. No half-intelligent person could possibly believe that.

And if that wasn't enough to convince me to forget what Davey told me, I might be charged with manslaughter – second-degree murder even, the old man wasn't sure which. The legal eagles he consulted, in confidence, weren't sure either. And then there was that spot in the derm program, courtesy of Foxy. I couldn't train as a dermatologist in jail.

They'd made their case. It was persuasive, but not compelling. Because here's the thing: I didn't feel like toeing the Cunningham line. It wasn't just Hands behind Davey's suicide. Charlie had been shafting him too. Why should I cover for Charlie Cunningham?

My old man would get over any public embarrassment at being a Capella investor. It was an imbroglio, no question, but he was a big boy, he could cope, just like I could handle people knowing I'd believed you could do a Pharma deal with one person's data, or remembering how I croaked in the first round of Wimbledon. I mean, shit, I didn't take a game off Gotaran, who went on to lose to Tomasi, who was a has-been by then, in the semis. Yet, somehow, life went on. If humiliation was the upshot of me speaking out about what Davey had told me, I reckoned the Southcotts would survive it.

And I didn't think I'd be going to jail for manslaughter. I'd made my own enquiries, hypothetically, in confidence, to some lawyer mates. They thought the Cunningham mob were putting the wind up me. So I was ready to roll the dice. If that meant Foxy got his knickers in a knot and I didn't get to be a dermatologist, so be it. I wasn't sure derm was for me anyway. Cutting possibly dodgy moles off the worried well, Monday to Friday? Nah, I couldn't really see myself in that picture.

But after my epiphany about Hands and Natalie's revelations, it was a whole new ball game. Davey had told me the Sino YingTech fairytale because he knew I would never believe he was testing his drug on himself to save some chimpanzees, no matter how special and how rare those animals were. Now I had no choice but to sign on to the chimpanzee story. The thought that David Tran had been thinking anything other than 'This is the moral course!' when EIGHT dripped merrily into his veins could not be allowed to cross the coroner's mind. The insurance wouldn't pay out if he'd committed suicide. And even though the possibility that I'd be charged with manslaughter was probably bullshit, I suspected that I would be charged with assisting a suicide if I spoke up about what had really happened.

Davey had finessed his suicide. Likewise, his murder of Hands. There was no paper trail, no script for the flecainide. I provided it. If I spoke up I would be charged with being an accessory to murder.

Davey had thought of everything. He'd set this up so that all I needed to do was what I did best. Nothing.

Then, Rosa Giannini's call. 'Let's do coffee again,' she said.

Rosa seemed nice enough, but I wasn't up for another coffee date.

'How about tomorrow?' she said.

How about never, was my thought.

Did she read that thought in my silence? 'I know what Dave did,' Rosa said.

So, the final piece of the puzzle. *She knows more about EIGHT than I do,* Davey had said. He had to have known EIGHT would kill him. Now, Rosa Giannini was going to tell me how.

I took her to lunch. I learned that there were secret experiments. Hers. All very cloak-and-dagger. And I was only the third person, after her and Davey, to know about them – the rogue experiments that she was running until Davey caught her out, the experiments that she'd now completed. They proved EIGHT was as good as a poison pill. Rosa's theory, her *hypothesis*, was that Davey did the final, secret experiment while she was on the gardening leave he insisted she take. So, he understood exactly what EIGHT would do to him when he shot up with it. Knowing the consequences, he went straight ahead. Topped himself. That was her theory. And of course she was right.

Seek first to understand, Foxy often said. I'd seen him walk that talk. Soon he knew your secrets, and your weaknesses. Then he exploited them.

So why, I asked Rosa, sitting opposite me, running her finger down the prices on the right-hand side of the menu, why would he have done that. Why would he have wanted to? Why would David Tran, superstar doctor, scientist extraordinaire, want to end his life?

'Because of the shame,' she said, 'the shame of his project failing.'

He did some secret experiment – that was hypothesis number one – so he knew that EIGHT was dead in the water, and he found the looming public humiliation, the certain stigma of it, unbearable. So – hypothesis number two – that was why he took his own life.

I breathed easy. I could sort this. Because, unlike her first hypothesis, Rosa Giannini's theory about his motivation was bullshit. 'Know your opponent,' my coaches used to tell me. And when I made the effort, studied their game and strategised my own, I usually won. It was time for me to walk that talk again.

Everyone has their price. Everyone can be persuaded. Even the earnest specimen sitting across the table from me could be bought. What would get my buddy's research assistant across the line? Should I go positive? Would a cheeky little injection of cash do the trick? Could I somehow make her a star, because who doesn't want to be famous, right? Or would I have to go negative? After all she'd been a naughty girl, doing those sneaky experiments.

I knew I'd crack it, I knew I'd crack her. Miles Southcott versus Rosa Giannini was a match I had to win. I needed to get in the game. And like Davey said, I needed to stay frosty.

Part 3

Before you embark on a journey of revenge, dig two graves.

– A QUOTE MISATTRIBUTED TO CONFUCIUS

In many ways you're lucky you know nothing about your father, Ly. Hands taunted me with stories of mine. I talked with Má and studied the histories written by my former compatriots. I eventually discovered that Hands was telling the truth. I'm ashamed of my father, so I didn't tell you, or anyone else, not even Miles, what he did.

He owned factories in Saigon that manufactured MSG. He was known as the Glutamate King. My father didn't treat his workers well. He underpaid, overtaxed and loan-sharked them. The Americans who were running Saigon turned a blind eye in return for the kickbacks he gave them. When Saigon fell to the communists, it was payback time for the people my father had taken advantage of. He heard that he would be arrested. He didn't wait to find out whether he'd be sent to the re-education camps or executed. He shot himself, leaving my mother and Má to fend for themselves and care for me on their own. My father was a coward.

I hope you don't think the same of me, Ly. I've done my best to provide for you and Má. I just couldn't let my fate play out the way it's doing for Má. I could feel myself losing control, ebbing away. I was behaving badly, especially towards Abigail, and I deeply regret that. So I decided to end my life.

I hope you don't judge me, but if you do, I hope you forgive me.
All my love,
Your brother Dung

Abigail

The coroner declared David's death accidental, although there was nothing accidental about it. David took some action and experienced the consequences. I know it sounds cruel, to summarise what happened like that, so when people ask me about David's death, which they do only rarely, I tell them it's still too painful to talk about.

Despite his finding, the coroner admonished Safe Medicines, who'd approved the trial of a drug that, in his words, had a devastating side effect. Did they miss some crucial piece of evidence? Or had they failed to mandate experiments that would have shown the drug was toxic? The coroner ordered Safe Medicines to conduct an enquiry into their own processes and find out.

Safe Medicines had also approved a protocol that specified only a ten-minute gap between administering David's drug to each patient, so eight lives could have been lost if the trial had gone ahead. The coroner was unimpressed. Make sure it doesn't happen again, he ordered Safe Medicines.

Blame had been apportioned, a scapegoat found. None of it helped me. The coroner's finding only briefly mentioned the chimpanzees who David saved by his actions. Probably, like

David, the coroner thought they were 'only animals', which they aren't. The scientific name for chimpanzees is *Pan troglodytes*, which means 'cave men'. Chimpanzees are people.

My Rwandan fieldwork stint was brief. Six months in, the director of Buranda decided he needed a white woman to meet and greet our many visitors. Donors, potential donors, journalists and animal welfare activists each paid two thousand US dollars for the privilege of spending a day with the chimpanzees. The visitors' money was a crucial supplement to the research grants that kept the project going. I was relieved: fieldwork is hard, and most of my fellow workers were scientists, only in Rwanda long enough to collect data for a career-making paper. I was their unpaid research assistant. That got tiresome very quickly.

So I became a kind of hostess. The visitors would fly in. My driver, Wilberforce, and I would pick them up in a white Land Cruiser. Then we would give them a tour of Kigali. All my charges wanted to see the Hôtel des Mille Collines, where more than a thousand people took refuge during the genocide, and they all decided they *should* see the new Kigali Genocide Memorial Centre, where the remains of the more than a quarter of the million Tutsis killed by the Hutu are buried.

Given the large fee they'd paid, the visitors needed to be coddled: bottled drinking water within arm's length at all times, clean toilet facilities pointed out, stops at good coffee shops. In Kigali it wasn't hard to please, and surprise, them. Miraculously, a clean, ordered city, with foliage manicured into box hedges and rooftop bars with views of the mountains, was emerging from chaos and tragedy. It was something I didn't emphasise to friends and family back home, who thought I was at least sweating in squalor, if not facing down mortal danger.

The Buranda project, scheduled for Day Two of the visitors' itinerary, was another story. The Buranda chimpanzees weren't habituated for tourism, and didn't interact with the researchers, let alone the visitors. There were strict rules: no one gets closer than five metres from the chimpans, no flash photography, no loud noises, only whispered talk. None of the cute stuff. Definitely no hugging.

The main purpose of the project was to monitor for inter-group violence. Jane Goodall had documented a brutal four-year war in the chimpanzee community she studied in Tanzania. A large group began invading a smaller group's territory, attacking its members and even drinking their blood as they died. Such violence was previously unknown, and some scientists believed it wasn't innate. Goodall had fed them bananas, which some researchers thought prompted the aggression. Others thought the war showed that chimpanzees are just like us: territorial, violent. Buranda was part of an Africa-wide study to find out who was right.

While I was there, our chimpans didn't fight one other. In fact, they were fairly relaxed whenever I saw them. The visitors, on the other hand, often expressed discontent on the late-afternoon drive back to Kigali. They'd braved a recently war-ravaged country, hiked in mud, been stung by nettles and bitten through their socks by ants. And while they were happy that the apes weren't murdering each other, they would still have liked a picture of themselves with a chimpanzee.

I empathised and would present an option for the next day: a visit to another chimpanzee community, one where touching and hugging were possible. Quintana and Tike's community. My charges got their happy-snaps and I was able to spend time with the two chimpanzees who'd become my friends. Buranda's director turned a blind eye until one visitor, a drop-dead-handsome French photographer, proved to be my downfall.

'They're only animals, Abigail,' David said on our last night together.

His offhand remark enraged me. And broke my heart. Because when I was forced to leave Rwanda I had to acknowledge that I'd been guilty of treating them as 'only animals' too: playthings, here on earth for my amusement. I'd oohed and aahed when Quintana peeled a banana, broke off a chunk and passed it to Tike. A mother feeding her baby! I'd smiled indulgently when Tike hopped on her back and they moved on to the next tree in search of more food. A parent piggy-backing their child!

And I'd taken Lucien, the charming French photographer, to visit them. He hadn't got saleable shots of the disengaged Buranda chimpans. He had a vision for the images he wanted.

He'd come equipped with the latest cell phone, complete with built-in camera. Cleverly, he'd rigged up a metal stick with a clamping mechanism for it. When Quintana and Tike came to greet us, Lucien made a show of taking pictures of himself. He ran his fingers through his hair. *Snap.* He pretended to pick spinach out of his teeth. *Snap.* He puckered his lips for a kiss, then grinned widely and ridiculously. *Snap, snap.* By the time he passed the stick to Quintana she was primed to follow suit. And of course Tike followed his mum's example when it was his turn to hold the stick: preening, proudly displaying his fulsome set of teeth, like Quintana and Lucien had done.

They're wonderful pictures. Lucien sold them to *World Wildlife* magazine. They put one of Quintana pretending to smooch on the cover. Lucien's two-thousand-dollar donation to Buranda was a good investment. I'm sure he'd heard on the photographer grapevine that it would get him to some friendly chimpans, via me. But the pictures weren't Lucien's to sell. On Quintana and Tike's behalf, the Friends of the Chimpanzees took Lucien to court claiming copyright infringement. They argued that Quintana and Tike were persons – admittedly nonhuman ones, but persons nevertheless, and entitled to the same rights as human persons and other nonhuman persons, like companies. Quintana and Tike had property rights.

The Friends of the Chimpanzees were major donors to the Buranda project. I'd facilitated a photo opportunity that had led one of our major donors to take legal action. I tendered my resignation and came home to Australia. Some months later, a judge found in favour of my chimpanzee friends. They were officially persons.

David knew all this. He knew how regretful I felt for letting Lucien use those persons for his benefit.

Living by your principles is hard. Every day I have to face the consequences of living by mine: the loss of David. Every day I have to wonder why he changed his mind about the relative value of animal and human lives. Every day I long to have our last discussion again, to have a second chance. But how would I want that discussion to end now?

We didn't speak again after our argument. I don't even know if he came to bed that Friday night. I didn't sense his presence. He was gone before I woke on Saturday. But he must have been home at some point before he went to the Oxford. Because, when I finally got back to our apartment from the hospital late that Sunday night, there was a note, propped up on our kitchen table by the carved chimpanzee I'd brought back from Africa.

> Dearest Abigail
> You're right. I will try EIGHT on myself.
> Love you
> David

I'm sure he meant those words to be comforting, and sometimes they are. Other times I wonder why he wrote the note. How did he know he would never get to say those words to me himself?

Foxy

I like to send Edwina flowers. I like to see her smile when they arrive, hear the girlishness in her voice when she says, 'Foxy, what a lovely surprise.' I get a little florist shop to drop off a bouquet just often enough to keep the home ambience warm and friendly.

The shop's known for its edgy arrangements. A dozen white roses, which you could be excused for thinking passé, and the girls add sea holly. Suddenly one has a very avant-garde offering. Their pièce de résistance though had to be the spray of black calla lilies, nestled on a tangle of dodda vine, with a miniature pineapple on the side, that I organised for Edwina when Katie left for Cambridge. 'The Star Trek bouquet', the girls called it.

Edwina appreciates such bohemian offerings. I like to think they remind her that there's life in the old fox yet. Of course I don't choose the flowers myself – I give the florist girls carte blanche – but I do make a point of remembering what they send, and I make sure to pay them a contextual compliment when I phone in my next order. 'Mr Good Taste', they call me.

We've been married thirty-five years, Edwina and I. You could say I've been lucky, but I always think one makes one's own luck. I made an excellent choice and I'm careful to treat Edwina well. Frankly, the alternative's too ghastly to contemplate. Flapping around trying to find one's socks in the morning, taking one's own shirts to the laundry, or, heaven forbid, facing the humiliation of dating, at my age? Not for me, thank you very much. No, I've stuck with Edwina, and thank Christ she's stuck with me, even through this ghastly incident.

We always travel Business. We're happy enough with that. The new seats are comfy and the vino is usually a passable drop. But I have seen a glimmer of longing in my good wife's eyes when we walk down the air bridge to board and some carelessly dressed slip of a girl slopes off to First, while we turn right and trudge our way to the upper deck. So, when I thought I'd closed off the SuperMab business, I decided to really treat Edwina on our winter trip to Europe.

We normally do Venice, or Positano, but Edwina had suggested we try Lake Como. She booked a lakeside villa in the Bellagio environs that came with a maid and chef. Katie was coming over to spend a week, bringing her new beau, who, I must say, sounded perfect. He was at Cambridge with her, reading economics, preparing for a career in the city.

We were all set. A couple of weeks before our departure, I met with CC at the club. CC was never a traveller – he got his kicks careering around his farm on a dirt bike – but Mary Lou travelled to Italy at least twice a year, with her sister. CC said the sisters had been to Bellagio and must have enjoyed it, otherwise he would have heard about it. 'You deserve a good break. You'll enjoy it, Foxy,' CC said while we were sipping our pre-lunch whiskies.

I was heartened by his remark, because it augured well for my fee. CC and I had a little tradition: I never billed him, and certainly never sought progress or upfront payments – a very tacky way to do business, in my opinion. I was on a monthly retainer for the three-plus decades I worked for him, and, in addition, whenever I finished any particular project, CC and I would have a one-on-one lunch at the club. We chewed the fat, often about the cricket. Over coffee and cognac he would present me with an envelope. In the envelope would be a cheque. The number on that cheque was what he thought my input had been worth. It's a system that I proposed, and it suited us both. CC was old-school to the core. Our arrangement tickled him. And he usually paid me considerably more than I would ever have billed.

Joe Unger hated our little ritual, but I'm sure he was always in the loop. No doubt he had a word in CC's ear about the number that appeared on the cheque. In any case, he and I always had a to and fro afterwards about the invoicing and receipting.

When CC and I met for what turned out to be our last lunch, I thought the outcome of the whole SuperMab debacle was looking quite reasonable, for everybody except Tran of course. CC was of the same mindset. 'Well done, Foxy,' he said, 'you've managed to snatch victory from the jaws of defeat.' That's when I made a mental note to upgrade our tickets to First.

I appreciated CC's compliment, although in reality, the fix – the chimpanzee story – had just fallen into place. I never believed it, mind you. No, my theory is that Tran gave himself the drug in a fit of pique after Charlie outmanoeuvred him with the planned SuperMab sale. It was an attention-seeking play and, tragically, he got more than he bargained for.

But no matter my speculative musings. The coroner bought the chimpanzee story and didn't bother with an inquest. The ClinHelp girl, Gigi, was shipped off to Eastern Europe, and I tied off all the other loose ends with that magic knot: money. Tran's assistant was back at BEST, completing her PhD courtesy of the Cunningham Family Office. The Professor insisted on that. But it was a trivial expense, literally decimal dust. And Capella was funding one of the Professor's new projects, as a gesture of goodwill. It's another of these monoclonals, this time for some type of cancer – but, thank Christ, not called 'super' anything. I always thought the 'super' prefix for the company was tempting fate. Better to be humble until you've got something solid to be proud about, I say.

Trying to fleece Tran – as well as being a tacky mistake – proved to be another expensive line item in the fix. We couldn't have Miles talking about the planned sale of SuperMab. He was the weak link in the chimpanzee story, and getting him on board proved costly. He insisted that we pay Tran's mother and sister the money that would have gone his friend's way if the trial had proceeded under SuperMab's banner. That was his price. I was sure it had eaten into the number I would soon see on CC's cheque, but nevertheless I felt proud of the boy. He was no longer the innocent abroad he had always seemed. Joe must have sweated blood though, having to stump up almost half a mill for the Trans, and I expected Joe himself would take a hit when it came to bonus time. When there was pain to be suffered, CC was nothing but fair. He spread it around.

We were eating dessert, an Eton mess that the kitchen always whipped up especially for him, when CC spoke frankly about

Charlie: 'Foxy, it's all turned out bloody well, but the tragedy is that this was all so unnecessary. Such a waste of money and time … and, of course, that young doctor's life. Saddens me to say it, but Charlie was a fool to try to sell SuperMab like that. You and I both know there was no need. We could have fixed the problem he created. Joe's doing it now, for Christ's sake!'

I was relieved. It had been the elephant in the room (our *private* room – the dining room was far too public for these debriefings). Now, CC had acknowledged Charlie's misstep. Somewhat obliquely, yes. 'The problem he created.' Goodness me, what an understatement! But it was out in the open.

'Joe's embroidering the books?' I asked.

'Yes, he's taking the loss off the balance sheet. The loss from the video business, and,' he paused, 'what followed. It can stay there until Capella has a win. No one will notice.'

CC was right. Joe's handiwork wouldn't be noticed. The investors had been primed not to expect a dividend for a few years – primed by *moi*, in fact – and, in any case, for most of them the financial statements may as well have been written in Mandarin. The few who spoke fluent finance never bothered to analyse the documents they received. They trusted the Cunninghams.

'You know that Joe's stepped up and taken over Capella,' CC said.

'Yes, he told me.'

CC looked at me shrewdly. 'Charlie's still my son,' he said, a tad defiantly.

CC didn't mention the latest news about his son that Joe had relayed to me. Charlie and Mercedes had officially separated, and Joe had the pre-nup at the ready. Still, since CC had been almost frank about his first-born, I decided to give him some comfort. I reminded him that, if the trial had gone ahead as planned, eight lives would almost certainly have been lost and the Cunninghams would have been looking at reputational ruin – possibly financial ruin as well – even with Joe and me on the case and in top form. So, one could argue, the chain of events young Charlie set in motion saved the Cunninghams' bacon.

CC seemed cheered by this thought, which, despite the wiliness he was famous for, didn't seem to have occurred to him. We parted company on excellent terms, me with my cheque – expenses had eaten into it as anticipated, but I was still a happy camper – and CC looking forward to his errant son's return from Hong Kong, where he'd been holed up at the Peninsula for the duration of my assignment. 'Foxy,' CC said, 'I sleep well at night knowing you're in my corner.'

So, *viva l'Italia!* Edwina and I were on our way. Ensconced in the Chairman's lounge at the airport, Edwina enjoyed a glass of her favourite bubbles – the Billecart-Salmon Brut Rosé. Then a lovely young lady escorted us right up to the door of the plane. 'Mr and Mrs Renard,' she said, passing our tickets to the head steward.

'Welcome aboard,' the fellow said to Edwina, giving my wife a look I thought a tad too appreciative. 'Let me take you to your seat,' he said, and turned to our left.

My wife's a very classy lady. She acted as if it were obvious. Why would Edwina Renard be turning any other direction than left?

As we followed her new best friend to our seats, Edwina turned back to me, pursed her lips and blew me a little air kiss.

It's precious, my memory of that moment, because we had to disembark literally minutes later. Edwina took it well of course. She really is a good sport. But disappointing her, having to abandon our trip – and in such a way: I hold that against Charlie more than anything else.

We were just getting comfortable. Edwina was flipping through a *Vogue* and the hostess had filled our glasses when my mobile rang. It was CC. 'Harry, we've got a problem,' he said. 'There's a video on the internet, on something called YouTube ...'

The shit had well and truly hit the fan. Vale not just our holiday but also my career, and of course, dear old CC.

Miles

Davey set it all up. His death. The web of lies he spun to those he needed to play a role in its sequel. The chimpanzee experiment he 'planned' then let Abigail talk him out of. The adrenaline that he 'checked' was on the crash trolley, but wasn't. Sino YingTech, the fantasy yellow knight. And finally, his pictorial message, delivered by Natalie, in case I couldn't connect the dots.

He set it up so that even a blocko like me would be hard-pressed to choke. And I didn't. I stepped up to the plate and played for my buddy's team. I followed his game plan and stayed frosty even when I had to return the curve ball that I doubt he saw coming. Rosa Giannini. Or did he? He gave me a heads up: 'she's smart'. Maybe he anticipated that her brains and doggedness would turn out to be the weak link in his otherwise foolproof plan. But I sorted it. I made it a win-win. She got the future she deserved, and Davey's secret is safe.

Then there was his enemy's murder. *Before you embark on a journey of revenge, dig two graves.* Davey learned the truth of that. He couldn't live with himself, Natalie said, after he had his Ma kill Hands.

That just left Charlie Cunningham. I didn't set out to get him. The ball got lobbed in my court, and I smashed it.

The last Friday in May, I rocked up to the Corner for my old school buddies' monthly piss-up. All the usual suspects were there, plus Rupert Stone, back in Melbourne visiting his olds, looking forward to a new posting in New York – a promotion – and plenty pleased with himself.

He put his hand on my back, did a little circle massage of my traps. 'Condolences, mate,' he said, 'but do you really think Tran did it to save the monkeys?'

'Chimps. And yes, I do.'

Stone said he never would've thought it, but I didn't bother trying to talk him around. No one cared what Rupert Stone thought.

'You got my messages about Cunningham?' Stone asked.

'Yeah. Sorry I didn't get back to you. There's been a lot going on. What's the story?'

'Well, he's been totally wasted every time I've seen him ... the Hong Kong nose candy is five-star. But in between stuffing happy dust up his nose he's been making good use of the chopper shuttle to Macau, hitting the casinos there hard, I hear. He's been trying to count cards at the blackjack tables.'

'Just for fun?'

'Nah. Turns out he did screw up on that video deal I told you about. Fucked up big-time, and now he's trying to recover the dough.' Stone laughed. 'Fat chance. But, I kid you not, that's what he's doing.'

There was no love lost between Stone and Charlie. The brains behind the two-up game at school had been one of Stone's mates. He was expelled after Charlie dobbed the organiser and participants in. I was surprised that Stone still spoke to Charlie, but maybe he was just biding his time, keeping his enemy close.

'I was hoping I'd catch you here tonight,' Stone said. 'I've got something to show you.' He whipped his phone out of his pocket.

The bar was getting rowdy, so we grabbed a booth. Stone had the latest-model mobile and it recorded video. He cued up the one he'd filmed of Charlie, and passed over the phone.

Like Stone said, Charlie was wasted and oblivious to the fact that he was on the record. His monologue started out in the woe-is-me vein. The card shuffling machines in Macau had thwarted his goal of winning big at blackjack. He had some choice words to say about the Chinese casino owners who'd installed those machines. Then things got interesting. Another freaking confession, and, unlike Davey's, bona fide. Four and a half million bucks gone-baby-gone, some of it my old man's too. Jesus Christ.

I paused the video and looked at Stone. 'Pure fucking gold, eh?' he said, grinning. 'Keep watching, mate, it gets even better.'

Stone was not exaggerating. Charlie makes another admission. He tried to sell SuperMab to recoup the dough he lost, but 'Tran', a 'conniving chink', fucked that up for him.

I handed Stone's phone back. 'I'm thinking of putting it up on YouTube. But given the unkind words Cunningham had to say about your recently deceased friend, I thought I'd run it by you first.'

It was considerate of Stone, but Davey was not the one who'd come off looking bad, in any viewer's eyes. 'Go for it,' I said. 'I think that video is something people need to see.'

Stone had a date in mind for the YouTube upload. He knew that Charlie had been summoned home to Oz, and he thought maximum impact would be achieved if it went live while he was en route. Stone had Charlie's flight details, courtesy of the attractive young female travel agent who looked after them both.

And Stone and Charlie had another contact in common too: their cocaine supplier. Knowing Charlie, and knowing that the Oz happy dust was far inferior to what Charlie had grown accustomed to, Rupert Stone believed there was no chance our nemesis would be heading home without secreting at least several grams, and possibly a lot more, somewhere on his person.

'Are there any stopovers on the flight?' I asked.

'You betcha.' Stone grinned.

He had all his – all *our* – ducks in a row.

'I'm in,' I said, and we shook on it like a couple of half-arsed mobsters.

So Davey, if you're up there looking down on your slacker friend, I hope you're pleased. Because, buddy, you should be. I didn't welch on my debt. I manned up. I looked after your people, just like you wanted, just like you planned. And I did better than that. Charlie Cunningham got what he had coming. One day, Lady Justice might have decided to draw her sword. But your friend, yours truly, got her in the fight. I did it for you, buddy.

Rosa

The YouTube video of Charlie Cunningham spilling his guts in a Hong Kong bar got 564,801 views in the eight hours it was online. At least a dozen of them were mine.

Charlie's ramblings were magnetic, all the more so for being out of focus, in an arty sort of way. At BEST, the boys and girls crowded around computer screens and gaped. Given that I 'knew' Charlie, my screen was a fave viewing location. I'd been repatriated from the BEST sin bin to acceptance, if not popularity, after the coroner's report named Safe Medicines, not me, as the party responsible for the incident.

Charlie looked ratshit. Unshaven. Unkempt. His probably-once-cream jacket sported grease stains. He was slurring his words but, unfortunately for him, not so badly that he couldn't be understood. Charlie totally let it rip. He claimed that Joe Unger – author of the your-services-are-no-longer-required email that I received – had screwed his video manipulation deal. Unger was a shit-arse Shylock. Spiros Economou, the peddler of the bogus technology that Charlie had purchased, was a goat-banging Greek. Awesome alliteration. Laughable logic. He was blaming Joe Unger for thwarting a deal with someone who turned out to be a fraudster. Charlie was obviously tired and emotional. And he couldn't stop himself. The never-speak-ill-of-the-dead road was not for my late boss's boss. Dave was a conniving chink who fucked up Charlie's plan to 'flip' SuperMab.

Charlie's rant clocked seventeen minutes. Occasionally the video zoomed in, and his face came into focus. Bloodshot eyes. Beads of perspiration on his forehead and upper lip. Seriously ugly. And at sixteen minutes fifty seconds, someone had added a special effect: a dissolve to black. Before his entranced viewers' eyes, Charlie disintegrated, like I'm guessing many of his own people wished he would do in real life.

A few hours after the video hit YouTube, Charlie was arrested in Singapore. By the time the TV news ran that evening, he was in prison. Other passengers on his flight seemed more than happy to share their Charlie stories. They'd heard him tell the narcotics bureau authorities to 'fuck off' when he was asked to step into a private room to be searched. 'You can't touch me. I'm in First class,' he yelled as he was led away. They apparently could. Their search turned up 260 grams of cocaine in a pocket of his jacket.

Soon after Charlie was arrested, the powers-that-be took the YouTube video down. But it had done its damage. When Charlie was charged with cocaine possession and trafficking, he got little sympathy at BEST, or, I'm guessing, anywhere else. Eighteen months previously, a Vietnamese Australian, Van Tuong Nguyen, had been hanged in Singapore for carrying heroin. *Those Singaporeans are targeting Australians,* people might have said if they hadn't seen Charlie's YouTube performance. Given that they had, the water cooler vibe at

BEST regarding his arrest was more: *It couldn't have happened to a nicer guy.*

Charlie's claim that he was planning to sell SuperMab got no airplay in the press or on the BEST grapevine. Was it true? If it was, did Dave know? If he did, was the impending failure of EIGHT even more devastating for him? I wondered. I guess it would have made his humiliation more public, because surely the sale would have been scheduled to happen after the trial. The trial would have failed spectacularly and put the kibosh on it.

But I'm only speculating. Parsing the finer points of a biotech company sale is way above my pay grade, and I had no one to workshop my musings with. Miles Southcott had insisted we go no-contact when I started negotiating with Prof to get back in the PhD program, so I couldn't ask him – not that I think asking him would have got me far. Miles never acknowledged that Dave committed suicide. He said I didn't even have proof that his 'buddy' completed my experiments. And he was right, I didn't. I had evidence – circumstantial evidence – but no proof.

The vials of EIGHT that had arrived from Switzerland the week before the incident were gone when I got back to BEST after the gardening leave Dave made me take. One was way more than enough for Golden Boy's self-experiment. What happened to the other two? I was sure he'd used one to run my final experiment. Then he'd probably tipped the remaining vial down the sink to stop me doing the final experiment myself and finding out what he knew. But I couldn't prove it.

A cytokine assay kit, a *whole* kit, went missing from Laycock Lab the week Dave stood me down. I thought he probably nicked it, used it for my final experiment and, *voila*: he saw that EIGHT stimulated an outpouring of cytokines from human blood cells. Again, I couldn't prove it.

He'd been pulling all-nighters the week I was off work. But no one had seen him in the instrument room where the assays were run – I asked. The Bio-Plex machine we used to run the cytokine assays was hooked up to a dedicated computer. There was no stray assay-results file on its hard disk – I checked. And no such files had been written to the BEST back-ups any night the week I was off – the IT nerds checked for me.

Thoughts. Suspicions. Speculation. That's all I had. But by the time Charlie Cunningham was charged with drug trafficking, I'd found the proof, the evidence, a compelling data point that convinced me, one hundred per cent, that Golden Boy had finished my experiments and knew what he was doing. He'd discovered that his super mAb was finished, or so he thought, and he'd found a way out: give the not-so-lucky EIGHT to himself. Like his friend Miles Southcott said, Dave was super smart. Smart enough to set up a close-to-watertight cover story.

We all had roles to play. Mine was a bit part. Dave told me he was planning to study chimps. 'Just tell the coroner's police what Dave told you, Rosa,' Prof said. 'That's all I had to do. Prof didn't want a scandal. Prof's role was to nod sagely and say, 'That makes sense,' when I told him about Golden Boy's let's-study-chimpanzees plan. That's all Prof had to do. Nod.

I ran the final experiment myself at Jude's lab in January while I was in limbo, sacked from SuperMab, awaiting reinstatement at BEST proper. I then re-ran that experiment when I was back at BEST, but I had to take two shots at it. The first time, the Bio-Plex machine was stuffed when I turned it on. *Shut down immediately. Cleaning procedure was not performed*, the on-screen message told me. The machine was clogged with crud. Whoever used it last hadn't run the cleaning cycle. It's a bummer, cleaning up after a hard day at the bench prepping samples, pipetting till your palm aches. It can take a half hour or more to flush out the tubing with bleach, then rinse it through. It's tempting not to bother. But it's a double bummer for the person who follows the slacker who succumbed to the 'I can't be bothereds'.

This time: triple bummer. I back-flushed with bleach to get the machine going, but it was too far gone, the crud too crusted on.

I called in the big gun: Linus, the lab manager. Linus took out the machine's probe, did the high-tech, stick-a-paper-clip-up-the-probe unblock procedure. No luck, the Bio-Plex was *totally* stuffed.

Linus called in the service technician, who took the machine apart and gave it a full-on rebore. That took time. My samples didn't last until the machine was up and running. I had to prep them again. A whole day wasted. I was seriously unimpressed.

Linus, even less impressed. The culprit, as well as the machine, would be flushed out. It was one of the medical fellows, he bet. He didn't care how important those doctors thought they were, he'd make sure they thought twice before wasting *his* time, *his* maintenance budget, again.

Dave was the transgressor. But I only found that out the week before Charlie's YouTube appearance. A random visit to the instrument room. Me to Linus: 'So, did you get to give the mystery slacker a bollocking?'

Linus to me: 'Oh, Rosie.'

Linus is an old hand at tracking down people who don't play by the rules. IT had obliged him with the Event Logs from the Bio-Plex's computer. David Tran had logged on at 1.04 am Thursday the 23th November. At 2.48 am he copied 'DT231114. rbx' – the assay results file – to a USB. At 2.50 am he deleted 'DT231114.rbx' from the hard disk. The evidence, so Golden Boy thought, gone. At 2.51 am David Tran logged off. Just in time. At three am every morning, as he probably knew, the BEST-wide system back-up kicks in.

Linus and I took a moment. We sat in silence, looking at the printout. Only one of us understood what it meant.

Golden Boy was smart, and possibly the smartest thing he ever did was commit suicide and make it look like a noble, save-the-animals, save-the-healthies self-experiment with a crazy-random, geez-what-a-bummer-but-shit-happens outcome. Dave Tran covered his tracks beautifully, but not perfectly.

Ly (Natalie)

Miles brought his laptop to my salon to show me the video of Charlie Cunningham. Miles's face was white, just like the time he came to our house to pay condolences after Dung passed. I suppose he was unhappy that Charlie called my brother a conniving chink. I didn't care about that. I turned the other cheek, because Charlie Cunningham was getting what he deserved. Jail.

Now Miles comes to my salon almost every week. I clip his nails, just like I used to do for Dung, and I cut his hair. He never wants a buzz cut like my brother did. Just a trim. He comes at the end of the day, and after I clip his nails and trim his hair, we sit out the back and drink whisky. One time, Trà My asked me if Miles was my boyfriend, but I told her no, he's not my type.

Miles was allowed to go back to work after the coroner said Dung's death was an accident, but he didn't want to be a doctor anymore. 'I'm chucking medicine in,' he told me. That sounded crazy. All the homework Dung did for him, all the help Dung gave him, all so that Miles could be a doctor. Now Miles says he will be an entrepreneur. People with ideas are going to come to him and, if he thinks their ideas are good, he'll lend them money and help them start a business.

He sometimes gives me advice, just like Dung used to do. 'You should quit smoking, Ly,' he says. 'It will make you sick. Probably kill you.'

Well, bad luck. I like smoking cigarettes while I sit with Miles, drinking whisky and talking about the happy times we had with Dung. Miles is kind, like Dung was, and he helps me with Má. He found a specialist for her, a doctor who looks after people with brain diseases. A neurologist. The neurologist gave Má a certificate so that she didn't have to speak with the police about what Dung did.

Miles thought Má might have Parkinson's disease because of the funny way she walks, or perhaps Alzheimer's because she's old, but the neurologist didn't think so. He did a special X-ray, called an MRI, on her brain. It showed that she probably has prion disease. Her brain already has holes in it. Prions are sort of like bacteria, little bacteria that eat your brain, and the doctor said that if that's what she has, her brain will get more and more holes until it ends up like the loofah sponges people use to rub off their flaky skin in the shower.

Miles wanted to be sure. Even though there's no treatment for prion disease, there are drugs for some of the other diseases she might have had. So Miles made the doctor take some fluid from her spine and test it. Just like the brain X-ray, the spine test showed she has prion disease. Some people call it 'Mad Cow'.

I already knew that's what she has. Dung had done the tests too. The results were in the parcel he said was a gift. But I didn't tell Miles.

Nothing can be done for Má. 'We just have to make sure she's comfortable,' Miles says. I know she wouldn't be comfortable in hospital, or in a nursing home, so Miles and Abigail have arranged for a nurse to come and live with us. Má will be at home when she passes, which is what Dung would have wanted.

Miles is still very sad that Dung took his own life. Sometimes, to make Miles feel better, I think about telling him the real reason Dung committed suicide. I told Miles it was because Dung couldn't live with himself after he made Má kill Hands. But that wasn't true. Dung was going to die soon anyway. He had prion disease too. My brother looked after me. He made sure Hands wouldn't hurt me again, then he took his own life.

I didn't notice my brother starting to go crazy, but Dung noticed it himself, and Abigail noticed too. One day after he passed she even said to me: 'He didn't seem the same person after I came back from Africa.'

Dung had the test on his brain done in America, so that there was no chance that anyone here, like the coroner, would find out. He put the results with the papers he left for me. I've looked at them many times. He used his real name for the test: Dung Pham. The results say that his brain had 'cortical ribboning' and 'showed FLAIR and ADC sequences'. I don't know what those things mean, but I understand the last sentence of the report: *The brain shows changes suggestive of prion disease.*

But I can't tell Abigail or Miles that. Even though Miles isn't a doctor anymore, and even though he says he was never a very good doctor, he probably knows how people get prion disease. And even though Abigail isn't a doctor, she is the sort of person who would find out.

Má was crying when I woke up on the floor the night Dung went on TV with Charlie Cunningham, the night Hands hit me. She was crying and saying '*Má thành thật xin lỗi*,' to Dung. I am so sorry. Over and over, '*Má thành thật xin lỗi*.'

Dung told her to be quiet. He had to sew up my face. He picked me up and carried me to bed. He put my head where my feet usually go and my feet on the pillow. Dung told Má to put an ice pack where Hands's ring had made a hole. Dung needed to go and get medicine and a needle. Then he would sew up the hole.

When he came back, Dung gave me an injection in my arm as well as my face and Má gave me whisky. Dung told her to sit beside me and hold my shoulders so that I didn't move. My brother kneeled on the floor and sewed up the hole. It didn't hurt, but when he finished I felt like I had drunk three whiskies, not just one.

'You need to sleep now, Ly,' Dung said, and he and Má went into the kitchen.

I didn't sleep. From my bed I could see Dung and I could hear what Má said, even though she was whispering. She told my brother what she told Hands many years ago when she was taken to the hospital in Hong Kong, crazy after being on the boat from Vietnam so long, like she's crazy now from the prion disease. It was bad luck for Má that Hands came to the hospital and asked Má what had happened to Dung's real mum, his boss's wife, Madame Pham. It was very bad luck for Dung and me that Má told Hands.

Sometimes people get prion disease for no reason. It just happens. Other times they get it from what they ate. In the letter Dung wrote to me and put with the papers in the parcel, he says he thinks his real mum must have had prion disease too. She loved eating beef steak and his father used to get it sent out by ship from England, especially for her, because the beef in Vietnam was so tough, often only buffalo. Some of the beef that came from England then could give people prion disease, but the doctors only found that out many years later, when it was too late.

Má never ate the beef steak, though. Dung thought she got prion disease from something else she ate, and perhaps that's how he got it too.

'*Chúng tôi ăn thịt bà ta,*' I could hear Má tell Dung in the kitchen, after he'd sewn up the hole in my face. I had no choice, she told him. Your mum was dead. You were hungry. I was hungry. We were both going to die. So, we ate her. We had no choice. We ate your mum.

'No,' Dung said. 'It's not true.'

'*Chân thành xin lỗi,*' Má whispered. I am so sorry.

Dung leaned over and put his head in his hands. It was the only time I saw my brother cry.

Epilogue

Geneva, 2016

Rosa

In 2008, I became Dr Giannini. Graduation night, I gowned-up and collected my PhD in person. When I stepped onto the stage where the university faculty sat, all gowned-up too, Frankie and Pep leaped to their feet and, like me, stood to attention while Prof read out my doctoral citation:

> Dr Rosa Giannini developed a laboratory method to predict whether candidate immunotherapies will cause devastating inflammatory reactions. Her method will ensure that groundbreaking new treatments become available without putting at risk the people who volunteer for clinical trial testing.

As I walked towards centre stage, where Prof and the university Chancellor waited to hand over the piece of paper I'd busted a gut to get, Frankie and Pep started clapping. They kept it up until I was back in my seat. The university's pre-ceremony memo banned standing ovations. I hadn't given it to them.

Miles Southcott didn't come to the ceremony, but he took the three of us to Società Italiana for dinner afterwards. Frankie was so captivated by Miles that she invited him to her next tomato-sauce-manufacturing day. I'd left the country by the time it happened, but Miles emailed after the event to say it had been fun, although harder work than he'd anticipated.

I moved to Switzerland in 2009. I was up for a change of scene. Charlie Cunningham had just been sentenced. The media had covered every day of the trial. His wife had divorced him, but his mother and sister sat loyally through it all. The pundits predicted Charlie would be found guilty, and he was. The sentence: death by hanging.

It seemed like a good time to leave the country. My ex was planning to come back to Melbourne with his American wife and their new infant. He'd made a splash in the US, publishing a bunch of papers, scoring the big grants, so Prof was creating a position for him. Nico would have his own lab. Bolt lab.

I had an offer from a Swiss diagnostics company that included a visiting Associate Professorship at the Université de Genève. It seemed like the stars were aligned. The Swiss company was Immunotest. They wanted to buy the rights to my method for screening monoclonal antibodies.

I say 'my method' because it is. I persuaded Miles Southcott to help me file a patent for it. And although I say persuaded, Miles needed little persuasion. When I called him after Dave's funeral, he suggested lunch, and this time he didn't stick me with the bill.

Miles didn't want me going public with my claim that his bestie committed suicide, and, as he pointed out, I couldn't prove it. What's more, 'Davey's dead. So how would bringing this up help anyone?' he asked. So, I put it to Miles: help me patent my screening method; fund my patent application.

In return for my silence about something I couldn't prove, I would gain acknowledgement for my own work. Miles not only jumped on my proposal, he conjured up a vision for my method's commercial future, which he sketched out on a table napkin. A bright future.

And that future has come to pass. Almost three hundred companies around the world now pay a hefty annual licensing fee for the right to use the 'Giannini Patterson Tran cytokine storm screen'. Yep, it's a mouthful. It's always referred to as the GPT screen.

Prof's name is right up there because, in the lingo of the lawyers who Miles set me up with, I gave Prof 'a piece of the action'. Those lawyers emphasised that I didn't have to include Prof on the patent as one of the inventors. The screening method was my idea, my work, and I'd done the crucial experiment while I was a casual at Jude's antibody facility, waiting to be, but not yet, re-enrolled as a PhD student. The mandatory assignment of students' and post docs' intellectual property to BEST didn't apply.

It could have been a real bummer for the mAb Meister. First, the Norbert–Pandaid stuff-up, then me – a former PhD student, and a failed one too – having a commercial win. 'History echoes' as someone once said, or should have.

But going solo would have been problematic for me. I still needed to be Dr Giannini. Prof held the key to my wished-for future. So, I named him on the patent. Prof re-enrolled me in my PhD and agreed that my testing method could be my new topic. Now he sings my praises from conference podiums around the world and sometimes even recommends me as a speaker, possibly because I also assigned BEST a percentage of the licensing fees.

My lawyers thought I was being too generous, but I wasn't overly troubled by the money. I wanted enough to fund Pep's hip replacement and pay off my HECS debt. I got all that, and more. I certainly don't have to sleep on Jude's sofa bed when I'm in Melbourne now.

That just left Capella. I'd used EIGHT to design and validate my testing system, which muddied the waters, because, even though SuperMab the company no longer existed, Capella owned the hybridoma I retrieved from Jude's freezer, as well as the EIGHT I extracted from it. The high-net-worth individuals at Capella might have decided they were entitled to a piece of the action too. So I suggested to Miles that he buy the patent for EIGHT from them. And he did. I doubt it cost him much.

I've never told Prof, or anyone else apart from Frankie and Pep, who my benefactor was. Miles didn't want his footprint on the patenting effort. Nor did he want even a token cut of the revenue from the GPT screen. My lawyers checked to make sure he was okay with me including 'Tran' in the testing system's name, and he said fine, it was a nice gesture, which it wasn't really. It was more of a message, a little shout out to 'Milesy' and the mAb Meister: 'Hey! I know what your bestie, your apprentice, did.'

So, here I am. Switzerland. And it's awesome. I work hard, but most Sundays I hike, often with a houseguest in tow. I'm the fave host now for BEST boys and girls travelling abroad. My loserism is history. All the old gang add a few nights at my pad to their European itinerary. A conference in London? Crash at Rosa's first. It's a top spot to get over your jet lag. A meeting in Frankfurt? Take a mini-break in Geneva before the long haul back to Australia. Rosa will put you up.

I'm okay with it. I give my visitors clean sheets in a room of their own plus a guided hike through von Trapp country, during which most belt out a woeful rendition of 'The Sound of Music', thinking they're being original. In return, I get the goss from back home, and the company I crave.

Jude was here last week. She emailed, said she and her better half were planning to do Croatia, sail up the coast on a catamaran with a bunch of friends, check out the islands. They'd heard Hvar was a blast. Post blast, hubby was having some 'me time' with his mates in Ireland, doing the golf courses. Could she come visit, have some 'girl time' with me? It would be fun to catch up. I agreed. It would be.

We rode the train out to Nyon, strolled through town to the rack and pinion station, took the little red putt-putt up to La Givrine then struck out for La Dôle, the cow bells tinkling encouragement. Soon we'd scaled a couple of ladder stiles and we were in wonderland, the air fresh, the landscape overwhelmingly green. In the valley below, Lake Geneva spanned the entire panorama, and when we reached the summit we glimpsed Mont-Blanc's snow-capped peak. It's hard to believe that this and the sunburnt country I left behind are part of the same world.

We stopped for lunch at La Barille, sat on the *terrasse*, ordered fondue and the obligatory white wine to wash it down.

Then Jude started in on her monologue. She and hubby were not on tour *en famille*. The next-gen Winstanleys are teenagers now and were left home alone, with no regrets from their parents. Despite all Jude's nurturing, her once-little darlings have grown into fuck-off-mum-but-drop-me-at-the-mall-first brats. A mother's unfulfilled goals for her offspring. Jude's still working through hers. After a decent interval, I interrupted. 'So what's new at BEST?' I asked. 'Give us the goss.'

That change in conversational course seemed to cheer her. She gave a precis of the latest interlab warfare and a *Who*-magazine-worthy rundown on BEST's latest romantic dalliances. Finally, she got to the real news. 'You know Charlie Cunningham died?' she said.

No, I didn't, and, bizarrely, it had taken Jude a full half-day to give up that intel. I knew that his sentence had been commuted on appeal to life, and that, after what I suspect was some serious behind-the-scenes haggling by the Cunninghams, he was returned to Australia to serve out his prison term. Charlie had health issues. That was the official line. Pulmonary hypertension, supposedly. But in the YouTube clip of him arriving back on Australian soil, a couple of detectives flanking his wheelchair, he looked fine. Totally faking it, I'd thought.

'So, he *was* sick then?' I asked Jude.

'Who knows,' she said, 'but it wasn't whatever weird hypertension thingy he was supposed to have that killed him. It was an overdose. Cocaine. He OD'd in prison. He was in one of those low-security places. There's going to be an investigation, but the word is that a guard smuggled it in for him.' Jude dipped another chunk of stale bread in the now-congealed fondue. 'So,

I guess that closes out the SuperMab story. A very tragic story too,' she added solemnly.

It doesn't close out the story, but Jude didn't notice my failure to acquiesce. She changed tack, segued to an upbeat vibe. 'But that's enough bad news,' she said. 'Look at you. Living it up here in Europe. An Associate Professor too! How does it feel?'

I chugged some more white wine and told Jude my news. My hard work has paid off. I've developed a new, improved version of the GPT. If a mAb causes a cytokine release you can use the GPT 2.0 to work out if there's a lower dose that doesn't, which is, obviously, good to know.

'Wow! Congrats!' Jude said. 'You're a real Golden Girl!'

We left the *terrasse* and headed for Saint-Cergue and the train back to Nyon. Our pace was slower than the morning. I blamed the heavy lunch, the middle-of-the-day wine.

There was more news, but I decided not to send it home with my friend. It would reach BEST soon enough. I've re-tested EIGHT, and in a much lower dose than Dave gave himself it doesn't cause a cytokine storm. Golden Boy was wrong. His super mAb wasn't finished. Because in the lower dose, as well as not being toxic, it still causes the much-coveted release of those magic regulatory T cells, the TREGS. EIGHT may still turn out to be immunology's Holy Grail.

Miles and I are now business partners. He rounded up investors, mainly his old school buddies, and we formed a company. We named it *Riprova,* Italian for 'try again', which is what we're doing. In the much lower dose, EIGHT will at last be tested in a phase one trial. When Miles arrives here tomorrow, I will run him through the plans I've made. But it will only be a top-line briefing. Miles says he's not a details dude. As far as the trial and the science go, I'm the boss. Since his tomato-themed trip to Strangeways I'm *Il capo* to him as well.

I was a sad-sack seven-year-old when Pep first called me that, a little dag in my sunhat and gumboots, doggedly shadowing my gruff newly acquired uncle from the chook shed to the manure heap to his beloved beehives. A trainee scientist desperate to get the answers to my own questions right. Because if I didn't, I might be sent back to where I came from, which of course was never going to happen.

How my life has changed. I'd be lying if I denied being pleased with myself. But the memory of Dave, *my* boss, tempers the pleasure and pride. My time working for him was fraught – absolutely – but he gave me a second chance when I needed one, something few others in our line of work would have done. Then, foreseeing failure, he used my work to kill himself, something I can't imagine ever doing, no matter how far my reputation looked set to fall.

And the more I think about it, the less what Golden Boy did makes sense. Because, as Paracelsus, the wise Swiss physician, alchemist and astrologer, said: *All things are poison, and nothing is without poison, the dosage alone makes it so a thing is not a poison.* Reducing the dose of EIGHT was a totally obvious strategy. Dave was smart. He must have known that. So there had to be something else, some sorrow he could no longer bear. What that was, I'll never know. What I do know is that EIGHT lives, after all.

Author's Note

Eight Lives has its origins in the first human trial of the monoclonal antibody theralizumab, also known as TGN1412. I say 'has its origins in' rather than 'was inspired by' because the trial ended tragically. Eight healthy men volunteered, and all six who received the drug suffered an immediate severe immune reaction known as a cytokine storm. They became critically ill with multi-organ failure and were placed on life support in an Intensive Care Unit. Fortunately, the men survived but one lost toes and fingers due to gangrene, and there have been suggestions that the damage to the men's immune systems will be lifelong.

The drug was being developed by the company TeGenero Immuno Therapeutics AG, and the trial took place in London on the 13th of March, 2006. By the time I read about it, the trial had been the subject of numerous scientific papers and a UK government enquiry. It had been labelled a disaster, a fiasco and a catastrophe. TeGenero was insolvent.

Having worked in medical research and the pharmaceutical industry for decades, I knew that first human trials are inherently perilous. No matter how rigorous the preceding animal testing, trying a new drug on humans is a leap into the unknown. But in the case of TGN1412 some scientists claimed that its propensity to cause a cytokine storm was foreseeable, and TeGenero itself warned about the possibility in the trial's Investigator's Brochure.

After reading the published material and talking with immunologists, my sense was that the trial participants had been betrayed. That feeling was the starting point for this novel. However, *Eight Lives* is in no way a fictionalised account of the TeGenero trial. The characters, institutions and events portrayed in *Eight Lives* are imaginary. The standard novelistic rider applies: any resemblance to people, living or dead, or to real events or organisations, is unintentional.

That said, the pharmacological effects of the fictional drug SMB1412, aka EIGHT, largely correspond to those of TGN1412, and the scientific concepts, medical conditions, and drug development processes referred to in *Eight Lives* are real. For readers who wish to know more about these subjects, I have posted a summary of the TeGenero trial and a chapter-by-chapter annotated list of sources on my website (www.susanhurley.com.au).

As well as these written sources, I consulted many people with expertise in immunology, the medical conditions referred to in *Eight Lives* or the biotechnology industry. I would particularly like to thank Ms Jamie Brady and Professor Jim Goding. Ms Brady allowed me to observe her in the laboratory, assaying samples for cytokines, and patiently answered my questions on numerous occasions. Professor Goding kindly reviewed the whole manuscript and critiqued my attempts to describe immunologic concepts. For their time and advice I also thank:

Professor Andrew Lew, Associate Professor Chris MacIsaac, Ms Kaye Wycherley, Professor James McCluskey, Ms Elle Hurley, Professor Stephen Kent, Dr Bob Anderson, Mr Don McRae, Mr Peter Turvey, Professor Terry Nolan and Professor Steven Collins.

The other area of research that underpins *Eight Lives* relates to the Vietnamese-Australian and Italian-Australian characters. In writing these characters I referred to the literature on Vietnamese and Italian immigration to, and resettlement in, Australia, particularly the exodus of more than two million people from Vietnam between 1975 to 1992. These written sources are also listed on my website, but the conversations I had with Vietnamese-Australians and Italian-Australians who generously shared both their memories and details of their current lives, were more important. I am particularly grateful to Dr Trang Vu, with whom I had many discussions and who read a draft of the manuscript. I would also like to thank Ms Ann Tran, who reviewed excerpts of an early draft and Ms Ngan Nguyen, Venerable Thich Phuoc Tan, Thuy Chau, Rosa Mitchell and Craig Terrell.

This novel has had a long gestation and I'm grateful to all those who have critiqued my efforts at various stages. *Eight Lives* really started to come to fruition after I attended the Yale Writers Conference in 2016 and I thank my workshop leaders, Marian Thurm and Erika Goldman, for their advice, and my fellow writers for their feedback. I would also like to thank Anna Boorstin, Trish Bolton, Tiffany Plummer, Josh Pomare and Lyn Yeowart for reading the manuscript, their thoughtful notes and always convivial company.

Clare Forster and Benjamin Stevenson at Curtis Brown, and the team at Affirm Press, particularly Martin Hughes and Ruby Ashby-Orr, have helped me bring *Eight Lives* to readers I don't know. I appreciate their support and confidence in me.

My husband Jamie La Nauze has stood beside me every step of the way. Thank you, Jamie.